Emma Willis Book III
I Can Help You

by

Joss Landry

Joss Landry Author Regd.

This book is a work of fiction. Any names, or references of events, past or present, and/or to existing people, living or dead, are purely coincidental and intended only for the message to the reader. All names, characters, places are the product of the author's imagination and used strictly fictitiously to enhance the reader's experience.

Copyright © 2019 by Joss Landry.

All rights reserved. No part of this book may be reproduced
or utilized in any form or by any means, electronic or mechanical, including photocopying, recording, e-book, or by any information storage or retrieval system, without permission in writing from the publisher.
Book cover design: Dar Albert of Wicked Smart Designs
Editing: Rey Dale of Book Beatles Publishing Ltd.
ISBN: Print book: 978-0-9959568-2-7 ISBN: E-BOOK: 978-0-9959568-3-4

Publisher's Cataloging-In-Publication Data
  (Prepared by The Donohue Group, Inc.)
Names: Landry, Joss, author.
Title: I can help you / by Joss Landry.
Description: Edmonton, Alberta : Joss Landry Author RGD, [2019] | Series: Emma Willis ; book 3 | Sequel to: Book 1. I Can See You, and Book 2. I Can Find You.
Identifiers: ISBN 9780995956827 (print) | ISBN 9780995956834 (ebook)
Subjects: LCSH: Psychology students--Fiction. | Women doctoral students--Fiction. | Clairvoyance--Fiction. | Time perception--Fiction. | LCGFT: Detective and mystery fiction.
Classification: LCC PR9199.4.A54 I333 2019 (print) | LCC PR9199.4.A54 (ebook) | DDC 813/.6--dc23

Two separate hearts beating sixty years apart, drawn to love, meshed into one soul.
Love to Hailey, grand maman.

VERY SPECIAL MENTION

To my lovely granddaughter, Hailey, who inspired this story and the character of Shad, the unicorn.

I am grateful for my husband Gilles' devotion. He is steadfast and a powerful motivator who believes in my stories. In short, he has slowly become the voice that drives me.
My children and grandchildren also drive me onward to improve, and not merely to do more, but to become more than I am. My personal cloud of angels.

Thank you to Darlene Albert for making this beautiful cover.
Thank you to all the prolific authors, beta readers and editors who spent time on this book polishing away the cobwebs. Last, but most important, thank you, Rabbouni for walking beside me.

***

Joss Landry is also the author of :
Mirror Deep
Exhale and Reboot, A Novel
Ava Moss, first book in the Manhattan Bad Boys Series.
Emma Willis Book I, I Can See You.
Emma Willis Book II, I Can Find You
What About Barnum? Book I in the Binary Bounty Series.
If you enjoyed this book, please be so kind as to leave a review. A review is the greatest praise an author can receive.
Thank you!

Prologue

Emma, eighteen years old.

Emma picked up the big book Granny Dottie left her, the one entrusted to her almost a decade ago. The tome didn't mean much to her back then, but throughout the years, she used it quite a bit to understand and learn some of the secrets of her trade—the trade of doing the impossible. Three years since she'd sat down and written on the technicalities of how to project herself, how to propel her body along with her mind, and the differences between the two modes of locomotion.

She also wrote down the magic spell needed to conjure and described the dangers attached to this particular talent. She at least graduated from the time she called her gifts a curse as they became lifesavers to many during her young years.

Emma considered the last three years to be the most selfish of her young life, aside from assisting Hank on a few of his unsolvable cases, she studied, and studied, and studied more. Very little time to do anything else and her friendships suffered also. On the brink of adulthood, her high school prom was already a blur along with all other activities a young woman is supposed to hold dear. "Memories," Tom would tell her. "At least stop long enough to make memories."

Of course, he was right. Forging strong memories is what Emma did at this moment, registering some of her souvenirs triggered by a visit from Dr. Fred Manson. Dr. Manson, an adopted name if she ever heard one, was a Devronair from the Devron system in another galaxy, one thousand light years away. He traveled at the speed of thought. Desperate, Fred stressed how he would never think of interfering with her life choices if this was an option, Fred required her help.

Her need to be selfish prevailed. Given too many assignments with little time to hand them, Emma promised Fred to help him as soon as she caught up with her workload.

She remembered the hurt look on his residual image and remembered the man's haughty glare. Devronairs were kind people who did not suffer awful traits such as pride and arrogance. Earth's atmosphere interfered with their emotions and with their abilities to get things done. Each one of them echoed some of Earth's biggest curses from time to time: fear, worry, conceit, anger. Of course, such emotions consumed all humans, more so when evil entities she had come to know as wizards, entered people's minds to disrupt their brain patterns and have them do terrible things. Devronairs, as well as other species were on Earth to help get rid of these wizards, and to help Earthlings attain the age of awareness so all versions of Earth might merge into one and create what God deemed to be Heaven—Nirvana.

She supposed he needed her help to get rid of some of these entities. He never specified what favor he wanted. She still had not figured out how to get rid of wizards, but she was willing to try.

Emma eyed the two pages she just jotted down in a breeze. She felt lighter somehow, more in tune with her innards. "Diary, my old friend. Please forgive this long absence. Now that we are all caught up, I promise to write more faithfully."

Joss Landry

—One—

Old Friends

Two Years Later.

Emma glanced at her navy blue suit in the mirror of a lady's washroom at Rutgers University. She smiled thinking the outfit made her appear more mature when visiting patients.

She checked her watch. Even in her comfy navy loafers, she would never reach the halfway house in time. She would need to travel on the astral plane to get there. Trouble was she'd never visited the area before and wouldn't know where to land while remaining invisible to others.

Her cell phone rang inside her briefcase. She hurried to open the little valise and grab the phone. "Emma, here."

"Doctor Rappaport, Emma. Forget about going to meet Anita Shelby. I spoke to her, and an old boyfriend caused her fears last night—not induced by her imagination. In fact, police arrested the man this morning. She's a little frightened, but she'll be fine."

Emma walked out into the busy hallway and breathed a massive sigh of relief. "Thank God. I was going to be late. My exam lasted longer than expected." Emma was grateful she could still project the answers from memory. Responses always appeared as a watermark finish on the exam page, and no one else could spot them. Of course, essay questions she needed to compose.

"I understand. I realize how difficult it is to juggle the work since we managed to turn your masters into a doctorate. I know this leaves you very little time to collect clinical hours. However, you'll be able to claim five hundred of the one thousand required hours of visiting patients from the ones done in your masters. Rest assured, the American Psychological Association board members have never encountered grades like yours."

"Lots to do before licensure."

"Yes, but the good news is that the board will allow you to take your Examination for Professional Practice in Psychology while you continue this doctoral internship. So, there are some sizable advantages in the less traveled, more difficult road we opted to take."

Emma nodded, the mention of her EPPP test tying her stomach in knots. She bit her lip considering the hour she would have spent with Anita Shelby no longer accountable. She wondered about the silence on the phone. "Professor Rappaport, are you still there?"

"Yes. Listen, I hope you don't mind, but I told Pauline Crenshaw one of the chairs at the APA that you are intuitive."

"What? Why? I told you this in confidence, more because you divulged you were intuitive."

"I understand. But you'll find many excellent psychologists can perceive people's thoughts—to some extent—as does Pauline Crenshaw. No one is going to ask you to prove it. However, this qualification can only help your career."

Emma rolled her eyes and hid a deep sigh. She would need not to be so cavalier with expressing her gifts and keep them concealed from now on, no matter what the prompt. She could not afford to release these secrets to anyone.

"And I want you to come to me when you are overworked. Dr. Reed is also going to help in any way he can."

"I appreciate your help, and Dr. Reed's assistance, but please don't tell anyone else I can ... sense people's thoughts." *If he knew how accurately I read people's thoughts, I would have a significant catastrophe on my hands.*

"No one else, I promise. The reason for my call is I have a unique patient for you to see—alone."

"You won't be coming with me?"

"I visited him last week, and I thought this might be a good experience for you. Besides, I have prior commitments this evening."

"Tonight? I reserved time to work on my dissertation this evening. I haven't been able to do this in weeks."

"Don't worry. No need to fear this meeting. The appointment is at the Essex County Hospital Center. Dr. Podero is well organized and can provide you with a nurse to assist if you wish."

"What's the patient's background?"

Emma Willis Book 3,
I Can Help You

"A little more complex. Let's meet at my office in a couple of hours. I'll fill you in. Oh, and this case may give you ample material for your dissertation."

Searching for the motivation she needed, Emma considered the time she met with her professor would add to the patient's time slot. Anything to climb this mountain of work she'd picked for herself.

These last four years at Rutgers flew by, although she found the more she studied, the more she needed to learn. Hard work did not discourage her. A lack of social life sometimes did. She hadn't spotted Amelia in weeks, not even in the corridors or in the classes they attended together. Text messages, the short and coded version, became their preferred mode of communication. Amelia was also busy with her double major.

As for Tom, she appreciated his nightly calls. He aced most of his computer courses and contemplated doing a master in computer science at MIT.

Emma decided she had enough time to go home. She would eat with her mom, and prepare for her meeting with Professor Rappaport. She put her phone in her briefcase, walked back to the washroom and invoked the little sentence to go home. "*Lift me away, oh universe, lift me away so I may fly home.*"

As usual, the astral world's portals drove her home while she kept her thoughts positive and peaceful. She landed in her room and stepped out to locate her mother.

Joss Landry

No answer. Emma checked her watch. Four o'clock, but her mother only worked mornings on Fridays. Maybe she had to babysit at Franka's again.

The doorbell rang, and she ran down the rest of the stairs to open the door.

Hank Apple stood at the door, with little Jarred in his arms. "Hey, Emma am I glad you're here. I need a big favor."

"Come on in." She laughed at Jarred's little sailor suit with the little square hat. "He is so cute that I just want to hold him and never let go." She stroked the baby's pudgy arm, and the little boy reached out to her, so she picked him out of Hank's arms. "Is he ever getting big. Looks more like a three-year-old than eighteen months."

"Trust me, he is eighteen months old, the way he walks and pulls everything at his reach to the floor. Then he flops down and anything on the floor, he puts in his mouth."

Emma laughed and squeezed him. "Where's Alex?"

"Gone with Mommy. He's such a momma's boy. Christina has parent-teacher meetings tonight, so she brought Alex with her. She sits him at a desk with coloring books and puzzles." He took back Jarred as the baby held out his little arms to him. "We had a sitter for Jarred, but she called saying she has the flu." He bounced the baby in his arms. "I've been calling around for the last hour trying to find a sitter. Friday afternoon. Where is everyone? Anyway, I'm glad you're home. I am holding my sergeant meeting tonight. No way can I bring a baby to the office."

Emma let out a huge sigh. "Come on in and sit. I'll get you a cup of coffee if you like. I have to make some for myself."

Hank walked in and followed her to the kitchen.

"Trouble is I can't babysit Jarred tonight. I have a meeting with my professor in an hour and a bit. Then I'm meeting with a patient."

Hank sat with the toddler at the table and reached into his bag for a cookie for him. "Where?"

"At the Essex County Hospital Center in Cedar Grove. I've never been there, so I'll need to take public transportation because I wouldn't know where to land. Sorry. I would much prefer babysitting Jarred."

"Never mind Jarred. Since you're going there, make sure to wear the oudjat, your eye of Horus."

"Really?"

"Hey, you don't fully realize what goes on in those places. Even though the center is relatively new, it is still a full-scale psychiatric facility. What better place to encounter our friends." His voice dropped to a whisper. "The wizards."

Emma pushed the coffee maker switch, leaned against the counter and turned to stare at Hank. "I haven't thought about them in such a long time." She nodded staring out the kitchen window. "I mean, you're immune, my uncle Jimmy and my dad both are, which is probably why I never gave them another thought."

"Didn't Manson contact you once or twice about them?"

"Once. Two years ago, during my exams. I told Fred I was

unavailable at the time. I must have ticked him off because I haven't heard from him since."

"Just as well. I have to go. I need to find a sitter for my little one. I'll skip the coffee." He turned to her. "Where's your dad, by the way?"

A sudden sadness engulfed Emma. She imagined the shrieks of her Grandma Abigail and her father in a fiery car crash. She shook the chills invading her and took a deep breath. "He's traveling, visiting house account clients."

"He still does that?"

Emma managed to relax again. "Not as often as he used to. For a week, every three months. They pay him huge bonuses."

"Both your parents still work so hard."

"Mom says working is what keeps them young." Emma laid a hand on his arm as he was about to walk toward the front door. "Wait. If my mother's not home yet, she's working late, or she's at my aunt Franka's babysitting."

"How old is Martha, ten years old?"

"She is going to be nine soon, but she's mostly babysitting Alyssa, who's one week younger than Jarred." Emma leaned against the table waiting for Hank's reaction. "I'm thinking she wouldn't mind taking care of your son while you're at your meeting."

"I forgot about little Alyssa. Fine Godparent I am." He laughed. "And of course, you can't ask a nine-year-old to babysit a toddler. Too much work."

"True. Although, Martha helps a lot. She can change her diaper, make her some dinner, even get her to sleep. She reads her stories, very sweet."

"You think your mother would mind?"

"Mom would love taking care of Jarred. The two babies could play together. And Martha would be in heaven. She's such a little mother." Emma paused as she noticed Hank considering this. "Of course, you'd have to drive him all the way to Soho."

"A twenty-minute drive. I've got lots of time, but I'd like you to confirm this with your mom first. I don't want to show up on Franka's doorstep with a child in my arms."

Emma laughed and dialed her mother's phone from her cell. "Hey, Mom. Where are you? I came home. I thought we'd have dinner together."

"I'm babysitting Martha and Alyssa. Jimmy and Franka have a soirée to attend. Why sweetie? Need my help?"

"Well, Hank's here, and he needs a sitter for Jarred, but I'm off again to the University and then to visit a patient."

Before Emma formulated the question, her mother offered. "Can he bring Jarred here? I would love to stay with him for a while. And tell him that if Franka and Jimmy come home before he finishes his meeting, I can bring Jarred back. Save him the trouble of driving all the way here. I have Alyssa's child seat in my car."

Emma rounded her eyes and gave Hank a big nod of her head. She indicated her watch, and Hank whispered his arrival time. "Hank should be there around five thirty, Mom. See you later." She blew her mom a kiss. Then, Emma communicated her mother's last words to Hank.

"Well, I hope my meeting won't last as long as a soirée which sounds a lot like what I'd need about now." He got up, swung the baby's tote over his shoulder, and walked to the front door. "Do you need a ride to the university?"

"Nope. Thank you, Hank. I can find my way there, no problem." She smiled lending meaning to her words.

He winked at her, knowing full well she would fly to school. "Just don't forget to wear your oudjat."

Emma considered Hank's words while she stared at him through the window pane in the front door, putting Jarred in his car seat, waving at her, then slowly driving away toward Soho. She spotted apprehension in his thoughts when she mentioned the Essex County Hospital Center, and wondered why. Hank, the chief of police, could read her pretty well, but not from any gift he owned. She sensed Hank became tuned in to her from the way they hung around for the last ten years. So, was she the one who worried about going there alone, and he caught the rumble in her mind? Or were his disturbing thoughts founded?

Shaking the doldrums, Emma ran up the stairs to secure the Eye of Horus around her neck so as not to forget. She did worry about going to the Essex Center alone, although she wasn't quite sure why. She would find out more from Professor Rappaport.

When Emma got to Doctor Rappaport's office, she knocked and walked in. He sat behind his desk going through a red-tagged file folder. "Come in, Emma. Have a seat."

She did, trying not to read his thoughts which she found difficult to do when his preoccupied state of mind filled the room around him.

"Is that the patient's file?"

"Yes." He pulled out an envelope from the desk's middle drawer and handed it to her. "I found this letter from a supposed ex-girlfriend of Eivan Baker, the young man at the hospital, tucked away in his office drawer."

Emma hesitated, then opening the letter, she checked the date. "A couple of weeks ago?"

He nodded. "I've been to the county hospital twice already since the letter, and only because the director of the facility is a good friend. He demands everything be above board and functioning efficiently."

Emma read the letter, her frown deepening as she did. Staring up at her professor, she remarked, "The letter has no stamp. It seems as though this Annemarie person handed her boyfriend the letter. The tone is one of complaint. She doesn't think a straight-A student in Physics, working at MIT should indulge in such dangerous experiments."

"She's not the subject of my concern. What I'm worried about is Eivan Baker who supposedly jumped off a building a couple of months ago. He broke a leg. Of course, the building is his parent's home and only three stories high, but police seem to think after the jump, he gave himself a boost to fall in a mountain of garbage at the bottom where he tucked and rolled, careful not to let his head hit the ground."

"Which means he either changed his mind, or someone pushed him."

"Correct. Since the boy has no history of histrionics, police can't agree with the suicide theory brought on by the stepfather."

"Stepfather?"

"Yes. Eivan's mother remarried, and Eivan stands to inherit from his biological father once he reaches twenty-five."

"How much money are we talking about?"

Professor Rappaport smiled and hesitated before he supplied, "Forty-five million dollars."

"No wonder police think this is foul play."

"There is more to it than this. The next day while in the hospital with a broken leg, Eivan apparently overdosed on sleeping medication. They had to pump his stomach to save his life—again."

"This is why they're holding him. They believe him to be a threat to himself and others."

"At the family's request, they are keeping him medicated."

"What do you want me to do?"

"Use your powers for good—your intuitive powers. I know intuition is not reliable. Works when we least expect it to work. I tried, but could not sense anything from him."

"Why have police stopped their investigation on the stepfather?"

"Nothing to go on. Steve Lemon, the stepfather, is a reverend in charge of a Presbyterian church. He's a dedicated man of God and has never crossed anyone in his life. Never had so much as a parking ticket." He drummed his fingers on the folder. "And, several people can vouch for him that evening. He was out ministering to flock members."

"Not an easy case. Do you believe Eivan's girlfriend, Annemarie? She seems to accuse Eivan of unjustified measures to feather his research. Can she be right?"

"Doubtful."

"I'll try my best. See what I can make out. As you said, intuition is not always reliable."

—Two—

First Contact

The bus to Cedar Grove was empty, Emma realized after she climbed the stairs and paid the toll. She chose a window seat wondering why only three people rode this bus. Emma sat down thinking perhaps because there weren't many stops along the way. She closed her eyes as a strange notion tugged at her, nothing she could shape or name, sadness, but with foreboding intensity as though a dark omen stood at her side, and she refused to stare the portent's way, choosing to ignore the message.

She must have fallen asleep because the vehicle's front wheels caught a pothole in the road and her head tossed left bumping against the window. She opened her eyes trying to gauge the countryside, a red clapboard house, a white auto-service building. She breathed with ease when she realized they were still headed west, toward a dipping sun. Her stop was the last one. Unless the driver turned around, she was on the right road. She glanced at the time and relaxed, her eyes fighting to close. Her appointment wasn't until eight o'clock. Only twenty minutes before she reached the hospital.

A quick survey of the people riding with her indicated one person had gotten off somewhere. Two people remained plus the driver. And her eyes closed again. The bumpy ride got the better of her.

A scream woke her. She eyed the man in the next row sound asleep, and the woman in front, sitting perpendicular to her reading a magazine.

A bad dream she thought clutching the oudjat bouncing against her chest.

Determined to remain awake, she caught a long shrill laugh followed by another scream. She held her breath. No one else appeared to notice. The driver's face in the mirror remained inexpressive, and she wondered why her pendant wasn't preventing these sounds. Dusk thickened quickly, the bleakness compounded by what appeared to be rain clouds moving in at high speed.

More sounds. Loud enough to shake the windows, and when Emma pressed her right hand against the pane, she burned her fingers.

Imagination? Too vivid, too real, she thought as she stared at the red and puffy skin on one of her fingers. Even as a child, she had never experienced creative visions of this magnitude—during sleep at times, in dreams, but never while awake and wearing the Eye of Horus.

As they drove on, the moans finally stopped. Emma stared out of her window wondering if sleep might have induced the bone-chilling cries when she came face to face with the vaporous, tortured, grim visage of an old woman. Emma managed to block a scream, but not entirely. She caught the driver's eyes staring at her, and she pretended a yawn to normalize the sound, the hand in front of her mouth shaking. Beads of sweat formed on her forehead, and the thought of abandoning the ride by invoking her little phrase strengthened. Emma's need to go home overwhelmed her. She dug deep inside herself for the resolve to be strong.

After all, this might be one of those dreams she occasionally found difficult to shake. The nightmare would explain why the Eye of Horus didn't work because if she dreamt she had her Eye of Horus and did not, the jewel would be useless. This made no sense. Was the universe attempting to convey a message?

The bus reached her stop, and she rose on trembling legs as she squeezed out of her seat. She walked toward the door, the only one getting off in this neck of the woods. Maybe not the bus's last stop.

She waited for the vehicle to go, and ran across the street. As she walked up the walkway near the parking lot, she cast her eyes left and right and almost sensed the dusk trying to seize her by the throat. When her phone rang, she jumped. She clasped her briefcase clutch and hurried to pick up. "Hello?"

"Emma? Where are you? I just went to your house, and no one's there."

"Tom," she breathed with relief. "I'm about to go inside the

Essex County Hospital Center. There is a patient here I need to see."

"At this hour? Are you alone?"

"Yes, I'm alone. Doctor Rappaport's patient, but he couldn't come with me."

"Who?"

"Professor Rappaport. I told you about him. He got my masters upgraded to a doctorate."

"Weird name. You would think I would remember a name like that. Stay put I'm coming to get you."

"No. I'm interviewing a patient."

"Well, don't you dare fly home in this state of mind. I know you, Emma. You're scared out of your wits right now."

Tom knew her well. But this also meant she needed to change her attitude and her tone to visit the patient. "I have to hang up. I'm about to go inside, and we're not allowed cell phones."

"I'll be in the parking lot closest to the front door. Call me the minute you're out."

Emma crossed her purse strap over her shoulder and gathered her briefcase. She walked to the reception area, smiled, and asked for Eivan Baker's room.

"Of course, he is still with a visitor in the smaller living room. You can wait in the antechamber until eight. Is that okay?" The reception nurse smiled.

"Perfect," Emma nodded.

The nurse called for an orderly to take Emma to the little salon. Emma followed the young man making sure to remember the way back. The layout, airy and modern, appeared vaster than what she'd spotted on the outside. She felt confident many corridors wound their way around the formidable atrium. Any sign she could detect, so as not to get lost on her way out, would be a bonus.

When the orderly brought her into the waiting room, she asked which way to the living room to meet with Eivan Baker.

"Just through those doors," the young man said. "When his visitor leaves, he will have to come through here."

She smiled and swallowed her apprehension as she watched him leave. Sitting down in one of the cozy recliners, she once more shuddered at the thought of going home. No one would be the wiser, but then she signed the book when she entered, so they would wonder what happened to her.

She rose to pace and shake the doldrums, all the while scolding her lack of bravery. What was wrong with her? She hadn't fallen prey to fears like these since the age of ten when she first met Hank Apple, thinking he was the devil apt to find out about her powers. No. The same fears plagued her during her father's long convalescence in the hospital because of a deep coma brought on by wizards.

Fifteen minutes later, the doors opened and made her jump. She watched a tall, broad man exit the room. He stopped as though surprised to see her and smiled. "Hello, I'm Steve Lemon, Eivan's father." He shrugged. "I didn't know he had another visitor scheduled for today."

"I'm just a consultant here to help—if I can." Emma smiled but then frowned. As the man approached, the scent of honeysuckle wafted around him, unmistakable. *My worst enemy, we meet again.*

Reverend Lemon smiled, but when he stared into her eyes, he became perturbed. As he held his right arm outstretched to shake her hand, he used it instead to grab his left arm, and a grimace of pain played on his face. After falling to his knees, he collapsed on the floor. The attendant in the small living room ran to press a beeper by the side of the door and began cardiopulmonary resuscitation on the man.

Emma backed up, eyeing the cowardly exit of a wizard leaving the Reverend's body. Had the evil entity inside Steve Lemon recognized her?

Barely one minute later, two male nurses arrived and lifted Steve Lemon to put him on a stretcher. They left the room immediately.

"Is he going to be all right?" Emma asked the attendant.

"He was breathing when he left. Heart attack. Don't worry." He patted Emma's shoulder, and she thought she must appear frightened. "They can happen without warning in any stressful situation." He turned toward the room. "This way, please."

She followed the attendant, and Emma knew this was no ordinary heart attack. Wizards ran out of the physical man leaving him vulnerable and alone. Their invasion had brought on his heart attack, and now, he would not come out of his particular coma.

The honeysuckle odor, still faint in the room, left with Steve Lemon. Soon, the sickening scent would be gone, which meant Eivan was not inhabited by wizards, at least not at the moment.

A tall shadow of a young man sat in a wheelchair in front of a table. His plastered left leg protruded from the chair while his head dangled with his chin resting against his chest as though he slept. Her heart went out to him. He appeared frail and abandoned.

The attendant parked himself in the room, in a corner hidden by the shade of a tall mahogany console dressed with a flat screen television and what appeared to be a state-of-the-art sound system. Whatever probe Emma intended to perform, she would need to do so silently using only her mind.

She sat in the chair facing him, on the other side of the coffee table. Out loud, she spoke, "Hello, Eivan. My name is Emma, and I was sent here by Professor Rappaport who is concerned about you."

His dark curly head did not budge, and when she looked toward the attendant, he walked over and squeezed Eivan's right shoulder applying his right thumb to the base of his neck.

Eivan's head straightened, and he looked at her or instead through her with a blank stare.

Emma took pity on the soulful green eyes and decided to project her voice making Eivan the only recipient able to hear her. A little trick she'd discovered two years ago which came in handy from time to time. *"Don't be afraid, Eivan. Professor Rappaport sent me here to help you. Can you hear me?"*

More words out loud to placate the nurse. "How are you feeling today, Eivan?" She smiled at the attendant, her eyes insisting she wanted privacy. He retreated to his place by the console.

"If you can understand what I say, Eivan, please move your right index finger." Emma spoke clearly and projected her voice so Eivan might hear her, making sure he was the only one who could.

Emma observed as his finger rose slightly. She bit her bottom lip hating how medicated he appeared to be.

"If you can't talk, try to form coherent sentences in your mind, and I will read them. When I project my voice, no one else can hear us, so don't worry about the attendant."

She continued her conversation for the sake of anyone watching from a distance. She had no doubt the session was recorded, "I hope I haven't come too late. You must be tired at this time."

His mouth moved as though he tried to remember how to form words. "Thank you. I'm fine."

Emma opened her briefcase and retrieved her digital pad to take notes.

This was when she heard Eivan's thoughts clearly. *"I didn't jump. Steve Lemon pushed me. I turned and saw him just before he rammed into me, shoving me off the roof. He was unusually strong, and his eyes were dark and empty, unlike him."*

"I understand you did a stint in the hospital also. How did you feel after the accident?" she spoke, adding with her mind, "*Who gave you all the medication that the authorities accused you of taking at the hospital. Do you know?*"

"*No. While I slept, someone injected the lethal medication into my tube. I don't think whoever did this meant to feign another suicide attempt. They wanted to finish the job and kill me.*" He answered her first question, "Happy, I was alive."

His strained voice appeared as though coming out of a tunnel. "*Why would you say this?*" Aloud she added, "I'm glad to learn you are happy. Your sense of gratitude simply means recovery is on the way."

"*The bell in my room went off almost immediately. I woke up and caught the shadow of a figure slipping out of my room seconds before the on-duty nurse ran in, rapidly unplugging my I.V. She spotted the person leaving. She sounded the alarm.*"

"Are you anxious to go home, Eivan? I understand your mother is worried about you."

"Yes."

"*The hospital knows this was not another suicide attempt. Why is no one admitting this?*" Emma could not believe the authorities' ambivalence. "Would you like her to come and visit you?"

"No. Don't want her to see me like this."

He'd coughed out the words, using what Emma considered to be an enormous amount of strength. Eivan then projected his thoughts to Emma. *"They want me dead. Something to do with my inheritance."*

"Don't worry. We'll get you out, somehow."

Emma rose. "Might be therapeutic to allow your mother to come and visit—for both of you."

She signaled to the attendant she was done, realizing the conversation hurt the young man more than anyone might measure. His head hung again.

Addressing the attendant, she told him, "He is drained, extremely tired. He needs to rest. I have what I need. Thank you."

The attendant, Mark, as per his name tag, wheeled him away and she followed him down the hall. She turned right at the elevators toward the reception, looking back at Eivan and Mark as they boarded the elevator. *"Don't be scared."* She projected her thoughts before the door closed. *"I won't forget you."* She realized despite the sincerity of her promise that she might not be able to get him out from this level of entrapment.

Emma walked toward the reception area and wanted to ask if she could wait inside for her ride when she spotted Tom pacing in front of the desk. "Hey, Emma. They wouldn't allow me to go any farther. Are you all right?"

Emma smiled. "Of course. I thought you were going to wait outside."

"Let's get out of here." Tom eyed the place with a frown.

Before he could drag her away, Emma turned to the receptionist and asked, "Do you know what happened to Reverend Steve Lemon? He apparently suffered a heart attack while I waited to see a patient—he collapsed right in front of me. Do you know if he's going to be all right?"

The nurse checked the forms she had on the desk. "Ah yes. Staff doctor revived him, and they rushed the patient to St Joseph's hospital in Patterson." The nurse smiled.

"Thank you." Emma turned to wave to the nurse. With Tom's arm looped with hers, she had no choice but to jog the rest of the way.

"Let's not take the same road that the bus took to get here, please."

"We're taking Reservoir Drive, faster and headed toward Forest Hills—complete other direction. I'm not going back to Rutgers."

"You're right. Sorry. I'm just a little confused."

Emma Willis Book 3,
I Can Help You

—Three—

Coming Together

*B*ack from the hospital with Tom, Emma stood by her living room window staring outside at the rose bushes her mother planted last year. Even though their bloom had grayed in the starlit evening, Emma smiled at the abundance of flowers, their scent intoxicating and their vivacity beyond her mom's wildest expectations.

"Will you look at the roses, Emma? How beautiful they are after just one year. They seem to be under a spell?"

Her mother had turned toward her daughter a silent question in her mind. "You did this, Mom. You obviously have a green thumb."

Emma attempted to make room in her mind for all the thoughts assailing her. The only way she imagined doing this was by recapping the latest events. She still wore her oudjat, and the jewelry appeared to be rendering the world silent around her while keeping her grounded.

Tom sat on the divan listening to television. He incessantly flicked the remote over the many channels which created a distracting flash in the background each time he did.

"We should turn on a lamp or something. You're going to hurt your eyes watching television in a pitch black room."

Emma stood in the back of him realizing she could not confide everything she learned about Eivan, but she needed to talk to Tom about some of her troubles.

As though sensing she wanted his input, he turned off the TV and stood to better stare at her. He walked around the sofa, turned on the small lamp on the console table, and gathered Emma in his arms. "I can always tell when something is bothering you. Talk to me."

Emma held onto Tom like a lifeline, taking in the male scent of him, and loving his big hands moving up and down her back. With a sigh, she stepped away to sit on the sofa, and he jumped over the back to sit beside her.

"What happened at the hospital?"

"Well, I can't discuss my conversation with a patient. I won't even be able to discuss what I know with my professor. I certainly can't tell him I communicated with the patient telepathically, can I?"

"No. You can't. But something else is bothering you. What is it?"

Emma let out a soft moan shaking her head. "I'm not sure. Weird things are happening around me. This afternoon, Hank came over with Jarred, looking for a babysitter."

"Always asking. Hank is always asking."

Emma ignored Tom's old feud with Hank, still going on whenever Hank needed her. "We had a nice chat. Then when he asked where my dad was, I got scared when I flashed on my father maneuvering away from a truck—just a glint of memory. My grandma sat next to him, and she screamed as the car plunged into a ravine."

"Well, if you know this is about to happen, you can stop it."

She shook her head. "Memory. I remember the accident killed them both—a year ago."

"Could be like the time you visualized me tumbling from my mountain bike on that wooden structure. You prevented that from happening."

"No. For a few seconds, I relived the funeral, my grief. My mom's anguish. But then just as quickly, the sadness lifted, and I told Hank my father visited house-accounts for the company."

"Whoa. I don't know what to tell you."

Emma stared at Tom and talked about the terrifying sounds and ghoulish faces she saw on the bus on her way to the hospital. "My oudjat did not prevent the apparitions or the screams."

She showed him her burnt fingers, and he stared at them his frown deepening. He deposited a kiss on her fingers, one by one. "I didn't even know you still wore the thing."

"Hank reminded me to take the pendant when I told him where I was going. He worried about me going to a full-scale psychiatric facility. Going to these types of places is hard for someone like me."

"Could this be because you haven't worn the jewel in a while?"

Emma gave Tom a raise of her eyebrows. "Of course, not." She laid her head against his shoulder. "When I got there, I had to wait in a little area. Someone else was visiting. I think the visitor came out of the patient's room and recognized me."

Tom moved a little to stare at her, placing his arm on the back of the sofa. "What do you mean?"

Emma took a deep breath. "The man came out, walked toward me with a smile, and guess what scent I picked up?"

"I forget the name ... honeysuckle?"

"Yes. The visitor came closer, his right arm outstretched in readiness of an introduction, stared into my eyes, and panicked." Emma turned toward Tom, eyeing his expression. "His weird dark eyes panicked, as though the wizard inside him recognized me. Instead of shaking my hand, he grabbed his left arm and rolled on the floor suffering from what appeared to be a heart attack."

"Well, it's certainly not your fault. Hospital can't blame you. Were you able to help him?"

"The attendant in the room gave him CPR, and five minutes later they wheeled him away. Obviously, the man's in a coma, and nothing anyone can do can get him out of there."

"Nothing you can do. You'd need to fight the wizards to bring this man back? I know you did this for Jimmy, but you knew him. He trusted you."

"You're right. Wizards left Steve Lemon. He never fought the wizards. How do you remember all of this?"

"A guy doesn't forget a thing like that. I used to be so worried they would get inside of me. That whole summer, I practiced patience, kindness. I tried to be the perfect gentleman."

"Poor, Tom. Never dawned on me you would worry about wizards. They got inside Hank once."

"You never told me this."

"Not something Hank wants me to broadcast, I'm sure. Occupation went on for days. The minute he would spot them inside of him they would leave. They almost killed him once making him collide with a fifty-three-foot truck in the Holland Tunnel.

Emma Willis Book 3,
I Can Help You

"Whoa!"

"We got to him in time a few days later. He collapsed inside St Michael's Church. He thought the Church would keep the evil away. Place of worship did not deter them one bit. But he fought them and won, and I was able to bring him back."

"Never knew this about Hank." Tom shook his head. "Come to think of it, you never told Amelia about any of this, your best friend."

Emma wondered if Tom's words were uttered to make himself feel better she'd kept him in the dark about Hank. "All these years, you were right, by the way. I should have told Amelia about my powers, from the beginning. Now, with each year that goes by, it becomes harder and harder to do so. I don't even know where to start." She let out a huge sigh. "Think she'll resent me when I do?"

"Depends on how you tell her."

Emma shook her head. "Trouble is I think she already resents me." Sad hazel expression stroked Tom's blue caressing eyes.

"You mean because she caught us kissing last month?"

"Yep."

"She knows we're in love. She wouldn't begrudge you happiness, would she?"

Emma hoisted her shoulders. "All I get from her lately are text messages, the coded kind."

"She's just as busy as you are with her dual major." Tom turned to face Emma. "Marry me, Emma. All these innuendos will go away. We can let the whole world know how much we love each other. I've waited a long time, Emma."

"You waited, but only until I was nineteen."

"Thank God you gave in when you did." He laughed. "I'm twenty-one, you're twenty. We can marry. What do you think Father Henley would say if he knew we were having sex?"

Emma laughed. A deep breath later, she added, "We're not having sex. We're making love. And it's not up to Father Henley, is it? All I can say is when two mature, consenting adults come together because of love and are not involved with anyone else God smiles on them, whether they have a piece of paper declaring it's legal or not."

"I know. Just thought I'd use a little maneuvering to convince you."

She laughed outright. "You're the best, Tom. You are."

"Then why won't you marry me? We could let the whole world discover how we feel."

"Well, my mother already knows we ... are committed to one another. So, does my dad. My aunt Franka knows also."

"So, why not make it official?"

"Truth? I wouldn't be able to live in close quarters with another human being right now. This doctorate is sucking all the energy out of me. I can't seem to focus on anything else. And what about you? You were supposed to be getting your masters at MIT already. Why this extra year at Rutgers?"

"My professor, my mentor," Tom bracketed the air. "Peter Range thought I could use a minor in administration before going to MIT. To tell you the truth, I would have ignored him if it weren't for you. I don't know how to leave you, Emma. Me, over at Tech, you here at Rutgers. I can't be apart from you, my love."

He lowered his eyes and pinched his lips. Emma recognized how troubled Tom was. She smoothed his face with her hand. "How long do you think it would take me to fly to Cambridge?" She tilted her head and smiled.

"Right. I hadn't thought of that. I would need to get private quarters—or coordinate with someone not to be there when you popped in." Tom's turn to smile.

"Simple solution."

He gathered her into his arms. "And there are solutions to your problems as well. We just haven't found them yet."

"I'm scared, Tom. I haven't been frightened like this for a long time." Her voice sounded muffled her mouth buried against his chest. "What if the wizards are trying to get inside me and they're running these weird picture shows in my head?"

Emma sensed Tom's shudder as he scooped her up close. "If you hold on to the fear, you're permitting the wizards to get inside you. You need to relax, be present, take life one day at a time."

She nodded, moving out of his arms. "Difficult to do when you're not around." She smiled at him. "I will miss our closeness when you leave. Perhaps more than you'll miss me. Who can say how much each of us needs the other?"

He kissed her lips gently. "Then, you're not going to like what I'm about to tell you."

Emma could not form the question mirrored in her eyes. When Tom wouldn't explain, she breathed, "What?"

"I had decided not to say anything ... now I think the more you know, the safer you'll be, better able to make heads or tails of this whole situation."

"So?"

"I looked up the name Rappaport in the staff catalog. Not there."

"What?" She hoisted her shoulders. "Can't be."

"Hey, might be a glitch. Maybe the professor is new, and he never got his name in before the thing went into print."

"Did you look online? Someone told me they update changes monthly."

"He's not online either."

"Well, he's not new. At least, he told me he'd been coaching students—good students he added—for two years at Rutgers. Does the catalog include all campuses?"

"Yep. Should."

A long breath escaped her. "Something else I need to resolve." Emma took off her shoes and curled her feet underneath her on the couch. "You know he did mention he spoke about me to Pauline Crenshaw."

"Who?"

"A prominent board member at the APA."

"So, call her. Talk about your work with Professor Rappaport. You, of all people, will know if she's never heard of him."

"This will have to wait till Monday. They don't cater to students on the weekends."

"What about Rappaport?"

"Works Saturdays sometimes. I'm not calling him until Monday. He's going to want to know about the patient I visited. I need time to make something up."

"Speaking of time," he took her face in his hands. "When is your mother coming back?"

"Franka and Jimmy went to a party. If all goes well, late." She smiled, staring deep into his eyes.

"What about your dad?"

She drew back, the odd sensation from the afternoon assailing her once more. "Usually comes back on Friday." Emma glanced at her watch. "He should be back already."

"Where did he go?"

"I'm not sure exactly. Mom said to a few places down the Eastern Seaboard."

"There you go. Your dad went further than expected and is too tired to drive home."

"Do you mind if I call him?"

"Suit yourself. Just don't tell him I'm here."

Emma rolled her eyes as she punched in the keys on her phone. The ring at the other end was long before her dad picked up. "Hello?"

"Dad, I was worried about you. Shouldn't you be home already?"

"Five o'clock this afternoon, I finished my last meeting in Richmond Virginia. Drove to Washington, had dinner, then found a place to stay for the night. Why? Need my help?"

"No. I'm fine. Just concerned."

"I already phoned your mom. She knows. I'll leave at five and be home around nine, nine thirty in the a.m. She has chores for me to do."

"See you then, Dad. Love you."

"Is Tom with you?"

She eyed Tom raising her shoulders in helplessness, refusing to lie. "Yes, Tom is here. We were discussing my latest project."

"Give him my best—as I'm sure you will."

"Dad!" Emma had shared a frank discussion with her parents about Tom. In fact, her father was ecstatic she'd turned down Tom's marriage proposal. He no longer minded the fact they were lovers. 'As long as I don't have to hear about it or witness your interaction in any way shape or form.'

"Just kidding, sweetheart." He laughed. "My way of saying you need to relax once in a while."

"Night."

Emma hung up and related the conversation back to Tom.

"What? Oh my God! The whole world does know. Your father has a big mouth."

"He also has a keen eye. He can tell the way we look at each other. And he's probably not the only one who can."

He stood and pulled her up toward him. "Come on. Let's not make liars out of them. I love you, my gentle Queen."

They clung together for a few minutes until Tom led her upstairs. In the old room where they'd studied as children, the room that used to house all her nightmares, the room visited by wizards, a pathfinder, optimal Earth humans and Devronairs, Tom claimed the woman he loved, and Emma spent a couple of hours of ecstasy in Tom's arms.

As the night deepened, their passion grew, and for the umpteenth time, Emma wondered why she'd waited so long to experience this total gift of herself to another human being, the man she loved. Ever since they got together, six months ago at Christmas, they kept trying to snatch a little time together now and then, which they both found difficult to do.

Tonight, for some reason, whether because of all her fears or her difficulties at school, the pleasure of loving Tom topped all her wishes.

Her eyes on the window, Emma embraced the full silver moon shining down through the branches of the old Elm tree. She turned toward Tom, already in his clothes, strapping on his summer jacket. "Do you have to leave right away?" Emma asked.

"Yes. I parked my car in your driveway, and your mom will be home soon. You say they know about us, but I would rather we keep this on the QT if you don't mind."

"So difficult to find the time to come together." She held out her hand, and Tom grabbed it, bent down beside her and Emma caressed his cheek with the back of her hand.

He kissed her lips, and Emma watched him stand and tiptoe to the door with shoes in hand, realizing this would have to do.

His hand on the door handle he turned to her. "Why do you think I asked you to marry me? So we wouldn't need to sneak around like this. As a married couple, we could share a room on campus."

"Okay. Food for thought." She smiled hating to say no to him as he was about to leave.

Joss Landry

—Four—

Time Shifts

Emma woke with a start. The clock on her bedside table displayed one o'clock in the morning. An hour since Tom's departure. Too many unresolved issues floated around in her head, and one of them yanked her from sleep, she supposed. Finding solutions made her edgy and dizzy.

The sound of the front door opening caught her attention. Still a decent hour for her mother to come home, she thought. She got up, looked out the window to spot her mom's car in the driveway. She doubted some of her senses of late.

She hesitated whether to go and disturb her with her thoughts. Finally, she put on her slippers and robe to greet her. She didn't need to mention anything about her weird life. A hug from her mother would go a long way to giving her the courage she needed.

Downstairs, Emma found Eloise sitting in the kitchen, in the dark, with her head slumped on the table, crying. The picture and sounds of her mother's sobs spun Emma around. She bit her lip to stop the tears from coming and prayed her mother was not mourning her father.

She went up to her rubbing her shoulders to try to soothe away her pain. "Mom, why are you crying?" She asked fearing the answer.

Her mother looked up and forced a pale smile through her tears. "Your father and my mother, your grandmother, would have loved this new little granddaughter, Alyssa. She is precious, sweetie."

Emma collapsed on the chair next to her, the pain in her chest poignant enough to hamper her breathing. She found challenging to restrain her sobs. Emma couldn't tell her mother how her whole world appeared to be collapsing around her. Shaky, frightened she might be going out of her mind, she strapped an arm around her mother's shoulders and tried to console her. "I'm sure he is aware of what is going on with all of us, Mom."

"I know, sweetheart. When someone passes after a lengthy illness or even a short one, it's easier to cope, I think. But an accident—so unfair, so unjust."

A flash of memory assaulted Emma. Her mom appeared stuck on this sentence because she must have uttered the words a hundred times in the past year. And Emma worried about her mother still riddled with this much pain a year after her father's death. One of them losing her mind was enough. She vowed to get to the bottom of her dilemma if only for her mother's sake. "Come on, Mom. Are you hungry? Would you like me to make you something to eat?"

Eloise shook her head. "No. I'm going to bed. I'm tired." She clasped her daughter's hands as she stood. "Thank God, you're still here with me. Don't know what I'd do without you."

Instead of receiving one of her mother's supermom hugs,

Emma gave a hug to the mother she loved so much. She held her in her arms, hoping to help her sobs subside. Emma's arm around her mother's waist, they left the kitchen and climbed the stairs up to Eloise's room. Once she made sure her mother changed for bed, she tucked her in the same way her mom had done for her when she was a little girl. "Things will be better in the morning, Mom."

Emma closed her mother's bedroom door and wondered about doing the same, getting some rest.

She walked into her room and eyed the cozy bed. How she would welcome the blissful peace of sleep. Then she wondered. If she indulged in rest right now, would she wake up in this timeline where Tom was her young man, and her doctorate was moving along at a rapid rate or in another unknown time and place?

Before she could change her mind, Emma got dressed in a hurry and tied her hair in a ponytail. With a hand on each shoulder, she invoked her little sentence. "Lift me away oh universe, lift me away so I can fly to a friend's house."

The ride through the astral world was bumpy. Emma realized her attitude needed to be more positive with fewer thoughts about how she headed for the psychiatric ward—as a patient. Filling herself with contented thoughts, she managed to land inside Hank Apple's kitchen without too many glitches, except in the dark, she hit the table and made what seemed like a big pot fall to the ground.

Immediately, she tensed and sent Hank a message that she was downstairs and needed to talk to him. The last thing she wanted was for him to barrel down the stairs with a loaded gun thinking a robber was on the premises. To help the process along, she turned on the lamp in the little living room and waited for him.

Another five minutes passed before she heard the stairs creak and Hank inquire in a big voice, "Who is there?"

"It's me, Emma. I'm in the living room."

Hank walked through the archway in his bathrobe and slippers. "Emma Willis? What are you doing here?"

He glanced at his watch and frowned waiting for her to say something.

"I need to talk to you, and I couldn't wait until morning."

Once Hank sat down beside her, she turned toward him and revealed the events of the last two days ending with his visit to her house with Jarred, and him bringing the toddler to Eloise to babysit. She also told him about going to the Essex County Hospital to visit a patient, and speaking to her dad who was visiting house-account clients for the company he worked for, on the Eastern Seaboard.

"Well, your father died last year along with your grandmother in a horrible accident caused by a fifty-footer." Hank got up and paced as was his custom to do when he needed to think. "As for me, I don't have any sons. Christina has difficulty conceiving. Last year we decided to stop trying so hard and make the best of the situation, be content with what we do have." He turned toward Emma. "What are you saying? In another life, we have two sons?"

"Two sons?" Christina's voice repeated in the salon's entrance.

"Sorry, Christina. Didn't mean to wake you."

"Tell me about my boys."

Emma glanced at Hank whose shrug didn't give her much direction. "Well, Alex is four and going to preschool, very proud of his mom the school teacher. Hank calls him a momma's boy because he follows you everywhere." Emma spotted the tears flowing out of Christina's eyes and wondered if she should continue. "He's cute, and he's a good mixture of you and Hank. Then there's Jarred. He's eighteen months old but looks like a three-year-old. He's so cute and adorable. Hank says he walks around and grabs anything he can reach to throw on the floor, and when he sits on the floor he puts everything he finds in his mouth."

Christina laughed, grabbed a tissue from her robe and wiped her eyes. "Sorry. These are exactly the children I thought I would have. Only, for some reason, I always thought I would have a daughter first." She took a deep breath and stood. "I'm going to make coffee. Would you like some?" She asked Emma.

"Sure, thank you."

Hank rose. "Let's go to the kitchen. Easier."

Emma caught Christina picking up the pot she'd knocked over on her way into the kitchen.

"Sorry. I knocked it over when I came in."

"Don't worry about it. Just a roast, defrosting for tomorrow."

"I'm sorry I came at this hour." Emma inspected both their expressions and understood they didn't get why she couldn't wait. Immediately Emma considered this was Hank Apple and Christina Tyler, her two best friends, aside from Tom, but of another time. She was in the wrong place at the wrong time. Emma couldn't divulge anything to them that might capsize their world. Already, she had oversupplied information. "May I use your washroom?"

"Sure," Christina smiled.

Panic-stricken, Emma locked herself in the washroom and traveled home. She couldn't talk to anyone in this wrong place. Emma needed to leave this timeline, but how? She figured sleep had brought her here, so she lay down and closed her eyes praying for peaceful dreams. As nervous as she was, the forty winks delivered her from all the questions and the fear she held in her grasp.

When she woke a couple of hours later, she tried Tom's number. A groggy voice answered her at the other end. She smiled with glee. She occupied her current space in time. She cooed to Tom, apologizing for the early morning call, and hung up once he said goodbye.

Emma got dressed and flew over to Hank's place, letting him know she was on the premises.

Just as previously, a creak in the staircase indicated Hank was coming down to meet Emma, only this time he knew it was her. His hands deep in the pockets of his white terry robe, Hank asked, "Emma, are you all right?"

"I need to talk to you, and this can't wait until morning."

"Let's go in the kitchen. Easier, and we can close the door not to wake Christina. She's tired lately with the boys and her classes, all those parent-teacher meetings."

Emma related her trip to the hospital, the odd occurrences, and finished with the fact she'd just met with Hank and Christina in another world, an alternate reality. Emma explained why and how she had left in a hurry, and that sleeping had brought her back to her own time.

"I'm sorry I came at dawn, but what if I wake up somewhere

else in the morning? How would I explain this to anyone?"

"You did the right thing coming over now. Besides, I wasn't sleeping. I just finished giving Jarred a bottle."

"How do I make people understand?" Weird memory flashes were all I experienced and very sporadically."

"Would you like a cup of coffee. I just made some. The only thing that keeps me from falling asleep with the baby still in my arms." Hank chuckled.

"Thanks. You make great coffee." She took a deep breath. "Hank, I don't know what's up or down anymore. I spent a couple of hours with Tom tonight trying to explain the situation to him. We hadn't been together in a while." She hesitated. "He asked me to marry him, but I can't handle marriage while I focus on my doctorate ..."

"Yeah. I didn't want to say anything when you mentioned the upgrade to a doctorate, but I had a feeling the work might be overwhelming."

"Not to mention that most of my stress is due to extracurricular activities—crazy shifts blowing me around like a leaf in a storm. Besides, the APA approved the transfer, so I guess it's a good thing."

"How can I help, Emma? What can I do?"

"I'm here because I need you to witness what's going on."

"Something or someone is responsible for the time switch."

"Well, I don't think it would have anything to do with the hospital I visited tonight."

"Did you wear your oudjat?"

"Yes. I hadn't worn it in a while." Emma recounted the occurrences that took place on the bus while she traveled to the center. She showed the burn on her hands.

"Good God," Hank exclaimed. "Those are real burns. This might be related to the hospital center for some reason. I've read reports written up on the place."

Emma realized Hank was fishing—techniques adopted by all good detectives. "I came across our friends, the wizards."

"No." Hank got up and paced from the window to the table, from the table to the window. "I can still recall what I went through when they invaded me, five years ago. I keep looking over my shoulder, you know." He regained his chair and refilled his coffee cup. "Can't believe they're still around. I hoped they'd be gone by now." He took a sip of his coffee. "What happened at the hospital?"

Emma shivered. She couldn't give Hank any details but could enlighten him on what she experienced. "While I waited to see my patient, a visitor came out of the room and collapsed in front of me from a heart attack."

"No heart attack," Hank breathed. "Wizards left him for dead. I always believed that when they relinquish a human, they take some part of us with them. Who is the patient you were asked to visit?"

"Confidential. I'm not allowed to reveal the details. I guess the name would be okay. Eivan Baker."

"What?" Hank's eyes doubled in size. "You need to tell me what went on in your conversation with that patient."

"Why?"

"The commissioner just dropped Eivan's file on my desk. He

hinted at foul play. Just doesn't know at what level the foul occurred."

"Well, several doctors have been assigned to his case. One of the doctors I am working with, Dr. Franklin Rappaport sent me there tonight."

"Irresponsible of him. He should have gone with you."

"I made the mistake of telling him I was also intuitive when he told me he could sometimes read people's minds." Emma shook her head. "I wonder about Professor Rappaport now."

"What do you mean?"

"Well, Tom found his name strange, and he looked it up in the Rutgers academic catalog, but could not find a Professor Rappaport anywhere. Not even in the online database."

Hank made sure his recorder was running correctly. "We'll need to keep an eye on this professor. Do you believe Eivan might have triggered all this?"

"I'm not sure. Looking back, I can see that there is more than a front and back door, more than a push and pull. There may be several issues involved."

"This all happened after you went to the hospital?"

"Yes. I was scared the whole time I was there. Good thing Tom came to pick me up. I wouldn't have been able to take the bus back."

"Well, whenever Tom is not available, you can call on me. Never forget this."

Emma smiled and squeezed his hand.

"What about the patient, Emma. You have to tell me what he

said."

"We communicated telepathically. I guess I can tell you, at least what's been in the papers. Eivan said his stepfather, Reverend Steve lemon, pushed him off the building. He also mentioned the weird black eyes when he did, which means the stepfather was under the influence of wizards. He said the reason for trying to kill him was the inheritance his father left him—forty-five million dollars he's not due to collect for another couple of months."

"Geez Louise. Bill said we were the only two people aware of this information."

"Somehow, in Eivan's state of mind, I found him too quick to admit to this theory?"

"To the fact, his stepfather pushed him?"

"No. To the reason why the stepfather pushed him." Emma stared at Hank. "Remember, his stepfather didn't push him, wizards did. And somehow, I think the boy is smart enough to realize this. Maybe not about wizards, but maybe about the possibility of his stepfather possessed by this evil he is attempting to pursue. I could sense his hesitation in the unspoken thoughts he kept aside. Besides, why would wizards be interested in money?"

"That's a damn good question?"

"They can't use any currency. Wizards can only use people. However, a quantum science project that might threaten their existence would be worth destroying. What better way to eliminate the threat than to do away with its inventor?"

"There you go."

Just as Hank said this, the kitchen door opened and Christina walked in. "I thought I heard people talking."

"I'm sorry we woke you, sweetie." Hank rose to take Christina in his arms.

"You didn't. Jarred needed to burp. The baby was crying. When I put him back to sleep, I heard you two talking. What's going on?"

Hank turned toward Christina bending to kiss her lips. "I'm getting dressed. Emma and I are going to Bill Frost's house. He needs to hear this before Emma changes again."

When Hank came downstairs with socks and shoes in hand, Emma had brought Christina in the loop.

Hank hugged Christina and grabbed his car keys.

"Hank, we won't need the car keys." Emma smiled as she took in his harried expression. "We're going to travel the astral route."

"I can't follow you there."

"You can if I hold your hand. I've been practicing with Tom, even with my dad once. They enjoyed the mode of transportation. Very peaceful, not at all scary."

"Christina, is that okay?"

She nodded, a frown on her brow and a smile in her beautiful brown eyes.

"Don't worry, Christina. I'll take good care of him."

Emma Willis Book 3,
I Can Help You

—Five—

Origins

*H*ank attempted to hide his nervousness at traveling through the portals of the astral world. He took Emma's hands in his, as she instructed, and smiled at Christina. Surprised there appeared no dizziness or sense of taking off as if he were flying through the air, he closed his eyes when he sensed his surroundings changing and opened them seconds later to catch the impression of a bright blue dome all around them.

Emma stared at him and wore a bright smile as she communicated telepathically about the flowered arches and the portals they traversed. He wondered how he could hear her. Then Hank remembered Emma learned how to project her voice to the person who needed her, a little like she did with her physical appearance. She had warned him to remain positive and keep pleasant thoughts of Christina, and he did, the whole experience relaxing and surprisingly joyous.

He smiled at Emma, and she nodded, giving the sign they were on their way down. Hank released a grateful breath she knew where they headed. He lost touch for seconds as they began to descend and the night stretched dark and mysterious.

They lightly touched down in Bill's yard in the posh neighborhood of Englewood Cliffs that bordered the Hudson River. A few streets back of the central area, FBI agent Bill Frost's expensive house appeared dark. Emma gave Hank the signal to remain still and quiet.

She listened as they took their first steps, and he wondered if she did this to detect an alarm of sorts.

"How was that?" She asked.

"No words to describe it." Hank glanced at his watch and remarked. "Took only seconds, but seemed longer somehow."

"The illusion of travel does this." Emma searched the area. "There doesn't appear to be anyone here."

"Should we ring, or knock?"

"Go to the back door, Hank. I'll open it for you." He didn't seem to understand. "I can materialize inside. Don't remember the layout enough to bring you along. Something to try later."

Hank did as she instructed, and waited for her to open the patio doors.

Once inside, Hank agreed with Emma. "You're right. The place appears empty."

"They might be on Earth Optimal. I'll try and summon Bill." She strapped her hands on each shoulder and closed her eyes, holding the thought of Bill Frost in her mind. Even if they were on Earth Optimal, Bill the Seraph from the Celeste Dynasty two galaxies away, traveled at the speed of thought. He would be there in a few moments.

A few minutes later, Bill appeared in front of them. "Hank, Emma? What are you doing here?"

"We need to talk," Hank breathed with his eyebrows hitched high.

"You were on Earth Optimal. Sorry to disturb you."

"You didn't. You know I don't need to sleep." He extended his arm for them to follow him. "Did you bring Hank along the astral route?"

"Yes, I did."

"This is urgent."

"Understatement of the year," Hank nodded.

Bill lead them to the living room, the one without any furniture Emma had spotted when Hank asked her to spy on Bill and his family five years prior.

Well furnished these days, he directed them toward a pair of lovely powder blue divans facing each other and encircling an oval marble table.

Hank and Emma sat on one of the divans, while Bill took the one opposite them. "What would you like? Coffee, tea, biscuits?"

"I'd love coffee," Hank said. "But never mind. It'll take too long."

Bill extended a hand over the table and a silver carafe brimming with hot coffee, and a smaller one with tea appeared as did a plateful of mixed little cakes and cookies.

"Okay, then," Hank said as he pinched the corner of his eyes. "No time at all." He poured himself some coffee and asked Emma to start. "You go, sweetie."

Emma gave the information as concisely and efficiently as she could, repeating almost word for word what she had told Hank and Christina.

"So, this is what's been going on." Bill also poured himself coffee.

"You knew? About the changing realities?" Emma asked, unable to mask her surprise.

"Nothing certain. Fred complained about wizards infiltrating more than their share, scared he wouldn't be able to stop them." Bill rose and walked toward the large windows staring onto the gardens. Not much to admire at this hour. He appeared lost in thought. "Tell me again what this boy said?"

"Not so much what he said, as what he didn't say."

"Explain, please."

"Well, he readily told me his stepfather pushed him off the roof, but of course the stepfather did not, wizards did. He mentioned Steve Lemon's eyes changing to black and weird, which indicates he knows about the evil. Then he volunteered very quickly that he'd done so, the stepfather, to get his hands on his inheritance of forty-five million dollars he is to receive in three-months-time."

"The only ones who know this, right?" Hank held his palms up and nodded Bill's way to show discontentment.

"Relax, Hank. They briefed me the same way."

"Of course, he wasn't pushed by his stepfather. Wizards did. And, wizards can't use money."

"You're right, Emma. They only use people." Bill came back to sit on the sofa. "So, Annemarie Hanover?"

Emma nodded.

"What would we do without you, Emma. You've been a bigger help in these crunches than anyone I know." He smiled.

"Yes, except now, I'm the one in trouble."

"This going back and forth?"

"Yes. Won't this affect you, or Fred Manson, or anyone else?"

"This is a time shift of Earth Refuse and a few contained changes, as far as I can tell. I'll have to assess the damage later." He eyed Emma, Hank, then Emma again. "Should you travel to other time shifts, you will retain everything you know now. I will not travel to any other timeline, neither will Fred. We can only exist within the current timeline. No other humans will be able to cross these thresholds."

"How come?"

"The likelihood of the situation being some sort of science project affects this Earth, and humans—only humans."

"Are you saying ... I'm not human?"

Hank scooted over to Emma and grabbed her hand. "That's not what he means at all, Emma," Hank said, his eyes menacing Bill not to continue this train of thought.

"I didn't want to tell you like this. Fred thought it imperative that we allow you to discover your origins on your own, in your own time."

She nodded. "I don't know the details, but I understand that although I am human, I'm not from here." She turned toward Hank. "I tried to tell you once, remember—when we visited my father at the hospital? I explained what the Devronairs mentioned during the trial."

He nodded, head down. He wrapped his arm around her shoulders and gave her a little tug. "Don't worry, Emma. Everything will work out."

"Okay, Bill. Since I already suspect most of it, how about the details?"

"You know what? I'm going to let Columba tell you this. She knows more than I do about your origins. She'll even bring you there if you wish."

"I've already been there a couple of times." She rested her head on Hank's shoulder. "Only problem, I've tried to reach Columba when all this happened, but I can't seem to get to her. Even my oudjat is not working properly."

"Ah!" He nodded. "The Earthly illusion is getting to you, influencing what you can and what you can't do. You need to come to terms with who you are, now, before the situation worsens and impedes more of your powers."

He put his hand to forestall her next question. "Don't worry, Columba admires you. She will be around to help you."

"Still something I do not understand. I was born on Earth.

How can I come from somewhere else?"

"There is more to it than this. Please wait for Columba to explain. She is the pathfinder, and she is well versed in all ancient rites."

Emma turned to face Hank. "This won't hurt our relationship, will it?" Emma remembered how terrified Hank was to work with Bill Frost and Tim O'Rourke when he found out five years earlier they were aliens from another galaxy.

"Of course not." He gave her a little squeeze his arms still around her shoulders.

Emma considered he remembered his former reaction to Bill and Tim, because he added, "I have matured a lot since then. I understand we are all the same, wherever we come from."

Emma smiled at him. She could always count on Hank, a formidable friend, and tireless worker.

She turned toward Bill. "What do I do now?"

"Go home. Go to bed. Wherever you wake up, you will be all right."

"What about Hank," she glanced at the chief of police sitting beside her. "If I wake elsewhere, will Hank be informed?"

"Best if this other Hank in another timeline doesn't know that you are shifting in time."

Emma released a huge breath. "I guess you're right. Hank and I will go now." She eyed Hank. "Christina will begin to worry if we don't hurry back."

They both rose, and Emma thought of something else. "By

the way, be careful how you bring this information concerning Eivan to others. This information came to me in strictest confidence, and I'm not allowed to repeat what I know."

"Who did give you this information—aside from Eivan Baker. Who sent you there?"

"Dr. Franklin Rappaport, my professor. He read the letter from Annemarie Hanover, and he has a real connection with Dr. Podero at the hospital. He said he visited Eivan twice."

Bill shook his head. "Are you sure about the name?"

"Yes, Professor Rappaport is the one who had my masters upgraded to a doctorate."

Bill took both her hands in his. "Emma, I don't expect you to understand, but inside this head." He poked his temple repeatedly. "Etched in alphabetical order is a list of every name on Earth Refuse I am likely to encounter. There is no Franklin Rappaport, at least none which works as a professor or as a doctor in any of the Rutgers University campuses."

"Tom was right." She eyed Bill. "My friend Tom said he searched the Rutgers catalog to verify the name of Franklin Rappaport and could not find anything."

Bill took a deep breath. "Do not report back to him anything that went on at that hospital. Okay?"

Emma nodded. "I'll tell him I couldn't go."

"Don't lie—at least not about being there. There are records. You signed your name when you arrived and when you left. Only tell him you found nothing amiss."

"Thanks, I will." As Emma and Hank prepared to leave,

she asked, "Will you let me know who he is when you find out?"

Bill shook Hank's hand. "I will, Emma."

"Love to Jeannie and the girls."

"She misses you too, Emma."

This last sentence they caught once Emma and Hank were airborne. This time, Hank kept his eyes open during takeoff and smiled throughout the voyage which took a couple of seconds. Since she was familiar with Hank and Christina's house, she landed in the small salon with him.

Hank put a finger to his lips. "Don't want to wake Christina," he whispered. "I'd be up until morning needing to explain."

"I understand." She put up her hand to wave. She disappeared almost immediately and landed at home in her room where she dropped on her bed merely kicking off her shoes. She wished for sleep to find her and keep her from thinking for the next couple of hours.

As she mentioned to Bill earlier on, Emma's dreams brought her once more to a familiar land. Purple skies on fire from the suspension of two suns facing each other like smiling collaborators struck Emma with a welcome-home tremor. No excessive heat emanated from the masses of light illuminating her world, only warmth and a generous amount of euphoria. As for the lush green valleys, the jumping, gurgling brook rolling at her feet, the poise of a red-breasted robin on her shoulder filling her ear with a delightful song, all filled her with a sense of peace, and a deep-seated wish to never leave.

As her hand stroke the feathers of the gentle bird cooing in her neck, she wondered in awe at the translucent quality of her limbs. No tiredness inhibited her movements. No headache or heart thumping sensation in her chest, no fear or discomfort of any kind. Just a smile that would not quit. As Emma looked down, she caught the glow emanating from her physical form. She could not distinguish an actual outline or even the clothes she'd worn to bed. Dreams could be so rewarding—at least the peaceful ones.

"*This place does not originate from the vapors of a dream.*"

Emma captured the thought in her mind, too loud to be her own. She turned to catch a familiar soul nearby. "*Columba! I searched the astral world for you. Could not find you anywhere.*"

"*I came to you, but you were unable to see me.*" She came closer the white dress she wore flowing around her. She extended her arms encompassing the surroundings. "*This world is your home, Emma, sweet Chavah.*"

"*What is that name you just called me? And what do you call this world?*"

"*The name has several meanings. I like to think of Chavah as the mother of all life, the desire to save life.*" She smiled. "*This world is named Capella—Quintus Capella, Latin for The Fifth Chapel.*"

Emma looked down at herself and indicated the odd

occurrence of her transparency to Columba. *"Why do I appear this way? What does this mean?"*

"Search your soul. The answers are there."

Emma nodded. *"Part of me remembers my quest to reach the source. This fifth dimension means I'm close, right?"*

Columba nodded as she smiled at Emma. *"Quite close."*

"Then, part of me gets bogged down with details of Earth. I need your help to bridge the gap."

"Think of my brother, Hawke. How he needed to cleanse after five years of Earth contamination."

"I Can't afford to stay away from Earth that long. And I've had more than a five-year exposure." Emma smiled, unafraid and content to be home.

Columba approached her and handed her an object. Emma admired the small jewel the pathfinder placed in her hand. *"What do I do with this?"*

"Take out your Eye of Horus. The black opal on top will join with the Star of Capella when you press the new jewel against it."

Emma stared at the small triangle glowing in varied hues of pink. Closer to her body, the triangle took on shiny facets of her physical form. She did as Columba suggested, and the stone affixed itself to the top of her jewel. *"What will this accomplish?"*

"This is your birthstone, Chavah. The jewel will keep you grounded and connected to the fifth dimension. This way, you will not get lost in any of the shifts occurring on Earth at

the moment."

"Thank you, so much. Are there others living here?"

"Yes, of course." Columba smiled. *"You will find them in due time."*

Columba whispered the last words as she disappeared from view. Emma gazed at her surroundings, traveling toward the sound of a waterfall tumbling into a vast lake flowing at the bottom of a cliff. She didn't want to leave, but she felt the pull of her body as she lay in bed on Earth.

The shift in her physical and mental weight sucker-punched her on arrival, the heaviness waking her up from a sound sleep, from her dream.

A dream? She wondered. Lifting the pendant from around her neck, she checked the Eye of Horus and smiled when she caught the gleaming pink of the small triangular Star of Capella. Would she still be able to target the wizards when they inhabited human bodies?

—Six—

Wrong Turn

A knock on her bedroom door woke Emma. She called out in a sleepy voice, "Am I late?"

"It's Dad. You're not late. It's Saturday, and your mother and I are going to round up some groceries. Just wanted to let you know."

"Come in, Dad."

Patrick Willis opened the door to his daughter's room.

Emma sat up in bed, her eyes still closed, acknowledging for the umpteenth time her father needed to oil the horrible squeak from the hinges on the door.

"Slept in your clothes again, I see."

"Yeah."

"Anything you need at the store?"

"No," she breathed out in a loud sigh. "Thank you." Emma smoothed her hair strands. "Tom and I plan to go swimming at Grandmas today. Going to be gorgeous, and she's had the pool heated since April."

"What?" Patrick walked into the room. "That pool is far from ready."

Emma paused. "What do you mean?"

"Well, since your grandmother's stroke, the grounds, including the tennis courts and the pool, have been neglected."

"Her stroke." she nodded.

"I told your mother and your aunt Franka to hire someone to maintain the grounds. They'll never be able to sell the house at the price they're asking if they don't." Patrick turned to stare at her. "And what's with Tom? He's going to come all the way from MIT to go swimming with you at Grandmas?"

Emma remained silent.

"Emma, are you all right?"

She stared at her room, at the old, worn furniture, at the broken lamp on her desk gone several years ago, and wondered why this other skip to an alternate life. "I'm just disoriented this morning. Too much studying."

"Too much studying and two jobs are more than enough to confuse you. Well, I have to go. Your mom's working part-time this afternoon. The flower shop is not doing so well, and they cut back her hours again. I don't mind telling you. The money your grandma Abigail left us is going to ease both our minds."

Emma gave him a little wave wondering with a slight edge of panic why she skipped lives again when Columba maintained she would not. No. Columba stipulated she would not get lost inside an alternate timeline. She lifted her oudjat from around her neck and discovered the little Star of Capella affixed to the black onyx.

She rose, showered and changed into her jeans and favorite blue T-shirt. At least she could adapt quickly from one time shift to the next.

As she was about to go downstairs, she bumped into Columba. "Ah!" she screamed. "You scared me. First, I can't get to you, now I bump into you twice in twenty-four hours," Emma said catching her breath.

Columba's pearly laugh sounded delightful in the middle of the mess surrounding her life. "I'm sorry, Emma. I need to be precise. Alternate jolts to your life are going on around you, but you remain the same, now aware of one more timeline."

"Yes. From what I can tell, my mother is still an employee of the flower shop and doesn't own it. My father never got his career off the ground, either because Hank never told that reporter why he was here so often, or that reporter was never here." She plopped on the bed. "I live in a mess." Emma extended her arms around her. "I am one year overdue to finish my Masters as I have two jobs aside from my studies, and I don't know how to get back to my timeline."

Columba bit her lip, her round eyes depicting she held back another bout of laughter. Emma admired her coolness under fire. She wore the same type of outfit her brother, Hawke wore all those years ago when she first met him. A peasant blouse with billowing sleeves, tight pants, and knee-high boots. Her dark hair, flowing as though she'd just been in a wind tunnel, framed a lovely porcelain face featuring ruby red lips and huge dark eyes. "Emma, take a look at your pendant."

Emma did and remarked, "Doesn't shine like it did when you first gave it to me."

"This indicates you are not inside your timeline, inside your reality."

"Good to know. Only, where is my reality? How do I get there?" Emma released a huge sigh. "More importantly, how do I remain there."

"I spoke to Bill this morning. He came to see me on Earth Optimal. He believes the experiment this young man, Eivan Baker began is still operating."

"Does the procedure need to be shut down?"

"Hard to say. First, we need to understand what Eivan did. Wizards may be operating behind the scenes to have it neutralized. We don't know."

"So, not shut it down. Might wizards be trying to acquire the project's help in any way?"

Columba smiled. "In other words, since wizards are interested in this project, Fred is attempting to discover why they are attracted to this, and how we can handle the process without getting into harm's way."

"This explains why they tried to kill Eivan."

Columba nodded. "To travel between alternate timelines, you need only to hold your pendant in your hand and use the same thought process you do to project your corporeal self into the astral world."

"I'll need a focal point of sorts. I hold in my mind the place where I wish to land when I travel through the astral world. What should I focus on to reach my reality?"

"Something that is unique to your time, something you haven't encountered anywhere else."

"Like a quantum signature of sorts."

"Bill Frost states he believes this signature to be your doctorate, and he mentioned the name, Franklin Rappaport."

"Yes," Emma answered enthusiastically. She got up to pace in front of the window. "This was the last thing I remembered before my life began to slide left and right." Emma turned toward Columba. "What about my other selves dispersed in other areas, will they return to where they should be?"

"You are the only one subjected to this transition. Once we manage to stop the multiplication of realities, you will remain in your original world."

"What about Fred Manson? Has he been consulted? Does he know about this development?"

"I can't reach him. No one can. He's nowhere, which could mean he is on Devron. No one is allowed on their planet except Devronairs."

"He works with others, though. I've seen them when they put me on trial, five years ago."

"You wouldn't get anywhere with any of them. Most of the Devronairs on Earth Refuse are drones, unable to perform anything else but the task assigned to them. The atmosphere inhibits their powers as well as their thought process."

"Yes, I remember that."

"Good luck to you." Columba smiled before she disappeared.

A deep breath later, a knot inside Emma's stomach indicated hunger pains. The curiosity to explore this timeline kept her glued to the place. She could just as well eat here and go home later. After all, she was in her house in a manner of speaking.

Going downstairs for a bite to eat and a cup of coffee, Emma wondered where Eivan Baker might be within this particular timeline. In the one she originally came from, she would have to visit him in the hospital again, possibly projecting herself into his room so no one would catch her on the premises. Would he be well enough to explain what was going on?

With a piece of her mom's blueberry buckle on a plate, she picked up her tablet to do some research. She walked toward the table while the coffee brewed. She took a big bite of the cake and putting down her fork she surfed on her tablet to find Eivan Baker. He was an MIT student. The thought crossed her mind to contact Tom, especially that she missed him more than she ever thought possible. She would welcome his well-rounded logic about now, not to mention how lonely she imagined her life to be without him. Still, she didn't want to interrupt whatever classes he might have today. Although, Saturday meant he possibly enjoyed a light day.

The coffee pot made its gurgle sound of evaporating water, and she walked over to pour herself a cup. Once more seated at the table, she could not find anything about Eivan in the news. A small article about a student making great strides in astrophysics caught Emma's attention. The article mentioned no one in particular, only that a second-year student worked on a particle accelerator to prove his theory of multi-universes. She wondered who wrote the story and when searching for a name, came across A. Hanover in smaller letters at the bottom of the story.

Then, Emma called up The Tech on her tablet, the Cambridge College newspaper, and scouted for any news on Eivan and on what project he might be working. Nothing.

She finished eating her cake, then searched her phone for Eivan's number, the one Dr.Rappaport gave her. She found his home number and remembered Columba's words their sense finally reaching her. For her and her possessions, such as her mind, her memory, and evidently her phone, information remained unchanged.

She punched in the keys to Eivan's home phone but stopped short of completing the call. Eivan might well be in school. She copied the MIT's number off the school paper, the only one she found and called. Had to be the wrong number. The thing just rang, ten times, fifteen times. As she was about to hang up, a click stalled her from ending the call. "Hello"

"Hello. I am the guard patrolling the hall. There is no one in this section of school today. I answered because the ringing is annoying."

"I'm trying to reach one of the students."

"Sorry. If you don't have the student's number, I will not be able to help you. You will need to call back Monday."

The click told her the guard hung up the phone without waiting for her to say anything else.

Emma got up to wash her hands and refill her coffee cup. Then she worked with her phone's settings to block her outgoing caller ID before contacting Eivan's home. An older woman's sweet voice told her Eivan was at Cambridge, in school. She thanked the person and hung up.

She reversed the settings on her phone and called Tom. A disconnected number message disenchanted her. Hank mentioned Tom had switched his number to a local one, and she wondered why. Tom always boasted how he loved the easy digits and would never change them. With unlimited talk and text phone plans these days, Emma didn't understand why Tom needed a local number.

Left with no choice than to show up on Tom unexpectedly, she decided on extra measures to make certain no one else was with him when she did. After packing a backpack and tying a jacket around her waist, she sat down on a kitchen chair and projected herself as close as possible to Tom as she could. Invisible, she would be able to detect someone else's presence without being spotted.

Tom was still in bed, and he wasn't alone. Stretched out beside him was Amelia, her best friend, sleeping soundly with her arm wrapped around Tom's torso. A tear rolled down her cheek, and she scolded herself. She wished nothing but happiness for Amelia and Tom, her two best friends. Perhaps Tom and Emma never got together last Christmas which was why he'd succumbed to Amelia's advances.

After a quivering breath, she left to retrieve her physical self still at home, sitting on a chair.

Now she understood to propel herself close to his door and call out to Tom making sure he was the only one who heard her.

She waited a good ten minutes before Tom finally came to the door and called out her name in a stunned whisper. "What are you doing here?" He turned to give Amelia a quick glance. "Let's go somewhere else." He closed the door softly behind him and led the way to one of the bright, airy atriums where several students had regrouped in what seemed to be a study session.

"I need your help, Tom."

"Listen, I would have told you about Amelia. She kept asking me to tell you. I just didn't know how to broach the subject."

"I understand completely. But why did you change your cell number?"

"Amelia. She maintains it's easier for people here to reach me."

He shrugged, and Emma remembered the pleasure of wallowing in those strong arms. She also recognized the jealousy that haunted Amelia. Perhaps the reason a for phone number change? Could this be why they hardly spoke anymore? "I'm in trouble. I need your help."

Tom rubbed his forehead. He picked up Emma's hand and brushed her fingers against his cheek. "I'm always here to help you, Emma. What can I do?"

"Do you know anyone by the name of Eivan Baker? I believe he is a second-year student in astrophysics."

"Name rings a bell." He shrugged, unable to come up with anything.

"Annemarie Hanover perhaps?"

"Annemarie. Yes! She helped me with some of my articles, some of my tech articles for The Tech—get it?"

Emma smiled waiting for him to continue.

"She told me about this ex-boyfriend in astrophysics, how she began to fear the experiment he was doing. I asked her about it, but she doesn't understand enough to explain. She's doing her masters in communications. She wants to be a journalist."

"And?"

"Just that the whole experiment appeared to be wild."

"I need to ask Eivan questions, this weekend. I have to go, but I also need answers before Monday. Do you think you could get his number for me?"

"I can try."

Emma's eyes ran over Tom's handsome features, and her heart beat faster when she remembered how much she loved him. She rose and checked out her surroundings. The students had left. Only she and Tom remained. She approached him and stared into his eyes. "Hide me while I leave?"

"What do you mean, hide you?" He scooped her up wrapping his big arms around her. "Do you ever think about us—about us being together?"

Locked in his arms, staring into his eyes, she could not prevent a smile.

"I'm not surprised. I sensed your disappointment when I admitted about Amelia."

"Here." Emma handed him the small jewel she'd conjured by mistake ten years prior, the one devoid of any powers. "Keep this oudjat with you at all times. The pendant will help me find you when I return."

Tom didn't take the jewel she handed him but gave the necklace a curious look. "What's an oudjat?"

"Never mind. I'll find you. Emma pocketed the jewel thinking it was better to keep the pendant than to leave it in the hands of someone who would not comprehend its worth.

Tom took Emma into his arms and held her close rubbing her back with his big hands. "Emma," he whispered, as though he didn't want to let her go.

With a heavy sigh, Tom moved away. "Do you know your way back?"

"Tom," she said surprised by his question. "You of all people know how I travel."

"How did you get here? Car, bus?"

"Tom?" Emma wanted some explanation. He didn't seem to know about her powers of transportation. He wasn't aware of the oudjat either.

Someone called out his name, and he turned around slowly. When he did, he moved, and she spotted Amelia, foaming at the mouth, appearing angry and hurt.

White as a ghost, she stared up at him, mouth opened, eyes as big and blue as mini oceans. She backed up when he approached her, and Emma wondered what she heard, what she spotted.

"You are with Emma. You held her in your arms. Did you guys kiss?"

She kept backing up, and Emma realized Tom would need to calm her down. "We didn't kiss," he mumbled.

"You're going to stand there and lie about what I just witnessed with my own eyes?"

He made one last attempt to hold her. Again, Amelia backed away. "Don't ever come near me again. Ever. You and I are over," she yelled. A smirk ran across her face. "And that goes for our friendship, Emma." She stomped her foot on the ground, and Emma realized how upset Amelia was.

"You would give up on your best friend without talking to her first, without getting the details of what you think you saw or what you believe you might have heard?"

"Oh, I'll give her a piece of my mind. But, I'm not stupid. Emma won't be able to cover anything up." Amelia wiped her eyes and ran in the direction of her room.

Tom watched her leave unable to run after her or walk back toward Emma. Amelia's bitter comportment left Emma with unsteady legs. Once more, Amelia jumped to erroneous conclusions and cast judgment without knowing the truth. What disconcerted her most was the fact Tom didn't seem to know about her powers, about her amulet when he eyed the jewel in a strange way. Tom even asked how Emma got to Cambridge.

When he walked back to her, the pitiful expression showed how unhappy Tom was. "I'm sorry about this, Emma. I'll get a hold of Annemarie. I promise. I'll call you as soon as I reach her."

Emma thanked him and walked down the hall toward the nearest door. Once in the shadow of two intersecting corridors, she flew home.

Joss Landry

—Seven—

Duality

Emma embraced the familiarity of her room after leaving Tom behind. Even if most of her keepsakes were missing, she hesitated to go back to her reality. She sensed she was in this one for a reason when she heard her mom call out that brunch was on the table. Emma walked out to the top of the stairs. "Don't you have to work today, Mom?"

Eloise shook her head. "Harry called. He is closing early today. He's going out of town for the weekend. But you're the supervisor in charge at the community center today. I thought I'd make your favorite brunch, chocolate chip pancakes with blueberries."

"Wow, mom. Quite the brunch. I'll be down in a second."

Once more, Emma debated going back to her own time. She didn't know how long she would need to wait for Tom to get the required number, and she hated wasting her whole afternoon at the community center. Usually, she would bring books there to study, but in her current timeline, she'd already done all those courses.

She donned the clothes she'd worn the day before, sat on her bed and held on to her pendant thinking of studying for her doctorate and of reporting back to Dr. Franklin Rappaport.

The transition was quick and impossible to detect, except that a second later, her room was tidy, well decorated and equipped with all the keepsakes she loved.

Emma gave thanks for a life she cherished while she keyed Tom's number, the number she knew well, and smiled when he answered with a cheery greeting. "I should block my number and catch you out of sorts when you answer some number you don't know." She laughed.

"Why would you want me to replace the greeting of, Emma, my sweet love?"

She laughed. "I appreciate the thought, trust me, I do. Anyway, I thought I'd have a bite to eat before we go swimming."

"Good idea. I'll be right over. Did you ask your grandma if we could swim there?"

"Of course. Grandma is always asking me to visit. I think she's lonely. My aunt Franka is not often around with her two-children obligations, and my folks still work hard, and when they don't, they leave the city whenever they can."

"Yeah, I can imagine she doesn't have too many friends, alone in that big house."

"Bring your tennis racket. I'll bring mine. Well-maintained tennis courts line the property at the back."

Emma hung up and ran downstairs. As usual, her parents were out. They would be shopping most of the day, so she grabbed a few toasts, brewed herself coffee she poured into her travel mug, and wrote them a note.

On the way to Abigail's house in Englewood Cliffs, Emma described for Tom the shifts she experienced. A frown marked his brow for the thirty miles they drove. "Science fiction," he spat out while turning into her grandmother's drive. "You're describing science fiction." He gave his and Emma's names to the guard at his post, and the man allowed them inside after verifying his list of family names.

"Your grandma believes in security." Tom parked his 2003 Ford Focus and eyed Emma before stepping out. "What are you going to do? I hope you don't intend to shift from one life to the next. That's crazy."

"I have been shifting—not by choice." She let go a huge breath she hadn't realized she was holding. "The good news is Columba gave me the means to reintegrate my own life when I need to do so."

"Here is a question. Where were you before you called me this morning?"

Emma smiled. "I was with you, at MIT."

"What?"

"In a couple of the other timelines, you're in Cambridge already. And now and then, you share your bed with Amelia."

"No!" Tom eyed her with disbelief. "I would never do that."

"You do. Amelia is a wonderful person, Tom. She's my best friend. And, I guess you and I never got together last Christmas in that life."

"You're right. Amelia is a terrific person, except she is insecure to the point of being neurotic. Easy to spot. The few times we went out, if I so much as mentioned your name, she'd sulk the rest of the evening. Not a pretty picture."

"I understand. Amelia can be difficult when she pouts. She's done this to me a couple of times. But, I can be difficult too, as can anyone else. Has to do with this atmosphere on this forgotten version of Earth. We all go through moods, and some of those frames of mind are difficult to shake. And I have life figured out more than most. So, if your friends don't stand by you when anger or jealousy strikes, who will?"

"Yeah, you're right." He pecked her lips. "We better go in. Your grandmother will think we're doing it in the car."

Emma laughed as she spotted Tom's eye-roll. He bent his tall frame to ease out, and they walked up to the big mansion hand in hand.

Before they reached the stoop, Abigail Tichy opened the door and pinned them with a narrow glare. "Quite a long time to be parking. Are the windows fogged up yet?"

Emma laughed, especially when she caught Tom's I-told-you-so glare. She moved up to her grandma and gave her a big hug. "I love your sense of humor, Grandma. We were discussing school exams, life, and time ran away from us."

"Well, that's what the pool is for." She replaced the inquisitive sourpuss with a bright smile. "And I love that my favorite granddaughter gets me." She kissed Emma's cheek, and with her arm around Emma's waist, she ignored Tom following a few steps behind.

Joss Landry

Once they changed into their swimwear and Tom had done a few laps of the thirty-five-meter pool, he came up underneath the raft Emma sailed on, and she jumped when he flipped her overboard. He laughed when she spat out water and wiped her eyes. "What are trying to do, drown me? I was sailing so peacefully. I fell asleep."

"Oh! Sorry. I had no idea you'd dozed off."

Emma smiled and shrugged. "It's okay. I came here to swim, not to sleep. I'll race you."

They'd each won a couple of races when Abigail showed up at the pool. "Emma," she called to get her attention.

Emma stopped, and she heard Tom claiming the win for this last lap. "Anything wrong, Grandma?"

"Hank Apple is here to see you."

Emma could tell by her grandmother's tone she worried something might be wrong.

"Can you have him come here?"

"I guess so. I'm warning you. Hank brought little Jarred with him. I hope he's not looking for a babysitter."

Emma laughed. Abigail had most likely heard from Eloise's last-minute services the night before. "No. Weekends he brings the toddler with him whenever he can, to give Christina a break."

Abigail nodded, and while she left, Emma got out of the pool and wrapped herself in a white fluffy beach towel. Whatever Hank wanted to say, she knew he would have questions to which she would need to provide answers.

Emma told Tom about her visit, and upon hearing the

name, Hank, Tom immediately climbed the pool ladder and grabbed a towel.

Aware of the long-lasting rancor Tom held toward Hank, proclaiming Hank used Emma's smarts for his glory, she mentioned this was just a social visit.

When Hank showed up with Jarred on his arm, she sensed Tom relax.

"Hey, Hank. Hello, little Jarred. You are too cute," she cooed to the baby in his arms. Once again, the child held out his arms to be with her, and she took him from Hank, Jarred grabbing her hair.

"No, no, Jarred. No grabbing the hair, little one." Hank gently opened the baby's fingers, so he could release Emma's tresses.

Jarred gurgled and held out his arms toward Tom.

Emma smiled at him. "He wants you to take him."

"I don't know what to do with him. Can I bring him in the pool?"

Hank thought a bit. "I guess it would be okay. He's off the diapers, and he's pretty good about asking for the potty. So, sure. How cold is that water," Hank asked as an afterthought.

"My grandmother keeps the water at 90°F."

"Definitely okay to bring him in the pool." Hank smiled. He picked up Jarred and took off his sandals, his little shirt, and pants. "He can go in his underwear. I have another pair for him in my bag."

"Wow, you've got this down pat."

"Second child. Always easier second time around."

Both Emma and Hank got closer to the pool to watch Tom go down the stairs in the shallow end with the toddler.

"I hope he doesn't scream. Alex hated the water at that age."

As Tom got waist deep, he dunked the baby halfway in the water and Jarred laughed and screamed with joy, hit the water and splashed Tom's face.

Hank laughed with relief. "First time. He's great. He's a chip off the old block." Then he turned toward Emma with a frown puckering his brow. "Bill just left my house."

He indicated the chairs at the table covered by a brightly colored parasol.

"Why? What did he say?"

"Well, to be honest, I haven't wrapped my mind around this yet. I finally told Christina. I almost couldn't leave. She was in tears."

"Why?"

"Bill explained some of the extracurricular lives there are, and how in most of them, Christina cannot have children."

"What matters is that she has them here and now."

"Yes, but once all these alternate realities are combined, reinstated, where will that leave us?"

A cry from Jarred interrupted their conversation, and they witnessed Tom going back into the water to the child's delight. Jarred demonstrated he didn't want Tom to leave the pool.

"I'll have to go rescue him. Tom must be tired of carrying him around."

"Wait. Tom's fine. Bill doesn't know, so it's not his fault he didn't tell you, but Columba did say once all these time fissures were eliminated, repaired, this is the original timeline that would remain." Emma took a deep breath. "Keep in mind. We don't know what we are dealing with or how the project went awry. May take a while before we fix this."

"There's more." He took a deep breath glancing at Tom sailing Jarred around the pool in a little floating tugboat, the baby's face utterly happy. "Bill couldn't find you, so he asked me to tell you that we can't find Fred Manson."

"I know. Columba also looked for him and could not find him. She seems to think this means he is on Devron. We can't get to him there. No one is allowed on that planet except Devronairs."

"Seraphs are allowed on Devron. They are welcome there apparently. Discretely, he found out Fred is on Earth." Hank got up and walked toward the pool.

Emma followed, asking, "What does that mean?"

"Bill thinks he might be imprisoned in one of the fissures."

"Held against his will, you mean?"

"Bill can't find him, neither can Columba as you just mentioned. He might be stuck somewhere unable to return."

"God, we have to find him."

"Before anyone finds out he is missing. If Devronairs discover their main emissary has been taken hostage somewhere, Earth could be in dire straits."

"Okay, here is a plan, the only one I foresee. I have encountered so far, three different realities. My own—this one, and two more. In one of them, I intend to return to get answers from Tom about how to reach Eivan Baker who is also at MIT."

"Sounds like a plan."

"With the new jewel Columba was kind enough to give me, I can easily travel between the timelines, and still come back to mine."

"You want me to ask Bill to figure out how many timelines there are and identify a unique property in each one of them?"

Emma let out a huge breath happy Hank was smart and quick to seize the right opportunities. She nodded. "I realize this is a tall order, but if he can do this, I will be able to travel to each timeline and see if I can spot Fred Manson in one of them."

"Rather than me trying to explain to Bill, and you getting the information third hand, we should hold a meeting later on tonight."

"I agree. Call me later. I'll make a point of being at the meeting."

Hank nodded and rushed to Jarred's side. The baby monopolized Tom's time, and clearly, Tom didn't know how to step out of the pool while avoiding the boy's shrieks and tears.

Emma Willis Book 3,
I Can Help You

"Come to Daddy, Jarred," Hank cooed to the boy with a smile, and the toddler held out his arms to him. Hank held a towel in front of him and when he wrapped the boy, Jarred put his little arms around his neck and squeezed him.

Emma smiled as she heard Jarred say, "Daddy."

"Ah!" Tom whispered as he came out of the water. "I was beginning to feel like a hostage to this tiny little fellow." He patted the boy on the head while Hank dried him, changed his underwear and put on his clothes. "Do you think Abigail would mind if I took him to the bathroom before I left?"

"No. Not at all. Follow me." All the way into the house, to the closest bathroom Emma could find, Jarred kept saying, "Potty, Daddy. Potty." Luckily, they got there just in time.

When they came out of the washroom, Abigail smiled at Jarred. "Would you like a cup of coffee Hank?"

"Thank you. I'll have to take a rain check. Christina's waiting for us."

Hank left almost immediately, and Emma watched him go.

"Trouble?" Abigail asked as she approached her granddaughter.

"Nothing Hank can't solve, Grandma. He's exceptional."

"With your help." Abigail smiled. "I know you're there for him, sweetheart. You two make a good team."

Emma gave her grandma a kiss on the cheek. "Thanks. I better see what Tom is doing. We brought our tennis rackets."

"Good. I'm glad. I enjoy a good game of tennis. I'll come outside and watch you play."

While Emma and Tom played tennis, each using their strengths to win a set, Emma's Bluetooth rang in her ear.

"Time," she yelled across the net. "My phone is ringing."

"You're kidding me. Who plays tennis with a Bluetooth stuck to their ear—my point then."

"Hello?"

"Emma, it's Tom."

Emma glanced across the net and stumbled from dizziness. "Tom Carson?"

"Of course. Who else?"

She turned to hide the shock on her face from her grandmother and from Tom standing on the other side of the court, flipping his racket's position in his hand. She remembered Columba telling her that who she was, her phone number and her mission, would remain the same throughout her slides.

She didn't know what to answer. She found her voice. "What's wrong, Tom?"

"Thank God. Amelia is distraught. She thinks you're trying to put the moves on me. You need to come back and stop her from blubbering. She's not herself right now."

Emma shuddered. Even though she realized this Tom Carson called from another reality, one liable to disappear as soon as they were able to shut down Eivan's machine, to have this second timespan deviate so much from the values of their current one might create an impossible dilemma—engender a permanent scenario they might not be able to undo. "I'll try and get there as fast as I can."

The moment she turned toward Tom, she found him inches away, concern coloring his face a dark shade of worry. "Was that Hank on the phone?" His tone came out as resentful.

She stared into his eyes, unable to keep the anxiety from creasing her brow. She shook her head to answer his question.

"Who was it?" Tom asked more forcefully.

"You."

Tom took thirty seconds before he understood the meaning of Emma's words. "What? I can reach you from another timeline?"

As incredulous as his question sounded, Emma realized she needed to be honest. "I didn't think this was possible either. I don't know what's going on, but I have to leave—now."

"You run. I'll make something up for your grandma."

"I'll keep you posted." Emma ran to her grandmother, kissed her as she told her Tom would explain.

Tom told Abigail Emma's professor scheduled an appointment for her in an hour. She had to run. "Would you like to play a couple of sets?" Tom offered Abigail.

"That's sweet of you, but I haven't played since last year."

"I'll just return the ball to you, allow you to practice."

Abigail's eyes narrowed, and her smile widened. "Well, then I'd love to play against you."

Joss Landry

While walking toward his side of the net, Tom remembered Emma bragging about her grandma's tennis exploits. He rolled his eyes, shook his head, and called himself a chump. He was about to be royally spanked.

Emma Willis Book 3,
I Can Help You

—Eight—

Annemarie Hanover

Emma prepared to land in the corner of Tom's room, the only place she hoped to find Tom alone. She reflected on the fact her grandmother did not ask how she would get to wherever she hurried. All her family, aware of her mode of transportation, never discussed the matter aloud. They accepted that Emma used the astral route to travel when she needed to do so.

Disoriented, and worried about this new turn of events, she figured finding Fred Manson in any of these time fissures would be impossible. The Devronair would not be changing with shifts of time. Not any more than Bill the Seraph or Tim O'Rourke, his assistant, did. She needed to re-examine the facts and try to configure where the good doctor might have gone. Discover what happened to him before Devronairs learned he was missing.

What worried her more was the fact this Tom was able to reach her on her cell. Not only did she appear to be the sole person traveling to and from these alternate lives, there seemed to be just one of her. What did this mean in the other scenarios? Was she missing? Did her family wonder where she was? Did they know about her powers, maybe wonder if she got stuck in the astral world?.

Tom was not in his room. Emma picked up a photo of him on his desk. He stood tall in his football jersey with the Engineers logo written across the maroon T-shirt, his hat in his left hand, his free arm wrapped around Amelia's shoulders. They made a cute couple, and she could spot the pure joy in Amelia's eyes. Something else to worry about—breaking Amelia's heart.

She walked to the door and peeked outside left and right of the long corridor, and when she found the coast clear, she walked toward the atrium where Tom and she first met. Tom stood his back to her as he stared out the window, hands in his pockets, legs apart, lost in thought. Without wanting to pry, she spotted in his concern for Amelia's sadness—his musings in a chaotic jumble, intermixed with the love he felt for her, Emma. No doubt about it. The dilemma of this particular triangle was an old one, but more potent now that they were adults.

"Tom," she called out.

He turned and ran toward her, scooping her up in his arms. "Emma. How did you get here so fast? Do you have a place on campus?"

He didn't know about her mode of travel. Unwilling to hurt his feelings, she eased out of his arms ever so gently. "What's going on? Were you able to reach Annemarie?"

He nodded. "I met Annemarie after you left." He pointed to

a couple of chairs by the window.

"Gardens are lovely this time of year," Emma declared.

"Yes, they are." He took a deep breath. "She's scared of Eivan Baker. She wants to be a reporter, and the boy paralyzes her with fear. She's even thinking of changing her major."

"Perhaps she's just scared of the true feelings she harbors for Eivan, and the fact she loves him is interfering with her better judgment."

"Well, I wasn't any help. Maybe you should talk to Annemarie. You're one of the bravest persons I know."

"Courage is highly overrated. Why does anyone do anything? Not bravery—bravado perhaps or rather because we have to. As in my case, I don't have a choice. I need my life back. Has nothing to do with fearlessness. I'm plenty scared. I guess determination better describes me."

"Serve Annemarie this speech, and you're golden."

"She didn't say anything at all?"

"Sorry. All Annemarie talked about was Eivan's father. An inventor who developed a lot of patents. Even sold a few of them, and in the process became very wealthy."

"So this is how he can leave Eivan forty-five million dollars."

"Forty-five million," Tom breathed, repeating the amount several times. "How do you know?"

"He will inherit the money in a couple of months. The information is in the papers—public knowledge."

"No wonder he dropped out of football and changed his

major."

"What do you mean?"

"He started off as an undergrad at MIT. The first year, he was an excellent quarterback. Freshman year, he thought he would take up science, but didn't know what field he favored. His second year, he changed his major to astrophysics, and dropped out of football."

"You didn't learn this from Annemarie. And what prompted the changes?"

"I searched for the name Eivan Baker in the school catalogs, and that's what I found. The changes happened the year his father died." Tom exhaled. "Annemarie said Eivan wanted to continue his father's work."

"Could you nose around and get me his number from someone on your football team maybe? Or a current teacher perhaps?"

"I can try. But this was before my time, so my teammates might not be able to give me an intro. Might be faster for you to talk to Annemarie."

She nodded. "Know where I can find her?"

"She's in the Hayden library right now, at least that's where she told me she intended to go. Tall, blonde, hair tied in a bun, slim and wearing jeans and a purple blouse. Oh, and she carries a red portfolio." He searched her eyes, releasing a nervous breath. "I'll take you there."

"Thanks, Tom." Emma smiled at him and kept the pace as they jogged to the door. Outside, they walked along the tall building serving as student residences and arrived at a vast, two-story structure surrounded by windows. A little out of breath from jogging with Tom, Emma eyed the enormous bike rack at the back of the building. No wonder students brought their bikes here. Made it more accessible to travel from one building to the next.

He stopped at the main door. "Best if Annemarie doesn't see us together. Good luck."

"I'll let you know what develops."

"Can you find your way back to the student residence?"

"Yes. I made a point of noticing my surroundings."

"Around the corner. Remember the gardens we admired?"

She nodded.

"Amelia's room is in the building across the gardens. I think you should talk to her before you leave." He gave her the number to her quarters and the floor.

Emma caught the deep sadness in Tom's blue eyes and realized he was a torn man. Ripped apart by his feelings for her and by the wish to be kind to the new woman in his life.

Emma decided she would do everything in her power to make him happy. "I promise to talk to her before I leave."

Once again he took her in his arms, and his expression replaced any words he might have attempted to say.

Emma watched him walk away, head down, shoulders hunched, and the heart tore out of her chest. She loved him so much, yet Tom was no longer hers to keep, at least in this reality. He belonged to Amelia here and now.

She entered the library her emotions in turmoil and searched the vast corridors for the description Tom gave her of Annemarie Hanover.

One figure stood out. A young woman with her hair tied into a bun on the nape. She sat in a chair with her books sprawled around her feet, some on her lap, facing the window her eyes fixed on the view of trees lining the banks of the Charles River. Emma also spotted the Harvard bridge in the distance.

"Excuse me, are you Annemarie Hanover?"

The young woman turned, and Emma caught a fleeting smile, surprise depicting the inquisitive nature of the light grey eyes staring at her. "And you are?"

Emma smiled and extended her hand in friendship. "Emma Willis. I am a friend of Thomas Carson."

Annemarie's smile disappeared, and she resumed her contemplation of the river and imagery beyond the window. "I love it here," she whispered.

Emma took this as her cue and grabbed a chair perpendicular to them at the end of the table and parked it close to Annemarie. "I can understand why you do. Not like a portrait. Alive, yet peaceful."

Annemarie nodded. She bent to assemble her folders and books and signaled they would leave to go outside.

Emma rose and followed her out the side door giving way to a lovely garden.

"Not many bridges can boast about the Smoot system of

measurements." Annemarie mentioned as she walked toward one of the benches beneath the foliage of a giant oak.

"The what?"

Annemarie chuckled as she sat down, sliding over to make room for Emma. "Oliver Smooth, MIT grad, as a fraternity prank, decided he would measure the Harvard crossing using his frat brothers to measure him across the span of the bridge. Turns out the Harvard Bridge measures 364.4 smooths plus or minus one ear, the plus or minus designed to indicate approximation."

"Wow! Is that actually written somewhere?"

"Yes, on the bridge since 1958. Quite an accomplishment, wouldn't you say?"

"Absolutely. Unusual, yet useful."

"I like to think of them out there, laughing, worrying a little about this enormous joke they were pulling on everyone, encouraging themselves to go on, to finish the project." She stared at Emma. "Turned out to be a prank that endured, one that is celebrated and has outlived all the other troubles."

Emma placed a hand on hers. "Something to live by." She took a deep breath, making sure no one around them lent an ear to their words. "I need to contact Eivan Baker. Would you be so kind as to give me the means to do so?"

"What are you studying, Emma?"

"Psychology. What are you studying, Annemarie?"

"Don't know anymore. I have a communication's major and I'm about to take a master in it. I wanted to be the best damn journalist ... Now, I may need to change my goals."

"Why? What happened?"

Annemarie rose, picked up her books and stacked them inside a red bag hanging her shoulder. Without saying a word, she walked away.

Emma pursued her and wondered how she'd spooked her. When she caught up with her, she asked again if Annemarie could give her Eivan Baker's number.

Annemarie took a deep breath. Let's walk. "We're drawing too much attention here."

"You're probably right."

"Besides, there are seats along the path by the river. Come, I'll show you."

Annemarie led the way and found a place for them to sit. Emma was surprised a paved, two-lane path stood before them. "This is wonderful."

"You should see this place in Spring when all the cherry trees are in bloom."

"I can imagine." A half a dozen cyclists flew by them, and Emma jumped a little startled. "Look how fast they're going—so close to the river." She glanced at the river and spotted many rows of canoeists sailing by wearing red and white shirts. Two men stood in the canoe, one at each end urging them on. "The river is quite blue."

"They've cleaned it up. You can swim in it now."

"More than I can say for the Hudson."

"You're from New York?"

"Newark, New Jersey. We enjoy Branch Brook Park, and of course, Central Park across the bridge, both lovely."

"What do you want with Eivan?"

Direct question Emma was not expecting. She searched her mind for the least troublesome explanation. "I'm doing my doctorate in psychology, and a small portion of my dissertation involves astrophysics. A friend of Tom's mentioned Eivan Baker to be quite brilliant in the matter." She shrugged. "Only, no one seems to know how to reach him."

"You're a long way from home just to drop some filler in your paper." Annemarie gave Emma a pointed stare. "You could have done this by internet. If you contact the chair at MIT's astrophysics department, they will arrange an interview for you."

Emma regretted having lied to the girl. Now, she looked incompetent and wasn't likely to obtain Annemarie's collaboration. But how could she tell her everything that went on? "Annemarie, I haven't been honest with you. I am not here to feather my dissertation. There is urgency in my request because of a certain project Eivan launched—one that is affecting us all."

Emma witnessed Annemarie's eyes widening with fear to render her expression unrecognizable. "Oh, my God. You know about time separating?"

"Something like that. How did you find out? No one knows."

"I was there when Eivan did his first tests. Some Machiavellian machine he built to get rid of evil, would you believe it?"

"Something must have happened to scare you like this."

She released a huge breath. "You can't blame me if something happens to you. I won't be held responsible for anyone else disappearing."

"Who disappeared, Annemarie?"

"Some doctor or other to whom Eivan agreed to give an interview. When the man examined Eivan's machine, this doctor got angry with him, treated him like some misbehaving brat. Eivan lost his temper and zapped him."

"Do you know the name of this doctor?"

"I did. Now, I forget."

"Could it be Dr. Fred Manson?"

Annemarie nodded her eyes terrified.

Emma wasn't overly worried. Fred only ever projected himself, traveled merely with his residual image. The boy didn't zap him. Fred returned to his current time and would attempt another way of stopping him later. So, where was Fred?

"Now, do you understand why I won't give you his number? If I do, and he finds out, he'll zap me to oblivion." She hung her head and cried. "I don't want to go like that."

"Listen. Nothing will happen to me. Please believe me. Nothing happened to Dr. Manson. He's also a scientist, and he never travels without," she hesitated, but then came clean, "projecting himself to the place he needs to visit."

"Projecting himself?"

"Like someone might use a projector to show an image on a wall. Not corporeally there."

"Wow!"

"You can't use this as material for an article. You can't tell anyone."

"I'm not going to tell. I don't want to have anything to do with Eivan which is why I want to change my major. There are a lot of criminals out there, not to mention all the dubious characters roaming around the universities. Fearing them all, I'll never report anything."

"Annemarie, these circumstances are not normal. The situation does not amount to black hats against white hats. Eivan's project is beyond the realm of understanding for most people."

"You understand this. You believe this."

"Let's just say this is my reason for wanting to meet Eivan. Find out what happened to him."

"He thinks he discovered a way to identify and destroy evil. His father first spotted the evil," Annemarie bracketed the word. "How can anyone measure, quantify, identify evil. No one can."

"You say his father began this project?"

"Yes. Only Eivan added to it—a lot of components. What can you do?"

"You'll have to trust me. I will never tell Eivan you gave me the number. I'll mention, Doctor Fred Manson."

"Okay." After a little more hesitation, Annemarie took out

her pen and scribbled the number on a piece of paper in her notebook. "Here." She tore the paper out of the book. "Please don't let anything happen to you." She smiled as she handed Emma the note. "If I'm going to be a reporter, I'll have to stick around to find out how this develops."

"I promise to give you the exclusive scoop on the story."

Emma's suggestion drew a smile from Annemarie, a bright smile. "Thank you for telling me about Dr. Manson being okay. I had trouble sleeping nights."

"A couple of things can always cause me problems with sleeping soundly," Emma smiled as she added, "Fear of the unknown, excitement, or loving a man deeply and worrying about that man."

"You will make a good psychologist, Emma. I do love Eivan. I worry about him. I wrote him a letter menacing I would leave him if he didn't stop his experiments."

"How did he respond?"

She shrugged. "Don't know. I'm still waiting."

When they got to the top of the stoop, Annemarie went her way, and Emma went hers. She doubled back to the student residences and strode for her meeting with Amelia. She hoped the girl would be in her room at this hour. However, the main door was locked.

A group of students was coming her way, and she waited for them to open the door. One of them asked if she lived in the building.

"No. I'm meeting someone on the third floor."

"Good enough," one young man said, giving her his most charming smile.

Emma took the elevator and walked up to Amelia's door. She hesitated, her hand skirting the wood. After releasing all the tension she harbored, she rehearsed a smile and knocked on the door.

A few seconds later, the door swung open. Amelia smiled, but she appeared disappointed, and Emma figured she expected Tom to come around. "May I come in?"

Amelia tossed a shoulder, and the smoldering anger and jealousy Emma spotted earlier may have evaporated because Amelia didn't flaunt any trace of a moue.

"About the hug, you witnessed Tom and me sharing. Good friends hugging was all that was."

Amelia nodded. "I know about our eyes playing tricks on us, especially when we're upset."

"Don't be. Nothing is going on between your Tom and me. We're friends, that's all."

"I'm so ashamed, Emma because you're the best friend I've ever had, and I keep thinking that you're standing between Tom and me. At least, you're not doing it intentionally."

"Tom likes me as a friend, but he is in love with you."

"That's not why I'm embarrassed. I suggested we attend MIT one year earlier to study, figuring we would see less of you. I hoped he might forget how much he loves you, Emma."

"Don't fret. Tom's all yours."

"Well, he and I both know you're the one he's been in love

with since he was a boy. He's the one I loved since I was a girl. We talked about it. I just have to stop going off half-cocked each time you're around, or he hugs you. My attitude is liable to push him away. It's not doing anything to cement our friendship or our love for that matter." She smiled. "I think it's time I grow up and start acting responsibly."

Emma wiped a few tears and came closer to hug Amelia. "I think you already have."

Amelia hugged her back and wiped her tears. "Would you like coffee or a soft drink?"

"I have time for a soft drink."

Amelia talked about her courses, her difficulties in specific subjects, and how she'd dropped the second major and was going instead for a teacher's certificate and a psychology major. True to form, Amelia never asked Emma what she was doing in Boston. Why she visited Tom so early in the morning. And Emma thought this might be the reason Emma never told Amelia about her powers or admitted to all the things she could accomplish. Perhaps, Amelia gave her the impression that deep down, she didn't want to know what made Emma tick.

One hour later, Emma flew home to Tom. In this life, he was her boyfriend, and they loved each other more than words might express.

Emma Willis Book 3,
I Can Help You

—Nine—

Emma's Lineage

Bill held the meeting at his house, and the place being empty, they could discuss the problem without interruptions. Emma once more brought Hank via the astral route to save him the drive there and the drive back. He was grateful.

The discussion became animated when Emma supplied the information she obtained from Annemarie Hanover. She gave them the details of Annemarie's conversation, the reason behind Eivan's project—finishing his father's work—and what she thought the repercussions might entail. Emma also revealed the fact she appeared to be the only one who traveled from one dimension to the next. Although when she did, she did not encounter herself anywhere, as though there was only one of her and she had not divided like the rest of them had.

"That's easy." Bill got up to pace, going around the coffee table and making Emma dizzy. "Emma, I could be wrong, but I believe you're inherent to this particular timeline and no other. You will not find me or Tim or anyone that came to Earth to help in any of those dimensions."

"But I am human."

"Columba didn't explain this to you?"

"She did. She showed me where I came from originally, and gave me this jewel, the Star of Capella to add to my Eye of Horus." She brandished her pendant tucked away under her T-shirt. "This is how I can travel from one timeline to the other. However, I was born on Earth from a human mother and a human father."

"You leaped here and seeded with the permission of the one who leaped here ahead of you."

"What?" Emma slapped her hand across her mouth restraining a shriek to a gasp. "My mother. She also came from Quintus Capella. I remember. We were friends living in peace waiting for our return to the source. She looked at Earth through the mirrored waters of Lake Tranquillum. She began to cry. I'd never seen tears before. She said Earth would never make the deadline, and she could not wait calmly to go to the Source when so many souls might perish." Emma took the tissue Hank found in his pocket and wiped her eyes. "I begged her not to go. She told me the memory would overshadow her happiness and pull her back down to the third dimension if she didn't ease her conscience and help."

"So, now you know. When your mother was ready, her body instinctually seeded you inside her womb."

"So my father ..."

"He's not your father," Bill said.

"He's the man who raised you, and the man who loves you as a father," Hank added.

Emma smiled through her tears. "He does, doesn't he?" She took a deep breath. "I wonder if my mother remembers?"

"Emma, you are a fifth dimension human, a Chavah favored to return to the source. However, this is not important now," Bill said, his tone eliminating all discussion of the subject. "What is significant is you understand how none of the people who came to Earth to help can split into different dimensions. The only reason you're traveling is due to your Eye of Horus, because of your powers."

"Not entirely true, Bill."

Emma and Hank both witnessed the effect of her comment weaken Bill's legs as he dropped in the first chair he found. "What?"

"Dr. Fred Manson was in the timeline I just left. Either he visited the dimension, or he is also present in that dimension. I don't know."

"Please, explain."

Emma did, including the part Annemarie mentioned about the small hand remote Eivan used to zap Fred Manson when he called him evil.

"Zap, Fred Manson. Where would he go?"

Emma caught Hank's worried expression and sought to reassure them both. "He either came back to this timeline, or he stayed behind to help. The three of us know you cannot zap Fred Manson anywhere."

Hank sat up. "That's true. The man never travels with his corporeal self. The jerkwad only ever uses his residual image. Five years ago, we incarcerated him for several weeks while he came and went as he pleased."

"Granted. Still, doesn't make sense," Bill breathed.

"Here's something else you won't like." She stared at Bill Frost, attempting to lift the incredulous glow in his eyes. "When I got to Tom and Amelia, both welcomed me like a long-lost friend when I visited MIT in Cambridge, although, Tom didn't know about my powers. Perhaps the Emma in that skewed timeline never developed her powers, or she never confided in Tom. Later, once I was back in this time, my original space—here," she hesitated unaware of the repercussion her statement would generate.

"What happened?" Bill appeared impatient.

"The other Tom, the one I left behind at MIT reached me on this cell phone."

"Unbelievable," Bill breathed. "Shoots my theory to hell." Bill made a point of releasing a huge breath. "I believe you, Emma." He rose and spread his hands in front of the coffee table. "Refreshments for everyone."

Emma eyed the variety of sustenance and remembered Jeannie, Bill's human wife, working in the kitchen, baking, stirring and preparing a meal with ardor and a smile on her face. She probably enforced the no-easy-magic rule for the sake of the children—and for her pleasure as well.

"Here's something interesting," Emma said as she poured

herself a cup of coffee. "Two years ago, Fred Manson came to see me. He needed help with one of his projects. Swamped with work at the time, in the middle of exams, I asked him to please come back later." She took a sip of the delicious brew. "I haven't seen him since."

"Your point?" Bill ignored the refreshments laid out on the table. Hank grabbed himself a coffee and something to eat.

Emma smiled. "Well, in this timeline, I just had my masters upgraded to a doctorate, not common practice, but the APA approved the bold gesture. The professor responsible for this advancement in my career is also supplying a list of patients for me to log the hours I need to pass licensure." Emma took a long sip of her coffee.

"So?" Bill asked intrigued by her tone.

"Well, although this professor just arrived on the scene, he tells me he taught at Rutgers for two years," Emma emphasized the last words. "And he has accumulated many contacts that will help me with the clinical hours I need to log to pass licensure. This professor is Dr. Franklin Rappaport."

Hank put his coffee cup down. "There is no Dr. Franklin Rappaport. You said so yourself, Bill."

"Fred Manson?" Bill mouthed incredulously. "Why would he play up such an elaborate charade?"

"Perhaps, he wanted my help, and he realized I'm busier now than I was two years ago?"

Bill hung his head as though he carried the weight of everyone on his back. "I'm going to have to go back to Celeste, my planet of origin. The Druids there will know what's going on."

"Meanwhile, I was dreading Monday morning's meeting with Dr. Rappaport, thinking I couldn't tell him anything. Now, I'll spend the better part of tomorrow writing down everything we've discussed—for Fred."

"You believe Franklin Rappaport is Fred Manson?" Bill needed confirmation.

Emma hoisted her shoulders. "Makes sense. He's nowhere in Rutgers' catalog, and he's not in the alphabetical list of the Earth people you are likely to encounter."

"List is extensive," Bill mumbled as though answering his argument.

"Can we meet here Monday night, Bill," Hank asked. "After Emma's consultation with Dr. Rappaport?" Hank turned the name into a funny set of syllables.

Emma chuckled.

"Sure. The time lapse should give me the time to seek the answers we need."

Emma wanted to know. "Bill, have you discovered how many rifts in time there are? I have a feeling there are more than three."

"Here's hoping the Druids will give me a clue. If not, I hope they can tell me how to obtain the information. As for finding a focal point on each segment, once we discover how many fissures there are, you can travel and identify a shortcut once you're on the spot—as long as you possess the means to come back."

"Perhaps. Although, over there looks a lot like here. Sometimes I get the feeling this is one thin line, and we're running around in circles. The impression is quite dizzying."

"Duly noted." Bill appeared ready to take his leave. "Anything else?"

Emma grasped Hank's hands. "No. Thank you. We're on our way."

They left, and Emma still got a kick out of Hank's happy expression. They landed in Hank's kitchen.

"Always surprised by this, though I'd love to be able to travel through the astral world on my own. I'd be on any criminal's ass in seconds. Imagine that."

Emma smiled. "I guess Christina is upstairs in the room."

"You can come up if you want to. The boys are sound sleepers."

"Say hello to her for me. I have to go."

Emma landed in her room, and for an instant, thought she'd come to the wrong place. Tom stood his back to her staring out at the old elm tree with its branches sweeping the window. Her room definitely, but why was he here?

"Tom, what are you doing here?" She smiled at him, happier to see him than she thought possible.

"I tried to reach you all day. No one was home. I came after dinner. Your mom said I could wait here for you."

Invaded with the impression of profound loneliness she

picked up from Tom, Emma shivered as she stared at the dirty walls and scruffy floor, at her keepsakes gone missing. She faced the fact that this wasn't her room, at least not the one she remembered. "Why didn't you try my cell phone?"

"You have a cell phone? Since when?"

She closed her eyes, realizing she was in the wrong world. She picked up her oudjat and discovered the Star of Capella devoid of shine as though the stone didn't wish to be here either. "Tom, what about MIT?"

"What are you talking about?" He came closer, a puzzled frown on his brow as he tried to understand. "I don't have any money to go to Rutgers. Think I can go to MIT?"

She remembered. In this timeline, Thomas Carson suffered a football injury that prevented him from obtaining a scholarship. In fact, he now walked with a limp and worked as a truck lift operator at one of the big warehouses in town.

Her cell phone rang. She looked at the number and recognized Hank's cell. "Emma, here."

"Emma. We're in the wrong place. My boys are gone, and I don't live here. I tiptoed up to my bedroom and Christina is lying beside some other man. Maybe we never got back together all those years ago."

Emma's response was stilted. She didn't want to give away the name of the caller, and she tried to impart to Hank that she wasn't alone. "I understand. Can you meet me downstairs?"

"I don't have a car here. So I'll have to walk over. Please, wait for me."

"I'll meet you somewhere along Grafton."

"Who the hell is that? And where did you get a cell phone?"

"I'll explain later. Right now, I have to go."

She ran downstairs and out the door, running toward Hank. She didn't want a big fight to resonate in her mother's house. She would keep track of the different timelines. So far, three, not counting her own.

Trouble occurred when she sensed Tom following her. She turned around and scolded him. "I said I would explain later. Please don't follow me."

Emma realized Tom would not allow her to go any farther. The determined look in his eyes frightened her. She turned and ran faster. With his limp, she would be able to avoid fighting with Tom by escaping and bumping into Hank if she had to.

"Whoa, Emma. Where are you running to so fast."

"Hank, thank God. I ran into a different version of Tom. We need to leave, now."

"Please, I am all yours."

As both of them spotted Tom emerging from the night's shadows, Emma grabbed on to Hank's hands and evoked her little sentence, while holding onto her jewel with her left hand.

When they opened their eyes, Tom was gone, and Emma immediately examined her jewel.

Standing once more in Hank's kitchen, she smiled when

she admired her pendant's bright shine. "I'm always going to have to check that this stone shines to its maximum potential as this means I'm inside the right timeline. We both are."

"No blue dome this time when we traveled. Love to see the blue sky at night."

"Time spent in the astral world was a flash of a second since we mostly changed timelines. When we do, no visible signs exist that we did—except for the brilliance of this stone."

"God," Hank enthused. "I was never so glad to hear someone's voice as when you picked up your cell. I nearly collapsed when I couldn't find my boys in their rooms, and my wife, my beautiful wife, lying down next to some other man."

"You're lucky they didn't wake up. You could have found yourself in a strange situation, the chief of police arrested for breaking and entering."

"I wasn't the chief of police back there. Just a plain-clothes detective."

"I'll go up with you to make sure this is the right place." Emma smiled and followed him upstairs. She sensed Hank's hesitation as he opened one of the boys' door. She smiled when she witnessed little Jarred sleeping on his tummy and making gurgling noises in his sleep. "He's an angel."

Hank let go a huge breath as he left and walked over to Alex's room. He too slept peacefully, and Emma heard Hank's small whisper of a prayer of gratitude he directed toward the heavens.

The door to the master bedroom opened wide, and Christina came through in her nightgown encircling her husband in her arms. "I'm sorry I went to bed. Exhaustion set in, Hank."

"Don't apologize. I'm so glad to be home."

They both turned toward Emma, and she waved as she disappeared to her own home while grasping the jewel around her neck. She would no longer take her Eye of Horus for granted. The profound changes churned wildly like treacherous waters bubbling over unexpectedly into her life and the lives of others. Until she better understood what was involved, she would no longer be able to take the slides in stride. They were dangerous and destructive. All of them would need to find a solution to this problem before there spawned too many outcomes they might not be able to undo.

Emma touched down inside her bedroom and sensed the same hesitation that overtook Hank earlier. Opening the light would give her an inkling if she arrived inside the right timeline.

She flicked the light switch and gazed at all her familiar keepsakes, on the lovely decorations of window treatments and designer colors her mother orchestrated for her and smiled. The calmness invading her lifted when she jumped, disturbed by Tom sitting on Granny Dotty's bench. "You startled me." She caught him rising, and Tom walked toward her, handsome in his Rutgers varsity jacket. No limp, just ruggedness, and deep affection rooted in his blue eyes. "Your parents are gone for the rest of the weekend. Your mom left you a note." Tom handed the note to her.

'Emma, I told Tom to help himself to a sandwich while he waits for you. Your father and I are going to the Jersey Shore. A client of his has a huge condo on Ocean Avenue in Monmouth Beach. Might be a little cold for an ocean swim in June, but he insisted we take it for the weekend. He bragged about his beautiful heated pool and told us about the well-groomed tennis courts. We'll be back late tomorrow night.' Eloise also left a number where Emma could reach her.

"We have the house to ourselves." Tom smiled, taking Emma into his arms. "What do you say we make the most of it?"

"I'll have work to do tomorrow, though."

"Me too. Let's just think about tonight." Tom kissed her, a deep lingering kiss and she sighed in response, loving the feel of his hands on her back, and the tickling sensation of his lips on her neck as he pushed her hair out of the way to rain kisses at the base of her throat. When he came up to her mouth again Emma's legs weakened from the knowledge the night was all theirs to do with as they pleased, and she surrendered, wrapping her arms around his neck.

Tom drew back, his eyes warm and hungry. "Did you have dinner?" He asked in the most solicitous tone. The inflection of care in his voice made her smile as she caressed his cheek. She shook her head.

"I'm starving for you, and for food. What should I eat first?"

She chuckled and took his face in her hands. Trying to

erase the weak, pathetic image of the Tom she met in the other life, she pecked his lips. "I don't want to think about anything else than loving you for a little while. Is that okay?"

"Perfect. I was hoping you would say that."

—Ten—

The Car

On their way to Englewood Cliffs to partake of her grandmother's hospitality, swim and play a few sets of tennis, Tom and Emma discussed the project she worked on all morning.

"I had to put down my thoughts on all the sliding issues on paper, just to make sense of them all. So far, I have encountered three alternate dimensions other than our own."

"This is getting out of hand."

Emma watched the road fly by as Tom drove at an alarming speed. "Slow down, Tom. You're going too fast. Something isn't right."

Tom glanced at the speedometer and braked immediately. "Sorry. I didn't realize I was driving this fast. Didn't even think this old clunker supported this kind of wind."

A sudden flash blinded Tom and had him jam on the brakes. He stepped on the brake pedal hard enough to go through the floor to avoid the glare of another car that appeared in front of them, out of nowhere. Swerving to the right, close to the turnpike's guardrail, he managed to avoid the vehicle in front of them slowing to a crawl before stopping by the side of the road. "What was that? I nearly drove into the car in front of me. One second the road is empty, next, this slow-moving violation of a jalopy is crossing our path." Tom got out of the old Ford to pace in the long reeds on the side of the road.

Emma got out as well. She checked her pendant for verification, and admitted to Tom, "We're no longer inside our timeline."

He released a deep breath. "We almost ended up in the Hackensack River." He grabbed Emma and held her in his arms. "I'm sorry. I shouldn't have been driving that fast."

"Not your fault. Take a look around you." She waited as Tom examined the topography, turning and scratching his head when he couldn't recognize where he stood. "Where's the bloody river? Where's the turnpike?" He leaned against his car, as though unable to find his legs. "No wonder the idiot drove at the speed of a turtle. We're on some side road to hell. Where are we?"

"I don't know. The GPS on my phone might give me a clue." Emma clicked on the settings on her phone and asked for directions from current location to get to Englewood Cliffs NJ. Emma glanced at Tom. "We're twenty miles east of Wichita Kansas."

"We're what? Fifteen—eighteen hours from where we are supposed to be?"

"Yep. Dead on with what the GPS is giving me."

"Can you get us back?"

"I am sure I can."

"Wait a minute. You can bring us back, but what about my car?"

Emma hadn't thought about Tom's old Focus, and she hoisted her shoulders in defeat. "I don't think I can bring the car back. We can sit inside, and I can try, but I doubt it will follow us home."

"It brought us here."

"Your car didn't bring us here, Tom. Weird circumstances did." Emma took a deep breath and stepped into the passenger seat. Tom walked around and sat at the wheel. "I can't leave my Rita behind, Emma. I have two payments left to make on it, and two new summer tires in the trunk."

Emma held back a chuckle. She loved the fact Tom christened his car with a girl name. "You still have your winter tires?"

"Yeah. It took me two months to save up enough money to buy two refurbished front tires." Tom turned in his seat to stare at Emma. "You get yourself back. I'll drive and get there eventually."

"You can't. You're not inside the right timeline. When you get back, there'll be one too many Toms. Look around you. You don't belong here."

"That much is certain, I would never, in any lifetime, come to Wichita Kansas, much less live here."

Emma couldn't stop a chuckle. Their situation appeared funny as nerves took over, and she couldn't stop the giggles pouring out of her, uncontrolled.

She wiped her eyes and said, "What we need to do is grab everything we can stuff into our pockets, license, registration, money. Then you can grab the tennis bag, I'll take my purse and my backpack, and we'll hope the car will follow."

Tom's turn to laugh. "The worst is I can't tell anyone about this. What will I tell my dad?"

"The car's in your name, right?"

"Yeah. Still, Dad will want to know where my wheels are."

"Got everything?" When she caught his nod, she made sure she secured her purse strap around her neck and her backpack behind her. She gave the car a once over and grabbed Tom's hand, and her oudjat in the other. "You won't feel a thing, won't even realize we've changed places."

A few seconds later, they found themselves sitting on the ground in her grandmother's drive. They both rose, and Emma couldn't help saying out loud, "Guess the car didn't follow."

"You think?"

She checked her pendant and recognized with a contented sigh that they'd arrived in their own time.

Walking up to the front door, laden with bags, Tom wondered. "What will the police do when they find my car by the side of the road? The plates are going to give me away, and I'll have to go down there to pick up the damn thing."

Emma stopped before she rang the bell to announce their arrival. They sidestepped the front gate, and her grandmother had no way of knowing they waited on the front stoop.

"They're not going to communicate with you."

"They are. Authorities are going to call the one who owns the car."

"Yes, but in that timeline, you're not the same Thomas Carson. There going to call someone else."

"Right, true. Tricky. Can't wrap my mind around it." He mumbled. "I just gave a perfectly good car and two new summer tires to some backwater Tom Carson. You're welcome," he shouted out loud for some far-away person to hear.

Emma smiled as she rang the bell. A few minutes later, a short, stern butler answered. He used the intercom to announce Emma and Tom's arrival and then allowed them inside.

"Grandma," Emma dropped her bags and squeezed her grandmother in a bear hug.

"Sweeties, did you take the bus here with all this gear? The guard said he looked up and spotted you sitting down in the middle of the drive. Did you walk for a long time?"

Emma glanced at Tom, and he nodded giving her the go. "A long story, Grandma. I'll tell you all about it."

Sitting at the patio table, flanked with tall lemonades and vanilla finger cookies, Emma and her grandmother watched Tom swim back and forth. Emma eyed her grandmother whose face paled considerably as the story of the world shifting in different directions filed before her.

Emma Willis Book 3,
I Can Help You

Emma wrapped the towel around her, the cool breeze making her shiver. "You can't tell anyone about this, Grandma. I haven't even told Mom and Dad yet."

"You have my word, little one. Besides, no one would believe me. People would call me crazy."

"Poor Tom. Works hard, has little money to spare, and the only car he was ever able to afford stayed behind."

"Well, that's unacceptable. You go back in the water. You're shivering. You'll catch your death. I'll be back in a little while. I have some calls to make."

Emma smiled as she dived back into the pool. The warm water invigorated and relaxed her at the same time. She too did some laps, until Tom suggested they towel off and play a little tennis.

"I hope your grandmother doesn't decide to play against me like she did last time."

"What do you mean?"

"When you left, yesterday, she challenged me to a couple of sets. She won them all. I could barely keep my serve."

Emma laughed. "I warned you. Why didn't you tell me this before?"

Tom gave Emma the raised eyebrows. "Voluntary omission."

Emma laughed more. "So, why tell me now?"

"Fair warning. I refuse to play your grandma again."

Emma and Tom had the time to each win a couple of serves when Abigail walked back toward them with a little shout and a wave.

Tom stopped his motion and ran to the net. He indicated for Emma to approach. "No. No. And no. I'm not playing your grandmother. She made me look like a fool."

Abigail neared them with shortened breath and a big smile on her face. "Children, I have excellent news." She waved for them to come closer. "I just got off the phone with a friend of mine. He owns the Cadillac dealership in Englewood Cliffs. He has a beauty in the lot right now. A used Audi A4, a nice coupe, monsoon metallic gray, black leather interior, satellite radio, sunroof, Bluetooth technology and all the appropriate safety features. Aluminum wheels, rear air and heated seats, everything you can dream of." She smiled, more excited than Emma had seen her in a while.

"What's the mileage on the car?" Tom asked incredulously.

"Forty-three thousand miles. Practically new."

"Mrs. Tichy, I can't afford an Audi. How much is the car?"

"It's a steal at sixteen thousand five hundred dollars. I told James to put it aside for you. We can go see it together."

Tom let go a huge breath, and Emma sensed his frustration mounting as he dropped his racket on the ground for effect. "I can't afford to buy a sixteen-thousand-dollar car," he repeated as politely as irritation allowed. "Not possible."

"Well, I will buy the car, and you and Emma can share it. My gift to you. You're only young once, and right now, you should focus on studying, on enhancing your future."

Tom's mouth opened, and his whole face dropped. The three of them were aware Emma didn't need a car as a mode of transportation. Tom did. "I can't accept a gift of this magnitude, thank you, but if you could maybe give me a loan of a couple of thousand dollars. I would buy an older car. And this way, I would be able to pay you back."

"Nonsense. Why should my granddaughter ride inside a vehicle that offers subpar safety? Enjoy your youth. Right now, is the time in your life when you need the most gifts, the most encouragement. Besides," Abigail gave Tom a crooked smile. "This is my way of apologizing for beating you at tennis the way I did. Not cool."

Emma laughed.

"Did he tell you?" Abigail elbowed Emma.

"Yes, he did."

"I don't know, Mrs. Tichy. A car is a big expense."

"You can start by calling me, Abigail." She winked at Emma. "Listen, Tom, there's no point arguing the matter here. First, we'll go to the dealership—just around the corner. You might not even like the car, so let's wait and see."

Emma coaxed Tom with her eyes while he rolled his, but Emma realized he could not seem to find the polite words to say no.

Abigail smiled triumphantly. "You two put your rackets down. We are going shopping."

Even though Abigail mentioned the dealership to be

around the corner, she still recruited her chauffeur's services to bring them there. When the three walked into the showroom, Tom appeared to lose his shyness, his glowing reticence as he eyed and stroked the cars displayed circularly. "Wow, quite the package."

James, the lot's owner, joined Abigail the minute she walked in the door.

A slight bow later, he explained. "We brought the car in from the lot, and it's being washed and prepped as we speak." He brought the three to his office, his arm encircling Abigail. "What would you like to drink?" He opened a mid-sized refrigerator and offered them wine, sodas, or champagne.

Abigail said she would love a glass of champagne. The two youngsters politely refused the drinks.

"I trust you will find the vehicle satisfactory. We can guarantee some of the main features for another 35,000 miles for a small premium, which pretty much gives you the same protection you might enjoy when buying a new car." He took some forms out, and Emma watched Tom pace the outer office. Unused to Abigail's high-roller tactics, a frown settled on Tom's brow, and he appeared on the verge of walking out and fleeing the scene of what he might consider a crime—a crime of wasting this much money on a kid Abigail hardly knew.

Fifteen minutes later, a man in gray overalls came out to tell them the car was ready and waiting at the back.

Tom was the first one out. Emma spotted him approaching

the vehicle slowly and gingerly. She realized this was love at first sight for Tom. She too thought the car to be spectacular.

He didn't dare glide his hand along the frame, he just stood and gawked at the superb Audi that Emma realized Tom didn't think he would own for many years.

"What do you think, Tom? Is this a car you might like?" Abigail smiled as she stared at him from the opposite side of the vehicle's shiny metallic hood.

"Like is too small a word. This Audi is magnificent. I mean what will I tell my dad? This car is three times nicer than his."

"Well, there is nothing I can do about that." Abigail smiled.

Emma considered this was as pleasurable for her grandmother as it was for Tom. Even more so as she'd tried to help Emma and her mother and father all her life, yet her father always turned down any hint of financial help. She found herself hoping Tom would be more gracious and realize how much giving him the car pleased her grandmother.

James stepped up. "Would you like to take the car out for a test drive?"

"Would I!" Tom's expression lit up, and he turned toward Emma. "You have to come with me. Let me know what you think."

"You coming too, Grandma?"

"You two go ahead. I'll wait for you here."

Seated inside the leather bucket seats, Tom breathed in the luxury around him. "Emma this is too beautiful. My dad is going to be envious." He looked around, and she told him that he didn't have to use the key to start the engine. "You only need to push the button as long as you have the key on you."

Tom drove the vehicle twice around the block, and with the dealership in sight, he told Emma. "I love this car. I truly love this car." He turned gently with one hand, the power steering doing the rest. "How am I going to explain this to my padre?"

"Well, just tell him my grandmother is a very generous lady, and you either accepted the car, or she threatened to play tennis with you again." Emma laughed at his expression.

"Are you sure your grandma is okay with this?"

"Please. Grandma tried to give my parents money all their lives, and my father always categorically refused, except for the one time when I was ten, and they were in a jam. Anyway, did you see the look on my grandmother's face?"

He hoisted a shoulder.

"When we return, check her expression. You'll notice she's happier than you are about this."

"Well, I certainly don't want her to hold a tennis rematch against me."

Tom parked the car, and both got out. He remitted the keys to James and addressed Abigail. "So that you know, I fell in love with this car." Unexpectedly, he walked up to her and gave her a bear hug. Abigail hugged him back, surprised raising her eyebrows while the warmth of Tom's embrace brought tears to her eyes.

"I'm glad." She turned toward James. "Let's proceed with the paperwork. My granddaughter and her friend need this car to go home tonight."

Driving home, Emma sat back and relaxed while listening to the stereo sound coming from the quality speakers. The evening's coolness prompted her to try her seat warmer, and she couldn't help smiling Tom's way. She found him preoccupied somehow. "You're not still worried about how to explain this to your father, are you?"

"No. I was just thinking about this morning. How the freaky flash flew us eighteen hours from where we headed."

Emma caught Tom slowing down when nearing the sign for the exit to Secaucus, where they'd suddenly found themselves some thirteen hundred miles away from home.

"How we almost ended in the Hackensack River." He glanced toward Emma. "What if this happens again? I mean, your grandmother paid for the car with her credit card. I didn't know anyone could do that."

"Tom, we just have to pray this doesn't happen again. If it does, insurance should cover the car's disappearance."

"If we can explain how it vanished into thin air."

"Let's not worry about this. Remember, what you worry about, you bring about."

"Yeah, you're right." With his hand on hers, Tom smiled at her and relaxed in his seat.

Emma caught him admiring the console all lit up and pulsing with sophistication. "Wow, Emma. I've got chills driving this vehicle. I love this car," Tom whispered.

"Registration states it's all yours."

—Eleven—

Where is Fred Manson

Monday Morning, Emma followed the beat of her mid-heel chunky sandals resounding loudly as they smacked against the tiled hallways of Rutgers University. Dressed in business attire to assist Dr. James Monroe all afternoon with clinical consultations, she was first meeting with Dr. Franklin Rappaport to give him a detailed report of her findings on Friday evening. Well, as detailed as she dared to dispense.

Standing at the door to Professor Rappaport's office, Emma hesitated before knocking. The written notes she carried in her bag did not afford her the ease she hoped they would. Suddenly, the thought of Dr. Rappaport being Dr. Fred Manson did not make any sense, and remembering Bill Frost's words, 'Why would Fred play such an elaborate charade?' deflated her confidence. Now, she would be unable to admit to the feat of telepathy she conducted with Eivan, or most of her findings.

After the prompt to enter, Emma tiptoed in and greeted her professor sitting at a desk obstructed with a mountain of files and paperwork. The mere thought he might be someone else evaporated into thin air.

"How was your weekend?" He asked without looking at her.

"Quite busy." Emma broke her rule and tried to read Dr. Rappaport's thoughts. Two years ago, she resolved not to do that to anyone again, mainly since this was something she would not like done to her. Still, rules were meant to be broken, and she peered into her professor's eyes as he looked up at her and smiled.

"I hope you found time to rest a little."

Emma could not find any thoughts in Dr. Rappaport's mind other than the memory of a dinner with friends on Sunday evening. "I traveled to MIT to meet with a friend of mine. I wanted to get a story on Eivan Baker."

"You went to MIT?" He appeared surprised. "That's a three-hour drive, one-way, even longer with public transportation."

"I wanted to add to the little I discovered on Friday evening."

"Well, I'm impressed with your determination, Emma. But what can you possibly discover at MIT?"

"I obtained help from a friend, Tom. He gave me the means to talk with a journalist over there." Emma proceeded to tell Dr. Rappaport about Eivan senior and the project his son agreed to take over after he passed away.

"All well and good. But I'm more interested in finding out about your visit with Eivan junior on Friday evening."

She curbed the bout of panic she sensed rising inside her and smiled as she admitted, "I learned very little from Eivan junior, Dr. Rappaport. He was heavily medicated, and as you know, intuition can do very little with such cases."

Emma witnessed Dr. Rappaport shake his head side to side, and when she peeked inside his mind, she put her hand over her mouth to prevent a little scream. Devronair encryption smacked her right between the eyes as she heard Fred Manson arguing with himself.

"Dr. Manson, is that you?"

"Yes," he said while retaining Dr. Rappaport's residual form. "I will deny this to anyone else."

"Why the pretense?"

He shuffled a couple of folders on his desk, keeping his eyes on the task at hand. "Different reasons, I suppose." He sat back in his chair and looked up at her. "I meant to take on a more pleasant residual form to replace the bug eyes and the large forehead," he added as he pinned her with a hard glare.

Emma sensed her shoulders drop a couple of inches. She remembered the teasing remarks concerning Dr. Manson. "I assure you, Fred. I've often defended your appearance."

"I am quite certain you have. Still, this won't help our time shifting situation, will it?"

"Is this why you came to seek my help two years ago?"

"Yes. My minions and I tried to resolve the situation but failed miserably."

Another one of the mocking terms Emma had often heard people say: Fred Manson and his minions.

Then she wondered since Doctor Rappaport did not exist whether the upgrade to a doctorate was even valid.

"Yes, the upgrade to your doctorate is valid. The APA approved the decision, and we are going forward."

"Thank you, Dr. Rappaport. I appreciate all you've done for me."

"Don't thank me yet. I did this to help you since you will be spending a lot of time helping us resolve the situation."

"I realize this." Emma opened her bag and pulled out the notes she'd jotted the day before—the visit to Eivan junior on Friday evening, the sliding turbulence she encountered by traveling to other timelines. She also divulged the name of the journalist she met while in another timeline as Annemarie Hanover.

"To support our new collaboration, I've copied down some relevant material over the last two years. I'm certain this information will enlighten you."

Emma watched as Dr. Rappaport, AKA Fred Manson, rose from his chair and walked to a couple of tall bookshelves lining the wall perpendicular to the long windows behind his desk. He rummaged the top shelf for a few minutes and brought back two big books filled with small, illegible scribblings, at least from what she could decipher.

He scanned the pages for some time, and Emma wondered if Fred remembered she was there. She checked the time on her watch and considered interrupting his reading. She had a class in less than forty-five minutes.

She cleared her throat, but to no avail. A couple of heavy sighs did not perturb her professor's research either. Arming herself with the patience to continue waiting, she attempted to read his mind to discover where his thoughts might lead him. The encryption in Fred's mind was in full force, and although she could always read through this encryption, with some effort, she concluded waiting for him to tell her what he knew would be less stressful.

"I came across the material Eivan senior began before his death. I'm trying to sum this up as succinctly as possible." He settled on a page in the book he was thumbing. "Says here he began with a theory on the flow of time. Particle entanglement, and how quantum uncertainty gives rise to entanglement."

"I read something about this. A hot cup of coffee for example. When it entangles with the air around it, brew cools down. Only the reverse is not possible. We are unable to warm the lukewarm coffee instantly." Emma waited for Fred to say something else. "Do you suppose if we had the proper equation to the equilibrium curve we might reverse the properties and turn the coffee hot again?"

"I cannot say. Devron does not function along the same physical properties Earth does. Even your scientists cannot agree on what creates entanglement or how to analyze the phenomenon correctly." Fred slipped a marker inside the tome and stared at Emma. "What happened Friday evening? I want to know everything Eivan junior communicated to you. After all, I am the doctor, and you are merely my assistant."

Emma nodded. "Eivan seems to believe that his father was killed by evil, or what we call wizards."

"Not true. Devronairs brought Eivan Baker senior and his partner Gerald Buttler to Earth Optimal. Nothing to do with wizards."

Emma sighed, shaking her head side to side, and rolling her eyes. "I'm sorry," she said when she caught Fred's raised eyebrows. "I can never get used to Devronairs bringing people to Earth Optimal. Was this what both of these men wanted?"

"Let's just say if I suggested that Eivan senior and Gerald Buttler might like to return to Earth Refuse, neither of them would comply."

"I see. Well, Eivan junior knows who tried to kill him. He admitted Steve Lemon pushed him off the roof of his home. He said he turned around and spotted his eyes colored an unusual shade of black, and he was convinced pure evil inhabited the man." Emma waited for Dr. Rappaport to say something. When he didn't, she continued. "He also suspects he was the one in his hospital room the next day, again, trying to kill him."

"Steve Lemon was never on that roof, or in Eivan's hospital room."

"How do you know?

"Steve Lemon is the well-known reverend, leader of an ecumenical committee and was ministering to flock members that evening. As a matter of fact, they testified on his behalf." Emma caught Dr. Rappaport taking a deep breath. "Devronairs pushed Eivan off that roof. He turned and encountered us. We were also in his hospital room the next day."

"No," Emma breathed. Change of residual image explained, she thought. He needed a whole new look when he visited Eivan in hospital. "Why would you do such a thing?"

"We figured this might be one way to have him admit where he hid the engine for the contraption he built. Once on Earth Optimal, he would not need the project anymore."

Emma hated to agree with the Devronair. However, what Fred said made sense. Earth Optimal being devoid of conflict and inhabited by the truth. They would find out all they needed to know about Eivan's infernal machine.

Still, she couldn't fathom how Eivan lied to her. As medicated and out of sorts as he appeared to be, he'd found the power to lie. "Why would Eivan lie to me? Doesn't make sense."

"The boy lied to protect his secret, not to reveal his project, and to safe-keep his privacy. You are familiar with the concept, yes?"

The words delivered a low blow, even for Fred. Emma hated to lie, the complex of guilt hanging over her head, and threatening to engulf her anytime she added one more lie to her repertoire. However, she recognized people weren't ready to learn about her secrets, about all the powers she manifested. So, lying was the only solution left to keep her safe from the outside world. Refusing to let Fred's comment bring her down, she thought aloud. "Do you suppose he is not really under, that he doesn't take the medication they hand him?"

"Well, if this is the case, he will need to be cautious. There are cameras everywhere, in the rooms and the bathrooms."

"So, you're after the engine that drives Eivan's project. When you met him at the hospital, did you ask about his work?"

"I couldn't. Instead, I tried to read the boy's mind, and I obtained nothing but a big blank. He did appear medicated more than someone might normally be in these circumstances."

"You went to visit him as Dr. Franklin Rappaport, right?"

"Yes, why do you ask?"

"Well, Eivan zapped you when you met him at MIT, although this was another timeline. Are you worried he might recognize you anyway? Or were you on that roof?"

"I wasn't on that roof. And, I didn't want to risk identification. Who knows what one person may retain from one timeline to the next. When I traveled to MIT, I wanted to find out more about his work. I told him I needed to obtain information about the engine he was using, the driving force behind the project skewing our timeline." Dr. Rappaport rose and stood by the window, looking at the lush grounds below his office.

"Unfortunately, I lost my temper." He turned toward Emma. "I was outraged when Eivan appeared to be cavalier about the time shifting. He laughed at me. He asked me to demonstrate. However, when I read in his mind that he knew about the shifts, well, that's when I raised my voice, and I guess he saw something in me that reminded him of those wizards. He pulled a component out of his pocket and zapped me. Of course, he didn't make me disappear. I just left."

"I heard about this from Annemarie Hannover. I had to reassure her saying you were a person who could project himself, and that Eivan had not killed you or made you disappear. She was extremely relieved. I was able to secure her collaboration."

"That's good work."

"Still, I would love to discover how his machine slides me around from one timeline to another."

"You've been sliding involuntarily?" Dr. Rappaport's kind face appeared troubled.

Emma told him about the slide she omitted, the one where Tom and she found themselves thousands of miles from where they were supposed to be. "To return, we brought everything we could carry, and I held Tom's hand. But the car never followed."

"I guess Eivan's machine works on a different frequency than your Oudjat."

Emma pulled the pendant from her blouse and showed it to Dr. Rappaport, wondering if he even remembered her original Eye of Horus. "This is what I use to make sure I'm inside the right timeline."

"The Star of Capella. The Pathfinder gave you this? Did she also explain where you come from?"

"Yes. Columba did. I even thought of bringing my mother there one day to show her where she comes from."

"Wait a minute. You can bring someone with you when you travel?"

"Yes. I brought Hank, Tom, even my dad a couple of times."

"Interesting, this might be quite useful."

"You brought some notes for me, and I have a class I can't miss."

"Yes." Dr. Rappaport sat down again at his desk and opened the volume he'd bookmarked before closing. "Eivan senior worked hard trying to discover a means to destroy the evil he caught by accident. When his brother suffered a heart attack, just before passing out, Eivan noticed his eyes changing. When he coupled this with the uncharacteristic demeanor his brother suffered the month before his death, he believed he'd uncovered the reason for this Earth's stagnancy. He calls this evil. We call them wizards."

"I guess I'm not the only one who can spot the wizards."

"He worked on a prototype, seven of them over the next ten years. He couldn't find the components he needed to solidify the electrical filaments he'd secured. So, he traveled to MIT to meet with Gerald Buttler, a renowned astrophysicist.

They still could not get their gearbox to respond with the force or the speed they needed to secure a free separate space, some sort of trap to attract and imprison the wizards."

"Wow. Ten years. That is some dedication."

"Then along comes Eivan junior. While traveling to MIT with Gerald Buttler, Eivan senior and Gerald suffered a car accident. The tumble did not kill Eivan senior, at least not right away. Gerald Buttler crash-landed with the Jaguar over the cliff, while Eivan senior was thrown clear. In the hospital, he gave his son the combination to his locked material, and to as much information as he could. His son promised to bring his project to term. Of course, the boy brought nano components to his father's project after he consulted with Luis Gonzalez, one of his professors at MIT. He increased the power of his father's project a thousand times over. Enough that we are now in turmoil because of the shifts his engine created."

"Oh, my God. What sort of nano components?"

"You can use them to enhance just about anything today. Eivan is using silver nanoparticle ink to form the conductive lines he needs in circuit boards. One utility of many. He is also using them to enhance the heat conductivity, as gold nanoparticle aggregates form in the solution to increase thermal heating and recover completely to the initial value upon removal of the heat. In other words, he's strengthened all the weak links responsible for stalling his father's project."

"Quite the little genius. No wonder he is unwilling to part with the information. I imagine he will want to patent his new invention before he tells anyone where to locate it. How do you know all this?"

"Gerald Buttler is quite informative. However, genius or not, this is where I draw the line. You have a class in ten minutes or so?"

Emma glanced at her wrist and jumped, grabbing her bag. "Yes. And I can't be late."

"After your class, come to my office. There is something I need to show you."

Joss Landry

—Twelve—

Lunch at MIT

Elizabeth Reardon, Emma's professor in Behavioral and Systems Neuroscience, held several classes each week with her more dedicated students. Emma needed to fly and land in the closest women's washroom just to make the session on time. Otherwise, Professor Reardon locked the door, so all tardies missed the precious information she handed out. Of course, the professor always made available the material she taught, filing her work at the library the following week. However, the in-class discussions provided a powerful research-oriented environment and brought on questions and discussions that far outweighed any scripted material.

Emma was the last one in, and the door locked in place by the time she sat down. Something was off, though. A shiver ran down her spine almost immediately—an odor seized her—one she came across for the first time in years when she visited Eivan Baker at the hospital. The overbearing, unpleasant stench of honeysuckle—not that the scent was particularly vile. Except, Emma, aware of what the odor represented, despised its carriers: wizards, the amalgamation of all the evil roaming the Earth. Rolled up into functional entities that penetrated the human shells to take over minds and bodies, their goal was to perpetuate human suffering.

Negativity, sadness, anger, all the baser human emotions drew the wizards to the person they now held under their power.

Emma tried to detect if she could sense where the scent originated, from where she might experience the most potent whiff. Impossible to do so while sitting in a circle of ten students without scrutinizing each one present.

At the end of the class, she was about to leave when her professor asked her to stay. Eyeing the room, Emma collected her books and approached Elizabeth. "Anything wrong, Ms. Reardon?"

"Have you heard from Amelia?"

Emma felt a twinge of guilt. She hadn't thought of Amelia lately, and her friend usually sat right beside her in Ms. Reardon's class. "We text each other once in a while. She's doing a dual major."

"I understand. I wouldn't mention this, but I left several messages on Amelia's cell phone. She never called me back."

"Never returns my calls either—any calls for that matter. I don't even think Amelia realizes she has voicemail. We text because that's the only way she uses her phone."

"I see." Elizabeth rose and gathered her folders and her attaché case. "Well, perhaps you'd be kind enough to let her know that if she misses another class, I will grade her next exam accordingly. The material covered in the test does not always reflect the handouts I leave at the library. A lot has to do with the subject matter we discuss in class."

"Thank you. I'll make sure to let Amelia know."

Emma walked toward the door. Her hand on the round knob, she considered how fast the room had emptied. Almost immediately though, she was reminded of the persistent aroma of honeysuckle. She'd discarded the problem during heated class debates, but she wondered about the odor still being this strong. She turned toward Elizabeth Reardon putting away the projector she'd used and walked toward her.

As soon as she inched close enough, she realized the scent came from her. No doubt about it. She spotted the outline of the wizard inside her, directing her thoughts, her movements. Such a kind soul Elizabeth Reardon portrayed. She wondered what the wretched creatures wanted with this kind woman.

Her heart fluttered in her chest as Emma stepped in closer. "I want to show you the gift I got for my birthday. I always forget when I'm in class. Then I remembered how much you love unusual jewelry, so I thought you might appreciate this family heirloom handed down from my grandmother."

"Oh, Emma. How kind of you to remember." The woman paused what she was doing and walked toward her. "I do love jewelry, especially the rare kind," she chuckled.

Emma pulled the pendant out of her blouse and showed

it to her professor.

"Beautiful," Elizabeth breathed, staring intently at the piece. "What an unusual little key on that chain."

"Yes, it activates the bezel and allows the two top stones to swivel, to turn. Watch." Saying this, Emma affixed the little key's oddly shaped bow to the minuscule head on the side of her jewel. She gave the bezel a quarter turn to the right and spotted the blue light only she could visualize as she directed the ray toward Elizabeth.

Her teacher's eyes blurred, and her expression changed a fraction of a second before the wizard stood outside her body with blank eyes and an empty stare. She directed the light toward the ghostly figure, and the evil turned into sparkling crystals that evaporated almost instantly.

Elizabeth put her hand to her head appearing slightly dazed. "Oh, I guess it's time I had a bite to eat."

Smiling, Emma realized the wizard had ceased to exist and would not be back to trouble this human as a bright glow enveloped Elizabeth from head to toe. Emma sensed the glow's presence would protect her teacher from more unholy unions.

"Did you want something, Emma?"

Classic, Emma thought. Once the wizard left a person, the victim didn't remember anything that went on while under the influence. This time, she hoped this person had retained her soul intact.

She quickly put the jewel back inside her blouse and

shook her head from side to side. "I just wanted to tell you how much I enjoyed today's class."

Emma ran along the corridors to regain Franklin Rappaport's office, or Fred Manson as she knew him. She'd traded in her jeans and T-shirt today for a skirt with a blouse and an A-line jacket. She dressed in readiness of logging five whole hours of clinical sessions with Dr. James Monroe. The time she booked with Franklin Rappaport also counted toward her licensure requirements.

She found Fred Manson standing his back to the door when she came in without knocking, the door being ajar.

They could communicate through telepathy when needed, and when they didn't wish anyone else to listen to their conversation.

"I'm ready, Dr. Manson."

He turned and acknowledged her with a head nod. He grabbed his valise and recommended she take her handbag with her. "I gather you have the means to take notes in your bag?"

"Yes. I also have a recorder on my phone if I need to collect important information."

"Very well. Please retain these coordinates inside your phone."

Emma did as she was told, and recorded a series of numbers, and letters. "Almost seems like URL addresses," she said.

"Yes. Each one of these timeframes has a specific address." He reached for the tablet inside his valise and told her to list all the different timeframes on her phone.

When she finished, she wanted to know, "How do I differentiate them?"

"With the numbers I gave you," he answered, frowning as though she had missed something.

Emma decided not to ask again. She would define little shortcuts to identify each timeline. Emma looped her arm into his to accelerate their departure but found he was nothing but a residual image. She wondered how other people shook his hand, or if someone bumped up against him if the other person might be surprised to encounter nothing but air.

"You of all people should understand how I can alter my residual image at will when it's time to secure someone's hand or … bump up against someone—although why would anyone wish to do this is beyond my comprehension. Also, you cannot come with me. You need to find your own way there. I don't travel the same route you do."

"How …?"

"Hold your jewel, as you would normally do, and repeat the sequence of numbers and letters I gave you."

Emma closed her eyes, and right now, she could well imagine Fred Manson's face after the sturdy repartee Franklin Rappaport just handed her. Fred, the Devronair possessed no patience for dilettantes or slow curves, evidently. Everyone needed to flash their mettle around him.

Holding her oudjat in her right hand, she focused on the

twelve numbers and three letters Fred had given her and transported to MIT in seconds, to the timeline where she'd met Annemarie Hanover. To the timeline where Amelia loved Tom, and Tom loved Amelia.

Her eyes opened, and Emma spotted someone's research, laboratory. Colorful beakers lined up on a corner table waited to be used. A Corning set of five Griffin-style beakers, made of borosilicate glass to withstand varying temperatures, stood in the middle of a pristine metal bench. She even spotted a few Reagent bottles topped with a white powdered substance.

Then she spotted her professor stepping out of the shadows. "You got here before I did. Impressive. What do you think?"

"Just lab paraphernalia."

"Turn around, and feast your eyes on the metal spokes mounted on the back wall."

Emma did and spotted a long lab coat propped against the wall. The cloth, dangling on a hook appeared as though the thick cotton blend had covered a lot of miles. No longer white, the garment displayed a multitude of vibrant colors. Beside it, secured against the wall like some mechanical, shiny skeletal head was a round object she could not identify. "Is this the engine you spoke of?"

Fred walked toward the back wall, and Emma followed. "Not the engine—just the gearbox. However, this component is a big source of our troubles." Fred waited for Emma to join him and indicated the item. "Eivan junior adapted a quasi-replica of a dual clutch transmission to propel his engine revved by nano components. He also amended the gearbox and the fuselage with nanotechnology."

"Can you elaborate?"

"In laymen terms?"

She nodded.

"General Motors would love to get their hands on this type of technology for their gearbox. They have a DCT that functions forty times faster than the blink of an eye when the system shifts the gears."

"Yes, I remember Tom mentioning something like that. His new car owns a dual clutch transmission—I think."

"This one operates at one thousand times faster than the human eye can blink."

Emma took a sharp breath. "The rapid speed is fluctuating our timeline."

"Yes."

"Still, if wizards are willing to kill for this, perhaps it is life-threatening to them."

"We both know wizards didn't end Eivan senior's life, nor his partner's life. And the attempt on junior's life was from Devronairs."

"Why did wizards leave Reverend Lemon's body that night? He collapsed right in front of me."

"I cannot say what the wizards wanted with a man like Reverend Lemon."

"Can you shut down these transmissions?"

"Not if we don't find the engines that propel them. And I've been told that shutting them down would need to be carefully planned."

"Meaning?"

"Well, there are twelve gears in that wall-mounted transmission. Only five are active. Should they remain active much longer, one or all of these timelines could supplant the reality we now enjoy."

"How do you know how many gears there are in the transmission?"

"In the current timeline, Luis Gonzalez is now on Earth Optimal—quite informative."

"Another timeline supplanting our own would be catastrophic," Emma answered thinking of where she'd been in the last few days—the last time shift scaring her out of her wits.

"More than you know." Fred walked toward the door. His hand on the handle, he added, "Bill Frost spoke the truth when he said all the aliens and kind souls, such as yourself, who are here to help Earth Refuse to merge with the other planets, are inherent of this current timeline only." Professor Rappaport's expression grew frightened and sad, emotions that didn't usually register on Fred Manson's face. "This place we call Earth Refuse would be much worse had we not tended to the world. Many of us have been here thousands of years, straightening out people, stabilizing emotions, educating the poor. Without us, three world wars happened in quick succession, incurring devastation, the decimation of its inhabitants, humans as well as animals. Had this occurred, we would no longer consider bringing this cluster with us."

"Earth would no longer be invited to participate in Heaven? Nirvana would go on without us?"

"Well, Chavah, you and your mother would be with the Source by now, or at the very least still on Capella Five waiting for the Source to open their arms to all on your planet."

"Strange how Bill maintains that none of the people who are here to help can reach these other timelines."

"Devronairs are the only ones who can, and just a few of us at that. Naturally, a fifth-dimension Chavah can pretty much reach whatever she wants."

They walked down a long corridor, and Emma glanced at the time affixed to her phone. "I need to get back. I work with James Monroe this afternoon." When Fred continued on his way and didn't answer, she asked. "Where are we going?"

The professor stopped in front of double doors.

Emma attempted to get her bearings. When she remembered the Hayden library Tom had pointed out to her, she asked. "What are we doing here?"

"You will need to talk to Annemarie. She is the only one who has seen the engine we are attempting to shut down. If we knew what we were looking for, we might be able to find it."

"There has to be another way. What if we simply go back

in time and prevent Eivan from doing this?"

"Impossible. I have told you. Devronairs cannot go back in time nor can we go to the future. Yes. We can go to any of these trumped up timelines, and we can go anywhere in several of our universes. But, we are not indigenous to Earth. We cannot align ourselves with her past or her future." He raised his eyebrows indicating her with a toss of his head. "However, you, Chavah can travel to the past and set things right."

"No. No way. I will not travel to the past and risk staying there. I tried to familiarize myself with the few explanations one of my ancestors wrote in the big book. Three paragraphs are all that exist on the subject." She searched the area around her. "I attempted a few times with baby steps. I went back in time one day. But then, I couldn't come back. I had to relive that day being careful to do everything the same way. Then I tried again, the year after. This time, I went back in time a whole week. Again, I could not come back—the longest week of my life."

"How old were you?"

"Sixteen, going on seventeen. I'm not doing this again."

"Perhaps you omitted a detail or other. You might spot the discrepancy, now that you're older and wiser. Going back in time would be the clean way to settle this whole mess."

"Even if I did. I wouldn't be able to change anything. To avoid all this mess, Eivan needs to go to Earth Optimal, and I can't bring him there."

"Why not?"

"What?" She caught the testiness in her tone of voice and hoped Manson also got the message. She didn't do well with coercion of any sort—especially his.

He did get the message. He raised his head and indicated the library's portal with his hand. "Let's get the information from Annemarie, shall we?"

She nodded and walked in. Never mind that the time she'd reserved for lunch before the long afternoon ahead of her would dissipate quickly. Better to be hungry than to attempt time travel again.

Joss Landry

—Thirteen—

Busy Monday

Emma walked a step behind the great Franklin Rappaport, AKA Fred Manson, as he walked into a small cafeteria in back of the Hayden Library at MIT.

They stopped in front of two tall stationary windows that helped the clerestory windows draw in more light—a lunchroom of sorts behind the library building where students could eat and discuss their findings.

"Annemarie?"

The girl turned and appeared happy to see her. "Wow, you look different, more professional somehow."

"The clothes. I have appointments all afternoon."

"Long way from home, though."

Emma turned to introduce Professor Franklin Rappaport when she realized the man was now invisible. Of course, he could choose to keep his residual image private, and she thought this man indeed was Dr. Fred Manson with his egotistical manner and his sink or swim attitude toward her. He would use her in every way he could. Jeannie, Bill Frost's wife, warned her more than once, and Emma laughed it away.

"May I sit with you for a few minutes?"

"Sure. I was just about to help myself to lunch. Did you have yours yet?"

"No."

"I have an extra salad. I bought it for my girlfriend, but she just texted me. She has a lab to make up." Annemarie took out a salad from her bag, and a second one she handed to Emma. She also gave her a can of lemon ice tea and a plum. "There, you're all set."

"You are a kind person." Emma smiled as she put down her handbag and opened the salad's plastic lid.

"Hope you like nuts and mixed greens with your veggies. I grabbed one I knew Carlie would like."

"Perfect," Emma answered her good mood restored. Let Fred Manson go to blazes, for all she cared. She would do her best, and he couldn't insist Emma do anything she did not want to do. Her life, her way. "I started to worry I wouldn't have time to eat."

"You have other appointments around here?"

"Yes, I do." She could feel the laser-sharp glare of Fred Manson realizing she partook in one more lie.

"Did you want to ask me something?"

"Yes. I needed to know if you ever spotted the engine Eivan uses for the project we discussed last time?"

"Hum," she pondered having chomped on two big bites. "I did once—ask him about this. Curiosity got the better of me. Only he never showed it to me. He said the apparatus, what he calls all his project tools, was in a safe place. Then he pointed to his neck. I thought he might be slightly unhinged." She twirled a finger to her right temple. "One of the reasons I walked away and never looked back. Although, Eivan called me yesterday, and I agreed to go out with him tomorrow night. He can be charming when he needs to be. He even said he was considering my ultimatum."

"Your ultimatum?"

"Remember? I told him he needed to choose between me and this project."

"For all our sakes I hope he chooses true love over a scientific nightmare."

"Thank You. I also hope he chooses to be with me."

"Annemarie, are you sure he meant an engine? In his neck?"

"To be fair, he did tell me once he'd put together the smallest engine in the world. He uses nano components."

"Ah! Then, his gesture makes more sense."

"Were you able to interview him at all?"

"No. Eivan is still trying to find the time."

"I hate to tell you this, but he may be using time as an excuse. He doesn't like people nosing around."

"Thank you for telling me. I'll try to bump into Eivan. Might be easier to snag him if I do."

Emma finished her lunch and didn't bother searching the area for Fred Manson. He'd most likely discovered the same thing she had. The remote Eivan had implanted into the base of his skull was both, an engine and a warning mechanism. She studied the road back in the numbers Fred had given her, and couldn't tell them apart, so she held on to her jewel and juggled with thoughts of home.

A few seconds later, after checking the brilliance of the star on her pendant, she sat at her desk in her room, content to be back in one piece. She had another hour to share with her mom, so she took the stairs two by two and flew down to the kitchen. "Mom, sorry I just got home, and I have to leave again. Just wanted to say, hey."

Eloise put the coffee pot on the burner and walked over to her daughter to give her a warm hug.

Emma hugged her back. "How was your weekend?"

"Gorgeous. Your father and I took advantage of everything they offered. We golfed, played tennis, swam to our hearts' content. Your dad even took me dancing."

"So happy for you, Mom." Emma chuckled, holding back the tears in her eyes. "You deserve to be pampered."

"Well, I never realized things could be this enchanting. I don't think I've been this happy in years." She finished her sentence with a great big smile.

Emma pondered her mother might regret discovering who she happened to be when faced with the ills of Earth Refuse. Suddenly, she found difficult to dispute the idea—not that Eloise might be unhappy because of the sad world around her, but because she finally achieved the happiness she craved all these years. Well, Emma didn't have to mention the truth this exact second. She didn't have to air her mother's origins today, or ever. "I'm glad you're happy, Mom. You've made my day."

As she sat down to sip a cup of coffee and share a chat with Eloise, both turned toward the sound of footsteps barreling down the stairs.

"Dad." Emma jumped up to hug him. "I thought you were at work."

"Took the day off. Wanted to spend a little more time with your mother." He smiled and winked at Eloise, and Emma gave thanks her parents appeared to be still in love, the way teenagers are, eyes only for each other while disregarding everything else.

Patrick walked to the counter and drained the coffee pot. "That was quite the weekend, Emma. Talk about luxury. I owe Bob Proctor big time."

He took a chair beside Eloise. "By the way, your mother and I spotted a fancy car parked in front of our house last night. Quite the set of wheels."

The way her father announced this after Tom parked on the street to leave the drive free for her parents should they arrive before he was gone, sounded more like a convenient prod rather than an actual question.

"So, Grandma told you."

Her mother laughed. "Yes, she did. She was so proud of getting Tom a dependable car."

"Dependable? El, the car is a knockout. Makes ours look

like a box."

"Now, your father wants to get a new car," Eloise winked at Emma and kissed her husband's lips.

"Did Grandma tell you why she did this?"

Her parents exchanged a curious glance, and Patrick hoisted his shoulders. "Come to think of it, no. She didn't."

With a few well-chosen, succinct sentences, Emma brought her parents up to speed with the timeline situation, the same type of explanation she gave her grandmother, Abigail. After relating what happened on Sunday afternoon, her mother's tears, never far removed, poured out.

"Emma," Eloise squeezed her hands. "Oh, my God. You said you are working on having these alternate timelines disappear. What if you're in one of them when they do?"

"Mom, listen. I'm working with Hank, FBI man, Bill Frost, and Columba. You remember Columba?"

Her mother nodded, Columba's name only bringing more tears. "Columba's implication means the matter is a complicated one."

Patrick had not yet found his words. When he did, they struck like thunder, loud and sudden. "FBI? Is Frosty helping you with this? Why did Hank bring the FBI into this mess? Is he crazy?"

Emma couldn't remember if she'd told her parents about Bill Frost's role in the world. Perhaps she had, and they'd forgotten. All she knew is she found it safer to hold onto most of her secrets except when to reassure the people Emma loved, she needed to let go. "Bill Frost is not human." Nope. She hadn't told them. Emma needed to clamp down on her jitters because all she wanted to do right now was laugh at the stretched-out expressions on her parents' faces, as though reflected by one of those grotesque mirrors in a circus funhouse. Her father's raised eyebrows up to his hairline, her mother's gaping mouth—she took a deep breath to explain. "He's an angel, a Seraphim, one of the highest-ranking Angels. He's from the Celeste Dynasty, two galaxies away. Like the others, he's here to help."

"Oh, my God." Her father's first words. "What about his wife and children? Didn't you spend one of your Thanksgivings at their home in Englewood Cliffs?"

"Yes. Bill and his family spend most of their time on Earth Optimal. The children attend school there."

"How do they get there?" Patrick wanted to know.

"Bill travels at the speed of thought. And their eldest, Brittany can also transport. She brings her mother and sisters to Earth Optimal when they wish to go home and Bill's not available. Her three little girls are what we call, hybrids."

"Unbelievable." Her father appeared the more surprised of the two.

"Perhaps if more people knew about this, they wouldn't be so judgmental when two people from a different race marry, or two people of the same gender fall in love and want to marry." Eloise's tone was adamant.

"An angel who makes love to a woman?" Her father shook

his head, having difficulty with the concept.

"They don't couple the way we do, Dad."

"I don't want to know," he said abruptly.

"Their souls join through holding hands, a simple touch. When they're ready, the woman calls forth the seed in her womb. When the baby is ready, she calls the child forth into her arms."

"Now, that is what I call optimal." Eloise turned toward Emma. "Why can't we have this?"

"Why all these aliens and angels are here to help us so that we can all be one and enjoy heaven together."

"I always sensed that this heaven business was a crock. There is no heaven, is there?" Patrick smirked.

"There will be when we're ready. We are building a heaven, Dad, Mom. We are building a heaven, one brick at a time."

***

Emma left for John Monroe's office, a few miles off campus. She landed in the supply room of the tall, narrow structure making sure no one was there. Then she slipped into the reception area to sign the arrival time sheet.

Knocking on James Monroe's door, she waited for his prompt to enter. None came. She backtracked to the front desk and asked Louise, the receptionist, if Professor James Monroe was on the grounds.

"He's at the hospital visiting patients today. Did you two

have an appointment?"

Emma dove to retrieve her agenda out of her handbag, at the same time checking on the brilliance of her jewel. The shine confirmed she was inside the right timeline. "Yes. I was assisting him with patients he was meeting here all afternoon. Can you communicate with him?"

"I'll try his pager. He doesn't bring his cell phone inside when he's at the hospital."

Emma sat down in one of the bright orange chairs and checked her watch. She still had ten minutes to spare. Had she misunderstood? The change in plans was unlike Dr. Monroe, the epitome of punctuality, a man who was known for his highly evolved work ethic.

The second's hand on the big clock to her left traveled fast, and if she needed to work beside the doctor at the hospital, she required Louise to tell her soon. She would have to get there quickly, and by ordinary means.

Another five minutes went by before Louise indicated with her hand for Emma to approach the desk. "He apologizes. A couple of emergencies are holding him up at the hospital. I misspoke earlier," she said, the pleated eyes and stretched out mouth confirming her words. "He said he made arrangements for you to assist another doctor. He is surprised this doctor didn't contact you to let you know."

"That's all right. I understand." As Emma prepared to leave, Doctor Franklin Rappaport walked in the door. "Am I late?" He glanced at his wrist. "I still have four more minutes to spare. Right on time."

Emma could not utter a word, so stunned was she.

"Good afternoon, Dr. Rappaport. Dr. Monroe said you would be replacing him. You can use his office. He left the door unlocked for you."

"Shall we," he addressed Emma, indicating with his hand that he would follow.

Emma thanked Louise, and lead the way to James Monroe's office. She walked in, put her satchel down, and waited for Rappaport to close the door behind him.

A little animosity remained from the stunt he'd pulled at MIT, leaving her with all the work. "How nice to see you again. Where did you disappear to when I held my meeting with Annemarie? Or did you stay behind, invisible while spying on us?"

"One of the reasons I changed my appearance. You showed a lot more respect when you thought I was Franklin Rappaport. Fred Manson doesn't hold the same candle, I'm afraid."

"I'm sorry. You're right. You're right. I have no business being angry or disrespectful after all the help you've given me. Please forgive me."

"I'm a Devronair. We may appear angry, moody, and uncooperative at times. The reason is due to your atmosphere. In truth, we do not harbor any such primitive thoughts. I also happen to understand a Chavah from the fifth dimension never harbors such feelings either. Therefore, no forgiveness is necessary."

Emma pinched her lips not to smile outright. Fred Manson could be colorful in his role of the alien helping poor unfortunate humans. "Dr. Monroe must hold you in high regard to trust you with his patients."

"Thank you, he does. Especially that he holds the same status that I do on Devron."

Emma meant to sit in front of him. Instead, she flopped into her chair with a thud. "Dr. Monroe is Devronair?"

"He is. I'm surprised you don't know this. He never encrypts his thoughts."

She exhaled a deep breath and hesitated to discuss her dilemma with Dr. Manson. Only she figured by now that he might already be aware of the vow she made. "I promised myself a couple of years ago that I wouldn't attempt to read people's minds anymore—not without first securing their permission to do so, as I did with Eivan on the night of our meeting."

"May I ask why?" He opened a drawer and grabbed some of the folders.

"I realized that I would hate for someone to read my thoughts without my permission." Emma gave Fred Manson the nod, her expression meaning the way he did to her. "So, I promised myself I would not do this to any other human—or human helper."

"The trouble with that sort of philosophy is the idea originates from Earth Refuse. Proof of this is on Devron and Earth

Optimal there is no such concept. There are no secrets. The need for privacy is non-existent. We derive happiness from oneness which we cannot fully achieve without eliminating all the walls."

"And the encryption."

Fred Manson smiled, a rare occurrence that Emma enjoyed nonetheless. "Consider your *prying* into other people's thoughts an endorsement which offers the same protection as *lying* to them."

Emma's shoulders slumped, and her eyes dropped to her lap. Manson was right. Her attempt to remain squeaky clean was nothing more than a cop-out. She needed to help others to become squeaky clean. To accomplish her task, she would need to work outside Earth Refuse policies. "You're right. I've been neglecting my duties. This is why I'm here, isn't it—to break Earthly rules, and to enhance this world to the status of Earth Optimal in doing so."

"Yes. Thank you. I'm glad you found your bearings. You're going to need them."

"Are you going to see Dr. Monroe's patients?"

"Read my thoughts," he told her with the slant of a smile.

She did and stated, "Not necessary to conceal your thoughts, I can read through your encryption." Emma smiled. Then she lost that smile. "What? We're going to see Eivan Baker at the Essex County Hospital Center?" Her head shook at the thought of the spooks she encountered there on her last visit.

"We will both be unharmed. Daylight will protect us. Not to mention, you have your pendant to secure your well-being."

"What about you?"

He rose, cornering her with an intense glare. "None of these ghosts will dare approach me. And our meeting with Eivan will be productive. I will do the talking, and you will capture his thoughts—not the ones he deigns to give you, as he did the last time, his real thoughts."

"Dr. Manson, you can read Eivan's mind. Why do you need me?"

"While I question him, you will draw pictures in your mind of the subjects you wish him to envision. This way you will prompt his thoughts toward what we want to know."

"Give me an example, please."

"You will picture the engine to his project, the nano components he uses, the transmission he operates. When you wonder how he turns off these apparatuses, pay close attention to his mind. Without realizing where the prompts originate, he will communicate quite a bit of information."

"I never pictured you as an optimist, Dr. Manson. I commend your conviction. I hope you're right."

Emma Willis Book 3,
I Can Help You

—Fourteen—

Afternoon To Remember

While afternoon light dispersed glorious rays over the city, Emma stretched out her legs while sitting comfortably in the posh leather seat of Dr. Manson's Maserati Ghibli. Emma considered driving up to the hospital problematic She worried about her last encounter with the ghosts when she traveled this same road Friday evening. She would have preferred to fly there using the astral route. "Why such an exquisite car, Dr. Manson?"

"A human gave it to me as gratitude for restoring his health. Since he accepted the life I handed him on Earth Optimal, he no longer needed a car, so he insisted I take it."

"Don't you usually travel with a mere thought?" At the same time, Emma wondered where Manson resided, and if he even stayed on Earth since he could be anywhere, quickly.

"Yes, I do. I just thought this might be more amenable to you than having to scramble to fly to the hospital. Then I, waiting until you found some spot to land."

Emma rolled her eyes as she considered this explanation pitiful. "Since you are in residual form, I find it hard to believe that you can maneuver physical forms, here on Earth."

"Since I travel at the brink of thought, it takes no time at all for my corporeal self to join me when I need to be whole. And today, I chose Professor Rappaport's image to support me." A small pause before he added, "Also, this car is equipped with a ghost detector."

Emma eyed the doctor with a worried frown. Was he also becoming unhinged—following in Eivan's footsteps?

He glanced at her. "Please, give me credit for my attempt at humor."

This time, she laughed outright. "Very well done. Great sense of humor. Although what you need is not a ghost detector but a ghostbuster." She chuckled at the sight of his crisscrossed eyebrows.

"Like the movie of the same name?"

"Yes! Have you seen the films? There are two of them."

"Have not had the pleasure. By the way, once we arrive at the hospital and cross that doorstep, I am Dr. Franklin Rappaport. Do not call me Fred or Fred Manson."

"I'll remember."

As they approached Grove Avenue, Emma reached for her pendant inside her blouse and held on to it. They drove by the red house she had noticed previously, and then Mick's auto service, and she braced herself for the wooded grove coming up. "This is where I spotted the ghostly disturbances on Friday night—coming up at the next turn."

Fred Manson slowed down. He made sure no cars followed him, and he slowed to a crawl. Once around the bend, he stopped by the side of the road.

"Why are we stopping?"

Emma tensed up, and even though she shut her eyes, she still sensed the paranormal activity going on around them. Invisible thumps bounced against the car, weirdly shaped hands tapped on the windows. The large crowd moaned and covered enough of the afternoon sun to make the wood appear dark and foreboding. "Why are we staying here?"

"A lot of mortals need help in this area. I lost count of how many. I need to alert the pathfinder. She will have to find a way to set these poor souls free."

Dr. Manson started the car, and slowly drove away from the grove. As they did, the shrieks and moans calmed somewhat, and Emma breathed again, her heart thumping in her chest. "This is how it was the other day, only worse since I was on a bus. I put my hand on the window and burned two of my fingers."

"They are trying to draw our attention somehow."

"What about all the people who live around here?"

"They can't sense anything. You and I are intuitive. The dead know this. Lost souls realize that you and I can help them." He glanced her way. "I can certainly understand your apprehension the other night, being here alone, at dusk."

"I wish I could help them all. I remember being caught in my grandmother's web of sorrow when I traveled through the astral world looking for my father. I was fifteen years old at the time, and she trapped my dad and me in a thick gray haze of pain and regret without even remembering who she was. I didn't know where I was until Columba told me later. These souls may be trapped in a few people's web of regret or worse, stricken with guilt, and they can't get out."

"Don't concern yourself with this at the moment. We need to concentrate on Eivan Baker, and you will need to exercise a lot of ingenuity to get him to reveal what he knows."

"Okay. Eivan Baker it is." She took a deep breath as the doctor hung a left at the fork in the road and arrived in front of the hospital. Fred had still not answered why he could not read Eivan's thoughts.

Emma had to up her walk to a jog to follow Fred Manson. She nearly tripped on one of the flagstones in the walkway, raised a little higher than the rest. "Dr. Rappaport, please slow down."

Fred glanced at her.

"You say I need to use imagery to trigger Eivan's brain. Are you aware that Annemarie said Eivan pointed toward his neck when I asked her about the engine?"

"Yes, I am aware. I read the conversation in your mind."

"Okay, please give me another example how to stimulate Eivan's mind."

"Well, creativity is not my forte. The humor you witnessed in the car is the extent of it, I'm afraid." His scrunched expression indicated he attempted to visualize some explanation. "Think of a nano. Some of these components are no bigger than a gallbladder stone."

She shrugged. "I need a comparison."

"Well, the head of a pin is one millimeter. The equivalent is one million nanometers. An ant is five hundred thousand nanometers while a DNA strand is 2.5 nanometers. A red blood cell is also close to 2 nanometers." He smiled.

No wonder Fred Manson had difficulty being creative. He walked around with an encyclopedia inside his head. "I get it. A nanometer is extremely small. I'm not surprised Eivan chose to have this implanted in his neck. Not something I would do, mind you."

With his hand poised to hit the automatic door opener, Fred said, "Hope this helps. The closest I can come to being imaginative."

Now, Fred didn't need to answer why he didn't want to prod Eivan's thoughts. He lacked the creativity to do so. He would need to capture the thoughts Eivan deigned him to hear.

They walked inside. Emma remembered the receptionist of the previous Friday night, thinking she worked the afternoon and night shift. After an orderly arrived at the front desk, they followed him to the same little salon where Emma waited to see Eivan on her last visit.

"From this moment on, we communicate telepathically. Too dangerous for anyone to overhear."

"I agree."

The door to the small visiting lounge opened, and a tall,

well-built man dressed in blue hospital scrubs invited them inside.

Emma recognized Eivan, sitting on the sofa this time, appearing relaxed and more alert than he did previously.

Two chairs faced the sofa separated by an oval glasslike coffee table. Emma admired the decor, though subtle, she thought the room appeared brighter and neater than she remembered.

Emma smiled at Eivan and waited for Dr. Manson to take the lead. Eivan remained stoic, she noticed, but his eyes shone with recognition, and he nodded her way as a sign of welcome.

"Eivan, I'm Doctor Franklin Rappaport. We met previously, only you might not remember. They had just brought you in and you were incapable of holding a conversation." Dr. Manson stretched to hand Eivan his card. "My assistant, Emma, tells me you would like to leave this place. Is this true?"

"Who wouldn't like to leave the hospital? Of course, it's true. And I do remember you, Dr. Rappaport."

Emma thought Eivan's last comment painted animosity toward the doctor.

"They aren't holding you against your will, are they?"

"No. I could insist on leaving, I suppose. Especially with what happened to Steve Lemon last time he was here. My mother needs me now."

"I can arrange this if you wish."

Emma reflected on the image of nanometers in her mind

through some of the objects Fred suggested. Eivan reacted almost immediately, pondering about his project and what might happen to it now that he was in the hospital. Emma perceived his worry about the unit being operational and someone else using it without permission. Then he pondered how quickly one might break into his system by reading up on his notes. *I should have secured my notes before going home that weekend. Anyone glancing inside my top drawer could jeopardize my project. Who knows what will happen now? The system needs shutting down until I can reopen again.*

Emma worked hard to contain her joy and worried about interrupting his thoughts. However, she had to take a chance and ask him the appropriate question they needed to know. "*How do we close your project, Eivan? I can help you without Dr. Rappaport knowing or anyone else for that matter.*" Emma smiled at him as he lurched upward, surprised she'd caught his innermost thoughts while she asked forgiveness for the lies.

Then his eyes narrowed, and Emma read that he remembered her telepathy from the last time she visited. "*Can you avoid the jerk in front of me, and shut down my system?*"

"*If you tell me how, I can. And no one needs to know. This information is strictly between you and me.*"

"*Do you even understand about this system, and what my work can do?*"

"*You never gave me details the last time I visited. But you were concerned about someone operating your project without understanding its scope."*

Fred realized a silent conversation occurred between his protégée and Eivan Baker. He could read Emma's thoughts, so he flicked through his notebook, pretending to find his next question. "Here's something that might help me get you released, Eivan." Fred waited until he had Eivan's undivided attention. "Do you plan to finish your doctorate in astrophysics? I know you were preparing your dissertation and writing a book on the discoveries you made when you were interrupted by this ... misunderstanding."

"Thank you for calling the hell that is overwhelming me a misunderstanding, Dr. Rappaport. Hell is hell, no matter what petty name you give it."

"I only meant to say that, in my opinion, this hell was not of your making."

"Thank you. To answer your question, yes. I fully intend to complete my doctorate as well as go through the infinite pile of assignments waiting for me at MIT."

Glancing at Emma, Eivan added. *"Go to my lab and look for the switch under the metal bench. Turn it off, and no one will be able to misuse my system. No one can turn it back on again without the input of my code."*

"I will try to do so. Can I contact you to inform you once I am successful?"

"Yes, you may do so. You know where I'll be."

Fred Manson rose and extended his hand toward Eivan. "I

will work fast Eivan to get you back out into the world again, working on the project you were meant to finish."

"Don't work too fast, Dr. Rappaport. There are some strange happenings in this hospital that I am investigating. I will need a few more weeks to do so."

"Perfect timing. A couple of weeks is most likely how long it will take me to get you out of here. Good day to you, sir." Fred turned and waited for Emma to rise and follow him.

After signing the outgoing sheet, and after letting the door swing shut behind them, Emma turned toward Fred, enthusiastic about what she learned.

Fred drew a finger to his lips while indicating the car with a toss of his head. Emma understood he wanted her to wait until they were on their way before she gave him details. Because he was driving her home, Fred took another route, avoiding going through Grove Street lined with the haunted, wooded park.

"You realize this trip took a mere couple of hours, far from the five hours I was due to spend with Dr. Monroe."

"You will be credited with the same amount of time."

"I appreciate this, Dr. Manson. Only this does not give me the experience I need."

"If it were up to me, I would afford you licensure immediately. You have more experience and more knowledge in your little finger than most psychiatrists possess in their entire brains. Earth Refuse academic certificates are antiquated and not indicative of a person's merits."

"Thank you. However, I still have to function in this society, and if not to acquire experience, I at least need to acquire confidence in the form of practice."

"What went on between you and Eivan?"

Emma grinned from ear to ear. "He may have implanted the engine inside his neck, but he told me how to shut off the system." She put up two thumbs in triumph.

"I'm surprised he did that. Isn't he worried you could flick the switch to start the project any time you wish?"

"Only his code will reactivate the system."

"Still, I got the distinct impression he wished to stay where he is."

"He does. He spotted a few evil dudes, was the term he used, inside the hospital. He wants to investigate further. Eivan also mentioned he was taking down all those names."

"Interesting. The boy doesn't realize the wizards travel in and out of humans at will."

"No. Eivan seems to be under the impression the evil is static."

"For now, let's not contradict him."

As they pulled up to her house, Emma wanted to know what Fred intended to do about the turn-off switch. "How are you going to do this?"

"I'll need to coordinate with other Devronairs since we're the only ones who can travel to these other timelines. I might ask for your help as well. We need to act in perfect unison, or there's no telling what might happen."

"Can you travel to the future of these alternate times?"

"No. Just as we cannot travel to this current version of Earth's past or future. Why?"

"I tried to reach Annemarie Hanover in this current timeline, and I can't find her anywhere."

"Why is this a problem? You realize all timelines differ from one another significantly."

"Yes, I understand this. In one timeline, my grandmother is gone, and my dad patiently waits for the fancy lawyers to divide my grandma's money between my mother and her sister. In another one of these alternate times, Tom, my boyfriend walks with a limp, attends community college while he works driving a forklift in one of the warehouses downtown Newark. So, I realize that life can change on the spin of a dime."

"Have you checked all the other timelines to locate Annemarie Hanover?"

"No. Perhaps I should. Something about Annemarie assures me she is a key player. Not sure why."

Emma eyed her house as she prepared to leave the car and spotted her dad coming out of the front door. He stopped abruptly recognizing her in the car, or perhaps he stood in awe of the Maserati. She couldn't tell. Men and their cars. She thanked Dr. Manson for the afternoon and his generous gift of time he would write in her transcript. "Please, let me know what happens."

"Of course."

She left the car and waved as he drove away. She turned toward the house and bumped into her dad.

"Emma, who belongs to that car?"

Emma laughed. "My Professor, Dr. Franklin Rappaport. I agree—a most comfortable ride."

"Comfort doesn't begin to do this car justice, sweetie." A heavy sigh later, Patrick walked toward his 2012 Chevy Cruze LS and mumbled, "I gotta get me a new car."

"Where are you going, Dad?"

"Grocery shopping for your mom."

"And car shopping for you?" She giggled as he turned to give her the head tilt and narrowed eyes, his as-if-expression glowing. "Later."

Emma hurried up the stairs. Her mother was cooking up a storm in the kitchen, proof in the mixture of aromas that welcomed her home, all with tantalizing scents. She had three hours left to study before she needed to have dinner and get ready for her meeting with Hank and Bill Frost. She would ask permission for Tom to come along if he could spare the time. She wouldn't need to repeat everything when she got home.

—Fifteen—

Family Matters

Two hours into her studies, hunger pains interrupted Emma's brain. Hunger rarely had this effect on her, but because she hadn't eaten anything since the salad she shared with Annemarie, she needed to ingest something, a fruit or a vegetable.

She ran downstairs to grab something from the refrigerator. She picked up a peach when she heard the doorbell and looked around searching for her mother, thinking she might answer the door. "Mom?"

"I'm on it, honey."

Emma rinsed the peach at the sink when her ears caught her aunt Franka's voice at the door.

Walking down the hall, she smiled when she spotted Franka, the two little girls, and her husband Jimmy walking in with a small mountain strapped to their backs and hanging on each arm.

"Aunt Emma," eight-year-old Martha called out, and Emma braced herself for the hug she would get while the little girl ran to her full speed. Martha wrapped her thin arms around her waist, and Emma couldn't help thinking how much she'd grown. Emma squeezed her niece in a warm hug. "Haven't seen you in a while, munchkin." She smoothed her long, curly hair. "You've grown, Martha."

The little girl nodded enthusiastically.

Franka handed the baby to her sister to unload some of the parcels she wore, and once done, she made a beeline for Emma. Gathering her niece in her arms, she greeted her. "Hey, munchkin, you've grown too," she laughed at Emma's stretched expression. "Well, you've grown famous. I'm so proud of you. The staff is buzzing about your phenomenal grades and the upgrade of your masters to a doctorate. I knew you would love Rutgers."

Emma rubbed her aunt's arm. "I miss you, Aunt Franka." She turned toward her mother and added, "We attend the same university. You'd think we bump into each other once in a while, but we don't."

"Hey, kiddo," Jimmy greeted her. "You're still the prettiest niece around."

Emma laughed. "The fact I'm the only one seals the deal, right?" Emma gave him both thumbs up.

Everyone laughed.

"What are you guys doing here?"

"Your mom invited us to dinner. We can't seem to coordinate anything since your parents are like runaway teenagers on the weekends, so we opted for a weeknight."

"Why didn't you tell me about this, Mom?"

"A surprise, sweetie. Truth is we didn't realize we could do this until the last minute. So, here we are."

Emma wanted to tell them about her meeting this evening but decided to keep it under wraps for a while. She didn't want to spoil everyone's fun. "Where's Dad?"

"Gone to the store to pick up missing grocery items," both her mother and aunt answered at the same time. They stared at each other and laughed.

Jimmy snickered. "Franka, don't tell your sister you usually have me park by the grocery store whenever you plan a dinner party. She'll subject Patrick to the same torture."

Jimmy's comment got the biggest roar from them, and Eloise eyed her sister. "You don't do that, do you?"

"Once. Once, I did this. And I have had to live it down for years. I think Jimmy wants me to do it again. He just doesn't know how to ask." She pecked Jimmy on the lips. Since they were all waiting for her to add an explanation, she did. "When Martha was little, we hosted a dinner for some of my faculty members, eight people, and so I asked him to park by the grocery store and keep his cell phone on." Franka chuckled and could not avoid the giggles while telling the rest of her story. "He sat in the car, reading, not having to run around or clean up the kitchen or cook or wash dishes. Anytime I realized I was missing an item, I would call him, and he would pick it up."

Emma was in stitches by the time Franka finished her story. "Oh, my God. How many items did you have next to you when you finally went home, Uncle Jimmy?"

Jimmy looked around, relishing the story, the attention, and answered, "Two full shopping bags. I went back in so many times, the cashiers started looking at me funny."

The roar continued. That was when the door opened, and Patrick walked in. "What's going on here. I could hear you guys laughing from the drive."

Emma tried to stop laughing as she asked, "Dad, do you have your cell phone with you?"

"Yes," he answered tentatively, his frown tickling them even more.

"Did you have to park by the grocery store until Mom remembered all the items she wanted you to get?"

Eloise was bent in two, laughing and trying to wipe the tears pouring out of her, and Franka roared. Even Jimmy laughed faced with Patrick's perplexed expression.

"I don't have to go back there, do I?" Patrick asked, panic on his face.

While everyone laughed so hard they could not answer Patrick's worried question, Franka added, "See, right there," she said while blowing her nose. "Patrick's terrified look. That's why I asked you to park there, sweetie." She kissed Jimmy's lips and both kept right on chuckling.

"Will someone, please tell me what is so funny?"

The roar got loud. It took several minutes before Eloise blew her nose and attempted to explain to Patrick.

"Dinner was lovely, Mom. And I love that I got to spend a

couple of hours with my family." Emma bounced little Alyssa in her arms, and the baby giggled and pulled her hair. "Unfortunately, I have a meeting in an hour with Hank and Bill Frost."

"What?" Patrick expressed his discontent. "You're not still helping Hank with all the work you have to do?"

Emma coined both her father and mother with an expressive stare. "Dad, Mom, I told you about this, remember?"

Patrick glanced at Eloise and nodded. "Yes, you did. I shouldn't complain about what you do with your time, Emma. It's just that you're always thinking of others, not that there is anything wrong with that. I'd just like you to be more selfish, think about yourself for a change."

"Thanks, Dad. Although, truthfully, this matter concerns us all."

Franka took Alyssa in her arms. "By the way, we heard about the great gift Mother gave Tom, and we are so happy that she did this. I didn't trust the old clunker he drove."

"Where is Grandma?" Emma wondered. "I'm surprised she's not here."

"Monday night, Bridge night. She's been playing with the same people for twenty years, ever since Dad passed away," Franka said as she put Alyssa down on the potty in the washroom.

"That's true. Mom's been faithful to her friends," Eloise chimed. She slid an arm around Emma's waist. "She said she'll come next time we do this on a weekend or a Friday night. She has plans every other night."

Emma slipped on her thin cotton jacket. "Here I worried she might be lonely." The bell rang, and she knew it was Tom. "We're driving up in that great vehicle of his to Englewood Cliffs, to Bill Frost's house." She kissed her mother's cheek. "We won't be long, Mom. An hour or so."

"We might still be here when you come back," Franka smiled as she handed Alyssa to Martha. "In case we're not, I want my hug," she added while giving Emma a big squeeze.

Emma waved to them, wishing she could stay longer. They so seldom spent time as a family anymore. She opened the door, and Tom entered. "Hey, good to see you all," he said.

Jimmy approached him. "Can I see your new wheels?"

"Sure."

Emma smiled spotting Tom's eagerness to show his new car.

"This is something I want to see too," Patrick said as he grabbed his glasses. "El, can you flick the spotlight over the garage?"

Eloise nodded and slipped out to the garage to turn on the outside light.

While the men poured over the car, Emma gave hugs to both her nieces, and stepped outside, waving to them as she did. She overheard Tom's animated explanation about the car and pondered on how much he learned about the vehicle in the twenty-four hours since he drove it home from the dealership. Men and their cars, she sighed. Emma hugged her dad, blew Jimmy a kiss, and sat in the passenger seat hoping her move would show Tom their need to leave.

He got the message. "Anyway, I have to go. I'll come by and show it to you over the weekend, Mr. Willis. You can take it out. Impossible to get a real feel for the car unless you take it for a spin."

More waves as they pulled away from the curve and Emma sat back in the seat and relaxed. Between studying, keeping up with everyone's conversation, not to mention traveling to Cambridge that same morning and meeting with Eivan Baker in the afternoon, she sensed fatigue creeping up on her. Her day started early, and she hoped it would finish on a good note.

"Hang a right, Tom. I told Hank we would pick him up." She smiled at his sudden enthusiasm to meet with Hank. Tom often treated Hank politely, but on the chilly side, and she pondered Tom reveled in showing one more person his new car.

Hank came out the minute Tom stopped in front of the house. He didn't get in immediately. Instead, surprise registered on his face when he spotted Tom at the wheel of this luxury car, and he walked around the vehicle with an appreciative whistle—reason for Tom to step out and explain with a lot of pride, she thought.

Still, Tom kept his joyful comments succinct—demonstrated in the smile on his face and the tone in his voice. He understood they needed to be at Bill Frost's house in less time than it took to drive there safely.

Both hopped in, and the conversation about cars took over as Emma used this time to rest her eyes, turn off her brain. The nod did her good.

When they arrived at Bill Frost's home, a glowing moon bathed the whole place. No porch light or soffit lighting—darkness reigned.

Tom parked in the drive and stared at the large house. "Is he expecting us, you think?"

"Yep. Bill will only get here once we ring the bell. He travels at the speed of thought, so he doesn't have to spend time here alone, other than for his job," Hank supplied.

The three got out of the vehicle, Tom giving his new car he named Trudy the once-over. "Still, you would think he might keep a few lights on to deter the punks from stealing."

"One movement in or around his house, Bill would know and scare the living daylights out of anyone attempting to rob him." Hank chuckled.

Tom turned toward his car, using the remote to make sure it was locked, for the third time while Emma rang the bell. A few seconds later, the porch lights and the soft lighting under the eaves turned on, and Bill answered the door. "Come in, please." Bill stared at Tom. "Haven't seen you in the last five years or so. You've changed quite a bit." He smiled and shook his hand. "Glad, you're on Emma's side, Tom."

Tom smiled and nodded, perhaps overwhelmed by the situation, the people, Emma wasn't sure. Tom had changed a lot in the last five years, but Emma considered he still had some maturing to do when it came to the people he didn't appear to like. She'd caught him cast a different glance at Hank tonight, as the two discussed cars. He would need to do the same for Bill, whom he would have to assess in another way once he got to know him a little better.

Bill led the way to the small salon they enjoyed on Saturday evening, and this time, he waved a hand over the coffee table right away. "I imagine you all had dinner, but you might like refreshments anyway."

Tom's eyes opened wide when he noticed the table suddenly fill with delights, Emma realized it wasn't the sight of the goodies so much as the way they'd appeared in front of them out of nowhere.

Hank, picked up a cup of coffee and sat down in the chair facing him.

Tom did the same. When he walked back to the sofa, he tripped on the coffee table leg and, though he managed to keep his balance, the cup and saucer went flying. A second later both items, including the coffee, were back in his hands. "Wow, handy little trick," Tom chuckled as he sat down beside Emma.

The only one not seated was Bill pacing up and down the small salon. "I imagine you're up to speed with what's going on, Tom?"

Tom glanced at Emma. "Yes. Although we haven't had a chance to discuss today's occurrences which is why she'll fill me in at the same time she tells you. This way, she won't have to repeat herself when she gets home."

"I understand." He paused, his knee leaning against a chair's armrest. "The Druids can't help us."

"Not at all?" Emma asked, remembering what Fred told her.

"That's why I'm here. Druids can't interfere with Earth Refuse or any other Earth for that matter. They confirmed whatever was ailing Earth would be cured with information found on Earth. Of course, they agree that we need vigilance to find this input, extract it to our benefit, and act accordingly." He sat down as though slightly deflated. "I couldn't even get how many different timelines we're looking at."

"Perhaps I can help," Emma countered. She explained how she discovered the whereabouts of Fred Manson, his impersonation, and what he discovered so far. She also related her meeting with Annemarie Hanover and her afternoon session with Eivan Baker. "There are five confirmed splits in the time-space continuum, excluding our own. Fred is going to need to put together a team that can turn off all the switches at the exact, precise time for this to work." She hesitated. "Also, he asked me to go to the future to see how all this develops."

"No way," Tom sputtered. "You almost stayed stuck in the past the last time you did."

"I know. It's not something I'm good at doing. I have very little knowledge of the two paragraphs written in my grandmother's diary. Not enough to attempt the trial one more time."

"Why should you go to the future?" Bill appeared outraged. "Just like Fred to demand you do all the work."

"Not really. Just as Fred can't access the past or future of this world, he can't access the past or the future of the various timelines."

"Here's a thought," Bill grabbed a cup of coffee in front of him and waved a finger over the brew to warm it up.

"Did you just reheat your coffee?" Emma asked, surprised by his gesture.

"Yes. I'm sorry," Bill smiled. "Would anyone else like their coffee hot again?"

Tom and Hank both nodded, and Bill complied.

"No," Emma said. "That's not why I asked. Fred said that our scientists are equating time flow with the way molecules from different items mesh with the universe around them. Like coffee molecules merging with the air around them and thus, becoming cold. Did you reverse this equation to make the coffee hot again?"

"No," Bill shrugged. "I just wanted my coffee to be hot again."

"Huh," she snorted. Emma deep in thought stared at the window treatment embellishing the room with a purple hue. "Perhaps it's that simple. Maybe, just maybe, all I need to do is to travel to the past and the future as though I'm traveling the astral route. Just as easy to return, right?"

Tom squeezed her hand to get her attention. "You're going to need to be careful, Emma. If you're stuck in the future or the past, no one can help you. I don't intend spending my life without you."

Emma smiled at Tom, squeezing his hand with gratitude. She liked that he wasn't afraid to speak up, even faced with the clout of both these men. "Perhaps I could try going back to the past for an hour."

"Good Idea," Bill breathed. "Hey, if you can't make it back, we can all wait around for an hour. That's no problem." Bill eyed Hank, then Tom to gauge their reaction.

"Sure," they both agreed.

"Can you bring one of us with you?" Hank asked.

"If this works, I can. I just rather do it alone for now." Emma held on to her oudjat around her neck and thought of today's date and the hour where she wished to travel.

When she opened her eyes, she was stepping out of the car and walking toward the house. Tom turned toward his car, using the remote to make sure doors were locked, for the third time, and Emma rang the bell. A few seconds later, the lights turned on, and Bill answered the door.

Emma smiled and, holding her oudjat, she closed her eyes and headed for today's date at the time specified on the clock before she left. Opening her eyes, she encountered Bill, Hank and Tom's eyes on her, appearing to wait for her return. "It worked. I went to the time we stepped out of the car and walked up to the porch."

"Well, here it appeared as though you never left," Hank whispered.

"That's because I came back at the same time I left. Had I come back five minutes later, you would have waited for my return. My question is, do you remember me standing at the door and walking in with Tom and Hank?"

"I do. Well done." Bill smiled.

"All this time, I couldn't understand why the explanation in my ancestors' two measly paragraphs didn't work."

Hank smiled at her. "These women aren't really your ancestors, are they?"

Emma glanced at Tom to read if he interpreted Hank's words, but he didn't seem to pay attention to their meaning. She hadn't told him she wasn't from Earth. She feared he might look at her differently.

Hank realized his gaffe and said, "They're your grandmother's ancestors. And they probably misconfigured this time conjecture."

Bill smiled at her. "Hank's right—on all aspects."

Emma let go of a huge breath and took in Tom's pleasant smile. She worried how he might react to learning that she originated from another planet.

—Sixteen—

Emma's Home

Emma returned home to discover her aunt and uncle had just left. Her mom and dad sat by the big screen television eating popcorn and watching a movie.

"Hey you two, want to watch the movie with us?" her dad asked. "We just started the DVD a couple of minutes ago."

"That's okay, Dad. I fell asleep on the way back. I'm exhausted, so I'm going to call it an early night."

"How did it go?"

Tom shrugged. "I'm sure Emma will fill in all the details when she's not so tired. I can't keep track of it all."

Tom and Emma walked back to the front door, and Tom took Emma into his arms. He ran his lips over her ear, and she shivered from the gentle touch.

He stared into her eyes and gently pecked her lips. "Thank you for including me, for always being yourself with me, for keeping it real. I love you."

Emma nestled in his arms, hiding her mounting emotions, fearing she still needed to tell him about her true origins. "I love you too, Tom, so much."

Emma Willis Book 3,
I Can Help You

Lying in bed, Emma contemplated the full day gone in a flash. She fingered the pendant around her neck, the piece of jewelry she didn't want to part with now, even during sleep, and decided she might like to fly home to the fifth dimension. Columba mentioned how Emma would find others when ready to do so and wondered how many more souls lived there while waiting to be invited to be one with the source. She could bring her mother there, and she could bring Tom there. She just wasn't sure of what she might find on Capella Five.

She closed her eyes and demanded her pendant and the universe to bring her home. Immediately, she recognized the two suns, the pink and purple skies with the tinge of blue toward the east. As her recollections deepened, she moved about without the use of her legs thinking of where she wanted to be. She came by Lake Tranquillum and sat along its edge on soft, dry loam. The mirror of the lake showed her the size of her planet, the cities, the villages, the fields of plenty. She gazed at the reflection of an outline of bright light, a young woman picking fruit from a tree. The instant she did, the peach was replaced by another. She remembered now. No hunger existed, no basic need to eat on this planet. Sometimes, one wanted to taste, but the desire to do so was almost eradicated.

A bee settled on her arm. "Welcome back, Mistress Cara."

"Is Cara my name here? Where I come from, they call me Emma."

"Whichever name you prefer, Mistress." The bee walked along her arm to settle on her hand. "I missed you. I worried about you not making the journey back. So many humans have disappeared."

"I'm glad to be back. I can't stay. Perhaps someday, I will."

"How are my fellow bees surviving in a 3D world?"

"I won't lie to you. The situation is critical. With the inclement weather of our winters, a high percentage of bees have perished. What's worse is many colonies are dying because of poisonous chemicals farmers spray on our genetically modified food. While the harsh chemicals kill pestilence, they are also killing bees and humans. The bees die quickly. As humans, however, we contract various diseases that can span our lifetime, putting us through a slow, painful death."

"You do not paint a pretty picture—at least for the humans who would not survive in a world without bees."

"You're right. No one would. Bees are responsible for the pollination of fruits and vegetables." She placed a gentle finger on the velvet-like back of the gentle bee. "I wish I could paint a prettier picture. Mostly, I wish I could leave that planet and come back to mine. I miss the communion of all our souls when loneliness never hovers near or far."

"Nothing stops you from returning permanently."

"Yes. My services are needed there. To help the others that have come down to do the same. I can't abandon them, no matter how difficult life can be."

Emma caught the sound of wings on the horizon. She

glanced upward and spotted a white unicorn coming toward her, its alicorn aglow in gold and silver dust. Coming down to meet her, Emma exclaimed, "Shad." She smiled at the slender beast who bowed to her the instant he landed.

She waved to the bee as it flew away, and Emma took a seat on the unicorn's back waiting for him to lift her away, and he did, setting her down on the fringes of a village in front of an adobe house. The pink house with white trim appeared magical. "Is this where I used to live with my friends?" Emma asked as she slid off the unicorn's back.

"Yes, Cara. The place is one of the residences you preferred. Many people like to live and sleep outdoors when the stars shine brightly, and scintillating colors on distant planets bear down on us with an enormous glow. Now and then, you would seek inner exploration over outside beauty."

Emma smiled as she twirled about the property. She didn't dare enter. She might never wish to leave.

"How are you surviving within 3D limitation?"

She turned toward Shad and caressed his flank. "Life down there will be harder now that I remember you." She closed her eyes and took in the warm air that lingered for all to breathe. "Even the air is different here. No pollution, no restrictions."

"What is pollution?"

Emma fingered the alicorn extending from the unicorn's forehead. Warm and sturdy, like the unicorn's soul. The last thing she wanted to do was discourage him from ever seeing her again. "Will you wait for me."

"You need to ask? You know my answer."

"I wanted to go to the village to say hello to everyone, but I don't dare visit. What if I can no longer leave this place?"

"You never answered my question, Chavah."

"Humans on Earth, still deal with the basic need of nourishment. However, our wellbeing is no longer measured by the accumulation of food. We need to amass things, and the more things we collect, the better we appear to feel. The occupation demands running, rushing through life without ever taking a breath. Most of the people I frequent are unfamiliar with contemplation, meditation, or exploring their inner self. No time left to do so."

"And your preoccupations?"

"Same as everyone else's. Too much work, not enough time to contemplate, meditate, explore my inner self. The results of this mad-hatter rush are what produce a dirty, unkempt world, which is what we call pollution."

"When are you coming back?"

"I cannot give you an accurate time. I will try to come and see you on a regular basis. I will bring a friend with me if I may, and we will remember old times."

"Come, I will take you to your point of entry."

Emma didn't remember where she entered this world. She left it up to Shad to bring her back, and he did, by the banks of Lake Tranquillum. After she slid off his back, Shad bowed to her and whispered, "I will not watch you leave. I wish to imagine you are still here with me, but I wish you a safe journey back, Cara."

Emma opened her eyes and looked around her room. At once Earth's heaviness slowed her thoughts, her movements. She sat up in bed to counteract the oppression weighing her down. She realized the impression was brought on by the 3D effect, one that didn't provide the lightness she felt on Capella Five. Still, an onslaught of sadness reached her, and she concluded once more, no matter how many people surrounded her, even when she stood in the middle of a crowd, loneliness prevailed. Unless humans accepted to bond at the soul level, they would continue to live in isolation.

Her head back on the pillow, she wondered how she'd be able to supply real help, one that didn't involve just undoing a knot in a rope. A tear streaked her cheek as she tried to sleep. No, she would not bring her mother to Capella Five.

***

Hank paced back and forth in his kitchen. He couldn't sleep, and Christina tried to make heads or tails of his story. "So, what did Bill say he was going to do?"

"There's nothing he can do. He went back to his planet to ask for advice, and the druids told him they could not interfere. The answer to this problem was to be settled by Earthlings."

"So, it's all on Emma's shoulders? We can't just let her

settle this on her own. Hank, do you know how much work a doctorate in psychology is?"

"Christina, I can well imagine. I just finished paying off my student loans. Believe me. I remember."

"Your student loans? Really?"

"Let's not go there."

"Well, when Emma plans to go to the past or the future, can you go with her? Make sure she stays out of trouble?"

"And here I thought you'd freak out if I suggested the solution."

"Ordinarily, I would. But this is Emma. She can't be in this alone."

Christina's ears picked up the sound of Jarred crying. "Our loud voices must have disturbed him. You know what a light sleeper he is."

"Go to him. Listen, honey. I'm tired. What do you say we take this up in the morning, or after I come home from work?"

She nodded and kissed his cheek. "I'll wait for you upstairs."

Hank walked into the living room, stopped by the window, and drew back the curtains. The night was dark, cloudy, and in front of him stood the muted grounds of the elementary school yard coloring a wide area a soft black no one could pierce. How many times had he stared at the field? He'd lost track. He didn't want to contemplate his life in the dead of night while staring out at an even darker realm. Chief of Police for five years, he marveled at how much he still retained most of his joy and his disposition to be grateful. One of the reasons he'd remained in touch with his inner self, and with the loves of his life was Emma. She went about her business with stoicism and lots of courage. Through all of it, he'd never seen her take a single bow.

Now, he sensed Emma's hurt, her pain at not being able to solve this mystery. Not quite sure why, his intuition told him she needed more than physical help. She needed encouragement, solidarity. Tom was in the background now, and this had to be a boon for Emma. But tonight, when Bill announced his failure to get help from the druids, loneliness wafted circles around her—her sad mood palpable.

Did she feel disconnected from them? Did she not realize how much he and Christina loved her? Perhaps it was time he had a heart to heart with her. Allowed Emma to read him correctly. He'd always forbade her to pick ideas out of his brain. Could this be why she kept to herself? She would visit Christina, but she only ever worked with him, present merely when he needed her help. Time for their friendship to reach new heights. He needed to let her know how the world would not be as pleasurable without her interference, without her love.

"That is an excellent idea, Hank. Something you should do."

Hank jumped, refusing to look behind him. The voice did not belong to Christina or Emma. The soft tone calmed him, and by the time he turned around, he realized who stood in his living room. "Columba." Her beauty was as he remembered, indescribable jeweled eyes, soft smile and gentle manner. Her inner beauty shone like a celebration fire. "What are you doing here?"

"Emma needs your help. You are right. She is lost and lonely."

"What happened? I'm used to Emma being the grownup."

"She went to her home planet a couple of times. I happen to know she will not go again for a while. She realized tonight how difficult it was for her to come back, to return to Earth when she didn't have to do so."

"What can I do?"

"Well, your musings were taking you in the right direction. You should let Emma see your heart, read your thoughts. She needs to discover that there are people on Earth who do live with their soul on their sleeve, their heart in their hands, just as the people do on Capella Five."

"What does her planet resemble? I ask because this might help me better reach her."

"I'm sorry, Hank. There are no words to describe it, none you would understand."

"Try me."

Columba chuckled, a delightful sound Hank thought as he waited for some response.

"Her planet caters to fifth dimension souls. Entities ready to reintegrate the Source."

"Ready to go to heaven, you mean."

"No. Heaven is something we are building. Why all of us are here to help Earth Refuse participate in the heaven we are painstakingly constructing."

"I don't understand what that means, fifth dimension."

"Well, Earth is what we call 3D, the third dimension. Surviving is still the basic instinct, and amassing possessions a derivative of that instinct."

"What dimension are you?"

"Same as you are—third dimension. Only on Earth Optimal, we have eradicated illness, disease, death. When people are ready on our planet, they ascend to the light of the fourth dimension, even sometimes skip ahead to the communion of dimension five."

"Why can't we have this?"

"You can. One of the reasons why we are here, to help you progress a little faster. You need to redirect your instinct and not focus on things or objects to measure happiness. You need to explore your soul, your emotions and how you can rule them, rather than let them dictate how you live." The pathfinder began to fade. "Go to your wife. Christina waits for you. When you fall asleep, find Emma. I will show you the way. Talk to Emma in her dreams. She will remember when she awakes, and this will brighten her days for a long time to come."

As she spoke the last words, Columba had already left. There was so much more Hank wanted to ask her. Then he realized, he would talk to Emma, ask her the questions he never asked Columba.

Hank tiptoed upstairs not wanting to wake Christina—her days filled with working and taking care of the children. He looked forward to those two summer months when she could take some time off and just worry about her boys.

To keep noise to a minimum, Hank undressed in the bathroom and slid into the blankets gently, without his usual bouncing around to find a comfortable position.

As he closed his eyes, he felt Christina turn and wrap her arm around his torso. "I love you, Hank," she muttered in a sleepy voice. Then Christina began to rub his chest as she rubbed up against him, her hand traveling to his southern region. He realized she was still mostly asleep, and though he tried to ignore her advances, they persisted. He turned to kiss her, at first, a soft peck on the lips followed by a more sensual kiss when she moaned and wrapped both her arms around his neck.

They spent the next twenty minutes making love, lost in a world of their own. Hank gave thanks, grateful that both Christina and himself kept their hearts in their hands and their souls on their sleeves.

—Seventeen—

Columbia's Help

Emma left the window facing her bed, and curled back between the blankets, her feet cold and her body shivering. The temperature was still warm at this time of night, but she attempted communication with the elm tree. The action, aside from draining most of her energy, produced little. The tree only smiled at her without communicating the pearls of wisdom she needed about now.

She realized the communion of human and animals, as well as their interaction with plant life, wasn't the same on a low vibrating energy-field such as Earth. Still, she needed something, someone to understand.

Sleep came once her nose warmed up, the satin rim of her blanket directly below it. She thought she might wander back home in her dreams, and this allowed her to fall asleep with a smile.

She realized she was in the astral world when she heard echoes of cries for help. She touched the pendant she wore and wondered why the screams were so loud. Were they her own? She floated under the blue dome of the sky, most likely toward the sounds because they became louder as she moved on.

"*Who needs help? Where are you?*" She understood not to speak aloud in the enormous space of afterlife. She sent her thoughts which had no limit of time or distance. No one answered. "*Please, answer using your thoughts. I catch your screams for help, but cannot hear any other words.*"

"*I am perched on a high mountain with a small ledge. I can't move forward or backward, and I am getting tired. I may fall. Please, help me.*"

"*Hold on. I'm on my way.*" Emma realized she had to keep floating toward whatever imaginary mountain this soul portrayed. There were no such mountains in the vaporous space of afterworld. Although she remembered a deep chasm, she fell into once. Perhaps the abyss was merely an impression of the hole or the bottom she believed she'd reached. Topography such as mountains and chasms could not exist in a space with no walls and no structure of any kind. The afterlife served as a passageway from real-time, or what people imagined to be real-time, to life on Earth.

Emma arrived at the sight of someone balancing on a cloud. To this person, the cloud might as well be a mountain, she supposed. "*I'm here. When I get close to you, grab my hand.*" Emma knew this exercise to be rhetorical—her rescue serving only to reassure this person, he or she would not fall. No one could get hurt in the astral world when traveling without their body. In dreams, bodies were back home in bed, asleep.

When she grabbed the person's hand, she sensed as though she already knew this soul. The familiarity prompted her to say, "*Hank? Is that you?*" No sooner had she said the words that Hank Apple's residual image appeared to reassure her statement.

"*Yes, that's who I am.*" He appeared surprised.

"*I will bring you back home.*"

"*I need to talk to you, I think.*"

Emma smiled at the hazy fog in his mind, remembering when she'd suffered the same effects. "*We'll talk there.*"

Once Emma brought Hank back to his room, she attempted to leave. Hank sat up in bed and whispered that he would meet her downstairs.

Hank grabbed a robe, and just now remembered his meeting with Columba as he fastened the belt of a white terrycloth garment. He couldn't visualize anything while in the astral world. Not even his reason for being there. Why perched on a mountain?

Hank grabbed his slippers and gazed at the love of his life, Christina, sleeping peacefully. He hurried downstairs unsure if Emma heard his request.

She was nowhere. Hank sat down in the chair he vacated hours ago and checked the time on his watch. He would give her a few more minutes.

Just as he was to walk upstairs, Emma appeared in front of him. "I thought perhaps we could talk tomorrow, but then I figured you must have something important to tell me, something that can't wait, perhaps?"

He nodded, searching for the right words.

"How did you get to the astral world?"

"Columba brought me there, although I never imagined she'd leave me perched on a mountain."

Emma laughed. "I don't believe she did. Your state of mind brought you to the top of that mountain. Besides, no such physical features exist in the astral world—not even the blue dome. Why did she bring you there?"

"So that you and I could talk." Hank worried about spooking Emma, but then he rose and gathered the strength he needed. "I sensed your sadness, your loneliness when Bill said he came back empty-handed. He had no advice to give us. Christina and I both worried about you going into this alone, and I believe part of my reaction came from sentiments you expended—unknowingly, but very real."

"I'm sorry. I certainly didn't mean to drag you into my nightmare."

"No. Don't be sorry." He took a deep breath measuring his next words carefully. "I am partly responsible for the reason you and I are not as close as we should be." He spotted the frown on Emma's brow and figured she tried to decipher his words without interrupting him. "Remember how I used to harp each time I even thought you might be reading my mind? You were ten years old."

She nodded.

"Well, I didn't want you going into my crazy, random

thoughts and be scandalized or traumatized by what you found." He pointed to his head. "This brain is not always censured for children, at least, not since I was a teenager." Hank began pacing. "I guess I always resented how easy it is for you to make out all my little bugaboos. Well, no more. You officially have my permission to read my mind any time you want."

Emma wiped a tear rolling down her cheek. "I don't know what to say, Hank."

"Listen, I'm no idiot. I understand that dumping my privacy at the curb is not going to make your life here any better. Just that, Columba said there are a lot of humans who live with their soul on their sleeve, their heart in their hands, ready to love unconditionally. Well, I'm here to say that Christina and I want to be a part of that crowd. We love you like a daughter, in fact, I'm glad we have two sons. If I had a daughter, I'd often be comparing her to you, and this might not work in her favor." He came closer to her. "My clumsy way of saying that you are like a beloved daughter to Christina and me, and I want you to count on us for all your needs."

Emma jumped into his arms giving Hank a warm hug, and he hugged her back.

"We'll figure out how to fix this mess. Don't you worry."

"Thanks, Hank. You've just turned on a light at the end of my tunnel. I realize now the tunnel is not so long, not so difficult to cross. To have you and Christina as wonderful friends is such a blessing."

"Tomorrow, we'll find a way, okay?"

She nodded, looking up as she gave him one last squeeze. "We'll talk tomorrow."

***

The morning arrived with a new resolve for Emma. By the time she readied to leave for her courses at the university, she'd already mapped out a plan to implement and compare different scenarios that might resolve the situation, and to pick the best one.

She hooked her bag to her back and ran downstairs to grab a bite to eat. She didn't have any visits scheduled today, just a class and two labs, so she wore jeans and a blue T-shirt with her hair tied in a ponytail. "Hey, Mom."

"You sound cheerful this morning."

Emma thought her mother and father might have noticed how drained she was the night before, so she took the time to reassure her. "I am. I slept well, and I have all sorts of great ideas I'm going to implement for school, and for life in general." She gave her mother a peck on the cheek.

"I'm glad to hear this, sweetie."

As she slid some of the pancakes her mother cooked onto a plate, her cell phone rang.

"Hello?"

"Emma, Rappaport. Your labs have been canceled for today, as has your one class. You have a free day."

Emma Willis Book 3,
I Can Help You

Emma wasn't sure postponing her classes was such a good idea. She suspected Rappaport, AKA Fred Manson, was responsible for this sudden light load, and she didn't want him butting into her life. Yes, thanks to him the board had upgraded her studies to a doctorate, but now, he needed to let her work to acquire said doctorate. "A free day? One of these labs would have helped me to understand one of the assignments I need to do. Besides, I have already carefully laid out the plan I wish to follow. I believe we need to obtain a little more information on the impact that closing the system might cause."

"What have you found? We can certainly accomplish more side by side than you can do on your own."

"Dr. Manson," Emma spotted her mother appearing to listen to her conversation, so she walked toward the living room. "You wish me to go to the future and take an accurate account of what goes on there. Still, I don't think we should ignore Eivan's work. I believe we should allow him to patent his invention. Something tells me this might be helpful."

"You know I cannot travel to the future or the past of Earth's time structure, although I would love to be able to do so. Yesterday, I had a difficult time returning from an alternate timeline to my current time."

The words were spoken in haste spewing a lot of bitterness, and when Emma asked him why, she already suspected the reason he would give.

"You know why. Eivan's project is affecting all Devronairs

in this quadrant."

Of course, she thought. The problem had gotten deeper, harder to handle. "I still think you should let me accomplish what I planned to do today, especially now that I possess more time to do so."

"Are you refusing my help?"

"Of course not. You're the one who liberated my day, so no, I'm not refusing your help. I believe that we will accomplish more if we divide to cover more ground."

"I also prepared an agenda, ideas I believe we should implement."

"That's great, Dr. Manson. Can we meet this evening at Bill Frost's house? Hank and I will be there, and we can separate the workload depending on which road we choose to take."

"Very well," he grumbled.

Emma thought the poor doctor, robbed of all his powers, appeared despondent. She could well understand this feeling, so she threw him a bone. "Here is something you could do that would be extremely useful. Can you still attempt to travel between the different timelines?"

"I can certainly try."

"We need to check a hypothesis I believe would save us some time."

"I'm listening."

"Could you go back to all timelines concerned, and make sure that on all the metal benches there exists an on-and-off switch? This action is crucial to continuing our investigation."

"I'm sure all his operations have that switch. I hope they do. We must shut them all off at the same time."

"One last thing, Dr. Manson. The letter from Annemarie Hanover to Eivan Baker, the one you showed me last Friday in your office. Did you get this letter from our current timeline?"

The hesitation lasted a long time. Emma thought the good doctor hung up. "Are you there?"

"Yes."

"You said you found the letter in one of his office drawers. Was this letter in our current timeline?"

"No. Why do you ask?"

"I can't seem to locate Annemarie Hanover in this timeline which is the reason for my question."

He appeared to ignore her query, and added. "I will get to work and will communicate with Bill about our meeting this evening." He hung up the phone and Emma wondered why he hadn't searched Eivan's office at present. Perhaps he had and simply found the letter elsewhere. She gave up on the riddle that was Fred Manson and called Hank. "Hank, how is your day today?"

"As usual, super busy. Why? Don't you have classes?"

"I don't anymore, courtesy of Dr. Fred Manson. He wanted us to work together. I'm not sure he's going about this the right way. Want to time-travel to the past with me?"

"Do I? Wow. I would love to go to the past with you."

"Mind you. We're not going back a hundred years. I only need to find someone, or find the reason I can't locate this person in the current time we live in."

"When do we leave?"

She caught Hank's excitement. Natural, she pondered. Who wouldn't be thrilled to take a peek at the life that shaped us? "I won't be ready until after lunch. There are a few things I need to check. You can do something before we leave, though."

"Sure, anything."

"Well, I've tried to find Annemarie Hanover on the Internet, searched the usual social media sites. Quite a few women popped up with her name, but none of them is the one I'm looking for. Can you help me find her? She studies at MIT, so obviously she might reside in the Cambridge, Massachusetts area. In another timeline, in all of them I believe, she's in love with Eivan Baker."

"I'll check the DMV and the other means at my disposal."

"Perhaps you can check the NCIC basis also?"

"National Crime Information Center? Isn't she just a kid, like you?"

"Yes. Just a hunch. I'm going to go to these other timelines and see if I can locate Annemarie. I'm going to find out more about her, about her parents, siblings, and we can compare notes when I return."

"Emma," Eloise called out to her. "Your pancakes are getting cold."

"Coming, Mom." She slipped the phone into her pocket and sat down at the table and poured a little syrup over her pancakes.

"Oh, I almost forgot," Eloise sat down beside her daughter, pleased to watch her enjoy the pancakes. "Amelia called you last night, late. She sounded upset. I tried to ask if she was all right, but she just hung up."

"How late?"

Eloise shrugged. "Dad and I were half an hour into our movie, so close to ten thirty. You were sleeping. I didn't want to wake you. I told her you would call her in the morning."

"I'll give her a call, Mom, thanks. I have a message for her from one of our teachers."

Just as she was readying to call Amelia, the doorbell rang. "I'll get it, Mom." Emma walked toward the door and found Tom standing at the door. She wondered what he was doing there. "Tom, I thought you had an eight o'clock lab this morning."

"Didn't Amelia call you?"

"She called me last night. My mom didn't wake me up. I was just about to call her back. Come on in."

Emma spotted Tom's awkwardness and began to worry. "Tom, you look like you haven't slept. Are you all right?"

Tom stayed pat in the foyer. "Amelia called my house late last night. Josh, her autistic stepbrother, left the house on his own. Someone forgot to lock the door like they usually do, and he just left."

"Oh, my God. Did they find him?"

"Mr. and Mrs. Swift took their car, bringing Emily with them, and went looking in one direction. I took mine and went into another, all the way to Branch Brook Park. Naturally, Amelia came with me."

Emma's frown deepened. "What happened?"

"We were still riding around in circles at three in the morning. Then, Amelia's mom got a call from the police station. Her dad had lodged a report with a good description. Someone found him agitated and screaming, so police picked him up."

"Is he okay?"

"I guess so. Josh is not ready to live on his own. They baby him too much. I tried telling Amelia they needed to have practice runs with him. She said it was a good idea. Are they going to do it? Don't know."

"No wonder you look like you haven't slept."

"That's not the worst of it. It was finally past four thirty when we left the police station." Tom appeared to hesitate but then began his usual tirade against Amelia's clingy friendship. "That woman. I felt as though I was in car-arrest."

Emma's shoulders slumped as she tried not to smile.

"Sitting in the car, parked at her door, she talked about everything under the sun. Her brother was found in Branch Brook Park, but when we got there earlier, she refused to go outside and check out different places to try to find him. All she wanted was for me to circle the Park while she talked and talked and talked."

"What did she say about your new car?"

"Don't even get me started. Amelia acts as though the car is our new car, hers and mine." A heavy sigh followed his comment. "The good news is I finally figured out why the girl is a bloody magpie around me. Truth is an inconsistency stands between her and me—nothing but a blank to Amelia—and the inconsistency states I, Thomas Carson, am in love with Emma Willis." He smiled and took Emma into his arms. "She doesn't hear this when I say it." He planted a kiss in her hair. "No matter how many times I say it. But, try as she may, she can't get past the blank, can she? So, she talks, and she talks." Tom kissed Emma, his moan indicating he was back where he belonged. "You're going to have to tell her that you're in love with me. You are going to need to emphasize how much we love each other—the only way she is going to accept our relationship."

Emma's sigh indicated how much the solution weighed on her. "I thought when she spotted us kissing the other day that she would come to realize this without me needing to dot the i's." Emma stared at her phone. "I guess this is not a phone call sort of conversation."

"No. It's not."

"Where are you off to today?"

"I have classes all afternoon. I just woke up. I fell asleep in my car, in the driveway. My dad woke me up banging on the window. Told me to get over my car and go to bed."

Emma chuckled when she imagined Rudy Carson's raised eyebrows.

"I'm going home to catch a few hours' sleep."

"I wonder what Amelia's schedule is like?"

"She's already gone. A class at nine, and I think she has two more classes in the afternoon. She also has a project to work on at the library after her morning class."

"I'll catch her later." Emma eyed Tom with a little reluctance. "I'm going to spend some time traveling to the past this afternoon."

"Are you sure? I know your little experiment worked well at Bill's house, but a lot of things could still go wrong with this."

"I'm sure. I need to check on some intangibles, and nothing is more intangible than all our lives at the moment."

"I don't want you to go alone. Fact is, I'm so tired, I don't know what kind of help I might be."

"I thought I might bring Hank along. He is desolate, worried, doesn't know what to do with himself. I told him I'd pick him up after lunch."

"Hey, you don't have to lay it on this thick. I understand. Tell Hank that I'm lodging an official request for him to take care of you."

Emma jumped into his arms to show how much she loved his new attitude.

When Tom got to his car, he waved. While still in the doorway, she sent a text to Amelia telling her she wanted to talk, and related their teacher, Elizabeth Reardon's message to her.

She ran back into the house to the kitchen and plopped her breakfast in the microwave. "Thank God for microwaves, Mom. These pancakes are the best I've ever tasted."

Joss Landry

—Eighteen—

Kidnapping

Emma, dressed in her jeans and T-shirt, grabbed her backpack, her water bottle, and cell phone in case she needed to record some notes. While Hank researched his data, trying to find Annemarie Hanover in their current timeline, she would slide to one of the timeline numbers Fred Manson gave her the day before. The same time sequence where she first met Annemarie in the Hayden Library at MIT.

After keypunching the numbers, she found herself outside, beside one of the trees lining the library's avenue. She checked her entourage, and no one seemed to have noticed her appearance. She always needed to be careful of quickly becoming visible to her surroundings without attracting attention. She didn't know where to start looking for Annemarie, but she figured someone at the library might know where she was.

She entered through the side door Tom had pointed out and walked to the oval front desk. "Excuse me," she whispered to an attendant who quickly put a finger in front of her lips. Then, the stern-looking librarian handed her a paper and a short pencil for her to write down her question. She did.

'I'm looking for Annemarie Hanover. I'm supposed to meet her here.'

After searching her computer, most likely gathering information from the list of attendants, the tall, bespectacled woman handed Emma her response. *'Annemarie is researching a project at the end of this aisle in row eight.'*

"Thank you," Emma mouthed. She tiptoed through the broad aisle, pausing to read the numbers over each row. Sure enough, when she rounded the row indicated, she spotted Annemarie ensconced in a mountain of textbooks, quietly communicating with a friend.

When Annemarie spotted Emma, her whole face expressed happy surprise. She scraped her chair delicately and ran to Emma, giving her a warm hug. Annemarie indicated her friend and whispered, "Carlie."

Emma nodded in her direction, wondering how she would ask all the questions she planned to ask her.

"We'll use the door here to slip outside. I'm due for a break about now," Annemarie whispered. Carlie didn't come with them, waving to them while her attention to the books never wavered.

Outside, Emma remarked, "Strict here on the silence issue."

"MIT is like that. Other students who visit here often say this is the quietest place they've ever attended. I'm so glad you're here. I wanted to tell you how right you were about my feelings for Eivan. I am in love with him. And, he's come around."

"I'm so happy for you. Do you mean Eivan abandoned his experiment?"

"Yes. Eivan already found another project he finds worthy. More to his liking—and to mine."

"Quite the coup. I'm happy for you. Listen, I was thinking about you the other day, and it dawned on me that I know very little about you. Would you mind if I I got to know you a little better?"

"Not at all. Fire away." Annemarie smiled.

"Well, I know you told me you grew up around here ..."

"Actually, I was born in Newark."

"Really?"

Annemarie opened her eyes wide and nodded. "My biological father died when I was four, car accident. He swerved to avoid a drunk driver. Two years later, my mother remarried. Then, Jerry Hanover, my stepfather moved us all to Boston. I was nine when we left Newark. Don't remember much of your city, though had I continued living there you and I would be best friends, I'm sure."

"We can still be best friends, Annemarie. I would like that." Emma rubbed her arm, then thought to ask. "Your last name is Hanover?"

"Yes. My father adopted me when we got to Boston. He wanted us all to have the same name. My mother agreed, and at the same time, she asked me if I wouldn't mind adding my middle name to my given name. She hated the sound of

Anne Hanover." Annemarie chuckled.

"I don't blame her." Emma laughed.

"Hey, I'm going to lunch with Carlie. The Flour Bakery & Cafe is right nearby—sticky buns to die for. Want to come?"

"Sure. I'm dying for a cup of coffee. Won't say no to a pastry, either."

"It will give us time to chat some more."

Annemarie signaled to Carlie inside with her hand to join them. When she did, she tapped her watch and said, "Time for lunch. Emma's coming with us."

They walked toward the Cafe, Emma in the middle of two talkative women, and she spotted the crowd of students sitting outside the quaint pastry shop with books and binders, discussing the different subjects of their various classes.

As they entered the establishment, Annemarie appeared to recognize a baritone voice echoing at a table by the window where three young men were discussing math equations.

"Hey, Emma, there's Eivan. About time you two meet."

Annemarie did the introduction. "Eivan, Carlie you know, of course, and this is Emma Willis. She is a fan of yours, and she has been dying to meet you."

The introduction put Emma on the defensive as she shook Eivan's hand with a ready smile. "Hello, Eivan. Annemarie told me about all the fun experiments you young men are conducting in astrophysics. No wonder I've been dying to meet you."

Two of the young men with him excused themselves and took the table across the aisle. Eivan made room for the three women. He extended his arm to shake Emma's hand. "You look familiar, Emma. Have we met before?"

The left-field comment took Emma by surprise, especially since they did meet previously, in another timeline. "I don't think so."

Emma sat down and ordered a coffee from the waitress who came to take their order. She turned toward Eivan. "So, what are you working on now?"

Before he could answer, Carlie chimed, "Thank God he's not working on chasing evil anymore." She gave Eivan a smug expression. "I'll have you know I don't believe in evil." She waited for him to add something.

Eivan ignored Carlie. "I was attempting to continue my father's research. Quite interesting from what he told me, and from what I read in his notes." He eyed Annemarie. "The research was complex and drove my girlfriend crazy." He kissed Annemarie's nose. "Truthfully, she's not simply my girlfriend. She's the love of my life."

"Congrats you two," Emma cheered. "I hope we can all become good friends," she smiled. Physically, Emma noticed Eivan was just as gorgeous as the one she met at the hospital, although his mind appeared different, less dedicated to his work somehow.

Lunch out of the way, Emma took her leave of Annemarie, Eivan, and Carlie. "See you soon. Oh, by the way, Annemarie.

What was your last name before your mother met your new father?"

"Well, Carlie and Eivan know, but don't tell anyone. It was Ripley, as in Ripley's Believe-It-Or-Not?" Carlie laughed, and Emma agreed not to tell.

Emma spent the next hour putting to memory sequences of numbers in her phone to make sure Annemarie existed in the other timelines. Emma discovered that in all of them, Annemarie had convinced Eivan to abandon his plans of catching evil entities and removing them from the face of the earth.

Then, curiosity took over. Emma wondered about herself, her activities, and her family. She had visited them briefly and understood she had two jobs to make ends meet in this particular sequence of time. She wondered if she might have courses at Rutgers today.

Once alone, Emma doubled back and slipped into the lady's room of the small pastry shop. She fingered her pendant and projected herself to this timeline to see what she was doing. A brief moment passed, and when she opened her eyes, she spotted herself talking to some professor at Rutgers, one she didn't know. Impossible to go up to that Emma and ask her without creating a wave of shock in the Emma standing five hundred feet away.

She would need to come back with Hank and have him ask this Emma some pertinent questions.

Emma was about to leave when the thought struck her to find Christina Tyler. She took out her phone and did a reverse search using her phone number, and reached the correct address. Only the name belonged to Christina Latham. Had she married someone else? Tyler was her maiden name that she gave up for Apple when she married Hank.

Unnerved by the search results, she nevertheless realized that in this particular timeline, any question she asked of Google, she would get this timeline's answers.

She headed for her native timeline, to Hank's precinct. Since the place was silent and he didn't seem to be around, she called him to let him know she waited for him in his office.

"I'll be there in five, Emma. Ask Cin to get you a cup of coffee."

An uneasy sense of gloom crept up to make her shiver. She wrapped her arms around herself and worried about her future. She'd already downed three cups of coffee today, and this most likely contributed to her suffering the cold jitters. Or did some other portent loom before her, some heavy burden she would not be allowed to square away?

By the time Hank entered his office, she might as well have been ten years old again, scared of her powers and even more frightened to discuss them with him.

She rose and smiled at Hank to allay her fears, to alleviate the cause of his deep frown. "Hey, Hank. What's wrong?"

"Another crazy. Every two years or so a couple of them surface and make me a raving, mad lunatic."

"Another Boleslaw?"

"Of sorts, yes. Different MO. Same results. Two young teens, fifteen-year-old girls, have already disappeared."

"No!" Emma found a chair where she readily collapsed. "I will help you, Hank. Don't worry."

"You have enough on your plate as it is. And I can't go with you this afternoon. At best, I can give you twenty minutes."

"I understand." A couple of deep breaths later, Emma asked, "Did you find anything on Annemarie Hanover?"

Hank dropped his gun on the desk and shook his head. "Nothing. Like you, a few women turned up, but they don't match the age or description you gave me." Hank sat behind his desk. "I even checked NCIC as per your suggestion. Nothing."

"She was born right here in Newark. Her biological dad died when she was four. Her mother remarried two years later, and Jerry Hanover moved the whole family to Boston."

"She carries the stepfather's name?"

"Yes. The man adopted her so they would all have the same name."

"No wonder I couldn't locate her." Hank rose and went to sit at his laptop on the round table beside the window. "Do you know her biological name?"

"Ripley, as in Ripley's believe or not." Emma chuckled. "That's what Annemarie said."

"Ripley?" Hank repeated the name like a mantra. "Mother Meredith?"

"Yes. Sounds like what Annemarie mentioned when we had coffee."

"Well, you're hunch to search the NCIC was correct. The reason we cannot find Anne Ripley Hanover is because in this timeline, Anne Ripley was Boleslaw's third victim."

"No," Emma cried. The gloom enveloped her like a shroud. The hidden suspicion she harbored, finally out and large. "No. Hank. No. Unacceptable." Upset, Emma rocked back and forth in her chair, dropping her face in her hands. She brushed away a few tears, but she couldn't stop herself from shaking.

"I'm sorry, Emma. All the crazies hunt down angels. Sweet, liable-to-make-a-difference angels. Remember how crazed the man was chasing you?"

She nodded.

"All the people you saved? They wouldn't be here today." He got up and walked over to her placing a hand on her shoulder. "Christina and I wouldn't be back together, and I wouldn't have my beautiful sons."

Emma rose and stared at him. "Tell me this. Why can't you and I hook up, and why can't I develop my powers unless Annemarie perishes in the hands of Boleslaw. Doesn't make any sense."

"I hear you, kiddo. Only I can't give you any answers, and I can't help you right now."

"I'm going to help you, so you can turn around and help me." She jiggled Hank's arm. "Bring me to the evidence locker. I need something from whatever belongs to those missing girls."

Surprise arose in Hank's raised eyebrows.

"Don't worry. I'll stay here in your office, and I'll project myself to the locker, so no one knows I'm there."

He nodded effusively. "Why didn't I think of that," he mumbled while opening his office door to head toward the evidence locker.

"Just make sure you lock your door on the way out. Also, you won't be able to bring me into this. You'll have to make sure whatever conviction you get sticks in court." Emma cautioned.

"I will. Don't worry about me." He jumped and turned to eye Emma. "I hope you're using your powers to make yourself invisible to others. There are cameras in that room."

"I'm still in your office, Hank. That's why I asked you to lock the door. No one can see or hear me, except you."

"Good times. Good old times." Hank chuckled as he pushed the door's twelve-digit lock code. "*Do your darnedest, sweet Emma.*" The chief of police deliberately used his mind to communicate with Emma. He didn't want anyone catching him talking to her.

Inside, he pulled a drawer in a wall of other drawers, some big and some small, and retrieved a watch, a small cosmetic case, a blue ribbon, and a few other items that belonged to the girls. "*Most of these were retrieved from the victims' homes. We found one blue ribbon in the high school's hallway. Might not *belong to either of the girls."*

Emma asked, Hank, *"Can you bring the items back to your office?"*

Hank nodded and took a small pouch in which he slipped the items.

In the office, Emma regained her corporeal form and grabbed the blue ribbon. "His name is John. Can't read the last name. The girls know him. They are comfortable with him." She stared at Hank. "He is a custodian at West High."

"A janitor?"

Emma nodded. She stared at Hank with a big smile. "The girls are alive, and he didn't harm them. He's unbalanced. He's lonely."

"Can you communicate with the girls?"

"Not without giving myself away."

"How about if they can hear you? You wouldn't need to show yourself."

"They might eventually recognize my voice, Hank."

"I can give you an apparatus that will disguise your voice."

"That won't do. I'll be in residual form. I'll just disguise my voice."

Hank handed Emma the voice apparatus. "Keep it anyway. Might come in handy. All you need to do is talk into the gizmo. The thing should make your voice tremble."

"What do you want to know?"

"The man's comings and goings. We do not want a slugfest when we retrieve the girls. We want to catch him in the act."

Emma nodded. She hated being responsible for this poor man's demise. Of course, he needed help since he had readily kidnapped these girls. Still, she hated him doing prison time, as down as he was on his luck. "Is it possible for you not to prosecute him?"

"Emma, sweetie. I understand how you feel. But the man is despondent. We're hoping he doesn't kill the girls and take his own life. He needs help. We're talking hospital time. He's not a hardened criminal, and often these lonely men do what they do simply to get our attention."

"You're right. I just wish there was another way. Kidnapping minors, he'll have the offense hanging over his head his whole life."

"Not necessarily. The man can appeal once a doctor states that he is back to normal. There are attenuating circumstances, especially if he didn't harm the girls."

Emma grabbed Hank's hand. "What if I find I can resolve this immediately? I will need your help to retrieve the girls."

"Okay, excellent question. I'm downloading an app that will keep you on my monitor at all times. This way, we'll be able to figure out where you are."

"Remember, you won't be able to locate me while I'm in residual form, only when I'm whole again."

Once Hank finished loading the application on her phone, he explained to Emma how to use it. "Should you feel the girls need to be out of wherever they are, as soon as possible, you push this button." He slid to the next screen. "The red button will alert my mobile that you need help, and we need to move in immediately. So, it won't matter if you're off my screen or in residual form. The alarm will give me your location."

A knock at Hank's door stalled his lesson. "Not now," he yelled.

The knock persisted. Hank jogged to the door and yanked it wide. "What is the meaning of this?"

A wall of an officer stood before Hank, and Emma bit back a smile catching Hank's rage making him appear taller and more menacing than the six-foot-eight-inches tall officer.

"Sorry to disturb you, but you told me to let you know if the girls' parents became disruptive. They're pacing the foyer up and down demanding to see you, threatening violence if they don't get their way. Want me to put them in the slammer?"

"Why would you want to bring them back here? Henry, these folks can't get past the foyer. The door is locked."

"They are threatening to go to the mayor's office. Mayor will call the commissioner who will dump this all on you."

Hank glanced at Emma, and she tried hard not to chuckle. "This is what I am up against."

She nodded staring down at her shoes, the only way she knew to stop the nerves from making her giggle.

"Okay. Give me three minutes. Then you bring them back to my office. You will knock once, and wait patiently. Understood?"

"Yes, sir. Thank you, sir."

Hank closed the door and stared at Emma, a smile pulling the right side of his face. "Trying not to laugh, are you?"

One smothered chuckle escaped, one she tried to turn into a cough. "I'm sorry." She smiled. "I have the knack for laughing at weird things."

"Nah. Christina would have laughed too. You laugh at the same things she does. Big Henry," he mumbled. "He should have been a stand-up comedian. The man's bigger than the wall, taller than the door frame, and his own shadow scares him." He released a huge sigh to Emma's soft chuckles. He came closer and nodded at her phone. "Do you understand how this works?"

"Yes, sir. I do, sir."

"I swear, if we weren't friends."

Emma thought it best to leave now rather than later. "Wouldn't want to be here when your guests arrive," were the last words she uttered while already on her way home.

Joss Landry

—Nineteen—

Assistance

Once in her room, Emma dressed in black jeans, a black sweater, and tied her hair back to slip under a black stretchy cotton cap. Making sure her phone was tucked in her hand, the oudjat fastened around her neck, she would project herself to the area imprinted in her mind while her body lay on the bed. She would not have her phone handy or her oudjat or Hank's gizmo to disguise her voice, but she would be able to hide from the girls while allowing them to hear her words.

Working undercover for Hank would free him to help her. The assist in this situation would also avoid other lovely, promising young women from being taken away. The memory of Anne Ripley's demise still resonated inside her, like a loud echo, a terrifying one. For the time being, she would duck in some dark corner with only her residual image that she would choose to hide from both girls.

Before leaving on her reconnaissance journey, she read up on the files of both students. Cathy Mendez, and Sandra Collins. The sixteen-year-olds did not attend the same classes, but frequented each other now and then. There was no evidence on how the missing girls had followed the janitor home.

Emma landed in a dark basement. One small window, protected with metal spikes, allowed almost no light through the dirt-smudged glass. The air was stifling, and she could not pierce the dark shroud around her. She moved about to locate the girls and caught a soft whimper nearby.

Both girls sat on a worn sofa of indeterminate color, and Emma caught their hands tied behind their back. She couldn't spot their feet, the ambiance too obscure. Emma took a deep breath and asked, "Are you girls, all right?"

One of the girls told the other. "See what you've done, Sandy with your constant whimpering, now I'm going crazy."

"You heard that too," the girl called Sandy said. "You're not crazy if we both heard the same thing."

Cathy asked, "Who are you? Where are you?"

"Witnesses noticed you two come in here, and they reported your presence to police."

"Thank God," Cathy breathed. "Why can't we see you?"

"Not important for now. We need to discover the man's comings and goings."

"He's never gone for long. He brought me lunch and dinner for the last two days, and yesterday he added a crying companion to the mix." She eyed Sandy next to her. "He allows us the use the washroom. When he's on the premises, he unties our hands and feet, and we can go about this basement with a little more freedom."

"Can you get out?"

"I tried. The window has bars on it, and the door that leads out of this basement is thick and locked."

"Did he tell you why he brought you here?" Emma wanted to know how emotional this man might be, liable to kill them all if he didn't get his way.

"He doesn't seem to be looking for any sexual favors if that's what you mean."

Sandy, the whimpering girl, added, "He said we remind him of his daughters. His wife left him and took their two girls. He's distraught and lonely. There's no telling what he might do."

"Does he carry a weapon?"

Cathy took over when Sandra cried as silently as she dared. "Yes. A gun he points at us now and then, and I've seen him pack a knife in a loop affixed to his boot."

"Can you deduce what time he usually comes home from work?" The time for lunch was long gone, Emma realized. She'd eaten with Annemarie and Carlie hours ago.

"No. Always dark here."

"I'm going to inform police that you are here. The authorities will close in on this man, and get you girls out."

"Tell them to hurry. The man said he was moving us today."

"Where to?"

"I don't know. The man didn't say. Please, hurry."

As Emma left to go back home to retrieve her body, she

heard the key in the lock of the basement door.

Once in her room, with her mobile in hand, her oudjat around her neck, and the gizmo to change her voice in her pocket, Emma donned a pale floral gown over her black togs, a gown she'd worn last year at her aunt Franka's Halloween party. She then propelled herself to the area, making sure only the man could detect her. Unafraid, she confronted him. Hank would not risk storming the house with the girls in the basement, and they could not afford to wait until the kidnapper moved Sandra and Cathy elsewhere.

***

In his office, Hank opened the door to allow Henry inside, but the girls' parents, harboring the intention of ramming Hank's office shoved the tall policeman inside the door, forcing Hank to back up in a hurry. When Henry made to leave, Hank told him to stay.

"Mr. and Mrs. Mendez, and Mr. and Mrs. Collins. You are now in my office, welcome." He took a deep breath and rearranged his suit. "I believe it is important to say that I will not tolerate an ounce of disrespect or the faintest threat of violence. If you cannot control your emotions, I will have Henry cuff you and haul you to jail, like common thieves." Hank's tone brooked no hesitation, not the slightest batting of an eye. He watched them with one eyebrow raised, his expression menacing as he waited for them to confirm they would behave. He almost wanted to be rankled, just so he could put them away. No scenario was ever more explosive than parents jumping the gun to save their children.

"I'm waiting for your reassurance on this matter."

Peter Collins spoke first. "Listen, I understand you believe you are doing all you can. What if you're not? How can we contribute?"

The parents chimed in, and while they did, Hank sat behind his desk. "First of all," he yelled after whistling with two fingers strategically placed inside his mouth. "If the need arises for me to do this again, a team of detectives will be at my door to put a stop to our little session. Do I make myself clear?"

Luis nodded. "We are good, Christian people. We go to mass every Sunday. Cathy is our pride and joy, our only child. We don't want her to suffer, and each hour that goes by..." He didn't finish his sentence. He picked up his wife's hand and lowered his head, overtaken by grief.

"I have two young sons of my own. If anything were to happen to them, I would feel as you do, as the four of you do, right now. However, my police training has taught me that emotions can be detrimental, worse than a bomb in any hostage situation."

The four nodded as they took deep breaths to release some of their tension. Carla Mendez, still squeezing her husband's hand, added, "This is a time for courage, I understand. We will help you in any way we can. We simply need to participate, not to be held out of the way while given very little information."

"Okay. Here is classified information I forbid you to give to anyone else. I want your promise this will stay with us."

The four consulted silently and agreed. Peter spoke first. "As for my wife, Debbie, and myself, we promise not to reveal anything that is said to us in this office. I am a man of honor, Chief Apple, and I will not do anything to endanger my daughter."

Luis hesitated but also complied. "As God is our witness, we promise not to talk about any information you share with us."

"Good enough for me." Hank got up and walked to the chair nearest the small group of people. "We have many psychics working with our office. One of them approached some of the items belonging to your daughters, and got an impression of the man who took them." Hank stop to gauge the parents' reaction. The Mendez's eyes were unusually big, but the Collins were smiling.

Debbie Collins said, "I applaud your sense of duty, Chief Apple. You have explored all avenues. My daughter is safe with you." She brushed a tear from her eye.

"Luis?" Hank asked waiting for his reaction to simmer down.

"I guess, God works in mysterious ways. We were taught to accept everyone. We are not narrow-minded individuals."

"Good to hear because this particular psychic who wishes

to remain anonymous does not want this matter disclosed outside this office. The person maintains both girls are still alive and the man did not harm them."

Audible sighs came from the women. "How do we get them back," Carla Mendez asked.

Hank got the beep on his mobile, and when he looked down, he smiled when the GPS gave him the direction to the custodian's house.

"I'm on my way to get them back. I'm traveling with a small group of detectives. If you can contain and control those emotions we talked about, you can follow behind the police escort. My proposal is not usual police procedure," he stressed. "You cannot leave your vehicles or make your presence known to anyone until Henry, here, gives you the go. Are we clear on this?"

They all nodded. "Quite clear," the four emphasized at the same time.

"Any attempt to do otherwise could seriously jeopardize our rescue mission and get your daughters killed."

"Chief, we will watch and wait for Henry's signal." Peter Collins affirmed.

***

Seconds after a slight hesitation, Emma pressed the button on her phone, the signal for Hank to move in. She hated signaling with this man present, but if they didn't act quickly, the complications might entail four teenage girls instead of two. Carefully, she called to John speaking through the gizmo and throwing her voice. He jumped and dumped three bullets of his gun into the wall beside her. While the girls yelled and Sandra cried, Emma, summoned her courage and smiled before she appeared around the corner, out of eyesight of the girls.

"Who are you? How did you get in here?"

"I think you know who I am."

"You're beautiful. What do you want with me?"

"I don't want you to ruin your life. By bringing the girls back, your actions will help you and things will go better for you."

"I'm not taking these girls back," he said outraged at her suggestion. "I need to bring them to my wife in exchange for my daughters." He pointed the gun around. "She won't give my girls back unless I replace them. I know her. Always what people can do for her."

"Why not show me the rest of your beautiful home. I know you work hard to pay for all this." She spread out her arms.

"You've never seen my house? What kind of guardian angel are you?" he asked in a suspicious tone.

"The kind who is more concerned with your soul than where you live."

"These girls need to use the washroom, and they need water, something to drink."

He untied their hands and feet, still pointing the gun at

them. Cathy and Sandra took turns using the washroom, and John lowered his packsack on the table and threw them each a water bottle. "I'll be back later with a snack. Then when it's dark, we leave."

Emma didn't follow him up the stairs. She disappeared and reappeared inside his house making sure no one spotted her.

Emma sensed Hank would follow the beacon on her phone to find her. Since this was Hank, she realized he would not arrive with guns blazing. Silence and stealth would be his approach. Hank understood that any threat might prompt John to pull the trigger on the girls before turning the weapon on himself.

Upstairs, John made the girls a grilled cheese sandwich and coupled the grub with carrot sticks and celery stalks. Emma thought he went to a lot of trouble to make sure the women were well treated.

Then she caught the distinct sound of several car doors thumping as they closed with a thud. John, used to the activity of neighbors coming home from work at this time, didn't pay attention. Only Emma realized this was Hank with a series of excellent detectives.

The doorbell rang.

"Who in the blazes is that? He attempted to peek from the kitchen but addressed her. "Guardian angel, go see, and report back to me."

Emma complied. "Looks like a delivery parcel. Are you

expecting one?"

"Yeah. Not due to arrive until tomorrow. Fast," John exclaimed. He stared at his gun not knowing what to do with it. He left the weapon on the table. "Guard my gun, guardian angel."

"*With pleasure, friend John.*" Using her conjuring sentence, Emma called the gun over and turned the weapon into a toy that fell on the floor. No one would be the wiser. She took a couple of seconds to go back home remove the gown and change her body into her residual form.

Two detectives walked in, and Emma spotted Hank outside one of the cars. Back to her basic black, she glided toward Hank and made her presence known only to him. "*The girls are downstairs in a locked basement. The door is thick and will be hard to open. The perp is neutralized, but he has a knife strapped to his right leg he can no longer extract from the loop on the side of his boot—at least, for now.*"

"*Thanks, Emma. Great job! I'll see you later at the office.*" Emma picked the words out of Hank's thoughts.

"*I'm going home, Hank. I need to figure out some things, and I'm behind on my school work. Plus, tomorrow, I have a heavy day at school. I'll have some time on Thursday afternoon, and Friday morning of this week.*"

"*Bill will be back sometime Friday, and we can hold a meeting with Fred later that day.*"

Emma watched Henry in the middle of the street, a wall of a man, raise his arm in the air with a sizable wave and a loud whistle toward two cars parked down the road. She then witnessed four people run from their cars toward them to welcome, with a happy grunt, two sobbing girls throwing themselves into their arms.

She caught John arguing with a police officer that his guardian angel had stolen his gun. No one listened to him as they shoved him into a police car, and remorse coursed through her at the rough way the officers handled him. Of course, they had no idea how desperate this lonely man was and how much he missed his children.

Emma got into Hank's car piloted by another police officer and thought she might give him details of how to better handle the man in custody. "He missed his daughters, Hank," she said making sure only Hank could make out her words. "His wife walked away with his children a couple of months ago. He misses them, but she apparently won't give him the time of day."

Emma realized if anyone were to understand John's predicament, Hank would. He gave her a nod to show he did.

"He was about to travel the hundreds of miles that separate them to try and exchange these girls against his daughters, believe it or not. He needs your help."

Again, Hank acknowledged in a way that left her satisfied justice would be adequately served. She trusted Hank to do what was best for everyone.

—Twenty—

Stay For Dinner

Emma paced inside her room, trying to find the peace she needed to unclench her fists and calm her breathing. She supposed she picked up the habit watching Hank pace often enough. The girls were safe, but what did Emma do for herself? She didn't dare ask Hank's help again. She understood he had a couple of rough days ahead of him with the press, the parents, and all the other cases clamoring for his attention.

The doorbell rang and interrupted her well-worn path of bookcase to window and widow to bookcase. Tuesday night, she thought. Her mother always ordered Chinese, and they would sit and make a lovely meal of all the individual boxes in the dining room on her mother's new dining room table. Eloise dressed the oak, oblong piece of furniture in adorable multi-colored placemats forgoing the thick tablecloth she used previously. Proud of her new furniture, Eloise wanted her little family to feast their eyes on the pieces each time they could. Two matching cabinets stood against the back wall holding new dishes, new candle tapers, and lovely ornate figurines that decorated the dining room with a lot of class.

The tempting aroma wafted up to her room, and she realized her lunch was long gone by now. She would sit with her family and partake of the delicious meal if only to renew her strength.

Again, the doorbell rang. Suspecting this might be Tom, she ran downstairs to answer. Emma opened the door with a smile, but the smile transformed into gaping surprise. Dr. Fred Manson, disguised as Dr. Rappaport, stood on the porch with a briefcase in his hand.

"Dr. Rappaport, what are you doing here?"

"I've come to hand you some of your books. Professor Cantor, your mentor in cognitive psychology, confessed about a surprise test he is handing out tomorrow morning. I thought you might like to brush up on your notes."

"Thank you. You're very kind to bring me my books." She couldn't believe this was the only reason he came calling. "Would you like to come in?"

He accepted with a gracious smile, and as she moved aside to allow him passage, she spotted Tom's car pulling into the drive.

Emma left the door open and offered Professor Rappaport to come to her father's office converted from a small sitting room. At this hour, the place would be empty, and she would be able to have a private conversation with him.

Once they were both inside the office, she closed the door behind them. "What did you find in your visits today, Dr. Manson?"

"We need to get together with Bill, Hank, and figure out a way out of this mess. Please, do not take any course of action before we meet. Could cause more harm than good."

"I understand. I have no time to do anything before Friday, anyway."

"What did you find?"

"I believe I came to the same conclusion you did. We are in a royal mess. I'm not sure how to interpret the differences in our current timeline, one where there is no Annemarie Hanover, versus the other five where Annemarie is alive, and I don't seem to have my powers."

"Until Friday, then."

Emma nodded as she led the way to the front door. When she turned to allow Professor Rappaport to leave, he was gone. His residual self no longer on the premises. Disappearing was one way of avoiding trouble, she thought. Unlike herself, the man would not risk getting caught in the intricate pattern of any web. He would escape with a minimum amount of scratches, and live to fight another day.

The imagery drew a smile on her expression, and as she walked into the hallway, she bumped into Tom.

"Emma, did you know your door was open?"

"I saw you drive up and I left it open for you. I was at the door because Dr. Rappaport dropped in." Emma bracketed the word and gave Tom a knowing look.

"In other words, Fred Manson dropped right out again."

"Yes. But don't let Fred catch you calling him Fred Manson or anyone else for that matter. He is supposed to be Professor Rappaport."

"Why is he so touchy?"

They walked toward the delicious aroma in the kitchen. "Well, I have the impression Fred is at the root of a lot of our problems."

"Really." Tom stopped walking and tugged on Emma's sleeve as he ducked in the little reading nook recessed from the hallway. "And here I thought he was most competent. I mean, he came in and saved your life five years ago when he reactivated the little oudjat for Columba to find you."

"Yes, I do owe him a great deal. However, Devronairs are on a mission, and they don't always realize that taking a life can lead to dire consequences for our future, even when they transplant the life they take on Earth Optimal."

"How was your trip to the past with Hank today?"

"Didn't happen. When I arrived to pick Hank up at the specified time, he was trapped with work—those girls that were kidnapped."

"Yes, I read about that. One disappeared day before yesterday, and another one yesterday afternoon."

"He was frantic. I hadn't seen Hank running on empty in a long time. I had to help him."

"Did you find them?"

"Yes, both are home safely, but don't mention this to anyone."

"What would Hank do without you?"

"He would have figured it out soon enough. The man didn't want to hurt them, he simply wanted to drive to his ex-wife's house, in some other city, and exchange these two girls against his daughters that she took with her when she left."

"What a nut job."

"Well, he needs help, which is why I'm studying to get a degree to be allowed to help these people." Emma looked around her as if just noticing the nook. "Why are we here?"

He shrugged. "Easier to talk. Mostly, I need a kiss, a real one."

Emma smiled, happy to comply with Tom's wishes. She wrapped her arms around his neck and brushed her lips against his own. When Emma heard his moan, sensed him trembling, she deepened her kiss, butterflies tickling her legs until they quivered like jelly. A kiss from the man she loved. There was no better encouragement, incentive to work hard and succeed. She could master the world with Tom by her side. His presence gave her wings like Shad did, her beautiful unicorn.

"Hey, you kids, this is not the invisible hallway."

Both jumped and ceased effusions immediately. Emma blotted her mouth with her sleeve and gave her dad an apologetic face, sad eyes with raised eyebrows. While Tom, his back to him, rolled his eyes over and over again, drawing a cross-eyed expression in the process which forced Emma to pinch her lips not to laugh.

Tom turned and directed his apology at her father. "Sorry, Mr. W. Won't happen again."

"Good. And how many times, Tom have I asked you not to call me Mr. W? Do you know how ridiculous that sounds?"

"You're right. For some reason, Mr. W doesn't sound as cool as Mr. C, or Mr. B. Why do you suppose that is?"

"The purpose of using the surname letter is one of abbreviation," Patrick Willis pointed out. "For instance, Mr. Cunningham would become, Mr. C. You might use Mr. B to replace, Mr. Buckingham."

"Hey, quite similar names," Tom exclaimed his purpose of making them laugh Emma realized.

"When you use Mr. W you are using more syllables than you would if you said, Mr. Willis."

"Right. Now that you've explained it so well, I understand." More friendly mocking Emma thought, hoping her dad wouldn't be offended.

"You can also call me, Patrick since I call you, Tom."

"Nah. If I called you, Patrick, I would have to call Mrs. Willis, Eloise, and I don't think I can do that."

Patrick released a huge sigh. "Emma, I think your mother needs your help in the kitchen."

"Sure, Dad. I'm on my way." Emma tugged on Tom's sleeve, rounding her eyes at him. "You know very well that you could use Mr. Dub as an abbreviation," she whispered.

"Of course, I know. Your father doesn't," Tom answered with a satisfied smile and a contented expression telling her he thought he'd won the argument.

Men could be such babies, she thought. "Mom, need my help?"

"Thanks, Emma. I just have to fill this cart with everything we need. Then you can roll it over to the dining room and start setting the table."

"We'll need to make two trips with all this food."

"El, why not use your fancy dishes. Save us the trouble of carrying them back and forth."

"I will, eventually. For now, I enjoy the fact the dishes are new and safely stored in my new cupboards."

Dinner spent together was lovely. Nothing Emma enjoyed more than when all the people she loved broke bread together. Something about taking the time to relax and sharing pleasant conversation ranked at the top of her list of real pleasures.

Tom appeared unfurled by her father's nervous temperament, frequently worn on his sleeve. Over the years, Tom got used to his moods and learned how to apply his brand of comedic fun to the mix. Of course, her dad realized the tall football major, as he sometimes called him, poked fun at him now and then. At least her dad didn't seem to mind. Perhaps he minded a little and pretended not to for his daughter's sake. Patrick accomplished much these last ten years in the success of his insurance commissions, and in his personal growth. Emma was proud of him.

"Apparently, Josh Swift ran away from home yesterday. At

least, this is what your dad told me, Tom."

Tom's dad and her father worked together and often traded stories. Except, that her powers were kept a secret from everyone, especially from prosaic, mistrusting Rudy Carson who did not believe in anything as grand as magic, at least as told by his son Tom. Anyway, her family's nightmare was that someone would find out and their lives would turn into a living hell, a dizzying and never-ending circus where they became the freaks everyone would condemn, as told by her father.

"Yeah. We spent half the night trying to find him."

"They baby him too much. Obviously, they need to lock their front door, but they should take him out more. Teach him the ropes."

"This is what I told Amelia. However, he can be a handful sometimes when he starts screaming for no apparent reason."

"Not apparent to us, Tom," Emma put down her fork and poured herself more water. "I've since learned that some autistic people can be frightened by the presence of too many people or when they believe they are lost like Josh was last night."

"Yes. Josh is big and tall, and if this happens, he would need someone strong enough to reign him in," Tom said between two mouthfuls. "Took two policemen to bring him in last night."

As they ate, the doorbell rang. "Who the hell would be calling at this hour?" Patrick said with a menacing pair of eyes.

"I'll have a look, Dad."

"Don't bother. At this hour, only someone trying to sell us something."

The door rang again, two more times. "This can't be a salesperson." Emma got up to answer. "The ring is too insistent."

When Emma opened the door, Hank's presence surprised her. "Didn't think to see you here at this time. Are you on your way home?"

"Yes. I am. I just wanted to thank you properly. Am I interrupting your dinner?"

Emma figured if Hank was at the door at this hour, Christina had to be still at school. "Yes, we're eating Chinese food. Come," she motioned while opening the door for him to enter.

Hank did, removing his shoes and following Emma to the dining room. "Everyone, Hank wanted to say hello on his way home."

All of them expressed a greeting, her father using a little hand wave. "Why don't you take a load off, Hank and grab something to eat," Patrick nudged him to do so.

"Do you have enough for everyone?"

Eloise chuckled. "Hank, there are only four of us, and we've got way too much food. Doesn't keep very long. Even with our best intentions, we usually end up throwing some of it away."

Patrick laughed. "First, we keep it around for a couple of

days, clog up our refrigerator, then we throw it away."

"Well, since you put it this way, I will have a bite to eat." Hank took off his jacket and slipped it on the divan against the far wall.

"Where's Christina?" Eloise asked.

"Parent-teacher meeting. The boys are asleep, and there's a sitter at our house right now."

Emma turned to him surprised. "Again. Didn't she have one last Friday?"

"Ah, she has one every night this week. She meets with the parents of the students that have difficulties. She does so individually to make sure they follow the strict guideline for their child to pass the state exams. She makes it a point every year to help all her students graduate. Not always easy."

"Oh, I bet," Patrick said, his face depicting recognition of the hard work Christina performed. He blew out air as if he was tired merely considering the fact.

"This is good, Eloise, Patrick. Thanks. I was heading toward a hungry man dinner." He slowed before his next bite. "I just wanted to thank Emma one more time."

Emma knocked on Hank's foot for him not to say anything. Too late, the gig was up.

Patrick hooked his glasses on the bridge of his nose. He wore them almost all the time now, forgetting to take them off when he wasn't reading or watching television. "What did you do, Emma?"

Hank realized he'd put his foot in the wrong place, but

then he came clean. "Listen, Emma would never toot her own horn, but she helped me solve the missing teenager case today."

"I read about this," Patrick said. "Two young girls, right?"

"Yeah. Emma identified the person who took them and was able to secure the man while we picked up the girls."

"Honey," Eloise said. "This is wonderful. Why didn't you tell us?"

"I meant to. Never had a chance."

Hank turned toward Emma, a goofy apologetic expression on his face. "I thought you might like to know how happy both sets of parents are. The scene where they held their daughters in their arms was primo."

"I witnessed some of it before I … left for home." Even though her parents realized she usually opted for the astral mode of transportation, she avoided expressing the thought out loud.

"Now that's what I call helping people, Emma," Patrick said slathering more rice and chicken on his plate. Turning toward Hank, he added. "She insists on working nonstop, struggling to make ends meet so she can obtain a doctorate, a piece of paper that will grant her permission to help people." He faced his daughter. "What you could do for Hank would provide people a lot of help, and you wouldn't need to work so hard."

"Pat, I understand why she wants a degree." Hank came to her rescue, probably thinking he owed her at least that much. "The man who took the girls is going to be reviled, stared upon as though he is a freak, and he's the one whose life might be ruined. Those girls will go on to thrive and be happy. It's people like the custodian, blind with the pain of losing his daughters that Emma wants to help."

"Yes! I so get that," Tom answered, spurred by Hank's speech.

"Besides, I hold a masters in psychology."

"Really." Patrick appeared shocked.

"Well, it's not a doctorate," Hank winked at Emma. "And I can't practice, but hey, I managed not to wring that custodian's neck."

Laughter arose from Patrick and Tom. Then Tom added, "That's why the requirement for policemen today is to have a higher education."

"True," Hank pumped his fist to Tom's. "An education helps hotheads like me keep things in perspective."

Emma stared at Hank. "I'm glad you were there when police picked him up. I'm not sure he would have had the same fair treatment had you not been there."

Patrick raised his water glass. "To my lovely daughter and her kindness toward helpless souls."

The rest of them cheered and raised their glasses, while Emma smiled. As she squeezed Tom's hand, she wiped an errant tear trailing down her cheek.

Emma Willis Book 3,
I Can Help You

—Twenty-One—

Brian Hayes

Wednesday morning, after her exam, Emma searched for Amelia. Her friend did not return any of the messages she left, even her text messages of Tuesday morning. She called Tom to find out if he knew where Amelia might be.

"Good question. Don't know."

"Tom, can you call her and find out where she is?"

"Won't return your calls, huh? I guess a little deception won't hurt. I'll call you back, love."

When Emma found out Amelia was eating at the donut shop, now waiting for Tom to join her, she flew there to meet her. Familiar with the grounds she landed in an oasis of trees decorating the picture window. When she walked out, she gazed at Amelia sitting by the window watching everyone go by, and she prepared her surprised expression.

"Amelia, finally we meet," Emma expressed with a big smile.

The surprise on Amelia's face was not as pleased. "What are you doing here? I can't talk right now. I'm waiting for someone."

Emma sat down in front of her, and Amelia appeared flustered. "Don't worry. I'll just stay until your friend gets here. Did you get my text about Elizabeth Reardon?"

"Yes, I did. I had a nice chat with Ms. Reardon. Not to worry."

"Well, since I didn't receive your text, I wondered."

"Sorry. I've been busy."

"I heard about Josh. Glad you found him."

"Who told you?"

"Tom did."

"When did he tell you? He left my place and was going straight home."

"He came by my place early yesterday morning before he went home to sleep for a couple of hours."

"Emma, are you trying to cause trouble between Tom and me?"

"Cause trouble?" Emma wondered about the question and shoved her hesitation aside. Amelia's words proved she'd waited too long before claiming Thomas Carson as the man she loved. "Amelia, Tom and I are in love. I thought you knew this. You caught us kissing a couple of weeks ago."

"Kissing doesn't mean anything. Tom and I kissed a few times. Doesn't mean he is in love with you."

Emma released a huge sigh. She needed the courage to explain to Amelia, not run away and forget the problem existed. "Tom and I have been a couple since last Christmas when we finally got together. At the time I realized how much I love him, and every day since. We have become one soul. We are extremely close."

"Not fair. I've been in love with Thomas Carson since I was a little girl. You know this. All along, all this time, it's been Tom and me. And now you're trying to put the kibosh on our relationship? I don't think so."

"How many times did Tom go to your place since you were a little girl?"

"A few times," Amelia answered defensively.

"How many times did he hang out with you at school?"

"We went out a couple of times."

"Tom practically lived at my house. We were tied at the hip in school. My grandmother just bought him a new car." When all Amelia did was shake her head negatively, Emma considered she needed to launch the big guns. "Tom asked me to marry him."

"What?" Amelia appeared winded.

Emma nodded. "He did, several times. We talked about it with my parents, and my father prefers we wait until I finish my doctorate, but Tom thinks it would be great for us to share common housing at the university."

Amelia leaned her forehead against her shaking hand, covering her eyes. Emma's heart broke when she witnessed the pinched lips and the tears straddling Amelia's cheeks.

"I'm sorry, Amelia. I kept my distances from him as much as I could because I sensed how much you liked him."

"Love him. I love him." She grabbed a napkin to blow her nose and wipe her eyes. "I tried dating other young men. None of them can hold a candle to Tom."

"Amelia, you are my best friend because you are a warm, giving and nurturing individual. You are beautiful inside and out, and you will find your true Prince Charming. The love of your life is not Tom. You only think he is because you haven't met the man who will sweep you off your feet."

Amelia planted her eyes on Emma. "Are you talking from prescience?"

Emma hesitated. If there ever was an opening to tell Amelia about what she could do, this might be the time. However, neither of them owned the leisure to talk all afternoon. "No. I only know that it's illogical to love someone with your heart and soul when this person's not ready to offer you the same privilege. Tom doesn't feel that way about you. Why would you waste one more hour of your precious life planning your future around someone who does not deserve your heart and soul—not because Tom isn't a kind and wonderful human being, but because he doesn't understand you."

"I know. Tom doesn't get me. I always sensed that if he could discover me, what's inside, he might fall in love with what he found. I've been waiting for some breakthrough or other."

"Say he wakes up one morning and realizes what a wonderful person you are, as I have already. He still wouldn't be prepared to give you his heart and soul."

"Why not?"

"That's what you've been waiting for, right?"

Amelia's head fell as she nodded her eyes glued to the

table.

"He would never do that, Amelia, as much as he likes you as a friend. He gave me his heart and soul a long time ago, and you of all people understand how strong the sentiment can be." Emma paused and caught Amelia's slight nods. "Even if one day, Tom should wish to retrieve his heart, we would still be forever soul bound. A type of love and devotion you still need to find. He's out there, Amelia."

Amelia shrugged. "I've been an idiot, haven't I? All these years. If this mystery man is out there waiting for me, I have to keep both eyes open. Problem is it'll be hard to stop thinking about Tom all the time."

"I understand. Time is a great healer, though. Meanwhile, you'll get to enjoy more of your dates as you meet new fellows. And when you least expect it, you will meet your Mr. Right."

Amelia squeezed Emma's hand. "Do you know who he is? What he looks like?"

Emma wondered about Amelia's strange question, her friend appearing to expect Emma to give her name and description of her mystery man. "Sorry. You will be the first to know."

Amelia rose, dropping some change on the table. "Thanks, Emma. I have to run, but I promise to return your calls and stay in touch. Please don't tell Tom about this conversation. He'll think I'm crazy."

Emma rose, realizing Amelia would need a while to get

over Tom. The process would be gradual, but thinking about someone else around the corner would also give her the courage to move on. She gave Amelia a big hug. "I'll keep our chat to myself. Don't forget, BFFs stay in touch, always."

"I love you, Emma." Amelia waved as she ran, and Emma hoped she would find shelter inside another heart like hers. She deserved love with the same formidable ardor Amelia used to lather on others. She waited for the coast to be clear, slipped between the branches, and flew home to change for her visit with patients alongside Professor James Monroe.

***

Emma arrived at Doctor Monroe's office, and Louise greeted her. "He's waiting for you—not that you're late or anything. That's just how he is." Louise smiled.

"Thanks, Louise."

She entered and promised herself she would interpret people's thoughts again, especially that this would help her learn about the intricacies of human behavior. She would also be in a better position to help them solve their problems promptly.

"Ah, Emma. Right on time," Professor Monroe smiled. "I've laid out a few files on the desk for you to browse." He rose collecting the folders and handed Emma the documents. Sitting on the edge of his desk, he continued, "Our first patient is a young woman who has difficulty socializing. She doesn't see the need to do so or understand the steps involved which means she is incapable of cultivating friendships, or even of keeping what friends she does encounter."

Emma sat down in front of the professor's desk and scanned the file mentioned. Each dossier included the person's name on top and the issue that needed treating, and on the righthand side, Dr. Monroe's notes, illegible to the human eye.

"The second case this afternoon is a young man who has trouble with exams, tests of any kind. Although he does learn the material well enough, and I have tested him on this issue, he cannot pick the answers he needs out of his brain under the pressure of taking an exam."

Again, Emma glanced at the file James Monroe handed to her, and though she read the subject's name, the age, and the issue, she could not make out any of Dr. Monroe's notes on the subject. "I can't seem to read your notes, so you'll have to relate your findings." Emma smiled.

"Well, they are encrypted. Fred mentioned he told you I am Devronair. If you run your thumb over the notes and perceive them as thoughts, your powers will take over, and you will read the file's content through your mind's eye."

"Thank you. I didn't even know this was possible. So, I can read any language, right?"

"Of course. I simply jot it down in encrypted form. This way, all Devronairs can read the content, as some of us can't read your language."

"Do you also read thoughts as Dr. Manson does?"

"No. Very few of us can. Your atmosphere interferes with our prowess." James Monroe smiled as he sat down behind his desk. "Both these first patients are light cases. Their issues are quite common, but I believe witnessing their interactions is still worth your time. The next three cases will be more complex. One of the young men is extremely introverted. I am hoping you can help draw him out."

"I can certainly try." She enjoyed James Monroe's company. She would never have pegged him to be Devronair. Polite, well-mannered and truly kind, he epitomized more the comportment of an enlightened human than he did an alien from Devron.

They worked hard as both remained focused and present while listening to patients. Emma did not ask any questions or supply any answers, even when she realized the patient said one thing while thinking another. Best to clear that up for James later. She made a note of it in her chart.

Three hours flew by before James stood, and offered Emma coffee and refreshments in the small kitchenette. "Louise makes sure the armoires are well stocked. I'm sure you'll find something you like. Don't be shy. Just go through all the cupboards and take anything you wish."

"Would you like me to bring you back a cup of coffee?"

"No. Thank you."

Emma left wondering what Devronairs ingested to keep their energy going. She'd never witnessed Fred eating or drinking anything. She would have to remember to ask him. Emma rummaged around the kitchenette and grabbed a few saltine crackers and made herself a cup of coffee.

A few minutes later, she wandered toward Louise's cubicle. "Would you like a cup of coffee, Louise? I just made a fresh pot."

Louise appeared preoccupied as she typed away at some reports. The frown on her brow ran deep. Perhaps she too had difficulty reading James Monroe's writing. However, a closer introspection led Emma to sense fear in her demeanor, something to do with her surroundings—out of character for her. Emma touched her shoulder to get her attention, and she jumped as though just noticing her. "Louise, are you all right?"

She nodded as she took in a great breath, eyeing the patient sitting across from her in one of the bright orange chairs. Turning her attention to Emma, she answered promptly. "Yes, of course. Trying to get through these reports."

"Would you like a cup of coffee?"

"I would love one. Thank you so much."

"Be right back." As Emma turned the corner, she concentrated on the young man facing the receptionist. For some reason, Louise feared him. In fact, the man's eyes, glued to Louise, indicated a fierce and unflinching scowl, his dark orbs like daggers apt to frighten or intimidate anyone. Emma hurried to fetch and bring back the coffee. When she did, Louise smiled as though glad she was no longer alone facing this young man. "Please tell Dr. Monroe that Brian Hayes is here."

"Certainly."

In the office, Emma closed the door and informed James Monroe, "Brian Hayes is waiting at reception."

"Thank you. Brian is the introverted young man I mentioned earlier, the one you might be able to help me read. I will go and get him."

"Of course."

Emma stood by the window, and when Brian walked in, she sensed the whole room's energy transform into a dark, foreboding place. Who was this young man and why was his aura so dark?

"Brian Hayes, one of our newest young doctors, Emma Willis."

Emma approached the young man with hand outstretched, but he merely sat down and ignored her.

"Our session will begin immediately, Brian. Were you able to finish the work I gave you during our last session?"

You stupid, dumb ass, freaky putz, you're the first one I'm killing on my list of people who need to die. "No. No time."

Emma tried not to jump or show she'd caught the boy's threats. Instead, she wrote down those thoughts, word for word.

"Did you bring the work with you?"

"No. I did not."

"How do you expect us to make progress if you don't do

the work?"

"Listen, I'm here because an asshole teacher recommended I come to therapy."

"Yes, and when you didn't comply, the school principal obtained a court order that forces you to seek therapy. If you do not cooperate or hand in the work I requested, I will need to go back to the courts. They will expel you from school. The authorities will send you to a reform type of school where therapy will be your main subject. Unfortunately, the school that your parents are proposing is miles away from your friends and family. Is this what you want?"

I will tear you to shreds, and kill that dodo bird brain in your reception. I just have to hold it together for two more weeks, and none of you will be able to put me away, like an animal. "Nobody tells me what to do? Do you hear me? Nobody."

Brian spoke the words in a soft tone which heightened his threat in more ways than one. Emma kept her eyes to herself. The boy needed help. She remembered the last time she sensed this much anger, a vile hatred for most human beings. Boleslaw, ten years ago, the maniac who went around killing little girls because he'd grown up sexually abused and ridiculed. She wondered about Brian's environment, about his parents.

"Well, you leave me no choice, Brian. Please leave. I will send my report to your parents, and your school principal."

Brian Hayes rose. "You do that asshole, and I'll make sure

you suffer from the pain I plan to inflict on you. I guarantee. I will have the last laugh."

He left, slamming the door behind him. Emma rubbed her arms to rid herself of the goosebumps. Of course, Brian would never be able to hurt or kill a Devronair, but he might be able to harm Louise.

"I wouldn't take his threats lightly. He has organized something. I read his thoughts. He needs two more weeks to put his murderous plan into action."

"I don't understand. Both Brian's parents appear to be from good stock. He's intelligent, capable. What is causing him to act this way?" James Monroe rose and sat in the chair beside Emma. "Did you spot any wizards?"

"No. No wizards. Rage churns inside him and Brian's anger runs deep. I have no idea what's causing it."

"Forgive the unusual request. Ordinarily, I would not make this demand of someone aspiring to licensure, but could you keep an eye on him? Perhaps check on these plans he mentioned in two-week's time. Might just be a surfeit of dark imagination."

"Really?"

"Yes. I've treated this before. Nevertheless, Brian appears quite sure of himself. He may be on his way to procuring the type of violence that would hurt a lot of innocent people."

"I'll keep an eye on him, Dr. Monroe."

"Good. I'll wait for some news from you before I lodge my official complaint."

Two hours later, Emma flew home, worrying about Brian Hayes, Eivan Baker, and all the work she still had to accomplish. Would she succeed in turning off Eivan Baker's experiment? Would Emma manage to prevent Hayes from carrying out whatever he was planning? Would she meet the deadline requirements for her school year?

Once in her room, Emma took a deep breath recognizing she was luckier than most. She did not need to work to support the expense of attending college. She also had powers no one else possessed to help solve some of these anomalies. Emma smiled. All she needed was to plan her time carefully and delegate some of her tasks.

— Twenty-Two —

Heartbroken

After finishing to help Eloise set the table, Emma answered her cell phone. "Hey, Tom. Are you at home?"

"No. Just finished my lab."

"Are you coming over for dinner?"

A slight hesitation had Emma repeat the question.

"How did your conversation with Amelia go?" Tom wanted to know.

"Excellent. When Amelia still didn't believe we were in love, I told her you asked me to marry you. The idea seemed to convince her, and when she left, we exchanged a big hug, and she told me that she loved me."

"Well, she has another version of your meeting. A different, altogether weird scene she said took place."

"What do you mean?"

"She called my cell phone while I was in a lab, balling her eyes out, saying that you're trying to muscle in on our relationship."

"You of all people know that's not true."

"Of course, it's a lie. Amelia's delusional. Can you give me more details of what was said? She is crying her eyes out and wants me to go over to her house."

Emma now realized Amelia's request not to tell Tom about their conversation was to feed her delusion. She promised her friend not to say anything to Tom about what was said, so she thought of a better method of educating Tom on what happened. "Where are you now?"

"In my car, in my driveway. Should I go over there?"

"Only if this is something you want to do. I'm not going to tell you how to handle the situation, Tom. You're capable of making your own decisions. If your wish is to console Amelia, then I recommend you follow your heart." Emma took a huge breath and exhaled it promptly. "Before you do, I might be able to help you make the right decision."

"How?"

"Come on over as soon as you can." Emma hung up and waited for Tom as she wondered how Amelia could have twisted everything around enough to confuse Tom this way. He had a tender heart, but Amelia purported herself to be her friend. She didn't appear to worry about Emma's life or her feelings, this after she said that she loved her.

She ran downstairs when she heard the bell. "I'll get it, Mom."

When Tom entered, Emma ushered him up to her room. Once inside, she closed the door. "Amelia made me promise I wouldn't tell you anything about our conversation. She worried about you thinking she is crazy."

"I already think she is a loon, no big change."

Emma smiled at him. His sad, puppy dog eyes told her more about Tom's concern for the crying and suffering Amelia than any words he might express. "Hold my hand, we're going to go back in time, and you will stay in the shadows, close enough to listen to our conversation without being seen."

"You can do that? Take me with you?"

"Corporeally I can. Residually, I wouldn't be able to do so. I'm doing this through my oudjat. Decorative trees form a little private island where we sat by the window. They serve to cheer up the place and make an oasis of a couple of tables on that side of the restaurant. We're going to land behind those trees. Don't worry. I flew home from there."

"I'm going to witness what went on between the two of you? Won't that be weird for you?"

Emma laughed. "Yes. But you need to be made aware of what's going on. So, instead of being a fly on the wall, you'll be Tom in a tree."

Tom chuckled and kissed her hand. "So that you know, I understand how manipulative she can be at times. And I have no doubt. You did the right thing."

"This journey is not about pointing out Amelia's reckless behavior. Our little trip to the past is to find a way out of this situation. I've explained all I could to her. Now, it's up to you to do the rest."

He nodded. "How long will this take?"

"Our conversation lasted five minutes and a bit. Not long."

"Good. Because I'm starving."

Emma took his hand in hers, gripped the pendant around her neck, and mentally evoked her sentence to travel to the time and place a couple of minutes after her arrival at the donut shop.

The instant they landed, tree branches brushed their faces and tickled Emma's nostrils. She had to pinch her nose to stop the sneeze about to alert every one of their presence. Emma planted her finger across her lips to indicate absolute silence.

Both of them glimpsed Emma and Amelia sitting at a nearby table while Emma tried to explain her feelings to Amelia. Emma eyed Tom as he witnessed with precision what happened between the two of them that afternoon.

At one point, Emma sensed Tom could not contain his temper anymore. He let go Emma's hand while silently asking for her permission to act. She hesitated, but then nodding, Emma stayed behind while Tom appeared as though from around the corner.

"Amelia. I heard everything you gals just said."

"Where did you come from?" Amelia gasped. She turned toward Emma. "Did you set me up?"

"No. I didn't know Tom was here. Did you?"

Amelia smiled smugly. "Yes, I knew he was on his way. He called me to find out where I was."

"When will you get it through your thick skull that I don't love you, Amelia. I never did, and I never will. All this time,

I've been pitying you, feeling guilty about the fact you like me so much. Well, no more. I'm not playing that game anymore. Our first dance when I was eleven, I did it to please Emma. I hated you hanging around me at school. All I ever wanted was to be with Emma. I am in love with her. I never cared for you that way. The only reason I called you today was so Emma could bump into you accidentally and tell you to back off."

Amelia rose staring at Emma, glaring at Tom. "So, you did set me up," she accused Emma.

"My intention was a private, one on one chat. I did not realize Tom was here."

"He just said he called you to let you know where I was."

"Yes, but he has a lab. I had no idea he was on his way here." Emma turned toward Tom. "What are you doing here? Why aren't you at the lab?"

"Something told me Amelia would wrap you around her little finger, and make you believe what she wants you to believe. She's done it to me often enough." He turned toward Amelia. "Listen, until you can be truthful with yourself, I don't want to be your friend anymore. It appears as though each time you call me for some advice or help to solve some problem you have, you imagine that I'm in love with you. No more." Tom walked away toward the door. He doubled back while the two argued their eyes hooked on each other.

Amelia rose. Her hands shook, and when she picked up her book-bag, she bit her lip and wiped the tears. "Well, I hope you're satisfied, Emma. Tom doesn't want to have anything to do with me anymore."

"Give him a little bit of time …" Emma never had a chance to finish.

Amelia threw money on the table that almost hit her in the face, and added, "And I don't want to have anything to do with you anymore."

She turned and left.

Emma rose on shaky legs and grabbed a tissue to wipe her eyes. Before she could turn and use the trees as camouflage to go home, Emma from the future grabbed Tom's hand and both disappeared.

When they arrived in her room, Emma caught a soft knock on the door. "Emma?"

Her mother must have been calling her, and since she wasn't on the premises, she had not provided her with an answer.

"Yes, Mom?"

"Is Tom having dinner with us?"

Emma stared at Tom and waited for him to answer. He smiled and nodded. "Yes, he is, Mom. We'll be down in a minute."

Tom took Emma into his arms. Her cheek rested against his shoulder. She sighed. "I can't believe I just lost my best friend."

"She'll come around, sweetheart." He paused and grabbed his phone. "Amelia's call is gone. The decision of whether or not I should go over there is moot."

Emma stroked Tom's cheek. This late in the day, she came across a little stubble on his chin and under his nose. "Those were harsh words, sweetie."

"Harsh words I should have spoken a long time ago. It's better for Amelia if she hates me. Every time Amelia was angry with me, guilt for what I'd done and worry about displeasing you would make me come around. If I hadn't been such a wuss, she'd have a better life today."

"I hope she can find it in her heart to forgive me."

"She will. Humiliated, torn, she overacted. Normal."

"I love you, Tom."

"I love you, Emma. And I want you to know, I never doubted you, not for a moment."

"What do you mean?"

"Amelia cried on the phone telling me how rude you were, that you were trying to dash all her hopes, and how upset you'd made her. She even said you laughed at her misery."

"At least, that part of her conversation no longer hangs over her head."

"Come on, let's go eat. I'm starving."

After devouring the lovely meal her mother prepared, Patrick disappeared into his office. "I'll help you clean up, Mom."

"No, you don't. You have an exam tomorrow, remember?" She left to bring the dishes from the dining room to the kitchen. "That nice Professor brought your books here. I heard him."

"What?" Tom's ears perked up as he waited for Emma to explain.

"That was yesterday, Mom. The exam was this morning."

"Time flies by, escapes me. How did you do, honey?"

Emma tugged on Tom's sleeve as she answered her mom. "Very well. I'm sure." She smiled.

"Well, never mind helping me. You have some studying to do. You always do, sweetie."

"That's true." Emma asked Tom. "What about you?"

"I need to buckle down tonight. I am presenting two papers this week."

Tom said goodnight to Eloise and walked to the door. Emma followed him.

"Listen, why did your father practically run to his office. I didn't say anything to offend him, did I?"

"No." Emma chuckled. "He brought takeout."

"He's going to eat greasy food after the lovely meal we shared?"

Emma laughed outright. She found Tom's face outraged at the thought and couldn't get the words out. "Takeout is work he brings home from the office. That's what he's always called it."

"Thank God. I was beginning to worry where he'd put all that food, even as wiry as he is."

"Yeah, well growing up, I was disappointed more than once when Mom would mention Dad was bringing home takeout."

Tom gathered Emma in his arms. "I hate to leave you." He kissed her properly, his arms holding her tightly. "I would love to study together and spend the night with you."

"I share your sentiment. I would love that too." Emma backed up to stare at him. "What about your dad. Is he alone all these nights for dinner?"

"Nope. He works overtime, most nights every week. He's trying to make enough money to help me with my tuition for MIT."

"Why don't you stay at Rutgers? The name MIT is not going to make that big of a difference when you're applying for a job, is it? Your grades are excellent."

"That's what the teacher, the one who suggested I take an administration minor this year, suggested. I applied already for a Fellowship."

"You never told me."

"Had to apply before March first." He shrugged. "I guess I forgot. Plus, I don't want to put my hopes up and be disappointed."

"Better than worrying about getting into MIT."

"My academic adviser suggested I also apply for a teaching assistantship. The position would provide the opportunity to work with the GSE faculty and staff, and they would allow me to collaborate on a variety of research and professional projects. I would teach or assist teaching and receive full tuition remission and an annual stipend."

"Well, that's it then. You can stay at Rutgers."

"If I get it."

"Hey, sweetie, your academic adviser suggested this alternative because he realized it's in the bag. They don't want to lose you."

Tom smiled. "I have to go, sweetheart while I still dare to do so." Tom kissed the top of her head and walked out the door quickly.

Emma stood by the door, waving at Tom as his car disappeared in the gloomy dusk of a sky laden with clouds. Shivering slightly under the weight of a firmament suspended with the eerie darkness of a moonless night, she wondered about Eivan Baker and Brian Hayes.

"Are you all right, Emma?" Eloise wrapped an arm around her waist and gave her a little squeeze. "Heart-wrenching when Tom has to go, isn't it?" Eloise poked Emma with her elbow. "He can stay, you know that, right?"

Emma smiled and planted a kiss on her mother's cheek. "Thanks, Mom. How did you convince Dad to accept the idea?"

"He didn't need convincing. He remembers what it's like to be young, and he is so proud of you." Eloise stopped to sniff a little. "We both are."

"Tom has two papers to produce, and I have a couple of exams to prepare. Mostly, I have reports to supply on the people I see. Hours I need to log. I don't think I could focus on anything else right now." She turned toward her mother.

"Tom has asked me to marry him, again." She sighed, letting out all her tension. "I just never thought this doctorate would demand so much of my time." Emma stepped up to close the door. Turning she added, "Besides, Dad would prefer we wait. He's very clear on the subject."

"This decision is not for your dad to make, nor for me. Your parents are here to give you suggestions. The final decision is up to you, Emma, and please don't allow either of us to influence you in any way."

"Thanks, Mom." Emma ran up the stairs to her room. She would check her agenda and proceed from the more to the less urgent tasks.

Emma Willis Book 3,
I Can Help You

—Twenty-Three—

Echoes

*E*mma worked on her laptop to finish an essay she needed to hand in for her behavioral pattern's class. Two more exams scheduled on her agenda also required study, but she wondered if she should inspect the immediate surroundings of one Brian Hayes, as requested by James Monroe. While debating the point, a sudden, slow shiver ran down her back. Someone was in the room. She turned and caught the beauty of Columba smiling as she waited for Emma to acknowledge her.

"Columba, great to see you. What are you doing here?" Emma closed her laptop and swung her chair around. She indicated the other chair to Columba.

"Thank you, but I don't need to sit. I came here to help you with your dilemma. I realize all the work you need to accomplish and I want to lessen your burden."

"Ah, wonderful," Emma breathed. She rose and went to sit on the bed to be closer. "How is your brother Hawke, by the way? I haven't heard from him in a long time."

"Hawke is thoroughly happy. He followed a young woman he liked from Earth Optimal to Kapera Laus, which is a planet in the fourth dimension. You were his first choice, you know, even before he realized you came from Capella Five. But, when he found out you were in love with Thomas Carson, he set his sails elsewhere."

"Wow, I never knew Hawke liked me that way." Emma sat up against her headboard to relax her stance. "Is he going to come back to Earth—this Earth—to help us?"

"He petitioned to ascend to the fourth dimension. His ascension also means he agreed not to come back to Earth in corporeal form."

"Why can't he come back. I am from the fifth dimension, and I did."

"You leaped here, to follow your friend. A friend who became your mother when she seeded you inside her."

"Does she know that she planted my seed inside her?"

"The soul part of her does. The human part of her doesn't remember."

"If I wanted to bring my mother to Capella Five, to help her remember who she is. Would I be allowed to do this?"

"You would need to travel there in your corporeal form. You would not be able to bring anyone with you in residual form."

"If I did, would she remember?"

"More than likely, she might not be able to visualize Capella Five, being on Earth Refuse so long. Emma, no human can see what they cannot expect, what they cannot believe, what they cannot understand."

"My mother recognizes my powers. She knows what I can do. So does my friend Tom, and I might want to bring him along to visit Capella Five one day."

"I can't give you an answer. Tom and your mother might be able to see your planet. Both may even aspire to go live there with you once they end their earthly stint." Columba smiled as she hesitated with the next sentence. "With visualization of your place of origin may come the dawning of some powers for your mother as well."

"I'm glad I can return home to Capella Five. It's breathtaking. I miss it every day."

"Your mother's contribution to helping Earth Refuse is immeasurable. Somewhere deep inside, she remembered she needed to implant you. She raised you well, and she is an inordinately good person to everyone around her. She has kept the imprint of the fifth dimension close to her heart."

"I heard only a few accomplish their mission after leaping."

"Sadly, very few leap to Earth and find a way to make a difference."

"Why, I wonder."

"We are not exactly sure why, but many are born physically or mentally challenged, or both. Something to do with the process of birth when a higher soul seeds into a human body. Of course, some make it through, but are attracted to money, independence, discouragement, depression."

Emma's thoughts jumbled as she thought about all the lures on Earth Refuse. She wondered if love might also be considered a lure.

"Does our little talk clear up some of your dilemmas?"

"What happened in this current timeline that allowed me to discover my powers? Other than Annemarie Hanover, or Anne Ripley being killed by Boleslaw?"

Columba smiled. "The domino effect. One little brick out of place can initiate the crumbling of many structures. Which is why there are so many different versions of Earth." Columba pondered Emma's question. "How well do you remember the emergence of your powers?"

"A bit blurry. I remember the dreams thinking they were more than bad dreams, especially when I spotted Ashley Miller, Boleslaw's fourth victim. Only, I didn't realize I visualized the future when I lived through the nightmare of that episode. I found out later when Hank told me."

"Do you remember the first time you conjured something?"

"I do. Only brought me trouble. I was eight years old when my granny Dottie told me about the little sentence that could make things appear out of thin air. She cautioned me against using this curse, she called everything a curse, saying it would be like stealing things out of the universe we inhabit. She also mentioned that this was why no one could execute the magic, even with the required sentence."

"Let's go back and look at your life—your current life. We'll be able to pinpoint what changed and why the sliding versions are different."

"This means we'll also need to search through the sliding

versions, or at least one of them, right? Strange how the versions all seem to be the same"

Columba nodded as she smiled.

Emma glanced at her desk, at a load of books piled up on the table beside her laptop.

"Don't worry, Emma. We'll come back at the exact time I entered your room."

"We can do that?" Emma thought of all the time this could save her. She'd never thought of using the past that way.

"Yes, you can. Only you need to make sure no bricks are removed or added to your life's structure while you are browsing through time. Otherwise, your future will be quite different."

"I guess cheating on time is a lot like taking from the universe," Emma added. She took a deep breath. There were a lot of instances in her young life Emma didn't care to remember, much less visualize. Still, she needed answers. "Okay. Let's do this."

As Emma agreed, with the wave of her hand Columba dressed them both in a strange robe. "We are going together with our corporeal form. This robe will keep us out of sight, out of harm's way, and since we are going as mere observers, in the strictest sense, we will not disturb the timeline as it expands and retracts."

"Like humans, breathing."

"Yes. Time's rhythm follows the beat of each heart, the pulse of each soul."

"How can that be?"

"Come, I will explain." Columba took Emma's hand and traveled back to the time she was eight years old.

Emma caught her Granny Dottie talking to a child—her. The little girl was her. Her granny appeared sad, tightly wound against her environment with her lips pinched and arched the wrong way. Her pleated brow and swollen eyes completed the expression of one fearing the world around her. "I didn't remember her this way, afraid, lonely."

Luckily, Columba glided speedily over the nightmare she encountered about Ashley Miller. Even so, Emma's heart beat wildly in her chest, and she wondered how she could have lived through such horrible moments.

Quickly, she snatched a glimpse of herself in the car coming back from the free clinic with a bandage on her leg. The episode brought memories of the bike accident while speeding through the old quarry trying to keep up with Tom. Inside the vehicle, she invoked the little sentence to conjure the bright, shiny new penny to satisfy the policeman's curiosity as to why she was on the floor of the car.

A clear picture appeared of Christina eavesdropping on her warning to Tom about the collapsing bike structure. Then Christina at the police station talking to Hank. Emma smiled when she encountered the vibrant attraction between the two.

In the dark, Columba shed some light on a figure climbing up the elm tree beside her house. "Boleslaw," Emma whispered.

She didn't get to see the rest of this picture, but this event she would remember all her life.

Her surroundings changed, and she found herself once more with Granny Dottie. The same picture unfolded. Everything remained as the first image.

Columba glided over the nightmare, yet the picture and the name had changed. She spotted Melanie Kramer instead. Emma turned her face away quickly—the image far too real to be futuristic. Strangely, Boleslaw did not appear to catch Emma on the premises. After she heard herself scream, Emma found herself in bed once more.

The same ride home from the free clinic followed, but no one stopped her mother's car, and she never conjured that penny.

At home doing her math homework on the bed, Tommy beside her, she made him promise not to ride in the next bike competition. Took some doing, but he agreed.

She spotted the old elm tree late at night, but the figure climbing the branches after the party was Tommy. Boleslaw never showed up.

Visions of Richard Kramer drunk and depressed showed Richard hiring a private army of detectives, four of them, and months later, Richard managed to track down Boleslaw. He killed him plugging him with five bullets. Then he waltzed over to the second precinct, and after he was allowed inside through deception, he pulled a gun on one of the detectives and murdered him. "Oh, no. Not Matt."

Later, Hank stormed into his captain's office and handed him his badge. "We told you the killer was Boleslaw, but you did nothing to stop him. I'll work at McDonald's if I have to, but I no longer wish to be a cop."

Hank later made up with his captain. However, heartbroken, Hank never showed his face at Matt's funeral. Christina attended the burial procession but never caught sight of Hank Apple.

Emma watched her teenage years speed by with Tom by her side, and she never attempted to fly home, or projected herself in the astral world or anywhere else.

The context, quite surreal as it unfolded in front of her, faded. Columba grabbed Emma's hands and flew away with her landing on a soft cloud in the astral world. "Can you pinpoint the changes that brought on the destruction of your current life structure?"

"You're talking about the alternate version, right? The one where Annemarie Hanover lives and breathes?"

"Yes. I understand how much you are fond of Annemarie. The fact that she died influenced a lot of new decisions, apt to draw on this Earth better scenarios, but her death wasn't the only reason you became aware of your powers."

"Why did I warn Tom at home while doing math homework? Originally, I warned him at school. I cautioned him about the frame of the structure he would use, and I mentioned that the man who kidnapped the little girl was not a bad man. These things Christina overheard and brought to Hank Apple."

"Well, Hank only gave his full attention to this case once they unearthed a third little girl, Anne Ripley. This was when police held the mandate to comb the streets, and the neighbors paid attention. When Jeff Hannigan picked up little Caitlin Castle at school, and Julia Castle barreled down the street after what she considered a rogue car, parents truly began to worry. Worry prompted Amelia's mother to spend the summer at home and to reassign her nanny for the summer, begging the Kramer's to hire her. Michelle Kramer finally did, instead of hiring Boleslaw disguised as big, chunky Marley Boleslava."

"What happened to Jeff Hannigan. He also appears to be a source of the changes."

"In the alternate worlds, the Governor's son died five years prior. He caused the accident with Ted Ripley, Anne's father."

"Oh my God. So, two factors are the reasons I am not aware of my powers in an alternate lifetime."

"Not being aware of them means not having any powers." Columba smiled.

"I don't understand why two people had to die for me to gain my powers. Didn't I come here to better Earth Refuse?"

"Yes, you did. Anne Ripley dies in the current timeline, but Hank and Christina are reunited. They bring forth two wonderful boys into the world. Matt lives on to marry Maria, and Richard Kramer doesn't spend the rest of his life in jail mourning his daughter's death."

"I guess we need to settle for the lesser of two evils. Very disheartening."

"Allow me to enlighten you, Chavah. Look around you," Columba whispered. "This world you see is an illusion. Earth and all of its versions are merely echo filaments of the Earth that once existed."

"An echo?"

"Yes." Columba appeared to search for the right words. "You are familiar with the Akashic records?"

Emma nodded. "The records of all past, present, and future events that have already happened."

"That's correct. Akashic records are why déjà vu is so exciting, why some people can visualize the past and even the future."

"You mean some people learn how to read the Akashic records?"

"Yes. Everything you see before you happened billions of years ago. In the heartbeat of one single moment the past, present, and future took place simultaneously. People living many lives, experiencing countless adventures all wanted to live through them again."

"Like a rollercoaster when one ride is never enough—no matter how scary it is."

Columba laughed. "Exactly. All who had agreed to enjoy life on Earth objected to the rapidity of the moment, arguing that with the means to reflect on their deeds, they could improve the outcome. The universe's Creator agreed. He called upon the spirit of time to follow the beat of each heart while respecting the gentle yearning of each soul. Time stepped in and released all the moments trapped in the Akashic records, slowed them down to a crawl, and allowed them to repeat—as an echo.

"I understand. Still, we can change this echo, right?"

"Yes. Change is the reason why the Creator allowed the illusion of time to appear carefully measured—the impression that time cannot be disturbed. Many people would be in a position to offer proof to the contrary. In fact, we all perceive the passing of time differently. And though time needs to obey the laws of its nature, the collective illusion makes us believe that we are all subjects of time's rules when we are the ones who imprint our intentions on time."

"If we live in an echo," Emma shook her head unable to grasp the whole picture. "How can we work toward reuniting all these echoes?"

"Well, time brought us the possibility to reflect, to repent, to change, to flex our courage and allow our souls to grow. In other words, we can modify Earth through the changes we bring to the echoes." Columba smiled, the reassuring smile Emma loved, and it prompted belief and a sigh of pleasure. "Time, ordered to follow the beat of each heart and the yearning of each soul, had to create many versions of different echoes many billions upon billions of Earth filaments. However, you cannot reunite mere echoes of Earth with other universes and planets waiting to join to participate in Nirvana. First, we must make a billion echoes whole again as one entity. Reassembling these odd intervals is what we are attempting to do. Reuniting these echoing clusters and bringing them to the quality of Earth Optimal will make Earth whole again, one single planet. Trying to change crows into nightingales to obtain the sounds apt to bring us, love. Love that will reunite all of us in peace and glory."

"In other words, Earth Refuse's echo is too cacophonous to join Earth's other versions."

"Nicely put."

"Still, I can't believe we live in an echo." Emma searched Columba's expression. "How do I fix the sliding dilemma without access to Eivan Baker's other machines in the alternate timelines?"

"I thought Eivan did not complete the other systems. Did he not merely finish this particular model?"

"I don't know. Fred Manson states that we must close them all at once so that the sliding timelines are all eliminated, and no harm overrides our current timeline."

"Yes. I can understand what Fred is attempting to do. He wants to prevent this enormous beat of change from affecting time as we know it. I believe that Time has already compensated for the pressure of Eivan's infernal machine by smoothing and shrinking a deregulated beat into smaller ones. The other reason for the different timelines might be that Eivan created them deliberately."

"Ah! The reason why the alternate worlds resemble each

other—one huge lump equally divided by time."

"I'm glad you are on our side, gentle Emma. You grasp a situation quickly. Although, somehow, I believe Eivan might have found a reason to create the discrepancy."

"Like ridding the world of evil being his reason to do so. I will need to consult with the others, and we will work to figure out the proper course of action."

Columba took Emma's hand and brought her back to her room. True to her word, Emma checked the clock on her desk, and no time had elapsed. She could now study without interruptions.

When she turned to say goodbye, Columba was gone. It's a good thing she remembered all these new possibilities or she would think Columba's presence was merely the impression of an overactive imagination, saddled with too much work. However, who could forget that life on Earth was a mere echo?

Joss Landry

—Twenty-Four—

Foul Play

Emma closed her book with a thud. She shut down her laptop and walked the length of her room feeling restless. The last thing she wanted to do was travel to Brian Hayes' house in her residual form. She needed to discover why this young man, of whom James Monroe spoke highly, behaved like a wild animal. More than just his actions, his thoughts resounded violent. Not since Boleslaw, or people occupied by wizards, had she sensed a rage apt to trigger a bloodbath somewhere in his surroundings. She even caught his timeframe of two weeks to kill a slew of people in his entourage. Although, James believed this type of violence, fantasized by some teenagers, seldom breeched the confines of imagination.

Dr. Monroe blamed the anger on a means to cope with too many expectations and a lack of a real support system. Emma had her doubts that too much work or a lack of friends could trigger this much hate. Perhaps Brian used his rage as a posture to appear brave, though most people thought Brian crazy. Being considered mad might suit him, she supposed—the exaggerated stance allowing him fearlessness toward anything or anyone.

Rather than debate this any longer, she decided to go and check out his living arrangement. Without an attempt to get closer to Brian to observe his habits, she would never solve the puzzle.

Emma decided she would allow Brian to listen to her but not visualize her. She could not afford to be recognized in future sessions with Professor Monroe—or anywhere else.

She lay on the bed, and focused on Brian's image—a task she found difficult to do. She met him once during the hour of one session while she worked hard not to stare directly at him. She would need to learn to read minds while keeping a detached expression, a poker face that her professor Elizabeth Reardon called the blank expression her students needed to practice. "The slightest hint of judgment will throw your patient's confidence."

Luckily, in this case, Brian would not see her. Emma embraced the astral world with the thought in mind and arrived near the Hayes house in West Orange. She recognized the affluent area. She could not mistake the luxury abodes. Of course, this grand cottage had to be the Hayes' home. The universe always delivered her to the right place.

She eyed the windows in front of her. At least, four to five bedrooms with the same number of bathrooms occupied the house. Finding Brian's room meant peeking in all the windows, like a voyeur—not something she relished. Brian's place likely occupied a smaller area, perhaps harboring one occupant inside, and because of the lateness he might be asleep in bed.

Once again, she debated going inside. What would she accomplish so late at night? If Brian slept, she would not be able to glean any information on his habits or why his rage disturbed everyone around him.

She stared at the moon, the circle around the globe blood red tonight. In residual form, she detected oddities not present when she retained her human form. Not quite sure why the moon's ring upset her, she peeked into the first room she spotted at the front of the house. A woman and a man slept in each other's arms, and she deemed them to be Brian's parents. She then found another room to the side of the house turned into an office and a library.

As she continued toward the back of the house, she found the grounds to be extensive. The property, what appeared to be a million-dollar estate, displayed a pool, a tennis court, and a lovely English garden.

Emma flew toward the room directly above the veranda. A flagstone staircase wound its way from the downstairs arbor to the lovely upstairs terrace that gave way to French doors. A luxury car, its bonnet blushing a soft red under the veranda's suspended lights, was parked below the staircase in a pea gravel driveway. This room had to be Brian's, accessible from the back of the house as to give him independence and freedom to come and go as he pleased.

One last moment of hesitation as Emma caught a muffled

sound like a blotted cry of protest or a scream during a struggle. Had Brian imprisoned someone in his room while giving him or her a taste of his violent temper?

As she entered, making sure to remain invisible, she spotted two shadows occupying the bed. One stretched out, almost immobile, while the man on top seemingly enjoyed himself. She left immediately thinking this had to be the parents' area.

But no. Emma had seen both parents sleeping just seconds ago. To make sure, she went back to the front bedroom and silently entered through the window. Emma recognized a man and a woman sleeping together. She searched the area, encountered the large walk-in closet, the attached bathroom, and decided this place had to be a master bedroom. She left through the window not knowing the layout of the house enough to attempt finding Brian's room again and headed toward the last bedroom she encountered.

Inside, she saw a man rise while what appeared to be a young man tearing away at the tape over his mouth. "You sleaze-bag. How dare you come in here again after I warned you not to. I'll go to the police if you persist."

"Who do you think they'll believe?" The man laughed. "Your dad gets his million-dollar financing, and you just got screwed." The tall man chuckled as he walked toward the French doors. He turned before stepping out. "By the way, you talk to the police, and you're a dead man. So is your mom, tough guy. I don't bluff. Any threat I make, you'll feel."

Joss Landry

Emma couldn't cry being out of body, but the sting of this situation would get to her later. She witnessed Brian fall to his knees and sob. Emma waited for several minutes before he got up again. Brian sauntered to the night table where she glimpsed him clutch a bottle of pills. He downed a few before he flopped onto the bed.

She hesitated, but then hurried before the pills he took could take effect. "Brian," she called. "You can't see me, but you can hear me. So, please, listen."

She caught him turn his head toward her, toward the sound. "Who's there?" He sat up in bed. He grabbed his head between both hands, shaking it from side to side. Fuck, I'm hearing voices again. "Leave me alone," he yelled.

"Don't be scared. I'm a good voice, and I'm here to help."

"Get out," he screamed. "Get out of my head or I'll jump out that window. Get out, get out, get out."

Emma considered leaving. Too distraught to let the boy wallow in his misery, she waited a few seconds and added, "I'm a good voice, outside your head. You need to listen. I witnessed what just happened. You need to talk to the police."

"Who the hell are you? And why can't I see you?"

"Not important. I'm just a friendly voice who's here to help you, Brian."

He lay back down in the bed. "Well, you can't help me. So, get out of my room, and leave me alone." He took the bottle of pills and threw it against the wall. "Stupid hallucinations. That'll teach me," he mumbled.

"Brian," Emma waited before he acknowledged.

"What?" She realized Brian's question was grumbled for him to glean peace.

"You're too important for me to allow you to suffer like this. I can help you."

"You heard what the man said. Now, get out of my life, and stay out."

"I have a friend who is a highly ranked police officer. You don't have to say a word. I will speak on your behalf and let them know what's going on."

"You don't understand. My bloody father sends them here. He needs money for the company he mismanaged. So, he uses me as a whipping boy, pimps me out whenever he needs to get more money."

"How many times has he done this?"

"Does it matter?"

"Is this why you act up at school, so they can ship you away to study somewhere else?"

"I plan to kill these men. I don't need your help."

"You don't want to become like that man, do you? Killing these people would make you one of them."

"I don't care if the freaks kill me. Dying doesn't bother me. But my mother is a sweet, loving woman. If she found out about this, she would die of shame."

"If your mother knew this was going on, would she allow this? Or would she put an immediate stop to it?"

"She would take me and run. We'd go back to Iowa to her

folks' house and live out our lives there."

"Why not give her a chance to do just that?"

"This is none of your business, you demented voice in my head." Brian moaned, a helpless sound. "Why won't you tell me who you are?"

Emma remembered what the custodian Hank arrested called her. "I might be your guardian angel for all you know."

"Right," he said sarcastically.

"All I want is your permission to talk to the high-ranking police officer. He'll make sure the information stays out of the media, at least as much as he can, and they'll put a stop to this. No one will hurt you. I promise."

"Who is going to stop them? You?"

"I have my ways—potent, angel ways."

"Why now? Why not show up sooner?"

"A lot of people need my help. I'm here now. Please allow me to talk to the officer I mentioned. He doesn't have to know the information comes from you."

"You won't tell anyone else, like the press?"

"Of course not. The good thing about Angels is we never lie."

"Okay. You can tell this police officer. I tried to tell one of my dad's friends, but he didn't believe me."

"Do you have these men's names?"

Brian hesitated. "I know who four of them are. And if you don't get them, I will."

"You need to promise me you will not use violence anymore. And you need to tell me about those pills."

Brian got up to retrieve the bottle he'd thrown. "A generic form of benzodiazepines. My mother got them to help me sleep. Only, I think the only reason I couldn't sleep was due to these nightly visits. Now, the pills have become a force of habit, not to mention I had to increase the dosage several times. An addiction I can't seem to shake." He palmed the bottle.

"You'll need rehabilitation to get rid of the cravings. Once they're gone, you'll be fine. Are you seeing a psychologist?"

"Yeah. Another idiot."

"He'll be able to help you settle the addiction you have. You need to trust him. He's not the problem, is he?"

"When will I hear from you again?"

"Soon. Please don't despair." Emma asked, "Does this happen every night?"

"No."

"Do you know in advance?"

He nodded. "I've come to guess by the way my father struts around me with that smug look on his face. He's the first one to die on my list. And don't give me any judgmental crap. Everyone would congratulate me for doing away with the evil he represents."

"If you kill your father, people at large might not blame you for taking action, but your mother would remain alone with her shame and her pain. You need to stay safe and let the law deal with him if only to take care of your mom once your father is out of the picture."

"Okay, so you're not judgmental. Maybe my angel is just stupid. I don't see how knowing the occurrence of a next attack can help in any way."

"We can record the next attack and catch whoever is doing this in the act."

"I would rather not. Not in the act."

"We'll come up with something. No one will proceed without first obtaining your permission."

Brian wrote the four names he knew on a piece of paper on his desk and left them there for Emma to take. He also stared at the bottle of pills in his hand and threw it in the wastebasket. "I don't need anyone's help to get rid of these stupid pills."

In seconds, Emma retrieved her body at home, and came back to land in the darkest corner of Brian's room. She stepped in and took the paper he'd left on the desk. Brian was already out cold. She thought of home and touched down in her room.

Past twelve on her clock, Emma yawned fatigue creeping up on her, tears streaking down her cheeks. Sitting on the lovely flowered bedspread, her arms wrapped tightly around herself, Emma rocked back and forth as she worried about Brian and all the other sexually abused young people. Emma sensed helplessness invade her, a form of discouragement she never allowed usually. But at the moment, a confused boy was treated like a commodity by the man who gave him life, and the situation appeared too far beyond belief to fathom. The worst for Emma was realizing that if she encountered one such case, many others existed. She hoped Hank would be able to help Brian without compromising his career. Whatever the consequences, she trusted Hank would make the right decision.

She suddenly worried about who these names might represent. She shed her shoes, untied her hair and slipped on a sweater to ward off the chills. Emma sat at her computer and went online to do a little research of her own.

The first name, Richard Ribeye, spawned a few people and many choices of cooking recipes. Without a picture or address, she wouldn't know who to choose.

For the second name on the list, Van Mortadel, nothing turned up. Perhaps a name Brian misunderstood or a name this man made up to keep authorities off his scent.

Then she checked on Ward Wagyu. Again, all that came up were restaurants and cuts of beef. She realized she would need more details to find any of these names. Emma gave up searching for Herb Porterhouse, another impossible surname to locate because of the multitude of choices, again mostly restaurants.

The most she could do for now was to hand this information to Hank and hope he would be able to implement something. Emma was about to log out when a box popped up in her search for Van Mortadel. "Who are you?" The directive asked.

Emma typed a reply inside the box, A concerned citizen.

The box disappeared. No other pop-ups and no other communication followed. Perhaps the connection was an automatic window to anyone who asked about this particular name. Might be interesting to find a program that would log back to the specific IP address, she thought.

Emma waited, but no one wrote back, and nothing happened. Instead, she performed the same search for Van Mortadel and waited for a pop-up. After five minutes passed, she abandoned the query and left her computer to shut down on its own.

She barely made it to bed before she passed out, still in her clothes minus the sweater she had donned to keep warm.

Dreams kept Emma between sleep and awake. She visualized cows, blood-red cuts of meat, all running after her. Mostly vegetarian, the parade of food made her nauseous, and when she woke up at seven, her stomach, distended and cramped, grumbled in protest as though she'd spent the night gorging on exotic food.

Emma rose and dizzily made her way to the washroom. Once there, those cuts of bleeding beef dangled in front of her eyes. Bare seconds to spare, she popped the lid to the toilet and hurled into the bowl. Sitting on the cold bathroom tiles, she grabbed a tissue on the lower shelf of the wall unit and sat back her head propped against the bathtub.

Eloise came in. "Emma, are you all right? I was getting ready to leave when I heard you throwing up. What's wrong, sweetheart?"

"I don't know, Mom. I'll be okay."

"Here, hold onto my arm." Eloise helped her daughter get to her feet and walked her back to the room. She pulled a little box out of her pockets. "Antacids. Take two. They'll make you feel better."

Emma grabbed the box and lied down on the bed still clutching the little carton in her hand. Eloise took it from her and placed the tablets close to her mouth. Emma opened her mouth, and her mother delivered the pills. "You'll feel better in an hour. I'll wait until you're up before I leave for the boutique." Eloise appeared to hesitate. "You work too hard, Emma. You rushed through dinner last night to study and study. It's no wonder you're sick this morning. Luckily you have a free morning today. I suggest you take this time to rest."

Emma thought it a blessing Eloise didn't know about her trip down alternate memory lanes with Columba or her visit to Brian Hayes' house where she witnessed a faceless, nameless man abusing a seventeen-year-old boy. "Okay, Mom. Thanks for staying. Please wake me in an hour."

"Why not sleep the whole morning?"

"I need to see Hank about a problem, one that a young patient is having. Please promise you'll wake me up in an hour?"

"I promise."

—Twenty-Five—

A Plan

Eloise tiptoed into Emma's room. She hated to wake her, so she watched her sleep, smiling as she did. She moved strands of hair from her face to the side and whispered her name. "Emma, you asked me to wake you, sweetheart." All she heard was a soft grunt. Emma slept.

The doorbell rang. "Emma," Eloise called out as she left the room and ran downstairs. She opened the door and welcomed Hank. "Come on in, Hank. Tom is already here waiting for Emma. She meant to get up at seven, but she was sick. Either something she ate, or too much studying, too much stress."

"Yeah, stress will do it to you. Emma is still young. She needs to take care of herself more."

"I agree." Eloise invited him to the small salon. She caught the noise coming from the upstairs bathroom. Had to be Emma. "I hope you're not in any hurry, Hank. She'll be down momentarily."

Eloise left to make sure Emma was okay and caught Tom

greeting Hank. She deemed Emma to be lucky to have such good friends as those two men. Exceptional characters, gentle manners. She realized Thomas Carson would make a warm son-in-law.

When she entered the bathroom, Emma was brushing her teeth.

"How are you feeling?"

Emma rinsed in the sink. "Much better. Thank you, Mom. Those antacids did the trick."

"Hank's downstairs. Hank and Tom."

"How come?"

"Tom knows your schedule, and I invited Hank here. Thought it might be easier for you to see him here than have to go all the way downtown."

"Thanks, Mom. That's sweet. We might have to go downtown to use their more powerful computers."

"Well, I'm off to work. Try and take it easy today."

Emma got downstairs as her mom was leaving. She hugged Tom and smiled at Hank thanking him for coming.

"Sorry you were sick, sweetie," Tom said keeping his arm around her waist.

"Too much to do in one day, I guess." Emma sat down and turned toward Hank. "What do you know about Brian Hayes?"

"Only what I read in the papers lately. The boy has a history of violent behavior in school. Prominent, well-to-do parents. Why?"

"He's one of the patients Dr. James Monroe is treating."

Tom placed a hand on Emma's arm. "Hey, I know Professor Monroe."

"Well, I found out he's also a Devronair."

"No way," Tom enthused. "He's not like Fred Manson at all."

"No. In fact, James Monroe is kind, compassionate, and he cares about this young man. But, he cannot read minds the way Fred Manson can, so he asked me to assist him. I hate to tell you. I read in his mind murderous plans to kill a bunch of people."

"Whoa. Does Monroe know about this?" Hank appeared concerned.

"I mentioned it. The doctor seems to think this is nothing but a boy's wild imagination. But, the therapy is court-appointed. So, he requested I keep an eye on Brian Hayes—before he hands in his report, which would not be favorable."

"So that's where you were last night," Hank smiled, shaking his head side to side. "You've got to take it easy, kiddo. You'll make yourself sick and won't be able to endure the long run."

"More than just traveling to Brian's house happened last night. Anyway, you won't like what I found."

She caught Hank bracing himself for the worst. "What?"

Emma glanced at Tom and grabbed his hand for support. "Brian is sexually abused by men his father needs to finance his projects. His father is pimping him out for money."

Hank took his head in his hand as though unable to support the idea. "Oh, my God. What kind of father would do this?"

"Why doesn't the guy just run, leave?" Tom asked, his tone determined and shaking with outrage.

"They threatened to kill his mom."

"Sons of bitches," Hank exclaimed.

"He loves his mother very much. He's torn between the shame a public scandal would cause her—if he told the police—and the threat abusers made to kill her if he runs. I was there in residual form. I told Brian I could help him if he allowed me to contact a high-ranking police officer of my acquaintance. I said I needed his permission. Took some convincing, but he gave me the go. He's waiting for us to do something without identifying him as the one responsible for the information. He gave me this paper with four names on it. He maintains he doesn't know the other names—more than four encounters."

"Bastards." Hank rose and took the paper from Emma as he began to pace, his favorite form of outlet to let off steam. "What's this? People's names? They're all cuts of meat?" He stared at Emma waiting for an explanation.

All she could do was chuckle. "I realize this." She eyed Tom. "This is what made me sick. I kept dreaming of bleeding cuts of beef chasing me all night."

"Poor sweetie. You should have called me." Tom rubbed

her back.

Emma smiled as she squeezed Tom's hand. "Either these people are hiding their identity, or Brian got the names wrong."

"Or he's sending you on a wild goose chase," Hank mumbled to himself.

"Somehow, I don't think so. One of the names I researched online, Van Mortadel, triggered a strange pop-up that asked me who I was."

"Wow," Tom jumped up and turned toward them, excited. "Yes. I know why you had the weird pop tart," Tom exclaimed. "This exists. It's a real thing." Tom began to talk with his hands and moving around in an agitated fashion. Emma realized they were entering his domain somehow, so technologically inclined was Tom. "My tech prof calls them pop tarts because they pop on the screen in the regular web when the tarts that configured them didn't do it correctly. Get it? Tarts? Pop?"

"So? What does it mean?"

"Well, a summary. A couple of weeks ago I handed in a project for my tech class that had to do with discovering ways to surf the Dark Web, which is no small feat as there is no search engine on the dark or deep web. You can only get in if you know the address you're looking for." Tom nodded to reassure Hank's bulging-eye expression. "Yes. Very tricky to penetrate. The founder of the Tor project updated security a couple of days after the FBI took the Silk Road offline, the drug cartel market. There are ways to navigate through the history directory. But this lesson is for another time. If you're online and you enter the sixteen digits to a site, let's say, any letter from a to z and any number from two to seven, you will then be asked for a password or some other related form of identification.

"Now, most deep web addresses are dot onion, so as not to confuse them with the real web addresses. But if the tech in charge takes a wrong turn, you can have what we call pop tarts appear on the natural side of things, which is what you found last night."

"How does that help us?" Hank demanded sitting on the edge of his seat.

"Well, I launched an account on the deep web to do my trials, and you can find a few links going through WikiLeaks' anonymous upload system."

"How?"

"I know WikiLeaks' URL address." Tom shrugged. "You can't surf, remember?"

"All this collection of drug dealers and pedophiles running loose," Hank grumbled.

Tom gave him a smirk. "For your information, there are more pedophiles and drug dealer sites on the regular web than there are anywhere else. A lot of people on the deep web are just fed up with having all their private information and their buying habits, their vacations, and the rest of what they do handed over to third parties everywhere. Can't say I blame them."

"How can this help us?"

Emma sensed Hank becoming impatient.

"In my project, I discovered a means to attain some of the nodes they use to make a site's location unattainable. They bounce IP addresses off these nodes around the world and make the sites' location impossible to find. Anyway, the pop-up proves that there is a site by that name, Van Mortadel, which I might be able to locate given the new information I found. The pop-up demanded a password, some key or other. They will only do it once per IP address, refusing to allow you entry once you miss."

"We'll never be able to guess a sixteen-digit password," Hank spat.

"No. But your FBI friend, Bill Frost, might know what to do."

"You have no idea?" Emma asked Tom.

"I don't want to jeopardize this teenager. All passwords that are tried and refused are logged."

"Ah, interesting." Hank turned toward Emma. "Did you try a password?"

"No. I never had the time. The pop-up disappeared after a few seconds. Never came back."

"So, we'll need a couple of IP addresses." Hank thought out loud.

Emma placed a hand on Hank's arm. "You can't write Brian Hayes' name or the activities they are doing. They would immediately suspect him and kill his mother. We need other sources of information."

"How do we get them?" Hank wondered.

Tom smiled. "Identify the man through cameras and IR. Once you know who one of these guys is, you can find something else on him that will stick." Tom shrugged.

Emma turned toward Tom. "IR? What's that?"

"Infra Red light. Gizmos that fit in the palm of my hand that can be attached remotely to certain cameras or placed strategically near a camera to light up an area covertly. I've seen it done. Spectacular imagery with very high resolution, depending on the camera, of course."

"Great idea, Tom. Once we know one of these guys, we can find out more about them. Anyone who is willing to take on this sort of illegal activity is more than likely involved in tons of other shit." Hank spat. "Completely immoral," he breathed. "Plus, I want Thornton Hayes. I've never wanted anyone in my life as much as I want him. I'd be ready to trade a couple of his men just to get my hands around his throat." Hank spoke as though to himself. He stared at Emma and Tom and added, "Figuratively speaking, of course."

Emma's turn to be excited. "Wait a minute. I remember last night there was a car parked on the terrace. I thought it might belong to Brian, but later when I picked up the names he left for me, the car was gone. I could see the fancy vehicle thanks to the lights on the veranda. A sort of red."

"Could you see the license plate?"

"No. The man left too fast."

Tom added, "The house might have security cameras all around. You could use them. They may already be supplied with IR."

"I doubt that. You're right about the cameras, Tom. But, since this man is pimping out his son, I doubt those cameras connect to the boy's room."

Hank turned toward Emma. "Can you find out from Brian who installed the security cameras at their house, if there are any. Tell the kid what we're trying to do. How we want to establish other motives on these people to pick them up without them being the wiser about the information's origin."

"I'll do that when he comes back from school."

Hank got up. "Excellent work, Emma." He turned toward Tom. "You too, Tom. I should hire you before you become unaffordable."

Tom chuckled and shook Hank's outstretched hand. "You wish. I'm going places." He wrapped his arm around Emma's shoulders. "I've got to take care of Emma. Make her the happiest woman alive." He pecked her lips.

"I'll see you later, Emma. Around eight o'clock at Bill's house. Do you want me to pick you up?"

Emma stared at Tom. "Are you coming tonight?"

"Don't think so, hon. I've got a project due, day after tomorrow. Serious work."

"I'll pick you up, Hank," she said with a smile. "We'll transport together."

Emma had classes all afternoon, but once she returned

home around dinner time, she sat down in the dining room penning all the ideas she needed to discuss during the meeting with Bill. Fred Manson would be there also. She wanted to discover if he had a hand in preventing the accident of Anne Ripley's father. Was he supposed to die as all the other timelines depicted?

Once she finished, she ran up the stairs to her room to call on Brian. Lying in bed, she crossed her arms over each shoulder and thought of Brian's room. She remained invisible to him as she had done the day before. She made sure he could hear her. "Brian, it's me. The spirit from last night."

"I thought I'd dreamt you. You exist?"

Emma spotted slight disbelief in the boy's tone. "Of course, I exist. I need information to help you while keeping you out of the loop."

"What sort of information?"

"Are there security cameras around your house?"

"Yes. But the ones giving access to my room are disconnected. When my mother asked my father why he'd done that, he told her he was trying to give me more freedom to come and go and to bring whomever I wanted back home."

"I'll admit. Pretty foolproof as an excuse. Do you know the name of the company?"

He got up and walked to his desk. He searched inside the bottom drawer. "I kept a copy of the invoice to show Mom the freak had not connected my room to the system."

"Does your mother wonder when you call your father

names why you do so?"

"She used to until he told her that since I'm a teenager and a hot-head, I choose to refute his authority." He tried to hand the invoice to Emma, but since he could not see her, he asked, "How do I get this to you?"

"Leave it on your desk. I'll pick it up later. Is there a person we should talk to at this security company, a code we need to use to get things changed?"

"Gregg Potwin takes care of our account." Emma spotted the boy's shrug. "If there is a code, I wouldn't know what that is. What are you going to do with this information?"

"We're going to look for other crimes these gentlemen committed. You can be sure depraved, greedy people like the ones you are acquainted with take part in all sorts of illicit activities. Don't worry. We'll get them."

"Well, until you show me some proof, I am still planning to kill these people. This way, they won't be able to hurt my mother, and she'll understand I did this for her."

"Yes, but Brian, she will be alone when she needs you the most."

"Then tell your people to hurry to get these guys out of commission, or else."

Emma Willis Book 3,
I Can Help You

—Twenty-Six—

Interesting Powwow

Landing in Bill Frost's living room, Emma and Hank saluted the two people already there, FBI agent, Bill Frost, and Devronair turned professor, Fred Manson.

"Greetings, Emma and Hank," Fred Manson said having regained his original residual form. "Thank you for your help. We appreciate it."

"Okay, what have we learned in the last week or so?" Bill wanted to catch up. He waved his hand and the coffee table filled with tea, coffee, and finger foods. "To tell you the truth. I haven't been working on this at all." Bill turned toward Hank. "We're swamped at the bureau with a rash of illicit activities—some of them dating back to our old friends, the body part snatchers."

"I thought we'd stopped their trafficking," Hank said as he grabbed a cup of coffee.

"Let's say we slowed it down. We seized the jerks' American operation. Remember me telling you we hadn't laid our hands on the ringleader?"

"You found him?" Bill got Hank's attention.

"Yeah." He smiled rubbing his hands together. "We did.

Only he doesn't know it yet."

"The ringleader, the one in charge?"

Bill nodded.

"Why didn't you tell me? I understand it's out of my jurisdiction since you're talking Europe, but I would have loved to be informed."

"Asia. And I am going to inform you, Hank. I've received the okay to do so since some of these men are in our territory."

Emma knew she would be up next, so she got herself a cup of tea.

"Anything to report, Emma?" Bill asked.

"I do. Last night I traveled, with Columba's help, to those alternate timelines. I was quite surprised by what I found. I am in those timelines, unaware of my powers, unable to use them. In fact, our timeline is unique, the only one of its kind."

Emma recounted what she'd found with Columba's help and how every other time continuum was the same except for their own. She also explained the reason for the nuances.

The explanation had Bill eye Fred, strangely. "Is this your doing, Fred? Helping Ted Ripley avoid the accident?"

Fred raised his head with disdain. "No. Jeff Hannigan who caused the initial vehicle collision and was charged posthumously with a DUI, five years before Boleslaw's arrival on the scene, was prompted by the hussy he was with that night to call a taxi to go home."

Emma's turn to ask, "Would you have been able to stop

the gruesome murder of Anne Ripley?"

"No. We can only bring to Earth Optimal people who are harmful to the fabric of what we are doing here. Even then, it is usually impossible to relocate them immediately. They first need to cleanse inside an alternate world." He didn't sit. No need, Emma thought as he showed up in his residual form. "Besides, twenty-two years ago, we were told by the Celeste being Thor …"

Bill rose as he heard this. "The head of our Celeste worlds?"

"Yes. Thoren asked us not to interfere with Earth's karmic activity for the next couple of years. He warned us to watch for a shooting star."

Bill addressed the questions in Hank and Emma's eyes. "A shooting star is usually someone who leaps successfully. They are rare occurrences, and we need to be advised." Bill turned toward Fred Manson. "Why weren't we told?"

"You will need to pose this question to Thoren. Even though he forewarned us, we never witnessed the emergence of the shooting star in question, and never suspected the birth would be female and occur on Earth Refuse."

"You're talking about me?"

"Yes, Chavah," Fred Manson answered. "Very few people attempt to leap to Earth Refuse anymore. The brave souls only ever encounter strife and challenges that they are never able to surmount."

"Where do they leap? Not on Earth Optimal?"

"On better versions of Earth, yes, in different clusters as well as on Earth Optimal. Once they rally their powers, they come down here and help out."

"Wow, so I came to the wrong place. We both did, my mom and I."

"None of the shooting stars possess the strength or variety of your powers. Your powers come from having seeded directly on this Earth and done so successfully."

"What do we do about Eivan Baker?" Emma wanted to know. "How can we shut down his experiment if he has not completed the system in any of the other worlds?"

"Did you visit all the laboratories?" Bill asked.

"Yes. I did. The reason why Eivan never completed his experiments in the other timelines is because Anne Ripley, now Annemarie Hanover, became enamored with Eivan and convinced him not to pursue his goals."

Bill turned toward Fred. "Okay, Fred. How do we get out of this mess?" Then eying Hank and Emma, he added, "I guess the druids weren't the right ones to ask. I should have gone to the high priest himself, Thoren. I might have learned a thing or two."

Fred took his most practiced, arrogant tone. "Thoren has no idea of the intricacies of Earth Refuse. If he did, he would not have told us to beware of a shooting star. He would have given us a name and a precise time of arrival. After all, Chavah wasn't a shooting star. The shooting star was already on Earth when Thoren advised caution, Eloise, Emma's mother.

The woman seeded Emma quietly and without fanfare when she became ready to do so."

Bill shook his head. "That's true. You're right, Fred. Now, what do we do about Eivan Baker?"

"It is a puzzle," Emma breathed. "We cannot simply shut off these timelines while hoping they will disappear."

"Why do they have to disappear?" Hank asked. "Would it be so wrong if they remained? Since these lines already exist?"

Fred turned toward Hank. "The action would bring chaos to our worlds. In fact, our friend Time might agree with you, Hank. Time might decide to keep the added beats of life as time now follows the heartbeat of each person alive in those alternate worlds."

"You once said that Earth clusters were comprised of all the possibilities that could happen. Can't we simply add these five timelines to our Earth?" Hank wanted to know.

"No. We cannot. Eivan's machine created them artificially and they are sub-processes of one timeline, which means they do not exist anywhere else, in any other Earth clusters."

"I'm not sure I understand." Emma applied all the logic she found to comprehend Fred's dilemma, but still couldn't grasp what he meant.

"Well, take Anne Ripley, or Annemarie Hanover as she is known in the fabricated timelines. In this reality, she has reincarnated and is living out her new life the way she should. To have the other timelines added to our own would risk destroying all the work we have done so far, setting us back five hundred years. Perhaps more when you take into account all the other twists and turns these timelines now breathe." Fred waited until he noticed Emma nod. "We need for them to no longer exist. Only I'm not sure how we can proceed."

Emma answered, "I believe I understand. In other words, while our timeline has continued to grow and reproduce, these recently created timelines grow in separate directions, right?"

"Yes. And should they continue to grow, they could very well pull us apart and destroy the fabric of this Earth Cluster."

"Wow," Hank breathed. "This is a dilemma. I can't believe no one knows what to do to correct the situation."

Fred added, "There are a few solutions which present themselves. Only I am powerless to act. These timelines have grown to the point I can no longer enter them."

Bill got up to stretch his legs. Emma could tell he was here on Earth in corporeal form. "Are there any other Devronairs who can help?"

Once again, Fred took on an overbearing expression. "I'm the most powerful Devronair on this Earth. At home, on Devron, we are all equally powerful. Here on Earth, well, none of us are."

"Except for you," Hank added. Emma read in Hank's mind how he felt sorry for the man so far away from home, working on this challenging case without ever enjoying the slightest respite.

"As I mentioned, Apple, I too have my limitations."

"Emma, what can you do?" Bill asked sitting down once more.

"I'm not sure." She turned toward the Devronair. "Fred, you mentioned you brought Eivan senior and his partner to Earth Optimal. What went wrong? Had Eivan senior passed immediately, he would not have consulted with his son, telling him about his project and where to find his notes."

"Again. None of us operate at full capacity. When we choose someone to make the transition from this world to Earth Optimal, it is usually done swiftly without pain or discomfort." Fred eyed his feet. Raising his head once more, he admitted, "We tried to bring Eivan junior to Earth Optimal to reunite him with his father, but we failed."

"News to me," Bill said sitting again. "In other words, this whole situation could have been avoided."

"Yes. We brought Eivan senior to Earth Optimal as he is an outstanding human being. He needed no cleansing whatsoever to join the others. Bringing him there, we thought, would do away with the problem of this evil entity search."

"Is this why you contacted me two years ago?"

"Yes."

"What could I have done?"

"We thought you might talk some sense into Eivan junior." Fred paused then asked, "Do you still have the coordinates I gave you to the other timelines?"

"Yes, on my phone."

"Here is one more coordinate you need to keep on you at all times." Fred gave Emma a series of letters, and numbers.

"A twenty-four-digit combination? Where will this take me?"

"To the ends of the Earth, this Earth."

"I don't possess your ability to grasp conundrums quickly, Dr. Manson. You need to explain."

"You need to go to each of the five different timelines. Once you get there, you need to activate this combination in your mind. Doing such will take you exactly where the particular timeline ends. Once you are there, you will need to take markers to gather time and place."

Hank rose and articulated with a forceful tone. "Fred, Emma can't do this on her own. The situation could be dangerous, and I don't want her stuck in the astral world again."

Fred took a deep breath. And Emma sensed impatience stirring him. "This whole Earth cluster is in danger of being sucked into the vacuum of these alternate worlds. No action will make this whole cluster and the other timelines implode. I guess the implosion might be one way of getting rid of all the work we still need to do to clean up this cluster." Fred stared at Hank and Bill with a smug expression on his residual face. He'd kept the trump card hidden. But now, Emma understood the problem. Understood and feared the solution, like staring at the loss of billions upon billions of people.

Fred turned toward Emma, his face kind when he smiled at her. "I suggest you enlist the pathfinder's help. She will enlighten you as to your location, the time segment of your landing, and she will make sure you return safely."

"Do I report to you afterward?"

"I will be Dr. Franklin Rappaport, available as usual at the university, and you will provide me with the time segments you found for each world."

Fred then crossed to shake Bill's hand, Hank's hand and nodded toward Emma. "I'm off." Under the tenth of a second, he was gone.

After Fred's departure, Hank took a good five minutes to clear his thoughts. "How did we ever get to this point."

"Doesn't take much to ruin the day," Bill said. "A young scientist who doesn't know what he's doing. Not his fault really, especially when you consider his reasons behind the project to be for humanitarian purposes, to rid the world of wizards he calls evil."

Hank refilled his third cup of coffee, and with the wave of his hand, Bill reheated the brew. Hank took a grateful sip before he said, "Emma came here to discuss something else with you. She has all the details."

Bill sat back and waited with a smile for Emma to speak. Emma related the case of Brian Hayes, how the matter was called to her attention by one of her professors, James Monroe, also a Devronair. She recounted the abuse to Brian brought on by his father and the mighty men with whom he dealt. When she gave Bill the paper with the names Brian listed, he jumped with an excited light in his eyes.

"Just like you Hank to come in here and save my ass."

"Entirely Emma's work. You know these people?"

"Yes. They are the men associated with the figure in Asia I mentioned earlier."

Hank rubbed his hand on his forehead, a gesture Emma recognized as nervous.

Bill addressed Emma. "Emma, Brian gave you these four names as his abusers, right?"

"Yes. He could not remember the others."

"Horrible. What are these people thinking?"

"What are they thinking with, you mean," Hank added. "We need to bring in one of these men, by arresting him for another matter other than Brian's abuse. They say they will kill his mother, and they mean business."

"Hank, the Bureau would have done this already if we knew how to reach these people with the phony names. Nowhere in our system."

"Tom mentioned something about the deep web. He said the pop-up I read identified them having a site on the deep web. Tom also thought the FBI might be able to access this site, as you already have."

"Would take us weeks to decipher this. We'd have to find another gateway inside."

"What about issuing a subpoena?" Emma thought she would ask.

"Well, first we have to find them, locate a name, an address."

Hank got up to pace. "We believe we have a plan that will

do just that." Upon Bill's nod, he continued. "Brian confirmed security cameras watch over his house, although he says the one to his room, adjacent to an upstairs terrace, is not connected. Tom came up with the brilliant idea of equipping these cameras with IR. Since the visits are nightly. It would be easy to get the make on the individual who first comes up the terrace staircase, and afterward get the license plate when he jumps into his car, parked in the drive under the veranda lights."

"Emma, did you see the license plate?" Bill wanted to know.

"Afraid not. I thought the car belonged to Brian. Later when I came to get his list of names, I noticed the car was gone. Figured vehicle had to belong to the man on the premises."

"What about the company who supplies the cameras?" Bill asked.

Emma handed him the copy of the invoice Brian left behind for her to pick up.

"Great stuff. Any name we need to contact?"

"Yes. Gregg Potwin. He's in charge of this account."

"Well, Gregg Potwin, you're about to receive a visitor from the FBI."

"You have to make sure no one traces this back to Brian or his family," Emma suggested.

"Not to worry. We can even take this man's picture on the way in, then zoom in on the car."

"I can do some stuff to scare the man away. As long as

you get your picture of the car."

Hank stepped in. "What are you going to do, Emma? I don't want you getting hurt."

"It's okay, Hank. I can pretend someone is walking up to the door, jiggle the handle and ask Brian if he's all right. Then, I can say that there's a policeman here to see him. Mention of the police should get our man hightailing out of there."

"God, you're good." Bill smiled. "Where do you get all these ideas?"

"Watched a lot of movies, once upon a time." Emma giggled. Tom and she had not been to a movie in years.

Bill rose and smacked his hand on Hank's shoulder. "Only thing left to do is to interrogate the sucker and hope he cracks."

Hank nodded. "We can make him believe the head of the operation is using him as a sacrificial lamb."

"Yeah. One way to go."

"Let me know when you're ready to interrogate a suspect in this case," Emma told Bill. "Fred taught me a neat little trick I practiced only once, but I could try it again. We have nothing to lose, right?"

Hank cocked his head. "What little trick?"

"Well, while someone interrogates a person, I can be present in residual form planting images in his mind. My prompt makes the person think of these images, and when he does, I discover names and places that I can relate to you."

"Tricky Fred," Hank said. "You know Emma we won't be

able to use this information."

"I'm thinking I could relate what I read in his mind and convey to Bill without the man being the wiser. Bill could use the information to shake him."

Bill laughed outright. He placed both hands on Emma's shoulders and shook her slightly. "Yes. Double yes. Let's do it." Bill walked away excited about the prospect of getting these people, already on the phone with Tim O'Rourke, his partner.

Hank shook his head side to side. He faced Emma and rolled his eyes as he whispered. "You've just given him a reason to rely on you for each one of his cases."

"Don't worry about me, Hank. I have learned how to say no. Wasn't easy, but I can refuse the work when I have too much of my own."

"Good girl." Hank put an arm around Emma's shoulders and told Bill they were leaving. Bill continued his conversation and waved their way.

Emma dropped Hank at home, hugged Christina, and transported to her bedroom. When she got there, her phone rang, and she answered Tom's call.

"Want some company, lover. I'm done for tonight. What do you say I come over?"

"We'll have to watch the movie with my folks."

"Why not sit on the balcony and have a chat. You can brief me on your meeting with these sharks."

Emma chuckled and agreed to meet Tom outside. She

breathed a little more relaxed that Tom was in her life. She needed his hugs about now.

Emma Willis Book 3,
I Can Help You

—Twenty-Seven—

Three Is A Crowd

Emma and Tom spent an hour chatting about the world around them while sitting in a rattan rocker, outside on the porch. Music from the movie her parents shared wafted toward them, and the setting relaxed Emma. She enjoyed the delicate tempo of this evening in Tom's company. Both deserved a little respite now and then. In fact, Tom stayed until her dad flashed the porch lights on and off.

"I'm going home, lover. I can't go up there when your father does this little trick of his."

"You know he doesn't mind if you stay over. He's just letting me know Mom and him are off to bed."

"I think he does mind. If he didn't, he wouldn't pull this trick with the lights—a clear case of intimidation, your honor." Tom smiled and hugged Emma as though she were his lifeline. "I'll see you tomorrow."

After her shower, Emma got ready for bed and applied a light salve on some of the mosquito bites she'd collected outside on the porch. She lay in bed unable to sleep. Too many images crowded her mind, and although she hoped she might latch onto one of these fleeting impressions and fall asleep, she remained awake and alert two hours later.

Emma rose and wrapped a robe around her silk nightie. She walked over to the window to stare at the moon, wondering about Columba and Hawke. Both were incredible human beings. This was why they inhabited Earth Optimal. Would Columba indulge her request to go to the end of time in all of the alternate worlds?

Devronairs, at least the one she knew as Fred Manson, worked in strange ways at times, and this, she had encountered firsthand. They shot first and asked questions later. Thank God this wasn't Hank Apple's MO. Kind and considerate, he weighed all possible consequences before attempting to resolve an issue—even so far as to worry about her safety. She smiled remembering his menacing tone toward Fred, unafraid the alien from Devron might erase who he was in a mere second.

Nevertheless, Fred Manson had come a long way since she'd first met him five years ago. No longer as quick to pass judgment or haul some heart and soul off to Earth Optimal on a mere whim, he nevertheless pursued his goals with stoic determination, like a dog with a bone, or like a brilliant computer with a blueprint to follow as Tom remarked this evening. Even so, Tom also shared the opinion that Fred's methods were likely to bring more trouble—trouble Emma would need to shoulder.

She remembered Tom's words. "There has to be an easier way to resolve this situation, Emma. A little like you resolved your traveling to the past and future of our current timeline. You tried for years while following your ancestors' false premises, remember? When you finally figured it out, the task became foolproof."

"You're right, of course. I was thinking the same thing when Fred gave me that twenty-four-digit combination." She turned and gave Tom her most beguiling smile. "You sure you can't stay?"

"I'm sure," he'd said while rising out of the rocker and giving her one last hug. "I'll call you first thing in the morning."

Emma sighed glancing at the orange moon suspended a little above the old elm tree. Tom was right. There had to be a more natural solution to settle this dilemma of splitting timelines. Of course, they needed to resolve this quickly. These other worlds possessed a past and a future and were growing at an alarming rate, at least as fast as their cluster was concerned. While there was only one of their Earth, these five potential other Earths growing nearby provided confusion. Emma couldn't even imagine the mathematic equations liable to spring from the two scenarios, likely to bring on the destruction of their cluster of Earth Refuse.

A niggling little thought came to disturb her musings. Why would a Devronair like Fred wish to know the coordinate markings of the endpoints in each new timeline? Was it to remove a billion or more people out of those worlds? Couldn't the gesture cause cataclysmic repercussions with what Columba called their friend, time?

"Pst, Emma"

Emma pushed her window up all the way. Someone was calling her. "Who's down there?"

"Me, Tom. Can I come up?"

Emma smiled and nodded. "Found a way around my dad's trick by using one of your own, I see." She laughed as she caught the grunts and bumps of Tom as he climbed the tree to her room, much less agile than he'd been at eleven years old.

"That old fart's going to be the death of me," he whispered. "I couldn't sleep. All I did was think about you and how long it might take before we're together again."

"I'm glad you came back. I couldn't sleep either. I keep wrestling with all the ideas we talked about until they make no sense, and I can't figure out what's right and what's wrong."

Tom took Emma in his arms. "Don't think about this crazy world. Not now, not tonight."

Emma stared into Tom's eyes. "Seriously, five alternate worlds exist."

"Compared to billions in this cluster alone," Tom answered understanding her logic and where she was going.

"Yes, of course. But, soon, these five worlds might outnumber our billions of worlds. As each world is growing, they are amassing clusters of their own. Still, is it right to condemn all those people to vanish? As if they never existed?"

"A moral dilemma I'll never be able to figure out." He paused as though a thought struck him. "Perhaps these people were never meant to exist. You said Fred told you that in this timeline, Anne Ripley has reincarnated and is living the life of her choice."

Emma nodded, a dubious smile hovering on her expression. A big sigh later, she nestled in Tom's arms. "Did you park in the driveway?"

"I walked here, or should I say tiptoed, afraid the old buzzer might hear me."

Emma chuckled. "He's not such a bad guy. Just trying to protect me."

"Know what? You can always check with Columba about the right path to take. She would know, or she would at least give you choices to make. Whatever you decide to do," he stepped back and lifted her chin to stare into her eyes. "You'll do it better after spending some time in my arms."

Tom smiled, and Emma couldn't help a chuckle. She pecked his lips sensing the flame about to ignite. When passion flared between them, little else mattered.

***

A knock on the door woke Emma. Her mother was trying to convey some message. The clock on her table read seven in the morning. "I hear you, Mom. I'm awake."

"I left you a note on the refrigerator, sweetie. Your dad and I are leaving early for that party tonight. The one I told you about in the Hamptons. This way your father will be able to play golf with the company's CEO and acquire more clients."

"Okay, Mom. Don't worry about me."

Emma was about to fall asleep again when her leg bumped up against someone else's leg. She jumped and swallowed a scream just in time. She turned and spotted Tom with his arm underneath her pillow.

She watched his peaceful expression as he slept, stretched out on his side, and thanked the heavens he didn't snore. She curbed the urge to run her fingers through his tangled hair messed up on the pillow, and the even greater need to caress his torso that appeared healthy and muscular. Looking down at the sheet covering the rest of him, she spotted his size thirteen feet sticking out from underneath, large feet that also didn't quite make the bed.

She lay back down with a smile on her face. She needed a bigger bed, one of those California Kings, longer than they were wide. Her room certainly had the space to support this, and she could bring the bed with her when she moved into her place.

A couple of sighs later, followed by a batting of the eyes that wouldn't stay closed, Emma realized the privilege of sleep had scampered. She got up, being careful not to wake Tom, and hurried to the bathroom. She would shower, brush her teeth, and make breakfast while she waited for her man to wake up.

Once downstairs, her head buried inside the super-sized refrigerator, Emma assembled ingredients to make pancakes.

Rummaging in the back shelves, she found fresh cherry tomatoes, maple syrup, orange juice, and slices of smoked ham Tom might like to eat.

Keeping the door open with her foot, she gathered the items two by two to place them on the counter beside her, the ham being the last item she hauled out. When she closed the door, Emma bumped into her dad. "Oh! My God. Dad, you scared me."

Emma clutched her heart while her father picked up the ham she dropped.

"Making a big breakfast, I see." He gave her a peck on the cheek. "Didn't mean to scare you, sweetie. Your mother's already in the car. Needed to add something to this note she hung on the refrigerator door. Now, I can tell you."

"What is it?" Her father sounded mysterious, as though he plotted some surprise or other.

"Tell your boyfriend, Tom, that his father's coming with us—not to worry about him."

"Rudy Carson?"

"Yes. I told you about this big client in the Hamptons, didn't I?"

"Yes. You did."

"Well, I explained to the CEO who invited us that I wanted to bring a colleague just as dedicated to his job as I am and that he was looking forward to meeting other potential clients. He said to bring him along."

"Wow, that's very generous of you, Dad."

"Don't sound so surprised. After all, when Rudy Carson becomes family, we'll need to look out for him, won't we?"

Emma hugged her father. "I love you, Dad."

"Tell that man of yours he doesn't need to leave and sneak back once we're in bed."

"He doesn't usually do that," Emma gave him a sly glance. "He hates when you flash the porch lights on and off, as though you want him to leave."

"Nah. Not my intention at all." A comical raise of his eyebrows, a sly smile of his own indicated to Emma that this was Patrick's way of making fun of Tom. Those two couldn't spend a day without using their comedic skills against each other.

"Have a nice time, Dad."

Patrick chuckled all the way to the front door.

Her father's turn to poke fun at Tom, Emma realized, wondering how he knew he was on the premises. Patrick and Tom each took turns to laugh at each other, yet they both held great respect for one another.

"Men," she sighed.

When Emma finished flipping over the pancakes on the sizable rectangular grill her mother used, she laid three on her plate and six on Tom's plate. Also, for Tom, Emma cut up slices of ham and placed them next to his over-easy eggs on a bed of Romain lettuce.

As she put the plates in the warming section of her mother's new stove, she heard Tom call her name from the top of the stairs. She ran to the staircase. "You bellowed?" She smiled.

"I was disappointed you weren't in bed with me anymore. For a minute I thought I was at my place, alone." Tom came down a few steps to show her there were no hard feelings. "Please tell me that aroma is breakfast. Smells so good."

"It is. Listen, you took chances coming down here dressed in your boxers. What if my folks were here?"

Tom smiled as he came closer to peck her lips. "I saw them pull out of the drive."

Emma caught Tom's sigh of relief. "Your Dad spotted me, so he waved, and I waved back. I had the last laugh."

Standing on a stair while exchanging barbs with Tom, all Emma wanted to do was skip breakfast and go back upstairs with him. Then, the doorbell rang.

Emma checked her watch. "Who could that be this early on a Saturday morning?"

"Who else. Your friend, Hank. Please don't agree to babysit for him, please?" Tom begged.

"I'm not babysitting for Hank. I can't babysit today, not when I'm Tom sitting," Emma gave him the dah eyes.

"Ah! Such a bad joke. Are you teaming up with your dad to get me? Seriously."

Emma smiled. "For your information, my dad took your dad with them to the Hamptons. This CEO invited my father there to glean more clients, and Dad asked if he could bring one of his colleagues also looking for new clients. Now, do you understand how much he likes you?"

"No way. Wow, my father's going to be ecstatic. You're right. Decent of your dad. He must like me a little."

The bell rang again for the third time.

"Don't let it ring again," Tom added, "I'm going to take a quick shower. Breakfast will still be good, right?"

"Of course." They could eat when Tom came back.

Emma opened the door expecting to find Hank, but instead caught a glimpse of a red-faced Amelia awkwardly switching from one foot to the next.

"Amelia, come in."

Emma moved aside to let her in. Amelia did enter while looking around her as though wanting to avoid Emma's parents.

"My folks aren't here. They're gone for the weekend. Anything wrong?"

"Everything's wrong. I'm sorry, Emma. You are my best friend in the whole world, and I can't seem to study, or eat, or sleep since I behaved so badly the other day."

"Oh, Amelia. I'm not mad at you. Honestly, I'm not. I understand how our emotions can get the better of us sometimes." Emma noticed Amelia's swollen eyes and figured she'd stewed long enough. She approached and gave her friend a hug.

Amelia hugged her back, collapsing into tears in Emma's arms. "I'm unhappy without you also," Emma told her. 'Why else do you think I would like us to see more of each other?"

Amelia blew her nose and wiped her eyes. "I didn't want to begrudge you the love of your life. Thomas Carson loves you. And I'm glad you found the one who makes you happy."

Emma smoothed her hair.

"And you were right, Emma. I need to find that person who will understand me and treat me with respect. A man who will love me unconditionally." She produced a pale smile. "I'm just scared sometimes that I'll never find him."

"When you're not looking, you will find him." Emma extended her arm. "I just made breakfast. Want some?"

"I'm not hungry. Besides, my mother needs me. She's baking a cake for my dad's birthday. She wants me to help her decorate."

"Help her decorate the house or the cake?"

"Both." Amelia's smile brightened. "Thanks for understanding, Emma. We should try to spend time together more often. Time goes by so quickly."

As Emma agreed, she heard Tom coming down the stairs. He froze when he caught sight of Amelia standing beside Emma.

"I thought you were alone," Amelia said.

"My parents are gone. Tom spent the night. We're just about to have breakfast, why I invited you to stay."

"Thanks, another time."

Amelia hesitated, but then glanced at Tom. "I hope we can be friends again."

Tom hardened his stance. He came down the stairs and

encircled Emma in his arms. "I was never your friend, Amelia. You're Emma's friend. I was nice to you because of Emma. I don't think we should go down that road again. No more misunderstandings."

Emma wanted to shake herself loose from Tom, but he held her tightly so she couldn't budge. She turned toward Tom to tell him not to be such a bully when she encountered a plea in his eyes. The message she read there compelled her not to argue with his motive. He attempted to restore Amelia's dignity, her self-respect. She needed to move on, and she would never be able to do this if he and Amelia were friends.

After Tom caught Emma's surreptitious nod, he released his hold on her. She approached Amelia and invited her once more. "You sure you don't want to have breakfast with us?"

"Sure. You and I will get together soon. I promise." Amelia kissed Emma on both cheeks, then she left, without saying anything else to Thomas Carson. She was taking a wide berth of this man. And perhaps this would be best for all concerned, at least for the next little while.

Emma watched Amelia walk away. She spotted Amelia blow her nose and wipe her eyes again. She figured she poured out grateful tears since she relished their friendship, tears of relief mixed with the bitter ones for the loss of her friendship with Tom.

Once she closed the door, Tom grabbed Emma's shoulders. "Trust me. I did the right thing. You and I both know

I was never Amelia's friend. I was simply friendly to her to please you."

"You're right. Once Amelia meets someone of her own, do you think we'll be able to hang out, the four of us?"

Tom laid a hand around Emma's waist, directing her toward the kitchen. "Sure. That'll be easier."

Joss Landry

—Twenty-Eight—

Help For Brian

Breakfast dishes washed and put away, Tom answered the door and came face to face with Hank. "You're early this morning," Tom said with a smile.

"So are you." Hank checked the time on his Rolex. "Here for breakfast?"

"As a matter of fact, yes. Come on in." He moved aside to allow the big chief of police to enter.

"Is Emma here?"

"She's upstairs, getting dressed. You don't have Jarred with you today."

"Nah. Christina brought them both to Jass."

"Where?"

"The unisex hair salon. Christina took the boys to get their hair cut. I am working on the Brian Hayes case, frantically."

"Yeah. Can't be a whole lot of fun to work on that grim story." Tom moved toward the kitchen inviting Hank there. "I've got fresh coffee on the burner."

"That'll hit the spot." Hank grabbed a cup and sat down at the kitchen table. "It'll be a whole lot of fun once we nab the buggers. I"m keeping my mind on the outcome."

Tom caught sight of Emma coming down the hall. She entered the kitchen and turned as she eyed the area. "Wow, Tom. You did a great job with this kitchen. Thank you so much. Hey, Hank."

"No problem. You made breakfast, only fair I help out with the cleaning."

"Help out? You did the whole thing. I'm impressed."

"Sounds like our household. Christina cooks up a storm, and I wash when she's finished."

"Well, I live with my dad who always hated washing dishes. Since he won't even buy a dishwasher, someone has to keep the kitchen half decent. Got used to it, I guess." Tom smiled.

Emma grabbed a cup and asked, "What's going on with Brian Hayes?"

"Bill is going all out on this one. He's already contacted the security company. Greg what's-his-name got the visit from an FBI agent this morning, at his home address. He's going to make sure Brian's room gets reconnected to the system sometime today."

"Does he know to keep Brian out of this?"

"Greg has been briefed and told to be silent—not to answer anyone's questions but Tim O'Rourke's."

"How fast can they do this?"

"Well, the physical connection is already at the house. All he has to do is reconnect the system from the base."

"Do they have IR in place?" Tom asked.

"They do." Hank smiled. "The quality of their cameras is unparalleled and equipped with infrared lights. The lights turn on automatically at dusk."

"Will that allow us to spot the person and the car—because of the lights in the veranda?" Emma worried about shadows.

Tom squeezed Emma's hand. "The porch lighting will serve to enhance the picture, not to worry, sweetie."

"I came here to ask you to communicate with Brian and let him know to advise us if he believes he is about to get a visitor."

"Should I tell him about the cameras?"

"No. Don't reveal anything you don't have to." Hank took a sip of his coffee.

"Do you want something to eat, Hank?"

"No. Thank you. Bill also communicated with a sister of Lorna Hayes—Brian's mother—Martha Crenshaw. She and her husband live in Fredericksburg Iowa. They cultivate and sell fresh vegetables, fir trees, and her husband Frank owns a small truck repair shop."

"He didn't say what this was about, did he?" Emma worried her sister would know before Lorna did.

"No. Bill mentioned he was a journalist doing a story on families living in the area."

"They could go there, Brian and his mom," Tom said.

"Yes, of course. Trouble is if we can find this place in Iowa, anyone else can. First, we need to make a few arrests. Then, mother and son will be able to vacate the premises."

"What about putting them in a witness protection program?" Tom asked

"Bill said it might come to that—as a last resort."

Emma nodded, eying Tom's concerned expression. "I'll look in on Brian this afternoon, Hank.

I'll reassure him that we are surveilling the area and that we are protecting him. Is that okay?"

"Well, that shouldn't be a problem. Although before you mention this, check Brian's thoughts. If you sense in any way that he's liable to brag about this to his father or the people connected to him, I wouldn't advise giving him precise information on how we intend to proceed."

Emma caught Tom's nod. He approved Hank's suggestion, and although her priority was to make the boy feel better about himself, and about the world around him, she tacitly agreed to wait before handing him too much information. As hurt and cut-up, as he was, he might give away the scent of the trap out of sheer retribution—if only to regain a little of his dignity. "I'll be careful, Hank. I promise."

Hank drained his coffee cup and rose. "I've got to go. I'm meeting Christina at Jass, the unisex hair salon—in case she should have problems with Jarred. It's his first haircut." He smiled giving the youngsters a hand salute.

"Give a hug to Christina for me," Emma said with a smile, as Tom returned Hank's wave.

Once Hank left, Emma moved toward Tom and rubbed his shoulders. "You're the sweetest, cleaning this kitchen the way you did. A quick question. Will my mother be able to locate any of her dishes?" Emma couldn't help a giggle as she spotted the interrogation mark on Tom's face.

He stood and took Emma in his arms. "Well, I rearranged her kitchen in a much more efficient way. Didn't put anything where it should be." He smiled at the look of horror on her face. He chuckled. "Relax. I know where everything goes. I've helped your mom with dishes before. Even told her she had created a user-friendly area."

"Really. What did my mom say?"

"She laughed. What can I say? Your mom finds me funny." Tom sighed as he stared into Emma's eyes. "When are you going to look in on Bryan?"

"I need to talk to Columba first. The mandate Fred gave me doesn't make sense. I want to run the idea by her before I do anything else."

"I agree with you. This problem is bigger than all of us combined and deserves your immediate attention. Is there any way I can help?"

Emma stared at the handsome, rugged face, at the unshaven fuzz on his cheeks and chin and remembered what little sleep they both shared the night before. "You should probably head home, at least for a little while, grab a change of clothes. I know your homework is like mine, piling up."

"Exactly what I wanted to do. I just wanted to make sure

you're going to be all right. Don't do anything drastic before I return, okay?"

"When will that be?"

"A couple of hours or so."

She nodded and walked him to the door. Emma watched him walk toward his house. She lost him when he cut across the neighbor's lawn to grab the shortcut home.

Closing the door, she locked it, turned and came face to face with Columba. Emma jumped. "Ah, my heart." She took a couple of deep breaths enjoying Columba's pearl-like chuckle.

"Sorry, Emma. I keep thinking you can sense me when I pop in."

"I'm too tired, somehow, mind too preoccupied." Emma walked toward the small living room. "But you're just the person I wanted to see." With a swipe of her arm, she invited Columba to enter the small room.

There, amidst her mother's big bouquet of red chrysanthemums and soft pink delphiniums intermixed with white orange sprigs, Emma sat and invited Columba to do the same. The Earth Optimal visitor did, present in her pleasant, human self.

Emma recounted what had gone on the night before while at Bill Frost's home. She gave the word for word rendition of Fred Manson's request and beathed easier when Columba's expression did not change while she regaled her with details of their encounter. But then, Columba's facial beauty rarely turned to anger or sadness or any other overpowering emotion. It was as though her lovely vision was rooted deeply in her character, flowing with harmony and contentment.

"I understand your moral dilemma," Columba spoke first once Emma ended the conversation. "This problem is why I'm here. We're already beginning to sense the effect of these other timelines on Earth Optimal. These five timelines are growing at an alarming rate."

"All the way to Earth Optimal? How can that be?" Emma could not prevent the shock from invading her expression.

"Well, some of our inhabitants have begun to sense themselves elsewhere, almost doubling their presence if you will, and they fear a process that can allow them to be in five different places at the same time could be detrimental to all of us."

"Oh, my God!" Emma sat back into the sofa's cushions, shaking her head side to side. "So, Fred is right. These worlds could implode and leave us with nothing."

"Fred is right about the outcome. Not necessarily right about the way to handle the matter."

"How do we handle this? No one seems to know. Bill asked the druids on his planet and they told him that this was an Earth problem that needed to be resolved by Earthlings."

"Yes. By Earthlings, or by a capable Chavah," Columba added with a smile.

"What would happen if I gave all the needed coordinates to Fred?"

"He would be able to destroy those worlds by deleting the range of those echoes."

"Wouldn't that bring on catastrophic results? All these people disappearing all at once?"

"On this, no one can agree—not even the savants from my Earth. The instant removal of these remote sections of time might produce dire outcomes on our worlds.

"So, what do we do?"

"Well, although I can show you what goes on in those alternate lines, as I did yesterday, I cannot enter them. Neither can Fred anymore. You are the only one who can."

"There has to be a way to do this. You know what I don't understand? I've shut down Eivan junior's switch in our current world. Why didn't this action cancel out all the other alternate worlds? Is it because his project was never turned on in those worlds?"

"You may have turned off a switch. Only Eivan's project is not shut down."

"What do you mean?"

"Eivan still owns the nanocomponents at the base of his neck, and the bioelectrical impulses that feed these nanos run through his body. So, as you can see, the system cannot be turned off with a switch."

"He led me to believe his system was no longer operative," she breathed.

"Perhaps he was merely protecting his project."

Emma rose to walk to the window. *A nice way for Colum-*

ba to admit that Eivan's admission was a lie. "I'm at a loss. I don't know what I can do."

Columba rose as well. "I sent a message to Hawke in the fourth dimension. I understand he can't help from where he is, but he's one of the brightest minds I know. If anyone can think of something, anything we can do, he will."

"I'll also try to find some solution at my end."

An hour later Emma still sat in the small living room staring out the window. She tried to relax as she allowed her mind to wander like a vagabond, uninhibited and unhampered. She realized that to stare bluntly at some trouble would only aggravate the problem, pushing back any possible solutions to the dark recesses of her brain. The free-flowing exercise brought forth all sorts of weird images, strings of unwanted drama peeping through in all types of colors—flashes of Fred changing into Professor Rappaport, Eivan junior's hard, rigid stare. She spotted Tom climbing up her tree to reach her room superimposed by Boleslaw's sick, red glare. But through it all, the gentle smile and wide-eyed innocence of Annemarie Hanover sprang forward, lighting up the imagery, making the tangled mess in her mind bearable. When images of her home planet shone through, she saw visions of Annemarie Hanover sitting with a book on her lap and a red portfolio beside her. She sat by Lake Tranquillum, and Emma wondered how she'd gotten there.

Phrases spoken throughout the last few weeks populated her mind, like when Annemarie uttered that had she grown up in Newark, the two of them would be best friends, and Eivan, trusting her with the combination of his lock—nothing but a lie when he stated the switch would turn off the system. Maybe all Emma needed to ensure was that the weird operation never saw the light of day.

The front door opened wide and brought her back.

"Tom, you're back early?"

He glanced at his watch. "I said a couple of hours, and it's been three. I thought you might be waiting for me. You didn't hear me drive up?"

"I think I fell asleep. I tried to meditate on some solution to put the world back the way it was, but I'm not sure I was able to accomplish very much."

"How about we go to Englewood Cliffs. We can swim, play some tennis. You can relax. Maybe your grandmother will know what to do."

"I'm not discussing this with my grandmother, Tom."

Tom shrugged as he waited for an answer.

"First, I need to check on Brian Hayes. The boy has no way to reach me so if something develops at home I need to know."

"Want me to go with you?"

"No. I only use my residual form. But when I come back, we could head out to Englewood Cliffs. We could have dinner with my grandmother."

"Okay." he deposited his bag on the floor. "I brought everything with me, in case you said yes."

"I'll just go upstairs and be back in a couple of minutes."

Once she relaxed in bed, Emma prepared to project herself to West Orange, and she landed, careful not to let anyone spot her, especially Brian Hayes.

Brian was in his room, lying on the floor and crying. Remorse for not landing on the premises earlier hit her with the force of a wrecking ball. "Brian? Why are you crying?"

"Where have you been, Angel. I've been calling you. No one is ever here when I need them. They just took my mom to the hospital. I heard her scream downstairs. When I showed up to try and help her, I found my father, her husband, beating up on her." Brian wiped his runny nose with the back of his sleeve, as a child might do. "I ran from him without being seen and called 911. I explained the situation to the operator. Minutes later, police and ambulances showed up at the door."

"What hospital did they take her to?"

"Saint Barnabas in Livingston." Brian searched the area from where the voice emanated. "My father told them I did this to my mother. He said I was enraged. Then he posted two goons at my room door and my patio door to prevent me from going to see her and from showing police that unlike him, who needs to wear gloves, my knuckles aren't bleeding."

Emma hated being there in residual form. She would have liked to comfort this boy in person. "I'll take you there. And you'll be talking to the Captain of police letting him know that you didn't do this. Your father did. They will believe you. Trust me."

"How can you take me there?"

"Don't worry. I will find a way to take you to see your mother, and if you can wait a minute or two, Brian, I will take you to your mother's hospital room." Emma went home and reintegrated her body. She had no choice than to trust that Brian would not look at her if she asked him not to. Emma wished that she knew how to bring people along in her residual form, but she had no idea how to do this. After a few seconds, she returned, warning Brian to close his eyes.

"Why do I have to close my eyes?"

"Bad luck for you to stare directly at an angel."

"Okay."

Before she landed, she made sure Brian kept his eyes closed. She took his hand and brought him through the astral space. She caught Brian's moans of fear and panic as he sensed he was in flight, but through it all, Brian kept his eyes closed. Emma found the way to his mother's room and landed inside gently. "Here she is. She will recover, have no fear. Be a gentle presence for her. I will contact the chief of police, and he will be here momentarily."

"Mom," Brian murmured sitting by her bed while holding her hand, never a thought for the angel who'd set him free.

Emma left remembering Hank had mentioned he was at the mall with Christina. She focused on their little family to locate their precise whereabouts. Emma spotted Hank towering over most of the crowd and found a dark corner close to him in which to land. She touched down and immediately got her foot stepped on. The surprise had her emit a little cry of pain, and the person in front of her turned with shock on his expression. "Oh, my God. I didn't realize anyone stood behind me. I must have missed you when I came here a few minutes ago.

Emma got that the man in front of her tried to hide the cigarette he was smoking.

"It's okay. I'm fine," Emma said with a smile.

She left the area and ran to catch up to Hank. After greeting the boys and hugging Christina, she took Hank aside. She whispered in his ear everything she had encountered.

"Sons of bitches. Brian's at the hospital now?"

"Yes. I've already sent a telepathic message to Bill Frost and Tim O'Rourke."

"Problem?" Christina smiled as her eyebrows rose in curiosity.

"I have to leave, sweetheart. I need to go to Saint Barnabas medical center. Bad guys are exploiting a victim, and I've got to stop this."

"What about all the bags, and the kids? Can't someone else handle this?"

"Call Matt. Emma just told me he's at this mall with Maria. He'll make sure you get home safely."

Emma turned to Christina with a smile. "While I was looking

for you, I caught sight of Matt and Maria. They're in the west wing of the mall."

"The matter is urgent. I'm sorry, Christina."

"Go. Quickly." Christina reached to peck Hank's lips and smiled, nodding as she did.

"We'll go to the nearest washrooms and leave from there," Emma told Hank.

Hank and Emma ran to the location, and when they got there, she grabbed his hand and flew away with him before anyone could spot them.

When they landed outside the hospital room, the corridor holding enough people to render them inconspicuous, Hank told Emma, "I wonder how long it will take for Bill to get here. Do you think I should wait before I talk to Brian?"

Emma turned to catch the loud footsteps of people running toward them. Bill and Tim both arrived promptly.

"Of course, they travel the same way you do," Hank mumbled.

They decided only two of them would enter the room and talk to Brian while Tim, the red-headed giant, would wait outside to prevent anyone else from entering the room for the next fifteen minutes.

Emma recounted how she had found Brian and advised them both of his state of mind. She also told Hank and Bill what Brian had seen, in case the boy might be too shy to express himself.

"Don't worry, Em. We'll get the son of a bitch," Hank

grumbled.

"Change of plans," Bill mouthed. "We'll use the father to reel in the others."

—Twenty-Nine—

Intergalactic War

Once again at home, in her room, Emma ran down the stairs to meet with Tom. He was reading one of his manuals and working on his tablet. He checked the time on his wrist and smiled as she arrived in the kitchen, out of breath and excited.

"What's going on?"

Emma sat down in front of him and recounted what she had spotted and what she had done.

"You've been gone less than fifteen minutes. How did you do all that?"

"I'm sorry to disappoint you, Tom. I can't go to my grandmother's just yet. I need to find Thornton Hayes III."

"Who?"

"Brian's father. He's out there trying to convince everyone Brian put his mother in the hospital."

"Wait a minute." Tom rose and tugged her toward him. "You can't deal with this man on your own. He's liable to do anything to make his story stick."

"I'm not going to confront him. I'm going to listen in on his conversations and create images in his mind that will get me more information on what we need, which will help Hank and Bill Frost. But mostly, his thoughts will help free his son." She jiggled Tom's hands with her own. "Don't worry. Thornton Hayes will not know I'm around, listening to everything he is saying."

"Is there any way I can talk you out of this?"

She shook her head from side to side. "But you can wait for me if you want."

"I'll be here when you return."

Emma left after a hug and a kiss from Tom. Trouble was the need to discover more about the elder Hayes quickly dissipated in Tom's arms—her little brand of Kryptonite. She smiled as she traveled through the astral world in residual form. She'd set her sights on Thornton Hayes III, and she found him talking erratically on his phone on some street corner. She searched the place to identify the area and memorized the name of the street and avenue, somewhere in West Orange by the looks of the affluent surroundings.

"I don't care about your rules," Thornton yelled in his phone. "Someone called my wife and gave her a message meant for me. This order for three kidneys and one liver was never intended for her ears." A slight pause and Thornton added, "When my wife told the man that he had the wrong number, the idiot gave her specifics on how we did business for years, purchasing and selling vital organs."

That's what happened, Emma concluded. Lorna received a message destined for Thornton, and all hell broke loose.

"No, she's not my secretary, you asshole, and she knows nothing about this. She's in the hospital thanks to you. She wouldn't let it go, and I had to do something to prevent her from going to the police."

Emma caught Thornton shaking, as though what he'd done was beyond his capability.

"This is why I need to speak to the man in charge. The Asian, as he is known. I demand protection. After all, protection for me will go a long way to protecting the big man himself, won't it?"

"He can leave you out to dry if he wants to, and you can't harm him. Especially if you don't know who he is."

Emma could no longer catch the conversation at the other end. The voice at the other end of the line stopped. She realized Thornton shook even more at this point.

"What if I do know who he is?"

Laughter came through the phone—a guttural, hateful sound. "You're nothing but an idiot who's shitting in his pants. How would you know who he is when I, the number one in his operation, don't even know his name?"

Thornton did a full turn to check his back.

"Besides," the firm tone at the other end of the line stated. "If you did know who the man is, we would have to kill you, wouldn't we?"

Thornton hung up the phone. Out of breath as though he'd run all the way from his house to this intersection, in the middle of a busy street, he pulled up his suit collar and walked over to his car.

Emma followed him, trailing on the roof of his vehicle like she'd done to Boleslaw all those years ago—anxious to discover where Thornton wanted to run.

Emma got off the car when she recognized her surroundings. The beautiful two-mile lake of South Mountain Reservation, the pride of several municipalities, outlined with a paved loop that skirted the lake and forest. She saw him park near the boathouse and wondered who he planned to meet there.

Searching the area near the lake, she found the powder red car she first spotted parked beside the veranda at Brian's house. She remembered the car. The top was down today, but she felt sure this was the vehicle they discussed. She waited by the car as two people argued, their flamboyant gestures leaving no doubt of a difference of opinion. The driver, definitely the man she spotted coming out of Brian's room, planted his anger-contorted-face inches away from an unidentified bald man sitting on the passenger side.

The voice of reason told her to go back to let Hank know of the little feather-plucking powwow, but she couldn't afford to leave and lose them. She moved to the back of the car and memorized the license plate.

They finally came out of the car, and the other man stowed a gun in his belt, under the flap of his jacket. The passenger's face appeared carved out of bronze. The man was tall and broad. Emma thought of him as a potential enforcer and worried about losing Thornton Hayes, whom she figured was ripe to spill everything he knew to cut a deal with the Feds.

Still, she needed to witness what was going on inside, so she followed the two men keeping a certain distance when she spotted the car's driver looking over his shoulder several times.

"What are you looking at, Mort?" The other man asked.

"Don't know. Have the oddest sensation someone is watching us."

"The great Mort Vandel afraid of his own shadow."

Mort Vandel, Emma's eyes opened wide. The name sounded like Van Mortadel. Could it be these fellows had merely twisted their names? Without a doubt, he was one of the men they wanted to find.

Inside the boathouse, they met up with Thornton. The two men didn't have time to sit before Thornton repeated the same story he'd told the other man on the phone.

"So, what are we going to do about this?"

"I told police my son had gone overboard and beaten up his mother."

The stone-faced man asked Thornton, "Why are you wearing gloves? To hide your banged-up knuckles?"

"I panicked. I didn't know what else to do. I didn't want Lorna to go to the police."

"But you didn't kill her. Now, she has police protection, and she is going to talk."

"Not if we threaten her son," Thornton said his eyes round and wild.

"You don't seem to care much about your son, do you?" the big man articulated.

"Stepson. I married the boy's mother when he was just a baby. He doesn't know."

"Okay then," Mort said with a smile. "I'll put a contract out on both of them. Make it look as though Brian killed his mother and then killed himself."

"Guess so," Thornton said looking at his gloved hands. "I hate to lose Lorna. I like her. The boy I never cared for, but Lorna ..."

Emma caught him wiping a tear that rolled down his cheek. And the other two stared at each other while a murderous expression registered in Mort's eyes.

"Okay, Rob, let's get out of here," Mort said still looking around at the empty seats around them.

"Why are you so shaky?" the big man asked again.

"I told you. The same girl I sensed in Brian's room that night is here somewhere."

The man called Rob gave Thornton a dubious eyeful. And Thornton extended his hand. "So, you're Rob Richards. Pleased to meet you."

Richard Ribeye, Emma pondered. That could be his name. Then, Mort's words sobered her. He was able to sense her presence. How was that possible? She decided to leave. When the three were outside, she hid behind a tree and waited to see if Mort could still feel her presence.

"Is the girl gone, Mort?"

"Not sure." He turned toward Rob and Emma realized what the big man was about to do.

When Rob pulled out his gun, she invoked her little sentence and turned the gun into a water pistol at the same time Rob brandished the gun on Thornton.

When water squirted, Thornton pulled his gun out of his pocket. He backed off spotting people on the lake, most likely not wanting to attract attention. "I trusted you guys. Why would you want to eliminate me when I've been a faithful and devoted business partner for ten years. People like me aren't easy to come by."

Thornton kept his gun out and backed up through the wooded mulch, at least until he found a clearing which was when he stowed his weapon and made a dash for his car.

Rob stared at the plastic orange water gun in his hand. "What happened, man?"

"I told you. A young girl is watching us. She did this. I spotted her the other night in the boy's room."

"I told you your love of pretty boys would get to you. Now, it's liable to get to both of us. And, if you're right about the woman, then she heard everything we said, names, for instance, license plates, the works."

"I'll just have to track her down and kill her, won't I?"

"How will you do that exactly? If she's an alien like you, she'll be able to defend herself."

"I'm more powerful than she is. I know I am."

Emma left promptly. She held too much information to

risk a fight with an alien. When Emma got to the hospital, Hank and the two FBI agents, Bill and Tim, were leaving. She showed herself to them. "I've got news. Can we meet at my house right away?"

"Sure. We'll bring Hank along," Bill confirmed.

Emma landed at home and searched the place for Tom. He was in the family room still working on his project. "Tom, I thought you'd gone. Thank God you're here."

Tom took Emma in his arms, and though she tried to stop shivering, she needed a couple of minutes encircled by Tom's warmth to shove the heebie-jeebies aside.

"What happened? You're trembling." Tom rubbed her back with his big hands, then pushed her slightly away to get her explanation. Just as he did, three people entered the house unexpectedly. "What the hell?" Tom recognized Hank, Bill, and Tim. "What are you guys doing here?"

"Emma needs to share," Bill said with a smile.

Emma did, without leaving anything behind. When she spoke about Mort's sensations of her presence, right down to her gender, she explained how his associate proclaimed Mort to be an alien.

Bill rose abruptly. "No! A dirty alien? Devronair?"

"Don't know. I didn't read encrypted thoughts. Come to think of it, I didn't read anything at all in the man's mind." She scoured the four people sitting in front of her. "He did say he would find me and get rid of me."

Silence followed that sentence.

Emma Willis Book 3,
I Can Help You

Tom shot up and came to sit on the arm of Emma's chair slipping his arm around her. "I'm not going to let the fool hurt you, sweetheart. He's going to have to go through me first."

Bill stared at Tim. "We have to contact Fred. He'll know what type of species this guy is."

"Oh, and Bill. I believe Mort Vandel is your leader."

"What makes you say that?"

"A conversation I heard between Thornton Hayes and a stranger who called himself the leader's number one man. When Thornton told him that without protection he would go to the police with the name of the leader, 'an Asian,' were his exact words, the man laughed and called his bluff. He said no one knew who the man was, not even him."

"So, what makes you think Mort Vandel is the leader?"

"Well, I believe the word Asian filtered down from the actual word Alien. The two got confused somehow, and since no one truly believes in Aliens, the leader became Asian."

"No wonder we can't find him. Five years we've been searching the globe for this elusive piece of shit." Bill took a deep breath and stared at Tim.

Tim shook his head from side to side. "Are we facing an intergalactic war? There has to be more than one of them here, collecting our resources."

Emma stared at Bill, then Tim. "There may be more than one. Rob Richards knew about Mort being an alien. He asked him what he intended to do about me and worried about the fact I may be an alien. Rob might be an innocent bystander, or he might be a partner."

"Just what we need. Two aliens who are out to get us."

Emma leaned on Tom's arm. "Whatever you do, don't let Fred send him to Earth Optimal."

Hank chuckled. Then, staring at Bill, he asked, "Anything I can do at my end?"

"Yes. We need to arrest Thornton Hayes, Robert Richards, and Mort Vandel. However, I'm going on the principle that Rob is an innocent stooge. And, I would hold off on Mort until Fred and I can assess who he is and what to do with him."

Hank rose. "I'll go back to the office. Put out an APB on Thornton Hayes." He turned toward Emma. "Would you like me to leave a couple of men posted here?"

"Thanks, but that won't do any good—not if he's an alien who can sense my presence." Emma grabbed Tom's pen and scribbled the red convertible's license plate number on a piece of paper. "This is the license to the car parked at Brian's that night. Mort Vandel's car."

Hank took the paper from her. "Great work, Emma."

"First we need to establish who he is and what he can do." Bill picked up his briefcase. "Tim and I are leaving. We're on his tail, Emma. Don't worry. Do you have your phone handy?"

"Yeah, I do." Emma took her phone out of its case. "Why?"

"I want you to take down this numbered sequence. Don't worry—not a twenty-four digit combination. Bill gave Emma twelve numbers, then told her to press down on the sequence for twelve seconds. Once she did, the number glowed with a strange light. "When you slide your finger across this glow three times, from right to left, you will immediately be transported to Earth Optimal. No one will be able to touch you while on that planet. Simply ask someone to direct you to Jeannie Frost."

"Will I land in the right country, the right city?"

"The number will bring you a block from our home. Someone will guide you there."

Emma nodded. "Thank you. Not that I don't want to visit Jeannie, but I sure hope the situation doesn't warrant the trip. I have so little time to study and do the work."

"I understand." Bill grabbed her hand. "We'll catch him before you need to run."

They all left with their designated tasks while Tom and Emma watched them go. "You're not scared being here alone with me?" Emma asked Tom with a pale smile.

"Since when have I ever been frightened by some ghoul alien? Let's not allow the evil dudes to spoil our lives."

"You talking about wizards?"

Tom shrugged. "May as well be. They're all the same. Out to make trouble, deplete our resources, control what we do and think."

Emma kissed him, her mind distant and preoccupied. She smiled at Tom, refusing her mood to sway her thoughts. "Let's go keep my grandma company."

Emma Willis Book 3,
I Can Help You

—Thirty—

Powers Revealed

Emma and Tom had just finished helping Abigail put her dishes away. A talented chef provided the meal they shared, duck confit with the tastiest little potatoes, accompanied by asparagus in a heavenly sauce. Although Emma tasted a tiny bite of the duck to please her grandmother, she had not eaten such a fancy dinner in a long time. Abigail having released the help earlier, Tom and Emma assisted her in putting the dinner fare away.

"The meal was delicious, Grandma." Emma hugged her grandmother. "Does your chef come to prepare meals just for you?"

"Oh, sometimes he does. He's never really motivated to strut out his talents just to please me. I invite my friends from the bridge club often enough." She tilted her head toward Emma. "They love to freeload." She smiled to lighten her words. "But, it's not the same. They don't bother with all the yummy noises you two performed, too stuck-up is what they are. Let me tell you, André was quite pleased that you were pleased."

Emma chuckled at her grandmother's enthusiasm at having them both with her. A little triumph for her that her grandchildren liked to be around an old woman like herself, as she often stipulated.

As they moved toward the game room, Tom wanted to play a little pool, Emma heard the feral cry of a cat outside. A strange sort of meow. Strong, foreboding.

"Are there wild cats around your place, Abigail?" Tom paid attention to spot another such call.

"I don't think so. Most likely a male cat warning another male to stay out of its territory. Although," Abigail listened to another, more defined cry. "Never heard them quite this loud before. Almost sounds as though the animal's at the door, doesn't it?"

Emma immediately realized this was no ordinary cat. The alien pursuing her would need to change his shape to get by the guards, wouldn't he?

"I'll go see what that's all about," Abigail said as she walked away.

"Don't grandma, no." Emma grabbed her grandmother's arm and brought her back in the game room. "Tom, listen. What I am about to say is very important. I believe the alien man we discussed earlier, the one who could sense me? Well, he's on the premises."

"What?" Abigail appeared shocked. "There's no way he can bypass my security system."

"Grandma. The man is an alien who has probably changed

himself into something else to get through your security. He's fast, imaginative and he's trying to get to me."

Tom picked his phone out of his pocket and prepared to dial 911. "I'll call the police. They'll be here in minutes."

"You won't have time," Emma insisted. "This being most likely operates at the speed of thought, and he can smell you."

"What are we going to do?" Abigail held Emma's hands in a panic, her eyes locked onto the windows in front of her.

Emma pulled out her phone and retrieved the application Bill Frost insisted she load. She displayed the bright glow on her screen for Tom. "Listen very carefully. I want you to touch the app for twelve seconds, and slide your finger three times over the light from right to left. Grab my grandmother's hand. The action will transport you to Earth Optimal. Ask for Jeannie Frost. Her house is a block from where you will land. She knows you, Tom. You can explain to her what happened.

"Oh, my God. I can go to Earth Optimal?" Tom appeared shocked

"You both can." She eyed her grandmother with a smile. "Don't worry. You'll be safe there."

Emma was about to leave when she realized Tom needed shaking. "Tom, now."

"What about my car?"

"Forget about your car, sweetie."

Tom smiled and nodded. Holding Emma's phone, he looped his arm with Abigail's arm, and Emma saw them both disappear. She prayed to God they would find their way once they got there.

As for herself, she held on to her oudjat and flew home, not her usual home, to her planet of Capella Five. She landed near Lake Tranquillum and immediately welcomed Shad, her unicorn who promised to always be there for her. "I need your help, Shad. I need to hide my physical self here while the residual me goes back to Earth."

Shad nodded and bent low to the ground so she could mount him. In seconds he brought her to the house he once showed her. She walked inside and admired the simplicity of the few rooms. She lay on a mat on the floor more comfortable than any mattress she ever slept on and transported back to Englewood Cliffs, Earth. This way, she figured the stranger would not be able to detect her smell or harm her while she lay asleep somewhere on Earth without the presence of her mind. Shad would stand guard over her.

The sound of wild cats screeching increased upon her return sounds that reminded Emma of fright and pain, and she wondered if the tactic might be hypnotic, the language meant to draw her out of the house.

She wished she had remembered to bring her oudjat, missing the item about now. Still, Emma searched the grounds using intense light only she could visualize. More sounds came forth. She counted five different, distinct calls. These were no ordinary cats. They were talking to each other.

She flew back home and told Shad she needed her oudjat. He gave it to her, and she was able to handle it even while in residual form. "Will I be able to hold on to this while on Earth?"

"This jewel is a part of who you are, attached to your very soul. It will serve you whether you are in residual or corporeal form."

Emma left again, and although only seconds fleeted by, when she returned to the grounds of her grandmother's large property, she spotted one of the cats transform into a man, the one called Mort Vandel. She took her oudjat and directed the blue flame on him twisting the jewel to the right, as she had done for her professor, Elizabeth Reardon. A terrifying groan breached the night's solitude, and Emma witnessed the pale outline of a wizard leave the man. Only, after the wizard departed, there was no man in her grandmother's yard, simply dust and an overpowering residue of honeysuckle scent.

Quickly she turned her unit on the four remaining huge, red cats. Screeches and menacing teeth and claws appeared as they ripped into each other. A few seconds and they dissipated into thin air.

Emma tried to make heads or tails of the situation as honeysuckle wafted toward her in the fresh, night air. To keep her dinner down, she left, not knowing with certainty if these men were gone or if they would be back in other forms.

She went home to Shad, to her peaceful abode, and

tearfully said goodbye to him once more. "Don't despair, my friend. I shall return."

Getting back to Earth, Emma flew to Bill Frost's house. She realized that by ringing his door, he would show up, eventually.

When he did, she walked in, tried to speak to him, but everything around her darkened. Little spots of green lights flew in front of her eyes, like the small trembling flames she spotted years ago, in the astral route outlined with oleanders—dark and foreboding.

When she opened her eyes again, she lay on the sofa while Bill dabbed a cold compress over her forehead. "Emma, thank God. You scared me. What happened?"

She sat up. "I need some water," she asked in a whisper.

A wave of Bill's hand and she held a glass of cold water she guzzled down immediately. "Thank you. By the way, Tom and my grandmother are on Earth Optimal. Can you bring them back?"

"Sure. The moment I saw Tom and your grandmother arrive, I knew you were in trouble. I was out in Englewood Cliff in residual form trying to look for you. Fred and I never found you."

"I suspected these men were not aliens. The night Mort Vandel occupied Brian's room—something about the threat Mort made—his mind was absent. More than that. At times, I read nothing but emptiness in his thoughts. An Alien would have at least encrypted his thoughts or held ideas in some foreign language. This man's head appeared surprisingly devoid of past or future, focused only on the present."

"Wizards. No longer content to inhabit humans, they are now taking human form. How? Where are they getting these people?"

Emma shrugged. "The honeysuckle scent was so strong, which was why I passed out when I got here."

"So sorry, Emma." Bill waved his hand and Tom and her grandmother stood in front of them. Tom ran to Emma and bent down beside her.

"Oh, Oh," her grandmother couldn't stop expressing surprise appearing to have problems to breathe.

"Are you okay, Abigail?" Tom went to her and strapping an arm around her waist helped her over to the sofa.

"Maybe you should lie down for a few minutes," Emma recommended.

"I'll be fine, sweetheart." She addressed Bill and told him, "One minute I'm talking to your wife Jeannie, marveling at the clean air and the wondrous sensation of oneness with these people, and the next I'm yanked through the astral world to find myself in some stranger's house."

"I apologize," Bill sat down beside her. "I should have brought you two back home more gradually." He turned toward Tom. "Are you all right?"

"Yeah. I can't believe how wonderful it is on your Earth, made doubly clear when we land back here."

"I understand, and if all of you would like to continue your lives on Earth Optimal, you are welcome to do so."

"Really?" Tom asked, his interest peeking through shyly.

Bill nodded. He turned toward Abigail. "Would you like some water?"

"Got something a little stronger back there?"

Bill smiled and confirmed she could have anything she wanted.

"Then, I'll have a scotch on the rocks. Get my heart going again."

"Good remedy for that," Bill enthused. "Hold out your hand." With the discreet wave of his wrist, the glass appeared in Abigail's right hand.

"Wow, quite the life."

"What about you, Tom. What would you like to drink?"

"Water will be fine."

A glass appeared in his hand.

"This is the best Scotch I've ever had. Who makes it?"

"Comes from Earth Optimal, as do all the things I conjure. On our version of Earth, everything we do is in the open, so it's not like stealing from anyone." Bill turned toward Emma, his smile gone. "Fred is going to be relieved that we don't have rogue aliens on our hands, liable to start an interstellar war."

"I don't know if the wizard situation isn't worse. Who are these people the wizards are flagging? Who belongs to those bodies? And why is there no residue left behind when I zap them?"

"All good questions I can't answer, Chavah. We'll have to put our heads together."

"This might mean your leader of the illegal trafficking of body parts you've been trying to nab is a wizard?"

"God, I hadn't thought of that."

Abigail had downed her Scotch, and while warmed up inside, the courage to talk welled up. "You can conjure all these things, travel between planets at the speed of thought, yet you can't find out anything about these ... wizards?"

"Conjuring is not difficult, Abigail. A lot of different races can make things appear out of thin air. Your granddaughter can."

"Bill," Emma breathed. She'd never told anyone except her father who had told her mother that she could materialize anything she wanted. And, she promised her father never to do that again.

"Sorry, Emma. Hadn't realized Tom and your grandmother didn't know about this."

Her grandmother sat there, interrupted from trying to suck the dregs of Scotch out of the ice cubes in her glass, her eyes and mouth competing for the most massive opening, mute in the process.

Tom put his water down and approached Emma, kneeling in front of her. "Wait a minute. You can make things appear out of thin air, anything?"

"Yes. I did it twice with dire consequences, and I promised myself I would never do this again. I promised my dad too."

Abigail's turn to react. "Your dad knows about this?"

"Both he and my mom know. He also made me promise never to tell anyone, and I never did."

Emma turned her eyes toward Bill who had left the scene of the drama he caused and seemed miles away talking on his phone with someone.

"Why did you stop conjuring?" Tom asked.

"Because it's taking things out of the fabric world we live in."

"Meaning?"

"If I conjure a car, let's say. Where am I going to get it? Yes, I can make it appear, but where do I get it? From some garage lot somewhere? This garage will report the car missing, and accusations, legalities will take hold. Someone might even be accused of stealing the vehicle."

"Oh, yeah. I thought you could make it from scratch. You're right. You need to get it somewhere."

"Oh, my God," her grandmother kept saying. "My granddaughter can conjure. Oh, my God!"

Bill was returning to their area, catching the last bit of conversation. "Abigail, you know that you can't ever tell anyone about this."

"I've loyally kept all of my granddaughter's secrets, even when my friends brag about their grandchildren. I would never break that trust. I don't understand why she never told me."

"I promised Dad, Grandma."

Emma Willis Book 3, I Can Help You

Tom rose and sat down beside Emma. "I can understand how touchy this might be—this conjuring. And it's not out of thin air. Whatever materializes is part of the resources we own—someone owns. I mean even if you took money from a bank, they would want to know where the funds disappeared. They might even blame some poor schmuck for the theft. Tricky."

"Exactly. Not anything to brag about, which is why I didn't tell you."

Tom wrapped his arm around her shoulders. "Yeah, well, you're off the hook."

"Thank you." She smiled at him nudging in closer.

Bill's broad smile suddenly made her uncomfortable. "You know how to conjure without taking things out of the universe, right?"

"Do I want to know?" Emma tried to silence him with her dubious tone.

Bill chuckled, and told her, "You tell me after I tell you."

Emma caught Tom and her grandmother's renewed interest, wondering what Bill's explanation might be to gain anything they wanted while avoiding theft from the universe.

"Simple, Emma. Earth Optimal has an unlimited supply of anything you wish to have while all things, possessions as you would call them, belong to Earth Optimal. They are yours for the taking. Think of it as materializing anything you wish, on demand."

"Wow!" Tom sprinted to his feet. "So, I could have a new

car, any fancy car I want?"

"Of course. All Emma has to do is order the car you want from Earth Optimal."

Emma rolled her eyes as she shook her head. "Bill, what are you doing to me? How am I ever going to educate the people I love to understand that life is not about the accumulation of wealth and resources? Life is about building friendships and long-lasting loyalties, and experiencing passion in what we do and who we are."

"Well, you're not going to tell anyone else, and I'm sure this might come in handy someday. I also realize that the two people on each side of you do not believe in amassing resources or wealth as you put it. They are passionate about what they do and who they are. Am I right?" He eyed Abigail. Then he glanced at Tom.

Both agreed immediately, nodding positively.

"Now," Bill continued, "Would you like something to eat with your water, Tom."

"I could use a cup of coffee—and a sticky bun."

"Good." Bill turned toward Emma. "Would you like to do the honors. Remember where you get this."

Emma blew strands of hair out of her face and gave Bill her most reproving, narrowed eyes. She didn't quite understand why he was doing this, but she went along with the gag.

She closed her eyes for a second and conjured coffee and a sticky bun for Tom. Both appeared on the coffee table in front of him.

Audible sighs came out of both people sitting beside her.

Bill eyed Abigail and added, "Now, do you understand how powerful your granddaughter is? She didn't even have to wave her hand."

Bill winked at Emma. Perhaps someday she would understand why he'd revealed this power of hers. For now, she pinched her lips not to laugh outright at the adoration on her grandmother's face or Tom's smug air of contentment as though the power also belonged to him. In a way it did. She prayed he wouldn't exercise his boyfriend privileges too often.

Joss Landry

— Thirty-One —

A Cross To Bear

Emma was invited to number eleven Center Place, the FBI Newark offices, to help identify the man she called Mort Vandel. Too many results showed up in their search for a name, and without an address or some other pertinent information, they would not be able to identify this person.

She showed up after her class, Monday morning, and wished Tom was by her side. In class until late afternoon on Mondays, he asked her to postpone the viewing, but Emma was in a hurry to get this done.

She came in the front door and found Bill Frost in conversation with a senior officer, one who looked familiar. The minute Bill spotted her, he welcomed her with a big smile and led the way to his office.

"I thought we would be more private here to discuss whatever we need to talk about rather than meeting in the screening room."

He opened a few books for her and slid to her his laptop computer to show what he'd found in the FBI's online databases.

Regaling in two cups of coffee, Emma spent an hour going through a couple of books and some of the information Bill logged on his computer.

"None of these men is the one I saw in Brian's room, or at the reservation that day." Emma took a sip of her coffee. "Are these one hundred and twenty-five people the only Mort Vandel's you found?"

"The only ones alive and kicking, liable to immobilize a young teenage boy. I mean, Brian is pretty big for his age and feisty. I doubt the man would be older than sixty."

"Yes, but if a wizard inhabited this man, he could have been much older and still strong enough to subdue Brian."

"You're right. The last wizard I encountered threw Hank against a wall as though he were nothing other than a peanut shell."

"Can I see all the pictures you have?"

"You ready to go through another hundred and fifty clips?"

"Do we have a choice? It will go fast. I have a detailed photo in my mind."

"Did you talk to Fred about the situation?"

"Yes, this morning before my class, I told Professor Rappaport."

"What was his reaction?"

"Not what I expected. I thought Fred would be furious, pace up and down. No. He just sat at his desk with a distant look on his face. Never said a word. I had a class, so I had to go." Emma shrugged as she dug in to view another group of pictures.

Before she did, she took in her surroundings. "I like what you've done with your office. Small but cheery. All these framed pictures of Jeannie and the kids make the place lively."

"Thank you, Emma. Jeannie had a hand in this."

Emma chuckled. Before she could buckle down to observe another batch of photos, a strange sound drew her attention. "Do you have a McCaw hidden somewhere?"

Bill laughed. "No. Fred's calling card." Bill picked up his phone. "I push number nine he knows he can enter. I push number one he cannot."

Emma didn't need to ask which number he pressed as Fred's projection appeared in front of Bill's desk.

"Emma, I hoped you would be here."

Fred turned toward Bill. "Dig up all the deceased Mort Vandel's you can find. Have Emma scan those pictures." He addressed Emma. "Emma, the Mort Vandel you spotted in Brian's room, and at the South Mountain Reservation on Saturday is a dead man. That was why there were no thoughts you could read."

Emma felt her heart skip a beat. She could hardly believe this. "A wizard operating within a deceased person? Impossible. I couldn't scan his mind because of the wizard, right?"

"No." Fred stared at Bill, imparting the Seraph to do as he requested. The senior agent nodded and reached for an other type of registry held in another cubicle. "I sorted these pictures, regrouped them and put them aside thinking them utterly useless."

He handed the small album to Emma, and she could not stop her hands from shaking, trembling when she took the black binder, still trembling when she flipped to the first page. A strange fear inside her made her recheck all the photos on that first page, glad she had not encountered what she realized Fred expected. For some reason, proving Fred wrong would serve to recuperate some of her sanity. The wizards encroached on all their lives these days, and she didn't know if she could withstand another problem in that area.

The second page did not bring up any recognizable photos either, and she continued to the third page thinking she had one more page to go and she was home-free.

On the last page of the little photo album, third row, fourth picture from the left, she found Mort Vandel. There was no mistaking him. Mort was the man in Brian's room, and the one she encountered getting out of the driver's seat at the South Mountain Reservation lake. Staring at Fred and Bill, Emma handed Bill the book, keeping her finger on the picture. "This is the one. I'm sure of it."

Bill nodded as he eyed Fred. "Mort Vandel, 1919 - 1951. How did you know, Fred?"

"Emma's description of the empty mind. The bodies residual forms remain as they were, propelled only by a soul and the wizards' will."

"Fred, how is this possible?"

Fred stared at Emma. "Remember the astral path, the one with the oleander gate, the one you traveled when searching the heavens for your father, where you almost got trapped indefinitely?"

Emma nodded. "Yes. Thousands upon thousands of little flames burning, waiting. I rescued my uncle when I located his flame, brighter than the others." Emma rose to walk toward the window. "My God, Fred. Are these flames bits of human souls?"

She turned to stare at him reading his thoughts, and she found confirmation to her question. "Can't be." Then Emma remembered Hank's appraisal of his experience with the wizards. "Yes, I fought them, and I won. Only when the wizards leave a person, they take with them fragments of our essence, which was how I got lost." What Hank called essence was a part of his soul. "Fred, how can that be? How do you know?"

"A few years ago when I approached you, partly because of Eivan Baker junior, but also because the universe's count of the souls of this cluster was off by a million or so souls. The discrepancy forbids us to form a loop with the other echoes to become one and join in Nirvana."

"How can people function without their soul? Impossible."

"Well, to people like Mort Vandel, deceased, they don't realize someone is running around with their soul while having copied their residual form—the one they enjoyed while they were alive. A soul is like any of your other organs."

Emma thought aloud. "A partial liver transplant will regrow and regenerate in each of the donor and recipient," Emma formulated.

"Yes. Except that the soul will never fail to do this. Therefore, even if someone were out in this world with Hank's body and soul, his body maneuvered by wizards, our Hank would never realize this. His soul is complete and the same that it was before the capture. However, the universe counts these as two souls instead of one."

"No." Emma's prompt derived from thoughts she read in Fred's mind. "You can't seriously contemplate destroying all of these alternate timelines."

"What is she talking about, Fred?" Bill's tone brooked no leeway.

Emma answered when Fred would not. "Fred, the pathfinder agrees with me. She says destroying the range of these echoes from beginning to end might bring catastrophic results to our world."

"Nonsense. The destruction would restore our current timeline while allowing it to breathe."

Bill spoke up. "You would be killing billions of people, Fred. There has to be another way."

"Billions of people that were never supposed to be. Not killing, simply erasing."

"By erasing them, where would their souls go? Souls cannot die or become erased, can they?" Emma wondered.

Fred appeared stumped for the next few seconds.

Bill chuckled. "How will that fare with your discrepancy on the count of souls?"

"Once the timelines are gone you will be left with ten times the discrepancy you and the universe encountered," Emma said.

"Emma's got you there, Fred. You can't always kill people to get to where you're going. You and I, and Emma, all want the same thing. We are working to have this version of Earth reunite with the planets and universes invited to participate in Nirvana."

"So, how do you suggest we go ahead?" Fred eyed Emma as though daring her to come up with a solution.

"Well, as a last resort, I was thinking I could go back in time, with Eivan Baker's permission, and find a way to prevent him from starting this project. To lure him to accept my proposal, I thought we might invite him to Earth Optimal. This is where Anne Ripley Hanover reincarnated, isn't it?"

"Yes. Annemarie lives on Earth Optimal. Although I don't advise you to take on such measures."

"Why not? Fred, Emma's got a brilliant plan. One that will work in our favor." Bill's outrage resounded in his tone.

"Chavah, once you make that change, you will come back to a future you will not recognize."

"What do you mean?"

"There will be no Eivan Baker, and who knows what else will have changed since you will need to go back two years."

"Can I preview some of the scenarios?"

Fred shook his head side to side. "Once you have succeeded in eliminating the swelling of those other alternate worlds, you will return to this time frame, and chances are you will not remember the current timeline. Part of you will remember certain fragments, but mostly, you will accept the changes as done, not quite understanding from where your impressions of loss originate."

Emma realized Fred scored the last victory.

He continued. "Everything you have learned in the last two years, every road you have chosen, all that you are ... liable to change."

"Everything I learned? As in where I come from, my relationship with Tom?"

"Yes. I can't promise the relationship will remain the same. No one can."

Emma walked to the desk and eyed Fred. "To come back to those souls in the astral world. Can you verify the tally of one of the errant souls?"

"Perhaps."

"When I attended one of Elizabeth Reardon's classes a couple of weeks ago, I was overcome with a strong smell of honeysuckle. When everyone left, and the scent remained, I spotted the wizard in her. With the pretext of showing her my jeweled oudjat, I was able to destroy the wizard. I witnessed him exiting Elizabeth and blowing up into little crystals that promptly disappeared."

"I'll check to see if she is the owner of another soul that would be trapped by wizards."

Bill smiled. "Emma, if you can do this, we can get rid of the sons of bitches."

Fred added, "If she remembers once she changes the past."

Emma sensed a little anger mounting inside her. "You know, Fred we never truly investigated the worth of Eivan Baker's infernal machine. You and I were more intent on shutting down the project than examining its value, right?"

"Worthless."

"You know this for a fact?"

"Yes."

"Fred?" Bill asked in his no-nonsense tone. "Even were you to gather these souls, the flames trapped by the wizards, How would you explain them to the universe?"

"Souls would automatically attach themselves to their original owners without causing any problems or changes whatsoever."

"In other words, we simply need to get them out of the wizard's hands."

"Yes." Fred turned toward Emma. "I will take my leave now and consider what you said about Elizabeth Reardon, and about the souls unable to be erased."

"Thank you." Emma smiled to lighten the air between them, although she realized Fred or Bill would never hold grudges or be upset. They did their job to the best of their knowledge.

"I'll give you more information on Mort Vandel as soon as I retrieve it, Emma," Bill laid a hand on her shoulder. "Go home and get some rest. You deserve it."

When Emma got home, the house was empty. Her mother and father were working, and Tom was at the university. No one present with whom she might echo her fears. Even so, she hesitated to talk to them about all this. Although, thanks to Bill's faux pas, her grandmother and Tom now knew of her ability to conjure. She could also conjure without worry, bringing all things and items from Earth Optimal. So much had changed because of Eivan Baker's arrival on the scene.

The whole mess only served to depress her. She didn't want her life to revert to ignorance—at least, not if it meant possessing less information than she did now. Mostly, she loved her relationship with Tom. He was her rock, the love of her life. Not to mention how Emma held renewed strength in having discovered her heritage, her mother's collaboration in this heritage, an enchanting development to say the least. Destroying two years of her life would mean all this new information she considered vital might no longer exist—even something as small as Tom's new car.

Tears poured out of her, and she didn't know how to stop them. The only happy stance in all of this, one that forced her to brush her tears away, was the fact that Brian Hayes and his mom were free. Those vile men destroyed, Brian no longer had to do their bidding, and the two could leave for Iowa and live a happy life. FBI agents had arrested Thornton Hayes, and Hank mentioned the man could not unload fast enough about the people he knew and their crooked activities. Arrests were issued while Bill and Tim set traps in several European countries as well as within the United States.

However, would this situation be resolved if she reshaped the future by going to the past? Or would Brian still be trapped in the hell his father fabricated?

Perhaps if she asked Columba, the Pathfinder might have some solution for her. She closed her eyes, crossed her hands on each shoulder and flew to the astral world. Once under the vast blue dome, she called for Columba. A few seconds later, the beautiful pathfinder stood before her.

They communicated silently through their thoughts. "I have a problem, Columba. It appears the only way I can stop these alternate worlds from invading our space is by going back and destroying two years of my past."

"Seriously?"

"Yes. Fred stated that while he can eliminate billions of people, he might not be able to erase their souls, which means unaccounted souls would exist in our universe, at least ones that wouldn't belong anywhere. Aside from giving the wizards access to easy prey, the errant souls might create a huge discrepancy that would prevent us from merging all echoes successfully."

"Emma, I'm truly sorry. However, Fred should have mentioned that the souls from these other realities will find their original owner and mend with them. No discrepancies."

"What about those that cannot find their counterparts, living or otherwise?"

"They will simply return to the Source where they will be prepared to take proper form on any of Earth's versions."

"Strange. I specifically asked Fred if he could erase billions of souls, and my question appeared to stump him. He left, promising he would ask and work to discover the answer."

"Fred's hesitation is strange. Unlike him to give false testimony." Columba smiled. "How can I help you, sweet Chavah?"

"I thought you might have a suggestion. Someway to have me remember my past, or keep it intact, as it is now."

"I wish I could. I'm sure you considered all the information this stint of Eivan Baker brought into your life, the star of Capella, your relationship with Tom, and your doctorate, everyone and everything you have encountered. The only place I might be able to help you is once you are in the past, you might no longer remember how to return to the future, as this is something you learned only recently."

"What can you do?"

"If you give me the exact coordinates you fly to, I will make sure to scan the area and bring you back to your own time."

"Is there nothing else I can do?"

"I'm afraid not. My powers are limited, Emma." Columba

smiled as she added, "One thing is certain, your idea will make all this pain go away. I admire your devotion. And, I don't quite know what we would do without you."

Emma smiled, knowing Columba's boon was meant to give her courage. She waved as she left. When she opened her eyes at home, she cried for all the ways her life would be different.

No one liked changes. But some of the differences would include vital pieces of knowledge that would disappear while she didn't know if they would ever return. In all the other timelines, two small differences occurred to alter the use of her powers as though they never existed.

Even if she confided in Tom, when destruction of the past indelibly modified the future, Tom would change also. A sacrifice she wished someone would remove, yet, a cross she realized she needed to bear.

Emma Willis Book 3,
I Can Help You

—Thirty-Two—

Fred Is Illogical

Emma waited for Tom to come home. She didn't want to interrupt his work, but at the same time, she needed his male presence in her life. After spending most of the afternoon studying, she called him just before dinner time.

"Hey, Tom. Do you have a lot of work to do tonight?"

"Some. I accomplished a lot yesterday. How did it go at the FBI?"

"There is something I need to discuss with you. Can you come over for dinner?"

"You never have to ask me twice. You know that. Your parents don't mind?"

"No, of course not. The folks don't mind if you stay over, either."

"Well, this is a little more difficult for me to do, but I'll see how things go with your dad."

When her parents came home, arriving at ten-minute intervals, Emma took the time to mention to her father that Tom would be over for dinner.

"On a Monday night? Doesn't he like to eat at home with

his father?"

"I invited him, Dad. I need him here tonight. Tomorrow I have to meet someone and, if all goes well, I'll have to go back two years in the past to destroy the alternate worlds created accidentally."

Patrick took the time to stop looking at the pile of mail on the hall desk, and turned toward Emma, taking her hands in his. "Can you do this and still enjoy the same life you have now?"

Emma's eyes rounded. She couldn't believe everyone thought of this detail when she tragically overlooked the problem when she first proposed the solution to Fred. She took a deep breath. "Yes. However, since I have to go back two years, traveling to the past may very well change my life—not that I'll realize any of it."

"Is there a way around this? Did you talk to Columba?"

"No. And yes, I asked her advice, and she confirmed there is nothing she can to do to assure me I will keep this same life."

"Sweetie. I'm sorry."

Her father's saddened expression appeared so genuine that Emma almost began to cry. She tapped into her resolve to remain positive and smiled instead. "Nothing will change for anyone else, at least, none of us will remember if they do. Plus, because I only learned to travel to the past and the future recently, I will give my coordinates to Columba, and she will make sure I can return home."

"Does Tom know about this?"

"No. I need to find a way to tell him."

"You two only got together last ..."

She nodded as her father did not continue his sentence.

"Well, I think he should not only have dinner with us, but he should also spend the night, at least for you two to work this out." He smiled. "Would you like me to extend an official invitation?"

Emma chuckled faced with her father's raised eyebrows. "Not necessary, Dad. Thank you."

Her mother brought dinner, fried chicken and all the trimmings. As delicious as the food was, the atmosphere around the table remained subdued. Her father stared at the chicken on his plate moving the pieces around before each bite, and Emma wondered if his silence meant he worried about saying something liable to make Tom uncomfortable. She realized he'd mentioned her dilemma to her mother as a permanent crease cropped Eloise's forehead, and the smile she always wore never showed up. Even when she offered Tom a second portion, her voice came out strained and teary.

Because of all these oddities, Tom shifted uncomfortably in his chair and appeared ready to flee. Emma pondered he might have already done so if he wasn't so tired and hungry. Tom eyed her father with an attempt at a smile. "By the way, my father's ecstatic over the three new clients Saturday's visit to the Hamptons procured him."

"Rudy mentioned it today. Glad I could help," her father answered without the courage to glance at Tom.

"When I left the house," Tom continued, "He'd already received calls from two referrals of these clients."

"That's wonderful."

Emma caught her father adding more coleslaw to his plate, and she suspected this was done so Patrick wouldn't have to face her young man. She turned to Tom. "Listen, I didn't want to mention anything here and now, but my parents already know, and their knowledge is what's creating the tension around the table. Has nothing to do with you."

Tom stopped eating and turned toward Emma, fear in his eyes. "Are you sick? Did someone die?"

"No." Putting her fork down, Emma told Tom what she had confessed to her father, giving him more details about Fred, and about the fact that their lives would not remain the same. "The changes will not appear different to any of us. No one will notice."

"All the things you've learned lately. They might all be gone."

"I realize this, but no one can help me. The only way to give our world a chance is to go back two years to prevent Eivan Baker from ever starting this project."

"God, the things I've learned. I know you can conjure. Wow!"

"What?" her father asked, his eyes bigger than quarters.

"Bill let it slip accidentally."

"And I went to Earth Optimal with your grandma. Now, we might never remember this."

Emma hoped telling Tom about her problem in front of her parents would excuse their odd behavior at dinner. All it did was put her on the spot, exposing the secrets she hadn't yet told them. She glanced at her mom, then at her dad, and said, "I'm sorry. I didn't have time to tell you yet. A threat occurred on Saturday night when Tom and I had dinner at Grandma's. I had to ship them to Earth Optimal. I destroyed five cats, wizards, in Grandma's backyard." She assessed that her dad and mom weren't angry or insulted, then she continued. "Bill Frost brought them back."

"Sweetheart," Eloise's tears glistened in the corner of her eyes. "What if you don't remember any of this?"

"Well, it's not as though I'll lose everything. It's only two years of my past."

"Wait a minute," Tom laid a hand on hers. "We only got together six months ago, after Christmas, before New-Years, and this was to celebrate the upgrade of your masters to a doctorate."

Emma nodded as she stared down at her plate. She had no courage to reassure Tom in front of her parents.

Patrick pushed his plate away. Emma caught that he hadn't eaten half what he usually did. "Listen, Tom. We're just going to have to hope for the best. After all, our real concern should be the success of Emma's trip. She's dallying with time, here. She'll need Columba's help to come back. Let's pray this solution works."

Emma could spot how Tom's nod wasn't convinced. He too pushed his plate away more upset than she figured he might be.

"Tom. Why not stay the night," her father said in his most friendly tone of voice. No hint of mockery. "The two of you can exchange ideas and work something out. What do you say?"

Tom glanced at Emma, surprise making his expression goofy. A little breathless that her dad brought their situation out in the open, he answered with hesitancy. "Sure, if this is okay with Emma. I'm sure we'll find a way around this."

At three o'clock in the morning, Emma wrapped in Tom's big arms still could not sleep. They'd debated the question left and right, discussing all angles while their preoccupations smothered their physical desire for one another.

"Maybe if I hold you tightly all night, I'll never forget being with you," Tom had muttered at one point, almost in tears.

Emma could not understand why Tom worried as much as he did. Then, she'd read his thoughts, a rare occasion between them—Tom being the one person in the world she found difficult to read.

He worried about one of the alternate realities she'd mentioned where he slept with Amelia while dreaming of being with Emma.

"Don't worry, Tom. The situation doesn't mean you'll end up at MIT with Amelia. You've found the purpose and the reasons for remaining at Rutgers. So that other side of your life is gone now."

"Remember that song your mother used to love? She would play it all the time, and I used to think it was the saddest song in the world. To me, songs need to be happy, motivating us to greatness or something. Otherwise, why be a song?"

"What song?"

"You know the one. This girl thinks this guy cheated on her, so they split. Then he tells her he has a wife, and for years they've been going strong, but at night he still sees her face when they make love."

"Ambrosia, *How Much I Feel*. I remember. Mom still hums it once in a while."

"Well, I don't know if there was ever some other great love in your mom's life for the song to strike her with such reality, but for me, the lyrics struck when you told me about Amelia and me sleeping together, in Cambridge. I never thought I could understand such a song. That day you told me about Amelia and me, I not only got the gist, but I also identified with the singer's desperation."

Now, Tom slept. Emma watched him and remembered the bitter words he'd mentioned just before falling asleep. "Won't even have my gorgeous car anymore, not that I'll know this. I'll be devoted to Rita and not realize I ever had an Audi named Trudy."

Unable to argue the point or reassure him—the Audi being a gift from an involuntary hook of those timelines—she'd hugged him for dear life. Then, Tom had fallen asleep.

Now, the side of her arm was numb, and she moved ever so slightly to retrieve her sore limb, not wanting to wake him. She was miserable, but Tom seemed to suffer worse misery than she did. She fell asleep wondering if Shad would understand if she didn't go back to visit him. She might not ever remember her home planet or the fact that her mother came from there also.

The next morning, Emma woke to find the space beside her empty. With an early lab on Tuesday mornings, the beep of Tom's watch undoubtedly woke him, not loud enough to elicit any response from her.

She stretched and came across a piece of paper on the pillow Tom used. She rubbed the sleep out of her eyes and read what he wrote.

'By the way, if I went to the past with you? Would that ensure we remain together? Please say yes. In any case, call me before you're about to take the plunge. Love you so much, my sweet Emma.'

Emma lied down on Tom's pillow stretching to put the paper on the nightstand. Even this note would be gone when she returned.

Unable to grab more rest, Emma rose and got ready for school. Today she was meeting with Professor Rappaport in his office. As for the three appointments she was scheduled to meet this afternoon, they would need to wait until Emma returned from her trip to the past. She might not even need to gather patient hours anymore. Who knew where this new life might take her? To someone who hated surprises, the disturbing thought turned her limbs to mush. She shoved it out of her mind. Nothing she could do would control the situation. She needed to accept whatever time threw her way.

Emma grabbed a muffin in the kitchen and filled the cup she carried with coffee. Both her parents were gone to work, and she flashed on how concerned her mother appeared to be last night—the proof of her mother's worry staring at her in the note she left pinned on the refrigerator door.

'Darling, whatever happens, your father and I are one hundred percent behind the decision you make. Always thinking of others, you rarely consider your feelings. Know that we are both proud of you and of who you have turned out to be. Love, mom, and dad.'

Emma smiled, dabbing at a tear in the corner of her eye. Best she refused to let them flow, or she would become a wreck.

The long corridors inside the familiar walls of Rutgers university cheered her up. She enjoyed the joyous groups of students walking and running to their classes. She saluted many friends on her way to Professor Rappaport's office, and each face she encountered, she attempted to stamp into memory.

Once the professor called out to enter, she did, sitting in

front of him and wondering if Fred had done due diligence with his investigation. Would he be able to stash the souls somewhere or keep them in limbo until some unspecified time in the future?

"Thank you for coming, Emma. I realize you have a crazy schedule today. I called Dr. Monroe letting him know that you would not be available for consultations this afternoon."

"Did you give him an update on the Brian Hayes case? I wanted to do this, but never had the chance."

"I did, Emma. I explained what had taken place, leaving out our dilemma, and he understood ... and is grateful you were able to help Brian. He and his mother have been whisked away to parts unknown."

"I thought they were headed to Iowa to stay with her sister."

"No. Hank didn't think it was safe for them there. Neither did Bill. I realized yesterday that there's an enormously large underworld dedicated to pedophilia. A group of them are even trying to amend the laws in the UK to acquire the right to pursue their cruelty."

"Unbelievable. What's this world coming to?"

"Well, when you consider the people that were molesting Brian were wizards, using deceased bodies, you understand a little more."

"What can we do to stop them?"

"Some people hold too much money, too much time on their hands, and then there are those who own too much entitlement."

"Entitlement?"

"High place leaders, rulers, monarchs. They are bored, and they are rich. They find their excitement in the forbidden. Never forget who they are, Emma or be impressed by what the world states they represent. They are mere shadows of darkness willing to lose their souls and the mere possibility of becoming more powerful."

"I will spend my lifetime stopping them any way I can."

"Strike without being observed. Bring the wizards down without warning, without letting them know who you are."

Emma thought she spotted a shiver run through Frank Rappaport. "I will. I promise."

He hesitated. "As per your suggestion, I went looking for the results of what might happen to the souls of the billions of people should we erase them from these timelines. You were right. The souls would remain. I was hoping you might be wrong—for your sake. Most souls will find their original counterparts and couple with them, without anyone being the wiser. A number of them, in the millions, will not find their counterparts."

"Why not?" Fred's answer did not mesh with Columba's statement. Emma remembered Columba's words, "They will simply return to the Source where they will be prepared to take proper form on any of Earth's versions."

"All those who never existed before this alternate life would be in danger of drifting into nothingness if the wizards don't grab them first. There are many—enough to draw our concerns." Fred hesitated. "You need to implement the plan I believe will change your life forever."

"The one time I hoped you were right, Dr. Rappaport. I did."

"I'm sorry, Emma. I wish I could help you. And, for your information, the Pathfinder does not know anything about souls and what happens to them."

"You read my mind. I hoped you would. I didn't wish to argue with you."

"When you return, I won't even suspect a difference. I may not be Dr. Franklin Rappaport." The professor smiled, and Emma could not chase away her doubts about his rendition of the facts. "Many things that occurred in the past two years are due to Eivan Baker's project. So, many differences will take place."

She nodded. She promised herself she would not wear the gloom she sensed envelop her. She smiled. "I'm ready for the changes, Dr. Rappaport. Thank you for helping me these last two years. All I need to do now is to contact Eivan Baker to gather his permission to retract two years of his life."

"Consulting with the boy is not something I recommend you do."

"I must."

"You must resolve the situation. I don't believe Eivan will give you that permission."

Emma didn't like part of the encryption she read in the

professor's mind. She rose abruptly. "I have to go. I have another class." She gave him a nod and walked to the door quickly, almost fearing he might stop her from going through with her plan.

As Emma was about to cross the threshold, Rappaport called out. "It is unwise to bring another human into this dilemma. You might be giving Eivan too much power to maneuver against the greater good."

Emma's only response was a slight pause as she considered Fred Manson's infallible logic. Of course, she did not believe his suggestion held merit.

—Thirty-Three—

Eivan Explains

Later, Emma communicated with Hank to find out if he still needed her help on the Brian Hayes' case.

"Thornton is pouring his heart out, Emma. We have gathered more information than we ever imagined possible. In return, we have agreed to an assault and battery charge against his wife."

"That's letting him off easy."

"He'll have to testify against these people, which means he'll be looking over his shoulder for the rest of his life. I wouldn't wish that on anyone."

"Isn't the FBI going to offer him witness protection?"

"Only during the trial. After that, Thornton's on his own."

"That's why you put his wife and son in protective custody."

"Yep. Brian and his mother are the ones who matter. Bill has set them up superbly. I'll tell you all about it, but not over the phone."

"I understand, Hank. So, since you don't need me, I'm off to rewind the past for the last two years."

A long pause followed her statement, and Emma sensed

one of Hank's fears. "This should not affect your second-born, Jarred, Hank. The birth of your sweet baby has nothing to do with Eivan Baker or what's happened in the last little while."

"Thank you, sweetie. Bill informed me of your generous offer yesterday morning. Christina and I spent the whole night discussing the situation, worrying about you and Tom, and about you losing the knowledge of all you've learned recently."

"No matter how I study the situation, there doesn't appear to be any other way to make things right."

"The worst part in all this is Brian and Lorna Hayes. Once the two-year curtain is pulled back, they may be trapped in the same hell as they were with Thornton on the loose, collaborating with evil minions all over the earth."

A huge sigh escaped Emma. "I asked Columba if there was some way we could send ourselves a message in a bottle or something."

"What did she say?"

"She didn't know of any. She did volunteer to come and get me in the past since I only learned to travel in time recently."

"Oh, Emma. Both Christina and I wish we could help you bear this cross."

"Hank. You have your problems. Don't worry about me. I'll resolve the situation. You take care of Christina and those wonderful boys."

Emma hung up the phone. To pursue the conversation

would only bring more heartache, make the task at hand a mountain she might not be able to climb. Fingering her phone to get her messages, Emma spotted one from Tom. As cold as she interpreted the decision to be, she decided not to call him back—another situation liable to make her weak and vulnerable to her fears, some of them real doozies. Aside from the one of not having Tom in her life, Emma worried about not having this new oudjat. How would she fare against the wizards without it? Would she remember about her home planet?

Emma closed her cell phone. She wanted no interruptions for what she was about to do. Emma took up a stall in the women's facilities at Rutgers University and counted to three as Emma called upon the universe to help her materialize on the front steps of the Essex County Hospital Center in Cedar Grove. A vast shaded area existed by the door, and she made sure no one spotted her. She entered the reception area and asked to see Eivan Baker.

"Is he expecting you?"

"I believe he is." Emma had mentioned to Eivan that she would drop by to see him, but neither of them had defined a specific time.

"I'll check to see if he is available. Afternoon visits are rare as patients are usually in session or assigned varied projects."

Emma regretted not having called ahead especially that the receptionist needed a good five minutes to locate Eivan.

When she did, and she mentioned the name of the person wanting to see him, the response came back affirmative.

"Eivan is in the courtyard. He says he's been waiting for you. I'll have an orderly escort you." The woman smiled and indicated where Emma could wait.

Emma sat down in a blue suede chair and stroked the soft armrest as she wondered why Eivan said he waited for her. She hadn't told him when she'd be here.

Her question would have to wait as the orderly stood in front of her. "This way please," he said, jolting her out of her thoughts.

Emma followed him to the courtyard. Flagstone flooring covered most of the large garden's trails, bordered with a great variety of flowers. Red finches, blue jays, and common yellowthroats flew over the area in droves, singing their joyous songs. Honey locust trees, intermixed with older white lilac trees provided a full bay where people could sit on wooden benches protected from the glare of summer sun by leafy arms extended overhead.

Eivan looked up when she approached, deposited his book on the seat beside him and stood to greet her. A warm smile played on his features as he waited for Emma to catch up.

When she did, the orderly left. Emma extended her arm to shake Eivan's hand, but he came forward and embraced her instead, planting a kiss on both her cheeks. "I've missed you, Emma Willis."

Joss Landry

Surprised by his gesture, her raised eyebrows made him laugh, and Emma couldn't vouch for the sincerity of this warm welcome.

"Beautiful garden," she exclaimed. "How far back does it go?"

"Quite a ways. Only, patients here never go the distance. Rumors of moaning ghosts back there keep them close to the building."

Emma stumbled face to face with the stories on her first trip there. They weren't rumors. She wondered if Fred mentioned the problem to Columba, and drew a mental note to do so, but then she might not remember this either upon her return.

"By the way, my stepfather, Steve Lemon, past away last night. His heart failed and no one could revive him."

"I'm sorry to hear that. Please, offer your mom my sincere condolences." Emma worried the wizards most likely possess a piece of the good reverend's soul.

"To what do I owe the honor of an Emma Willis visit?" Eivan bowed from the waist, and with the sweep of his arm, indicated the bench behind him.

Emma thought his gesture somewhat sarcastic but didn't mind Eivan letting off steam. A brilliant mind such as his, cooped up in this place, needed to find ways to entertain himself. "Well, I need to ask you for a favor."

Eivan plopped down on the bench abruptly, as though her words winded him. "A favor? You?"

She nodded. Remembering where she stood, she looked around and spotted others coming their way. "Let's walk toward those lilacs. The scent is intoxicating."

"Sure." He grabbed his book and followed her lead to one of the more massive trees in the garden.

Once safely hidden behind the big tree's trunk, Emma took Eivan's hand. "I need to bring you somewhere. Is that okay?" Emma realized shocking Eivan with her powers would all be erased when she changed the past. Her actions needed no explanation or preparation. And for now, she needed the element of surprise on her side, if only to convince him to agree to erase two years of his work.

He smiled. "I'm ready."

Eivan should have questioned her statement, or at least showed surprise. She was once more the one left wondering about his intentions.

She looked around making sure they were invisible to everyone there. "We need to go somewhere private where we can talk."

"I'm ready." Then as though to reassure her, he said, "The astral world is beautiful all year 'round."

More questions Emma didn't have time to consider. She invoked the little sentence, and both found themselves sitting on a cloud under a big blue dome.

"Blue roof, puffy little clouds as soft chairs ... how do you shape the astral world to be what you needed it to be?"

"Thought process," she answered a little peeved. The element of surprise she hoped might rally Eivan to permit her to erase his two-year-long project would not hold. "Who are you? And how do you know about the astral world?" Staring at him while waiting for an answer, Emma suddenly read his mind and realized Eivan was no ordinary human being. "You can read my mind," she told him breathlessly.

"Yes, I can. I can read most minds, even the sophisticated thoughts of a fifth dimension Chavah."

"You're not from here, are you?"

"Before I answer, I'm still waiting for you to ask me for that favor."

"You already know what I am about to ask you. I need to know who you are."

Eivan laughed a strange sound that made her shiver. "Of course, I know what you're going to ask me. My curiosity pertained to how you might word the request for a man, an unstable man at that, to destroy two years of his life, annihilate the time as though he never existed."

"Erase time, not you."

"I am my work. The work is a part of me, the main part of me."

"Then you are also aware that you created five other timelines that are growing at an alarming speed. Their growth could implode this whole cluster."

"They will not touch your world—this cluster or any other cluster."

"Explain, please."

Emma Willis Book 3, I Can Help You

"I deliberately created an echo within an echo, five separate echoes to be precise. The shape is a pentagon, and although I will not explain the meaning of the numbers present in a pentagon, I will tell you that I did this on purpose. No accident."

"What do you mean about the numbers present in a pentagon?"

"I could give you a detailed mathematical analysis, and I'm quite sure you would understand and find the knowledge fascinating. The explanation would take us a full hour and more. To save time, in all figure of speeches, I will sum up by confirming that the numbers contained in a pentagon add up to human weakness, man's lawlessness, and an overall penchant toward atheism. In other words, a pentagon is a perfect symbol to attract evil, or what you call wizards."

"So, I was right. You built your construct to kill wizards."

"Yes. And you're thinking, why didn't Fred recognize this?"

Emma nodded.

"Fred hates me. He hates all Quatars."

"Near Saudi Arabia?"

"No. Quatar the planet, in another universe."

"Another universe. How many are there?"

"Don't know. More than one. When our universe created planets, two of them turned out to be identical: Quatar and Polaris, sister planets. Over the next millennium, both grew in population and knowledge. Quatar devoted its time toward mathematics, science and understanding the ways of the

Creator. Polaris grew to research emotions and the understanding of the heart and the many elements that fabricate those emotions."

"In other words, you grew apart."

"Yes. Quatars would travel to Polaris with a single thought. Having learned to conjure, we brought gifts every time we visited."

"People of Polaris began to envy you. Thus jealousy prompted their actions."

"Polarians stopped coming to Quatar, and our scientist told us to expect the worst. Finally, one thousand of our best scientists rounded up the means to leave their home planet. It was not easy to do." Eivan stopped as though remembering a little more. "They reunited in a big ship they propelled through thought."

"What about the others, the ones remaining on Quatar?"

"They agreed to share all they knew with our neighbors. Their knowledge was not on par with the scientists who left. They thought their lack of knowledge would contain our friends the Polarians from using what we learned scientifically into emotional upheaval."

"How do you cross a universe?"

"Well, Quatars didn't realize that their planet stood at the edge of their universe. When they propelled themselves through the universe's border, they were jolted many galaxies away into another universe. My great, great grandfather said when they arrived here, all they spotted in this system were the sight of bright filaments. When examining the space a little closer, they discovered many other filaments, some less colorful, some veritably dull and hardly visible at all. When they processed the information through their mathematical computers, they discovered the filaments to be echoes or particles of what once belonged to a huge planet, ten times the size of Quatar."

"Earth."

"Most scientists decided to join the brightest filaments they could find. My ancestors and a little over one hundred of their followers opted to land on the dullest filament they found with the purpose of helping them shine. Since then, my grandfathers, my father, and I have been trying to rid this cluster of evil."

"Your ancestors aren't still alive, are they?"

"Yes, but they've been hoisted to Earth Optimal by Devronairs."

"How do you know about Devron? More importantly, how do they know about you?"

"Devron is a planet in our old universe. Lo and behold when my ancestors came here, they realized a Devron planet existed in this universe as well."

"How can that be?"

"They are much more advanced than most of us realize, I guess. Devronairs blamed Quatar for the feud with Polaris. Since Devronairs seem to have appointed themselves as guardians of both universes, they sometimes forget not to judge. As you know, judgment is bound by prejudice and interpretation."

"Quite right. Although some Devronairs can read minds, no one can visualize what conspires in the human heart."

"Except for a fifth dimension Chavah, who knows better than to pass judgment."

Emma smiled. "Okay, so what do we do about our problem. I, for one, hate the idea of going back two years to prevent you from beginning your quest. I have a lot to lose in the process, and I would much rather not destroy your life's work—or two years of mine." Emma thought for a bit. "Are you what we call a hybrid child?"

"Yes. The first in my line. My father married a human. I'm lucky I retained most of my father's mathematical prowess." Eivan took something out of his pant pocket. "Take a look at this gizmo."

"What is this? All I see is thirty-eight percent, I think. Numbers are small."

"You are correct. The number of evils trapped in the pentagon I created."

"No! That is amazing. I mean one hundred percent would be better, but this is amazing. And they are trapped there?"

"Yes. All I have to do is press this button, and those worlds cease to exist as do the wizards."

"Where did you find this?"

"I built it." He pointed to his neck. "A friend implanted a nanoparticle behind my right cochlea."

"Through the tympanic membrane?"

"Yes. I just asked my friend to remove it. When he did, I continued to get the information, externally, on the number of wizards entering the pentagon. Once they enter, they are trapped and cannot leave to warn the others."

"You're getting this through the apparatus, right?"

"Yes. It's exciting. Once I press this tiny red button, the pentagon will disappear, and thirty-eight percent of the wizards will be destroyed."

"What about all those people and their souls? Where will they go? And how will your destruction affect our echoes?"

"The people in this pentagon are nothing but mirrors. They do not exist. Their duality does, elsewhere on other filaments, which is why Optimal Earthlings have begun to sense this duality. Once the pentagon is destroyed, whatever souls cannot find their original counterpart will move toward the Source where they will be repaired and reprocessed."

"That's what Columba told me." Emma stared into Eivan's deep green eyes. "However, Fred has maintained that the souls who cannot find their duality will perish, or risk being taken over by wizards."

"He is lying to you. Perhaps he wishes my project destroyed at all cost."

"That doesn't sound like Fred. He is not a prevaricator, especially with matters of this importance. There has to be another reason." Emma rose to prepare to leave. "I understand how you feel about Devronairs. Would you be willing to come with me and talk to Fred?"

Eivan hesitated. He took a deep breath and gave her a slight nod. "I won't let him intimidate me. I'll go with you."

"Can you let me do the talking?"

"Meaning, you don't want me to insult him." Eivan smiled. "I promise to behave."

Destruction

Traveling through the astral world, Emma brought Eivan with her to meet Dr. Rappaport, also known as Devronair, Fred Manson.

She knocked on his door and breathed a little relief when he told her to enter. First, she did so, slowly. Moving aside toward his desk, she allowed him to cast his eyes on Eivan Baker who came in behind her.

Fred rose and lost his poise. "What is this man doing here?"

"He is with me. I told him about the problem his machine caused." Emma waited for Fred's remonstration. When no words came, she added, "Eivan meant to draw a pentagon with echoes of our echoes, Fred. He specifically drew the five-sided geometric figure to attract the wizards—trap them inside."

"Fred exhaled loudly and said, "I know."

"You do? You would have allowed me to destroy two years of my life. Worse, you would have forced the release of thirty-eight percent of this cluster's wizards back into our world. Why the duplicity?" Emma attempted to prevent the shakes from taking over her body, but couldn't quite pull this off.

"Please, both of you sit down."

Emma did, wrapping her arms around herself. When Eivan took a seat, he first laid an arm around Emma's shoulders looking into her eyes, communicating not to worry, and that everything would be all right.

Eivan had promised her he would not speak, and Emma realized he waited for Fred's explanation, hands steepled, eyes avoiding direct contact with the man facing him.

"Believe me, Emma," Fred answered while he stared at his hands. "To detect close to forty percent of the wizard body reintegrate our Earth cluster would be devastating. Still, the high council of Devron held a meeting with your ancestors, Eivan, on Earth Optimal. Your ancestors have agreed to help us grow this number to sixty percent. We have accepted their cooperation and look forward to their precious help."

Eivan smiled. "And here I thought you hated us, Devronair."

"We are incapable of hating anyone, Quatar. Our program is a simple one. To take on the battles and help those who are vulnerable and unaware of how the world turns, how the universe proceeds. This was why we came to the rescue of Polarians. Not because we thought you exploited them, but because they happened to be in a dire situation due to their follies. Many of your race understood this, why they packed up and left, to allow the Polarians to grow and become more substantial beings."

"Well, this is not the way I understood how the confrontation happened, as told by my ancestors," Eivan scoffed with a rigid smile.

"The human side of you misunderstood. It is natural since you have no way of knowing that on Devron, there is no judgment. We merely distribute the help where it is needed. If Emma goes back to erase your project, your father agreed to trap sixty percent of the wizards for elimination."

Eivan could not hide his surprise any longer. "You would encounter the same problems."

"No. Your father and grandfather admired your pentagon, Eivan. They have since streamlined the project so that no one would become affected by the other timelines. In other words, these alternate worlds would be invisible to everyone else here on Earth."

Emma could not contain her outrage. "These measures would not give me back two years of my life. Why take all these chances of building this contraption again? Because you wished to erase two years of my life? Why?"

Fred hesitated. Emma found Fred's hesitancy awkward, inappropriate. She worried he might never tell her the truth.

Eivan reached for her hand and gave the ice-cold limb a warm squeeze. "Tell her what you know, Man from Devron. You owe this Chavah the truth."

The barb appeared to jab Fred's awareness, and he nodded agreeing with Eivan's request. He rose and circled his desk to sit closer to the two youngsters with worry painted on their faces. "I looked into your request about Elizabeth Reardon's encounter with the wizard."

"And?"

"The good news is that there is no discrepancy of souls regarding her. The wizard disappeared, died, without bringing back a piece of her soul."

"Thank God for little miracles. One saved."

"Yes, and this event would likely have gone unnoticed."

"What's that supposed to mean?"

"Remember the five cats in your grandmother's garden?"

Emma nodded. She sensed Eivan's hand tightening his grip slightly around hers. "How did you hear about this?"

"Please." Fred didn't have to say. She figured Bill told him. "Well, the wizards now know who you are. They will band together to take you out."

"They can't. I have my oudjat."

"They can get close to you and your oudjat through a loved one, anytime, anywhere, in any place of their choosing."

"Oh, my God." Emma remembered how terrified she was wizards might harm the people she loved were she to take them out. Then, she ignored their threat and proceeded to eliminate them anyway. "They tried to intimidate me before. I didn't let them. I have no intention of allowing them to scare me now."

"Except that now, they realize you can kill them outright. It's one thing to interfere with the wizards' plans when their minions can still bring back a piece of a human's soul. They could still walk away with a part of their essence. It's quite another problem when you erase them and prevent them from collecting the souls they seek." Fred took a deep breath. "Keep this up, and their number will dwindle dramatically."

"What about Eivan's contraption. His machine is much worse. Are they also after him?"

"Eivan has agreed to go to Earth Optimal. They can't touch him there."

Eivan's surprise came through. "Is this why my ancestors and my father are on Earth Optimal? To prevent the evil from attacking them?"

Fred nodded. "Emma, you can also live on Earth Optimal with your father and mother, and with Tom and your grandmother."

"What about Tom's father, and his aunt? What about Hank Apple, Christina Tyler, and their two children, my aunt Franka and Jimmy and their two children? My best friend, Amelia?"

"We need Hank in this cluster. As for your aunt and uncle, they also need to remain here for now."

"I can't go to Earth Optimal and leave these people behind. My mother and father won't want to leave Earth knowing Franka can't come, and there would be nothing to stop the wizards from attacking the people I love. At least when I'm here, I can prevent the attack."

"Yes. So far you can sense the creatures through sight and olfactory senses. They may work on changing these facts."

Eivan touched her arm. "Can you detect wizards through

scent and sight?"

"Yes. I can."

"Fred, old man, this changes everything. "I'm staying on Earth Refuse. I'm not afraid of those creatures. I intend to kill them all if I have to. And if you have my back, Fred," he turned toward Emma. "You also, then we'll watch out for each other. We'll whip them good."

Emma smiled through her tears. She turned toward Fred with a smile on her face. Placing a gentle hand on his, she was surprised to encounter a limb underneath hers. "Was this the reason you wanted me to erase two years of my life? To get the wizards off my back?"

"Yes. No one deserves that kind of pursuit. Trust me. You don't know the wizards as well as I do."

"I'm getting to know them, as I did five years ago while trying to find my dad." Emma smile. "Thanks for worrying about me, Fred. Only I refuse to go elsewhere, and I'm not going to run from a fight." She glanced at Eivan. "Thank you for your support, Eivan, but all the people you love are on Earth Optimal. Makes sense for you to go there."

"Makes more sense to stay here and help you."

"What about Annemarie Hanover. She's on Earth Optimal."

"Annemarie Hanover is a mirrored subject I created inside the Pentagon. She may exist on Earth Optimal, but my place is here, beside you."

Emma wanted to tell Eivan about Thomas Carson, but

decided now was not the time. She turned toward Fred instead. "How sure are you that the wizards are out to get me?"

"No uncertainty. You will need to surveil your surroundings constantly."

"Emma," Eivan tugged her shoulders to turn her toward him. "I can fabricate some alarm that would allow you to spot them before they can do any harm. I can even supply you with a special tool that will let you kill more than one evil at a time."

"I can sense when they are in the room with their honeysuckle scent. However, if I could pinpoint who the carrier is within a group, this alarm would be welcomed."

"I'll work on this for you, Emma." Eivan turned to stare at Fred. "Tell my ancestors, and my father I'm staying here. If they wish to build something to annihilate the evil and would like me to test it, I'm their man."

"I gather you're not going back to the hospital?"

"No. The doctor released me days ago, and I'm going to stay on my own with the money my father left me. There are a couple of good labs around here that I'll use while I set up my own."

"You're going to set up your own lab?" Emma was impressed.

"Yep. Quite a few friends of mine will want to participate. I've got the money to do this now, so I'll indulge and build one of the best technical, astrophysics labs anyone can find."

"Well, your decision. Emma, this means I will still be Professor Frank Rappaport. I will pilot you to licensure." Frank Rappaport smiled, the way Fred Manson never did.

"Thank you. As much as I'm frightened of these wizards coming back to ruin me, I'm most happy my life won't be going in another direction. So, again, thank you—for trying to protect me, and for telling me the truth."

"Well, then I guess it's time to eradicate these wizards. Such a pleasure," Eivan mentioned as he pressed the red button on his nano-component.

"No," Fred had the time to yell, then everything went dark for Emma, in the blackest sense of the word.

She couldn't detect anyone around her except the pale, sick green, tiny sizes of the wizards surrounding her, eyeing her with black, reddened eyes.

Images of people fighting the wizard invasions, writhing with fear once they'd been boarded and occupied while changing to do the evil's bidding, broke Emma's heart. Moans and groans scared her beyond reason. She had difficulty holding on to her identity, and she wondered who she was and why an ominous dark cloud covered everything. Not night time, not in the throes of a nightmare, she tried to gauge where she'd landed. She called for help but found herself mute, unable to utter a single sound.

The honeysuckle scent overwhelmed her, and she waved her arms to stop the wizards from coming near her—waiving and turning, spinning without control until she could no longer remain erect, until she fell in some abyss unable to yell, incapable of screaming or crying.

Visions of armies of wizards taking over large cities and poisoning people's minds whipped her with pain, helplessness rendering her dizzy and lost. The throbs continued for a long time. She didn't know how long, only that she tired and sensed her body floating to a cottony bunches of clouds where a soft smile drew her in. She felt as though she knew this person—a beautiful angel of mercy so different than the evil she'd encountered.

"*Emma,*" the soft, lyrical voice called to her. "*Remember, Emma. You are safe. No one will harm you here. I promise.*"

"*Columba?*" She still could not form words, but she somehow remembered the pathfinder and realized she would hear her silent questions. "*How did I get here? Where am I?*"

"*Protected by two friendly planets, in the astral space between worlds. Your instincts brought you here. The wizards cannot harm you in this free space. Nor can they harm you on Quintus Capella.*"

"*My home planet.*" Emma smiled as memory returned. "*Eivan activated the destruct sequence to eliminate the wizards and the alternate worlds.*"

"*Yes. Fred could not stop him in time. The elimination needed to be done in a protected area, certainly not with an emotional fifth dimension Chavah in the vicinity.*"

"*The wizards. They attacked me. Horrible visions went through my mind.*"

"*I'm sorry, sweet Chavah. You were never meant to bear*

the brunt of this destruction. However, the wizards did not attack you. They fought their demise holding on to life any way they could, and in so doing released the baggage the creatures carried, the ugly truths they engendered throughout the centuries. The pain and suffering inflicted on others are what you experienced."

"Where is my body? How did I get separated?"

"I searched the heavens to find you. You are at home in your bed, and your mother and father are quite upset by your inertness. You need to return."

"If I do, I will visualize those images again. Columba, I don't think I can."

"You will need to focus on the people you love and pray to the Creator that he remove these wicked thoughts from your mind. He will do as you ask."

"Perhaps it's best if they are present for a while. I worried in vain about the results of my doctorate, about doing all the work. Then I worried about losing it all. I am not sure why I hesitated to embrace a simpler life. None of that matters, not after what I experienced."

"Ready to go?"

Emma nodded.

A few seconds were all she needed before she opened her eyes. Cognizance slowly returned when she caught her mother's screams to her father. "Patrick, come quick. I think Emma's waking up."

Then, Emma had difficulty breathing. Her mother lay down

on top of her, squeezing her into a tight hug.

"El, let her go. You're going to choke her to death."

"Oh, I'm sorry, Emma." Eloise released her daughter and sat down on the bed.

Patrick approached, and Emma read the worry in her dad's eyes. "How are you feeling, kiddo?"

"Better, Dad, Mom. Thanks for standing by me."

"We're not the only ones." Her father added his eyebrows far above his eyes. "We've got two cocks downstairs in our living room, facing each other with hard glances. I've been strutting to the staircase to catch a peek now and then, make sure they're not rolling around on your mother's rug in a death grip."

"What are you talking about, Dad?"

"This new boy you brought home, Eivan? Well, he's acting territorial toward you and your projects. Tom is also behaving like he owns the place—and you. Told the boy he was your fiancé."

"I didn't bring this boy home, Dad. And Tom did propose, and I accepted his proposal, telling him we would get married when I got my degree. In a way, I guess this constitutes an engagement."

"Tom should make it official. Your engagement would discourage all those other contenders from intruding into your life."

"I hear you. Although, sometimes preventing people from taking part in our life is not an easy task."

Eloise smiled as she picked up her daughter's hand. "Can Tom come up?"

Emma nodded realizing her mother favored Tom over most young men her age.

—Thirty-Five—

Joyous Reunion

Still too weak to rise, Emma waited for Tom to enter. She asked her father to tell Eivan she wasn't well enough to talk to him just yet and to ask him to come back later.

"I'm sorry, Emma," Patrick said gruffly. "This boy believes the accident is all his fault. If you ask him to come back later, you'll be reinforcing his worries."

Emma smiled, quite surprised her dad held such a soft spot for someone he hardly knew. Then she remembered how Patrick Willis garnered the reputation of being a hothead all these years. Being forgiven for his flareups was most likely something he'd craved on many occasions.

"You should probably reassure him sooner rather than later," he added.

"Okay. I guess you can send Eivan up once Tom leaves." Emma rethought her instructions. "No. Once Tom leaves, I'll go down to the living room to talk to him."

"Best idea if you feel up to it?"

She nodded, and Patrick left when he caught Tom hovering outside the door.

Tom entered and closed the door behind Patrick. He knelt beside Emma's bed and kissed her lips. "Are you going to be okay?"

She nodded, tears pouring out of her.

Tom lay down beside Emma to wrap his arms around her.

In the comfort of Tom's strong embrace with his big hands moving up and down her back and arms, she cried, releasing all the sorrow she'd imbibed.

Tom riffled his pocket and handed Emma some tissues. "No worries, they're clean. Want to talk about this?"

Emma took the tissues to blow her nose and wipe her eyes, and with a small hiccup told Tom how much she loved him. "One good thing about all this is that we won't have to change our lives. I never needed to travel to the past and change anything." Then she admitted to Tom what Fred had done to protect her from the wizards.

"The man's paranoia came very close to splitting us apart."

Tom rose and pulled on Emma's hands to help her rise. Doing so, he took her into his arms again. "How much danger are we talking about here?"

"Nothing I can't handle, I'm sure."

"Your father told me I should make our engagement official. He said, this would keep the sharks from circling." He chuckled. "Speaking of sharks, who's the stiff downstairs?"

"Eivan Baker."

"The psycho from the loony bin?"

Emma couldn't help a chuckle. "He is the astrophysics

student who created a pentagon that echoed our world. A five-sided figure that attracted forty percent of all wizards and trapped them there."

"Huh! Loonier than I thought." The big smile on Tom's face was difficult to resist. So, when he bent down to kiss her lips, Emma gave in, glowing with the love she felt for him.

"I love you, Emma. The reason I never made our engagement official is you never gave me a definite yes. You only mentioned that you might consider this later."

"And here I thought you knew how I felt, how much I need you, miss you when you're not around, and how much I want to spend the rest of my life with you."

"If this is your way of accepting my proposal, I will hawk everything I own to buy you a ring."

"Don't you dare do that. Just give me some token circle and seal the deal with a kiss. That will make me happy."

"Making you happy makes me happy. Getting a ring would make me proud, though. I'm only human, Emma. You can't expect me to forego tradition that demands the guy take care of the woman he loves, can you?"

"I believe I can. You and I are different. We are building our future, using our money for books and courses, and whatever else makes us advance in life, right?"

"Our engagement is something that will make us advance in life. Give me a chance to get something nice for you."

Emma let out a huge sigh and nodded reluctantly. In love with an Earthling, she needed to understand about his ego and leave him room to grow.

Still on wobbly legs, Emma held on to Tom's arm as she accompanied him downstairs. She walked him to the door.

In the small vestibule, Tom asked her, "Want to me to get rid of that joker for you?"

"No. Eivan is a friend, Tom. That's all. Still, you need to be nice to him. He's going to help protect me against the wizards."

With a telltale sigh, Tom nodded. He kissed Emma and left quickly, as though forcing himself to do so.

In the living room, she greeted Eivan. "Sorry about the delay. My fiancé just left."

Eivan rose and walked toward her. He picked up her left hand and stared at her fingers. "No ring."

"He is a student. He is in university thanks to a full football scholarship."

"I see. Seems like a nice guy."

"He is." She released a drawn-out breath. "What happened is not your fault. Please don't blame yourself. I'm fine."

"I realize this. I like you a lot, Emma. You're the first woman I've befriended in a long time. Don't get me wrong. I'm not into guys or anything like that."

Emma laughed. "I know you're not."

"My mistress is technology."

"Then you would like Tom. He is the brightest in all his classes, in IT. Nothing he doesn't know about computers."

"Really. I don't know anyone with those qualifications.

Tom's talent would be a good add-on to my company."

"Could be. Are you sure you want to stay on Earth Refuse?"

"I'm staying. Took me all my life to meet up with the most interesting bunch of humans I've ever come across. I'm staying." Eivan rose and kissed Emma on both cheeks. "I'll forward my new address once I'm out of the hospital. The cell phone number will be the same." He walked toward the front door. "Meanwhile, I'm going to start working on that alarm I promised you." As he was about to open the door to leave, the bell rang, and Emma unlatched the lock to see who it was.

"Emma," Amelia stood on the front porch. "I heard you had an accident. Are you all right?"

"I'm fine. Come on in." She moved aside and did the introductions. "Eivan Baker, Amelia Swift."

Emma watched Amelia extend a hand while staring at Eivan's towering presence, curly black hair, and bright green eyes. He wore an unattainable smile, and even so, Amelia wore her come-and-get-me grin, her eyes attempting to send him all sorts of sensuous signals.

"Amelia," Eivan spoke with a mechanical tone while throwing her inscrutable eyes. Emma understood a little better why Eivan didn't have a girlfriend. He turned toward her, ignoring Amelia's playful advances. "I have to go. I will call you later." He smiled and kissed her hand before running out the door.

Amelia watched him leave. "Who is the hunk?"

Joss Landry

Emma hesitated not wanting her best friend to become smitten with another impossible conquest. "He's already engaged." She thought of Eivan's answer to his girl comment, how he was engaged to his work.

"Oh. I hope I didn't come on too strong. The man is going to think I'm a nutcase or something."

"Don't worry about it. Want to go to the Mall?"

"You know it. My favorite place in the world."

***

Two days later, Emma, still looking over her shoulder every chance she got, worrying about wizards, got off the bus to meet Tom at the 27 Mix restaurant. A classy place to dine along Rutger's strip of eateries, one Emma never thought Tom would choose for dinner. Tom offered to pick her up, but she told him she would hop the bus and take the five-minute ride to meet him there. Tom sounded excited. Said he wanted to treat her to a great meal.

The aroma of sizzling fajitas and homemade salsa, mixed with the salty spray of beer on tap toyed with Emma's senses. She hadn't realized she was hungry until she walked through the door. An austere-looking place with a brick wall to her left and the bar's exposed bottles on the right stretched into one long and narrow corridor. The tables would be at the back where she would find Tom. But, when she got there, she did a complete turn to search the area without success.

"Are you Emma?" One of the waiters asked.

"Yes."

"Your friend is sitting outside." He brought her to the big patio doors at the back and indicated a quaint table under a tree. The dipping sun toyed with the umbrellas over each surface and peeked in occasionally. The busy, jovial atmosphere drew a smile from her, and stepping outside, she spotted Tom and waved hurrying toward his table.

"You never want to sit outside. The decor is lovely," Emma enthused.

"Well, it's a decent-sized table, and inside is cramped. I thought this would be nice."

Emma smiled and realized he sat in this courtyard to please her. "It's perfect," she said as he rose to kiss her properly. He pulled the chair for her to sit beside him.

"What's this all about? You sounded excited over the phone."

"Well," Tom tapped his two index fingers on the table repeatedly. "Drum roll." He smiled. "I got a teacher's assistant contract in the IT department."

"Oh, my God. Congratulations. You won't have to worry about money for your master's degree."

"Nope. Also means I've decided to make Rutgers my home. No more MIT. Rutgers has been good to me."

Emma blew out a sigh. "What a relief. We won't have to be apart."

"Something else. Psycho from the loony bin called me."

"Eivan?" Emma chuckled.

"Yeah. Sorry. I realize I should call Eivan by his name. He offered me a job." Emma could tell how happy Tom was with the offer.

"You told him you were doing a master's, didn't you?"

"Absolutely. Eivan said the job would be part-time for now. My turn to be relieved. Every student wonders, no, worries while studying, will I get a job in my field? Great news."

"Wonderful news."

"And I know he can pay me. He told me how you'd plugged me last time he saw you. Thanks, Emma."

"I also told him we were engaged to be married. I didn't want any misunderstanding to sneak in between us."

"Which brings me to the other reason I'm excited," he chuckled. "Nervous is a better word. I asked a lot of people for help on how to do this, and I don't mind telling you. Most offered extreme scenarios to go about this, so I'm just going to proceed in the most natural way I can." Tom pulled out an old-fashioned velvet box out of his pocket.

When Tom flipped the dark, square lid, Emma drew in a loud gasp, shocked to her core. "Tom, where did you get this?" She didn't dare reach for the dazzling ring she ogled, mesmerized by its shine and its beauty. "Is this real?" No way, could Tom ever afford this ring.

Tom smiled, picking up the ring in readiness. "Emma, Louise Willis, will you marry me?"

Emma's words trapped in her throat could not be released.

She stared into Tom's blue eyes and nodded as he wiped the tears from the corner of her eyes.

He picked up her left hand and placed the ring on her finger. No fudging, no stumbling, the ring was a perfect fit. "Wow, it fits."

Emma eyed the ring on her finger and realized the ring came from a place of love. Still, she recognized Tom or his father or his aunt could never afford a ring like this. Not unless the ring was a smart piece of costume jewelry which Emma wouldn't mind a bit. She was already carrying an oudjat around her neck that Luigi, the diamond expert, evaluated upward of a million dollars. "Where did you get this?"

"It's genuine, by the way."

"Such a beautiful cut. So many different colored facets," Emma whispered playing with the diamond under the light. "Is this my grandmother's doing? Did she force this ring on you?"

"No. Well, it's from your grandmother, your granny Dottie."

"No way. She never had any money."

"When she died, she had a couple of things. The house she left to your father, the oudjat she left for you and this ring. Apparently, your grandfather was a banker."

"I think I knew this. But I never saw my granny wear the ring."

"She took it off after her husband took his own life."

"No. Granny told me he was hit by an automobile."

Tom shook his head. "After the crash of 1930, he was a

banker who lost everything. Heavily invested, he owned the house your grandmother lived in, and he had given her some gold she used to live over the years."

"Who told you this?"

"Your dad. Apparently, she left a letter with the ring. She tried to conceive a child for twenty years. She was planning to tell your grandfather she was pregnant that night at dinner when she got the news he jumped off a building. She took off the ring that night and never wore it again."

"No wonder she was unhappy. Poor granny."

"I'm sure she's stepping with joy at the thought her Emma will be wearing the ring she never did."

"Gorgeous ring."

"Circa 1930 with a platinum band. What creates the light is the cut of many stones. They equal 2.9 carats in total." Tom put his finger on the stone to describe it. "Four prongs hold four flush baguette cut diamonds, and then here is the center stone surrounded by twenty round, single cut diamonds."

"Did you learn this by rote?"

Tom made a face to hide his shyness. "On account of I read the ring's evaluation your father gave me over and over again. I couldn't believe I was giving you a thirty-thousand-dollar ring." He hesitated. "Well, it comes from your granny, but she stipulated that the love of Emma's life should give her this ring." Tom took Emma's hands in his and bent to kiss her lips. "Maybe you don't have to tell everyone where the ring came from."

"Are you kidding? I'm going to tell everyone I can find. I'll tell them this ring comes from you, the love of my life."

The waiter approached the table. "Please don't think I forgot about taking your order. I realized you shared a moment, so, I waited." He bowed from the waist eying Emma. "Congratulations."

"Thank you." Emma gave her order of portobello mushroom ravioli over spinach, then Tom ordered the lobster ravioli.

"Both excellent choices. They will go fabulously with this complimentary bottle of champagne the maître d' wishes you to enjoy." Saying this, their server turned toward the tray he'd wheeled to their table and distributed napkins and utensils, and two champagne flutes before he proceeded to pop the cork and fill their glasses. "I will return quickly with your apéritifs."

The meal was delicious, and Tom went all out once they'd drained the champagne and ordered a bottle of white Zinfandel as suggested by their waiter.

Emma discussed the time she spent with Eivan, then her visit to Rappaport's office.

"Why the hell did the Devronair lie?"

Emma shrugged, unwilling to put a spoiler on their lovely evening. However, once she was picking at her crème brulée, she decided there could be no secrets between her and Tom.

"The reason Fred lied is that he wanted to protect me. You see, by going back two years, I would have canceled out a lot of the things I did. Remember those five cats I killed in my grandmother's backyard?"

"Yeah, when she and I went to Earth Optimal."

"Well, this alerted the wizards to my presence and what I can do. Fred says that now they will be after me, and I need to be vigilant, constantly look over my shoulder."

Tom dropped his spoon on his plate. "Great, and here I thought we were going to be happy."

"Love, I'll never let anything happen to you. You know that, right?" Emma rubbed his hand.

He nodded. "Never mind me. I'm worried about you. Can't they do anything?"

"Eivan and his ancestors on Earth Optimal are working on something that would alert me to their presence much faster than I might normally spot them."

"I hope he comes through quickly."

Emma could see how this information disturbed Tom's joy. She added, "They have offered us to live on Earth Optimal. You, me, my father, my mother and my grandmother."

"Earth Optimal? Wow."

She nodded waiting for the realization to hit Tom as it had done for her.

"Wait a minute, what about my dad, my aunt?"

"Hank Apple and Christina Tyler and their two boys?"

"Your aunt Franka and Jimmy and their two girls?"

"Amelia, and all our friends."

"Did you ask about them?"

"First thing I did. Only the four of us are allowed to go."

"Well, we stay. No question about it."

"That's what Eivan said. I'm still not sure why he's staying. All his ancestors and his dad are on Earth Optimal. He says he wants to help."

Tom sat back in his chair knotting his hands in one big fist. Emma read the thoughts brewing inside his mind wondering what sort of trickery Eivan held up his sleeve. She would need to refrain from mentioning Eivan in front of Tom. Still, she thought it best if she told Tom everything there was to know.

Joss Landry

—Thirty-Six—

Love Conquers All

Sitting in the 27 Mix restaurant near Rutgers University, Emma and Tom were down to sipping their second cup of strong coffee. The champagne before dinner and the wine with their meal had taken its toll, and they needed to sober up before traveling home. The sun had dipped behind the trees, and dusk was creeping up on them.

Emma smiled as she eyed the small lamps on each of the outdoor tables. So romantic, she thought. "Something I need to tell you about Eivan Baker."

"Please don't tell me he has the hots for you."

"Of course not. Eivan is a hybrid child."

"A what?"

"A hybrid. A blend between a human and a Quatar."

"What the hell is a Quatar?"

Emma educated Tom on Eivan's background and how they came from another universe. She told him how Eivan's ancestors came to this universe and found Earth to be strings of filaments, and while most of the one thousand refugees opted to live on the brightest filaments in the echo system, his ancestors chose the dullest, darkest thread so they might be able to help the people here.

"So maybe he does want to help."

"I'm sure he does. He is more Quatar than he is human and he's never had a girlfriend. I believe he is in love with technology and with the need to help the people around him."

"Thank you. I'm glad you told me. And I'm sorry for thinking you could ever love anyone else. Remnants of my mother abandoning my father and me. I'm slowly getting over this, by the way."

"I understand, Tom. I hope you realize. I can never be like your mother."

"I do. I even stopped blaming my mother. Besides, my father and my mother were never a good match. She is a romantic, and he is dry and unimaginative."

"You're not saying this because of their different color, are you?"

"No. Of course not. My father's mother was white while his dad was black, so the color was never an issue."

"Especially that your dad has the most incredible jeweled, green eyes I've ever seen on a man."

"Yeah. Dad does. I guess I took after my mom. Light brown hair, blue eyes, fair to medium complexion."

"Don't sound so disappointed. You inherited your dad's muscular build, his tallness, along with your mother's svelte figure. The best of both worlds."

Tom nodded. "He was a good football player in his day."

Loud noises attracted their attention, and both searched

the patio door. Patrick Willis, Eloise, and Rudy Carson stood there arguing with the waiter that they were joining their children for a drink.

Tom stood and waved to them. "Dad, over here."

"Did you know about this?"

"I forgot. The three spent some time at McGovern's tavern, and said they might stop by on their way home."

Emma stared at her ring with a big smile. She looked forward to sharing her happiness with her parents.

When her mother reached the table, Emma rose and hugged her. "I'm engaged." Then she showed the scintillating jewel on her finger. "So beautiful."

Patrick came forward. "Now you'll have to let me get you a proper ring, Eloise."

Emma caught her mother rolling her eyes. "I'm happy with this one."

"I know what you mean, Mom. I would have been just as elated with a ring from a box of popcorn." Emma chuckled.

"Don't I get a hug?" Patrick's sharp tone indicated he too wanted to participate in the news. Emma wound her arms around his neck and squeezed. "Yes, you do. Thanks for remembering Granny's inheritance, by the way. I love this ring. Mostly because it was hers."

"Then I won't tell you the story revolving around this ring."

The five sat down at the table, and when the waiter came to take their order, Patrick ordered a bottle of their best Champagne.

Emma Willis Book 3,
I Can Help You

"Dad, we're into our second cups of strong coffee because we already drank a lot of champagne and wine with dinner."

"Ah, you can always have a little more. Rudy, your mother, and I have a gift for you." Patrick handed Emma a small white envelope.

Emma took it from him, eying Tom for some idea. He raised his shoulders as though he didn't know what was inside.

"Hotel reservations?"

"At the Langham, midtown Manhattan."

Emma stared at Tom in shock. "This suite is worth thousands of dollars a night. Dad, what did you do?"

"Your mother, Rudy and I are happy to do this for you. And if I were you, to take full advantage of this offer, you should head there tomorrow around noon. They will keep your bags handy while you tour the hotel, go for a swim, and take full advantage of the facilities. Once you're settled in, you can call for in-room massages."

"How do you know about this place?"

"Your mother and I enjoyed this one weekend. Nice to be pampered now and then."

Rudy slapped Tom on the back. "Especially that it will be a while before you can afford any luxury like this, right son?" He chuckled at Tom's worried expression.

Tom hesitated, but upon Emma's prompt to go ahead, he told the three about his new position at the university. "They'll be reimbursing all the costs for my master's degree, and paying me a stipend. Plus, Eivan Baker hired me to set up the computer network for his new company. And once I finish my master's, he says he wants to put me in charge of his IT department. That's the equivalent of a couple of hundred grands a year." He raised his shoulders hesitantly, faced with the shock on their faces.

"Whoa," Rudy said his green eyes as big as saucers. "You're going places, son. You're going to be famous."

"Hum. Don't know about famous, but I'll be able to support Emma and myself."

"Plus, Emma will also be contributing to this support." Emma sensed her father needed to establish her role in this marriage early.

"A big part of that support," Tom added.

Emma noticed her dad slurring some of his words. "Are you all right to drive home, Dad?"

"No. Of course not." He laughed.

"Are you driving home, Mom."

"Less capable than your Dad," she giggled her eyes round and glazed.

Rudy spoke up. "Don't worry. We all took a cab here. That's how we're going back. No one can drive in this condition." The three of them laughed hysterically faced with their inebriated situation.

Then, the champagne arrived.

"Listen, honey, please clear your Saturday evening."

"Why, Mom?"

Emma Willis Book 3,
I Can Help You

"Grandma is throwing you a surprise engagement party. Please don't tell her I said anything."

"I'll act surprised." She turned toward Tom. "You ready?"

"Yeah, let's go."

After saying their goodbyes, and after they reached the parking lot, Tom stumbled on a small rock on the ground. "I don't think I should drive, Emma. I never drink. All this wine and champagne was too much for me. How are you feeling?"

"I'll drive home. We'll be fine."

Emma pulling into her driveway, Tom mentioned, "Too bad this room our parents reserved isn't for tonight." He smiled.

"I have a lab tomorrow afternoon, but I'm going to get out of it. How about you?"

Tom got out of the car and followed Emma to the door. I have a nothing day tomorrow. If I hadn't agreed to a summer semester, I would be free the whole week."

When they reached the balcony, Bill Frost and Tim O'Rourke suddenly appeared in front of them. "What are you guys doing here?" Emma searched her perimeters to check on any shock their appearance might have caused. No one was around.

Bill apologized for the surprise. "Here is a small component Eivan promised you. He modified his own and used the technology his father developed on Earth Optimal.

Emma took the little component Bill handed her and asked, "What's with the number six blinking on the little visor?"

"Six is the number of wizards inside your house right now.

Press the red button, and they'll all die."

Emma's panic-stricken eyes stared at Tom, almost hoping he would say something. She was tongue-tied.

Tom grasped the component Tim handed him. "I have one also?"

"Yes. Check it before you enter your house, and do the same thing."

"Bill, what if they enter the house while we are sleeping?"

Your house, Tom's house, your grandmother's house, and in total, six homes were domed."

"Seven," Tim added.

"Of course. Hank asked us to put a dome over Matt and Maria's home. He's going to provide them with a couple of units and explain to them what to do. All homes will be impenetrable from now on, once the wizards inside are gone."

"Did you inform Hank that our current time has not changed?"

"I did. I don't mind telling you, Hank is relieved."

Emma shook her head, lost in thought. "How did Eivan work on this so fast?"

"Eivan's father and grandfather have been working on this for months."

Tom still couldn't understand. "What about when we travel outside the home when we're at university?"

"Point the unit to yourself, and press the blue button. You can protect yourself and anyone you wish, like a sitter for Hank's children. He can protect them before he leaves."

"Wow." Emma found her hands were shaking. "The wizards didn't waste any time."

"They are not smart. Wizards do not plan or organize tasks. This assault proves it. They will not be able to report back as to what happened, and chances are, no one will miss them." Eventually, they will forget all about you."

"What do I tell my Dad?" Tom was outraged. "He doesn't know anything about this."

"Well, Tim and I will contact him in the morning."

"What will you tell him?"

"We're from the FBI, and we are dealing with a secret, urgent matter of the utmost importance. He will be made to understand that he cannot discuss this matter with anyone, except with you, of course. He will follow the procedure just as you do."

"In other words, he doesn't need to find out that this is about Emma."

"It's not about Emma. It's about wizards." Bill smiled. Until he gets his unit, you can blue coat him for his protection."

Emma pressed on the red button to destroy the evil inside her house. Slight dizziness overcame her, but she remained standing. Tom secured her by putting an arm around her waist. "I wanted to do this while you were here in case something happened to me."

"You, all right?" Bill asked.

Emma nodded. "What does blue coating mean?"

Bill smiled. "The quick explanation is the blue ray emitted

by the component is invisible but blocks human electrical impulses that the wizards need to enter a person and alter their behavior."

"How long does the effect last?" Emma wanted to know. "I'm sure it's not permanent."

"It's not," Bill answered.

Tim chuckled. "Otherwise, we'd zap everyone around, sit back, relax, and gaze at the changing world before our wondrous eyes."

"We don't know how long. The ones we were able to test lasted twenty-four hours."

"Good to know," Tom answered.

"And don't you worry, Emma. Right now, you're the soup du jour. Once enough of them have disappeared, the rest of them will forget you even exist." Bill patted her shoulder.

Tim nodded. "Yeah. It's a good thing that six of them are trapped in there. Another four or five are at your house, Tom. The more, the merrier right now. Eliminating the wizards means the others will soon look the other way. Most of them don't even know about you. Remember, they don't communicate on any specific level, especially when out of a body."

"Thank you, Bill, Tim. It's wonderful how all these people are working to help us." Emma slid the little gizmo inside her jacket pocket. "Where are you going now?"

"To talk to your aunt, Franka, and uncle Jimmy."

"Good."

Tim handed Emma a small cloth bag. "Here are the components for your mom and dad. Make sure you tell them how to use them properly."

"Yeah," Tim added. "If your father goes to a meeting and checks the small component and reads a number, all he needs to do is press that red button."

"Wow," Emma breathed. "This means I can do the same wherever I go."

"Absolutely." Bill smiled.

"Thank you." Tom and Emma watched as both angels vanished into thin air.

Tom took Emma into his arms. "Bill never noticed your ring."

"He's got other things on his mind."

"So do I." Tom sealed their newfound engagement with a passionate kiss that left Emma breathless. "I was hoping to spend the night, but I won't be able to. I have to get rid of the wizards in my house, then wait for my father to come home so I can coat him with this blue light."

"Why not protect him in the morning before he leaves for work? The house is protected, remember?"

"Yeah, you're right. And Bill and Tim will talk to him in the morning." Tom squeezed Emma in his arms. Okay, I'll be back in half an hour."

Emma watched him leave on foot as she unlocked the door to her house. Closing it behind her, she sensed her heart pounding in her chest. Wizards back in her life to cause her grief. Still, Emma breathed a little more relaxed that she and Tom were still together, and that she didn't have to forego all the information she'd amassed these past two years.

Once upstairs in her room, she bumped into Columba, and as usual, jumped out of her skin. "Columba, ah you scared me. I thought you might be a wizard."

"I'm here to give you an important precision on Bill's instructions. Whatever you do, do not coat yourself with the blue light when wearing the oudjat. You must warn Tom not to perform this operation on you, and also tell your parents. You might even need to tell Hank, as I'm sure all of you will be bluing anyone you encounter." She chuckled wholeheartedly.

"Would the action disrupt my oudjat?"

"Possibly. Besides, the oudjat is all the protection you need. The wizards will want to take possession of the ones you love since they cannot get to you. So, let everyone know not to raise that blue weapon on you." Again, she giggled.

"Thanks. I have an engagement party planned for Saturday night, and I suspect that all the ones who are armed and dangerous will be present. I will talk to them."

"Congratulations on your engagement, Chavah. I wish you all the happiness in the world."

Before Emma could add anything, Columba disappeared.

When Tom returned, Emma told him about Columba's instructions. He rolled his eyes and mentioned. "I almost blued you before I left. Wow. You'll need to warn everyone, especially since you're always wearing that oudjat." Tom took her in his arms. In fact, I think you should leave your oudjat home on Saturday night. I'm betting once you go through that door, that blue ray will come from Hank, your aunt Franka, perhaps even from your grandmother."

"You're right." Emma hugged him warmly. "We'll have to find a way to explain to my uncle Jimmy and your father why they should never point their blue ray at me." She backed away slightly and realized the time had come for her to admit to Tom who she was, and where her original planet resided.

They both sat on the bed, and Tom's frowned remained during her whole story. She talked about Shad, her unicorn and all the other differences that existed on her planet, about her mother being from the same place. She witnessed his expression grow to one of sadness, and his shoulders slumped as though he'd lost all his confidence—the stubborn courage he carried everywhere in his broad shoulders and straight demeanor gone.

She shed a few tears at first, then felt her body rock with sobs. Release from the long day? Pent-up fears going haywire?

Her sobs gone, her eyes dried, Emma recognized Tom's valiance rising to the occasion as he put an arm around her shoulders to bring her into his arms. He held her until her hiccups subsided.

"I'm sorry I didn't tell you sooner. Columba only brought me to my home planet a couple of weeks ago. I suspected I came from somewhere else for a while, but I only found out for sure recently."

Emma waited for Tom to say something.

He appeared to rally, love shining in his big blue eyes. "When I found out about Bill, and Tim, and Columba, and that big oaf, Hawke, I suspected it, even while I hoped you weren't that different from me, but thinking you might be." He smiled. All at once, the frown puckered his eyes. "You're not a hybrid child, are you? You're nothing like Eivan, right?"

Emma shook her head side to side.

"Because of your mom. You said she seeded you inside her."

"I'm still human, just not an Earth Refuse human. I'm a fifth-dimension human."

When the truth dawned on Tom, he appeared dazed, his eyes rounder and more prominent than she'd ever spotted them. "Your father is not your father."

"Dad is my father—not biologically, but he's the one who raised me."

Tom nodded and smiled. "That explains it. And here I worried about you giving birth to a little Patrick."

"Tom." Emma pulled on his sleeve to get his attention.

"Don't worry. Mr. Dub will never hear this from me. He is your dad. He provided for you, took care of you. He's the one."

"Thank you. We can never tell my dad about this, okay?"

"I promise, sweetheart. Although." he appeared to hesitate. "I can't imagine what you see in me. Why you love me. You have all these possibilities."

Emma Willis Book 3,
I Can Help You

"My biggest possibility is you and me. Let's not ruin our time together by worrying about where I come from, please."

Tom gazed into Emma's eyes, and she witnessed him closing the blue jewels while taking a deep breath. "I love you so much, Emma. Will you teach me to make love as they do on your planet, and on Earth Optimal?"

"I will. I promise."

Tonight, they would consecrate their union the old fashion way. Only Emma realized her soul would call out to Tom's soul, and their two essences would mingle on a whole different spiritual plane.

Joss Landry

Emma Willis continues...

Not the end. Emma Willis' next adventure will be titled: I Can Save You. She will help Fred and others. She will encounter other daring experiences, and Tom and her friend Amelia will be a part of these adventures.

CPSIA information can be obtained
at www.ICGtesting.com
Printed in the USA
LVHW040032161019
634321LV00008B/59/P